Tap Dancing at the Bluebird

A NOVEL

CHRISTINE WALKER

Sibylline
DIGITAL FIRST

Sibylline
DIGITAL FIRST

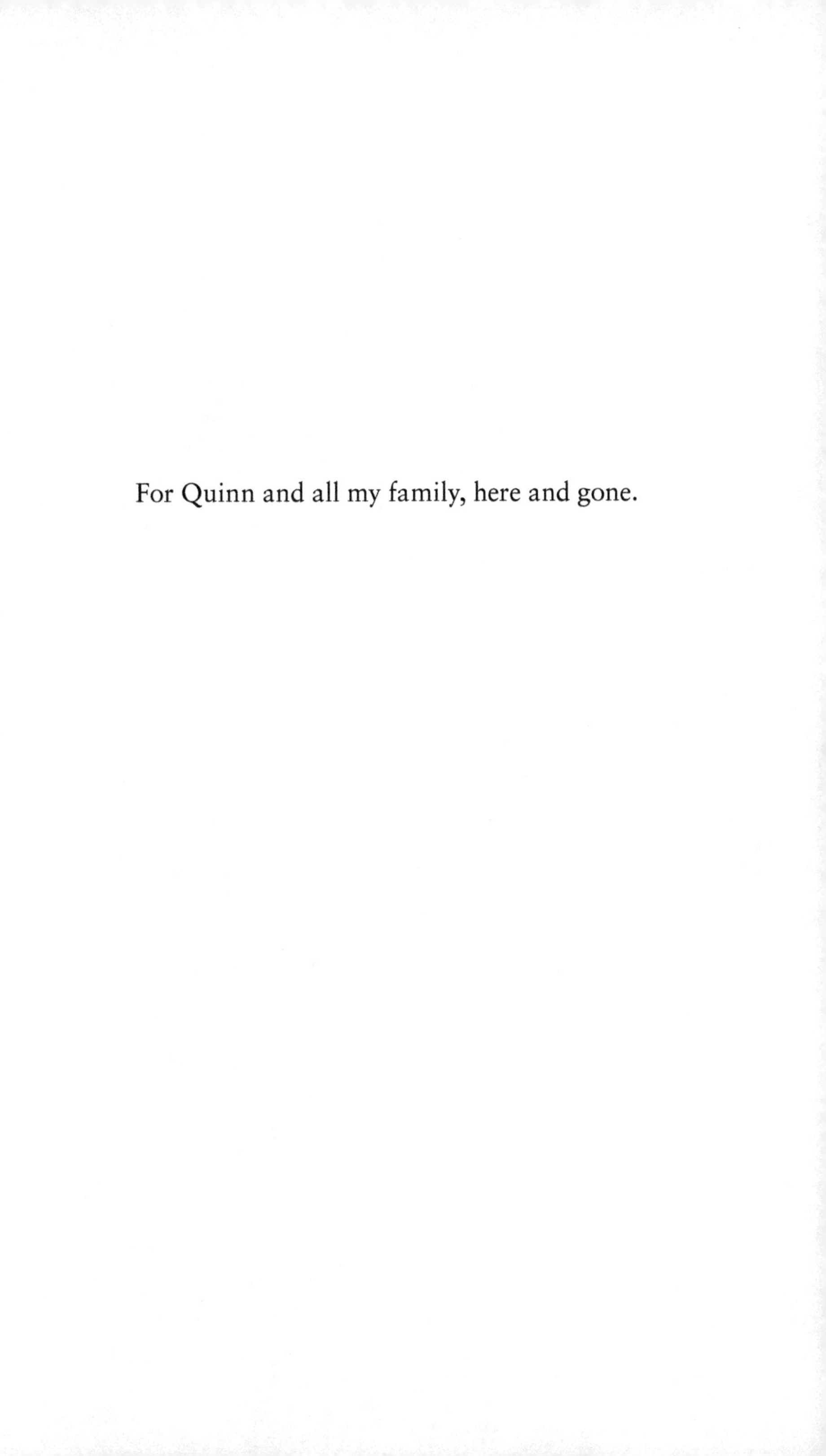

For Quinn and all my family, here and gone.

Praise for Christine Walker's *Tap Dancing at the Bluebird*

"An epic novel about lives intertwined, unraveled, and re-woven, driven by the power of dance that shapes and transforms personal histories."

—Kimi Okada, Tony Award-nominated Choreographer,
Director of ODC School

"Beautifully rendered, *Tap Dancing at the Bluebird* is a heartfelt evocation of time, place and family with prose that shimmers and characters that resonate across the generations. Walker manages to capture both the desperation and hope of those who endured the Great Depression and the profound place of memory and longing in bringing those stories alive for contemporary audiences."

—Ken Wells, author of *Meely LaBauve* and *Swamped!*

"Kip and Mattie's story crosses time and distance to weave a beautiful and deeply moving portrait of both a nation in flux and of personal resilience. The writing is lyrical, the characters are real and complicated people, the historical detail is perfect, and the action is page-turning. I re-read many passages several times for the insights and wisdom about dance, aging, and life. It's a wonderful read, and highly recommended."

— Sheri T. Joseph, author of *Edge of the
Known World,* a USA Today Booklist best-seller

"I like the way [Christine] captures how every little thing matters and how a person of good will and heart can get through difficult times so much better than a self-centered person. The entire novel with the re-found love reminds me of a Shakespearean plot. We do believe in it because the author and characters compel us to."

—Barbara Baer, author of *The Ice Palace Waltz*
and *The Ballet Lover*

Tap Dancing at the Bluebird is very satisfying story. I stayed interested to the end. Love, love, love these characters. I wanted to keep reading . . . didn't want the story to end."
—Marlene Cullen, Editor of *The Write Spot*
anthologies and host of The Writers Forum

"From the very beginning, I was interested in finding out Kip and Mattie's story. I really felt the precarious times for people during the depression. Great descriptions of tap dancing! I could visualize and also hear the actual tapping."
—Susan Hillery, Library Specialist,
Sonoma County Library

Praise for Christine Walker's *A Painter's Garden: Cultivating the Creative Life*

"Intelligent, evocative, elegant, and articulate . . . The parallels between lesson in the garden, the studio, and life ring true."
—Eleanor Coppola, filmmaker, artist, and author

PART ONE

CHAPTER ONE

Solo

Kip. He arrives in Mattie's memory with a shimmer, the way he appeared at her family's restaurant one morning in 1932, sunlight edging his hat, overcoat, and bundle slung over one shoulder. His black leather shoes, with taps at heel and toe, fit his feet like a second skin.

"I see work here I could do for a meal." He enters and sets her life in motion. *Click-clack.*

Her body still knows all the dance moves he taught her— leaping bells, trading fours, tanglefoot, rubber legs, falling off logs. In the decades since, she hasn't allowed her thoughts to linger on what might have been with him. He was here then gone, their time together as ephemeral as the fireflies on a warm summer evening in Kansas City, her parents watching from the lamp-lit porch, and eternal as the stars that night on the cold, dark mesa, coyotes howling in the distance. By then, Kip and she had been traveling for days, and he let spill bits and pieces about himself. She gave him the silver bird peppershaker for good luck and kept its mate for her own.

Today, on her bedroom balcony overlooking San Francisco, Mattie swirls her pelvis and hops. Snakehips with a spring. Feeling the catch in her hip joint as she lands, she steadies herself against the railing. She opens her hand to the little bird saltshaker, which has been tucked away in her desk at the university. The tarnished silver catches a sparkle of afternoon sun, igniting dormant sensations—the screech of metal, sudden pitch of the train. Salt glitters her palm. She closes her hand over the rounded breast, etched feathers, tiny beak, and holes in the head.

Tek tek. Perched on the railing, a bird with a beating heart pecks a tiny caterpillar, lifts on a breeze, and wings toward the downtown skyline and the new Memory and Movement Center beside the bay, where Mattie's young research assistants in the neuroscience department are relocating.

Her phone pings. She takes it from her pocket and reads the text. *We need you here. You're living proof of our theories.*

She depends on their tech savvy and tips for her playlist, which she brings up now. Tapping her foot to "Can't Stop the Feeling," she again tries to envision leaving this city. How will she manage without her daily work and colleagues or her salsa pals?

When she was a girl, long before research showed how anticipating another person's moves fires the neural synapses, she felt for the first time the magical sensation of oneness when dancing with a partner. Decades passed before she learned about the hippocampus and its role in balance, learning, memory, and emotion.

Her team has documented the benefits of spinning apart and twirling together with another human being, and Mattie has summarized them for her doctoral students. "In those moments, a feeling of total fulfillment arrives hand-in-hand with a belief in all possibility. You resonate with the other. Simply put, it's joy."

The wind whips, and she steps inside. She tucks the silver bird into a travel bag and whispers, "Give no thought to limitations." She takes her childhood diary to the armchair and settles, expecting a call. Her phone screen brightens with *Sunday, March 8, 4:00* and chimes.

Abundant dark curls halo Genet's smiling face. "The news is scary, Gram. I need you to tell me how people dealt with the hard times back in your day. We'll have the whole week to talk after you land in KC tomorrow, of course, but I need to hear it now."

"Won't we be busy with wedding preparations?" Mattie's face reflects in a corner of the screen—her tousled white hair, rosy cheeks, and eyeglasses rimmed with polka dots. She smiles at Genet.

"Ravi's mother has it handled. Imagine me, a California girl, marrying a boy from India she met in Missouri. He's good at calming me down, but he's away on a bug hunt, so I started cleaning the attic. I found a photo of two kids at a diner and showed it to Uncle Wiley today. He kept saying 'dancing boy.' I think the girl is you, Gram, but who is the boy in the tap shoes?"

Mattie has never confronted the horror of what happened, never revealed it to any family member or friend, and certainly not to the man who recently interviewed her about train-hopping youth of the thirties, saying, "So few of you left." She wonders how soon her granddaughter's questions will lead there.

Mattie shivers and draws a blanket across her lap. "That would be Kip the day we met." The touch of wool propels her to a vivid memory. "Let's begin the evening before. Your great-uncle and I were huddling in the closet behind the coats, breathing the scent of cedar and shoe polish, listening for Father's return. My other siblings had outgrown the game, but Wiley still delighted in it."

"How old were you?"

"Twelve and five. Such a dear little brother. Always has been. My world was there with him and the family and at the Bluebird Buffet, where I worked after school and on weekends."

"Hold on, Gram. I want to record you—Okay. Ready."

"Perhaps the memory of the closet is palpable because we hid there every Friday night, or because this time was the last, although I didn't know it then. The knob rattled as Father opened the door to toss his hat onto the shelf. We jumped out, and he pretended to be scared, but he was pleased as punch and took us in his arms. I shouted, 'She's on her way!'

"Had it not been for a brave woman soaring above the Atlantic, the evening might not have stood out from the happy blur of memories at home, but I know the date. I'll try to recall for you the flavor of those days and how one thing led to another. Part of it is here in these pages." Mattie thumbs her diary, releasing mustiness and a taste of bittersweet. "Can you hear me okay?"

"Crystal clear. Continue."

"I can say with certainty that the next morning—Saturday— when Kip Kelly walked into the Bluebird, my world split into what was before and all that followed after he came to us. But I'll start with that Friday evening, May twentieth, nineteen thirty-two."

CHAPTER TWO

Home

Every day the newspapers conveyed greater suffering across America, but if times had been different, Kip would not have been among the thousands hopping trains and stopping in Kansas City to ask for work. I believed it was synchronicity that brought him to us then, although I didn't yet know that word. I didn't yet know that my sense of anticipation was like sitting beside a train track with your hand on the cool smooth metal. Before you see the train, you hear a distant rumble. Before you hear the sound, you feel the surge through the track, the tremble in your hand, and you know something's coming. I can say that some things in life remain mysterious, even if they are meant to be. Some things we must leave behind unexplained.

On that Friday evening, the house was warm and bright. In winter, when our coal bin had been empty and the electricity unpaid, we retired early, layered on blankets, and read by candles. Though Mother was clever at stretching meals, we had often gone to bed hungry, but it was now late May, vegetables grew in the yard, and I wanted to believe that we would not be facing the unbearable any time soon.

We sat down for dinner eager to hear Father's news from his travels that week to towns in Kansas and Missouri. After giving a blessing, he regarded each of us around the table—Mother, Aunt Irene, my brothers and sister, our boarder, and me—and said, "I'm happy to report that I was able to submit several excellent bids."

We children thought of Father's architecture business as a game, like a spelling bee. You could be best in your class but lose the prize if you made one mistake. He never told us when he lost bids, only when he won. This time he said again, "I'm confident that things will improve."

"How can you be so sure?" I asked.

"If you put your power of mind on it, Mattie, it will manifest."

I wanted to have that power for my own. He had envisioned building a skyscraper, publishing a book of poetry, owning a restaurant, and making a fortune to pass to his children. He had fulfilled these dreams, other than becoming rich. If times were different, he might have done so.

He took a spoonful of peas and noodles and passed the casserole. "Who could have predicted these lean months would last so long? Now the Bluebird is our cushion against slow times. People can wait for buildings, but they have to eat."

Aunt Irene threw him her nasty look. "It's a mighty thin pillow, Elliot." They had opened the Bluebird in spring of 1929, and Father had never voiced regrets, but she often said they were fools to do so in those heady days before the Great Crash because nothing good lasts forever. Father let go of the lease on his office downtown and moved his drafting table into a storeroom off the restaurant's kitchen. He drew his plans there, but weekdays he was usually away on projects or seeking new ones. Aunt Irene ran the Bluebird, working every weekday and most weekends. She liked to play the martyr, but she truly needed help. She turned to Mother. "Wouldn't you agree, Clara, that the cushion has lost its feathers?"

"We're rich in essential ways, Irene." Mother, who had been watching Wiley help himself to a large portion, guided his hand on the spoon to spill some back to the dish. "We have family, stirred with love."

"Indeed." Father passed the bread. "And art and faith. Offerings of the mind and spirit."

"Those won't pay the price of coffee beans, Elliot. With your big heart and heaping the customers' plates, our profits are a pittance." Aunt Irene glowered. "I can't mix in any more chicory and barley and still call it coffee. Soon we'll be roasting dandelion roots."

"A hot beverage can add hope to a day, and that's our true wealth." Father spoke to Irene and included all of us. "People have always reached for the stars, as we're witnessing tonight."

He checked his pocket watch. "We have just enough time for what's cooling on the counter." He knew I was excited to dial up the Philco for any news of Amelia Earhart, who had left Harbor Grace for Paris in her Lockheed Vega a few hours before we sat down for dinner.

I had made a mock apple pie the way he and I liked it—extra tangy and spicy. The mix of lemon and cinnamon still tastes to me like times with the family before everything changed.

After dessert, our boarder retreated downstairs. My sister stepped onto the porch with a new suitor, and my brothers ran out to play hide-and-seek with the neighbors. Of the girls, I was usually the first to sniff out the boys. They smelled like freshly dug, damp dirt.

I took my turn with the dishes and rushed to the living room, where the Philco sputtered. A man's voice broke through singing "Bye Bye Blackbird."

Aunt Irene knitted at her spot on the spindle back settee. Her needles darted in and out. A sleeve dangled. "Fiddlesticks." She picked up the dropped stitch with her crochet hook. She was forty-one, only three years older than Father, but her hair was thin and graying, while his was dark and wavy. He had a ready grin, and her mouth settled in a frown.

Mother worked at her tole-painting table. Lamplight shone on her face and auburn hair, loosely gathered into a bun. She hummed as she painted roses on the lid of a tin box for me to save the letters from Eugene, who had been my best friend since we were babies. In January, he had moved to New York City. I envied his adventures and yearned for Scout camp in July so that I would have some soul-stirring events to write about to him and in my diary. "I want to see *Tarzan the Ape Man* tomorrow," I said.

"It's not appropriate for young girls." Aunt Irene glared at Father and at Mother, who continued painting.

"I'm almost thirteen, Auntie."

"You're barely twelve. And it's time you cease being a tomboy."

"It's been more than two months since my birthday. That's not barely."

"Now Irene, Mattie knows about right decisions. She's a Toft and a Swenson. She has our English stalwartness and Clara's Swedish tenacity. She won't soon be swinging through trees." Father smiled at Mother, whose immigrant grandparents had been part of a group who founded a town in Kansas. To me he said, "As long as your brother goes with you."

He opened the jumbo atlas on the card table, and I joined him. We tracked Amelia's route over the night ocean toward the dawn. I turned toward the window to send a plea for her safety, unsure if it would help her, but certain it couldn't hurt.

The announcer's voice boomed. "Quaker Oats. Delicious. Nutritious. You'll feel ambitious."

My ambitions reached to the skies as a pilot and to Broadway or Hollywood as a singer and actress. I wanted to believe that one day my dreams would take me far beyond Kansas City. Knowing how to get to wherever I was going would help me get there.

"This young woman is making history," Father said. "Think of what your future holds, Mattie. Things we can't possibly imagine. Why, you may see the twenty-first century."

"If I live to be eighty—"

"Horsefeathers." Aunt Irene interrupted. "When I was born, Margaret Ann, most people didn't live past fifty. Now it is close to sixty. That's long enough to wear a body out. People weren't meant to carry on much past that. Certainly not our lineage with the weak tickers and excess of bad luck." She turned the dial, and "Dancing in the Dark" sounded along with static.

"What if we could enter the next century together, Father? You'd be one hundred and four."

He chuckled. "I'd like that. Miracles do happen."

He was a cup-more-than-half-full person who strove for high ideals. Partial to a touch of elegance, he wore white shirts, which Mother starched and ironed. If he spilled even a spot of gravy while at the Bluebird, he tied on a fresh apron. When they opened the restaurant, he commissioned a silversmith downtown to craft sets of sterling salt and peppers formed as small birds. Their companion sugar bowls were made from silver twigs soldered into nests with smooth lids topped by little twig handles.

I polished the sets weekly until the first Saturday morning in May when Aunt Irene left the Bluebird and returned with boxes of plain glass shakers and sugar bowls. May Day flags that I'd cut from my sister's gingham fabric remnants hung across the restaurant windows in tribute to the union men. Aunt Irene told me to wrap the silver shakers in the flags and newspaper, put them into a flour sack, and then wrap the bowls. She placed the sacks on the top shelf in the pantry room, saying she would sell the sterling if things got worse.

Aunt Irene glared at Father and cast off a stitch. "All I know is some customers are sitting too long over their cups. We're fools to think we'll be able to go on forever this way."

Mother, who was humming to the tune of "As Time Goes By," looked up. "Well, of course, Irene. None of us will go on forever, will we?"

CHAPTER THREE

Bluebird

The next morning at the restaurant, I was serving the men who had lingered past breakfast. After school and on Saturdays, I worked to earn money for camp and clothes, setting aside enough pennies to see a moving picture once a month. Filling their cups, I was imagining how Amelia, according to the papers, had met with bad weather and a faulty altimeter and landed in a Northern Ireland field miles short of her destination. The Bluebird sparkled, and I sensed something wonderful was about to happen. Or had it happened? Maybe it was Amelia being victorious, even if detoured. A mirror behind the walnut counter reflected the overhead globe lamps, all but the one dangling unlit. Sunshine bounced over the blue leather stools and booth cushions, brass coat hooks, Formica tabletops, and blue-and-white checkerboard floor.

I heard a click and clack from the doorway and saw a backlit shape. The man's brimmed hat obscured his face. He stepped in. His shoes looked like those of a professional tap dancer. The scuffed black leather had formed to his feet. "I see work here I could do for a meal." He gestured to the window. "Repaint your sign?"

He appeared to be younger than the railroad workers and

roving men who usually came our way. The customer I was serving turned to look, unsteadying the mug in his hand, and caused me to dribble on the table. A few drops splattered on my dress. I'd neglected to wear an apron, but the spots disappeared into the fabric's flower pattern.

Father came from behind the counter, wiping his hands. "It has needed a touch-up for a long while, but I haven't taken the time."

"Take some of mine?" The visitor spread his arms.

Father chuckled. "Gladly. I'm Elliot Toft."

"Kip." He placed his hand over his heart and bowed.

"Do you have a surname, son?"

"Uh—" He shifted his bundle, looking toward the window and back at Father. "Kelly."

"Good to meet you, Kip Kelly. Welcome to the Bluebird. This is my daughter Mattie."

My hands were full with the coffee pot and mopping rag, so I waved the rag. Kip touched his heart again. From the pantry, Father fetched a brush and an unopened can of blue paint that Aunt Irene had bought.

"When you're done, sit down for a cup until the corned beef and cabbage is ready."

"Is there a ladder?" Kip glanced at Father and then me.

I set the pot on the counter and dashed to the pantry for the stepladder. Kip hung his coat on a chair, carried the supplies outside, and propped the ladder in front of the window. BLU_ BI__ BUF__T skipped along the top. Our menu on the door displayed the name, along with our specials and hours. We once offered a fixed-price, all-you-can-eat buffet, but we'd eliminated it in favor of a bargain special. When Aunt Irene wasn't watching, Father ladled bigger portions for those who appeared to be eating their one meal of the day or, perhaps, of several.

Kip studied the sign, as if to consider the right approach to a task worth doing well. He hitched up the suspenders of his corduroy trousers, stepped onto the ladder with the paint and brush, and began working. He concentrated on a gap, painted a missing letter, concentrated, and painted. He tilted his head and leaned in close, checking his work. His careful movements made me want to watch him. As I poured, some customers kept an eye on Kip too, instead of their cups. I glanced up from wiping a table, and Kip was looking at me. I squinted at the now complete name and nodded. He finished and carried the equipment inside, click-clacking as he walked across the checkerboard floor.

He stowed the paint in the pantry and held up the brush. "Is there turpentine?"

Aunt Irene darted out from the kitchen. "I'll see to that." She plucked the brush from Kip's hand and motioned to the counter. "Take a seat." She opened the back door and stepped into the alley, where we kept a can of kerosene behind the trash bin.

"That's my aunt." I said it as an apology.

Kip swirled onto a stool, and I darted behind the counter to pour his coffee.

"Thank you." He dashed in sugar and milk and stirred. The cup overflowed. "Sorry about that." He lifted the cup, his gaze following me over the rim, and slurped.

I wiped the counter. "It's not your fault. I filled the cup too full."

"Even-steven. I poured the milk. Don't take the whole rap." His smile showed teeth that were not stained yellow like those of the other transient men, but white and nearly perfect. One incisor angled slightly forward.

Father emerged from the kitchen carrying a plate heaped with fragrant corned beef and cabbage and set it in front of Kip. "That's a fine job, young man." He lingered behind the counter, polishing clean glasses with a white cloth. "On the road long?"

"A bit." Kip lay his hat tenderly on the counter. It was black felt, as other men wore, but had a band pieced from scraps of fabric with red, blue, and green polka dots. Kip's dark hair was disheveled. His thick dark eyebrows nearly met above the bridge of his nose, as did my older brother's, but Kip's eyes shone copper, like pennies, while Mickey's were as blue as Father's, as blue as the bird in the painting that I could see on the wall past Kip's head. I'd guessed him to be as old as my sister and her friends, who were about to graduate high school. Hatless, he looked closer in age to Mickey, who was fourteen, but Mickey's cheeks were smooth, and Kip's showed a few whiskers.

"How old are you?" I asked.

"Fifteen."

"When is your birthday?"

"Saint Pat's."

"Oh, mine is the day before."

"Is that so. And you are—?"

"Thirteen. On the next one."

He nodded. "That's about right. Might have guessed younger."

"Mother says I'm growing like a weed." I stood as tall as I could. "Are you a tap dancer?" I then wished I hadn't asked the obvious, because his face clouded with sadness.

"I once thought I would be." Head down, he began eating, soaking up juice with a biscuit. When finished, he looked up at the loose ceiling lamp. "Where's the fuse box?"

"In the pantry," Father said. "Tools are there too." He feared electricity or he would have fixed the light himself.

Kip found a screwdriver, placed the ladder beside a table beneath the fixture, and stepped up. He stretched to reattach the wires and secure the globe. The ladder wobbled, his foot slipped, and he fell onto the table in a crouch. He grabbed the edge, steadied himself, and leapt to the floor, landing on his toes. *Click*. He fell back on his heels. *Clack*.

I clapped. His face flushed and he bowed. As if attached to marionette strings controlled by an invisible puppeteer, his knees shot upward and his whole body lifted off the ground with a jolt that rippled through him and dropped him down on right toe and heel, left heel and toe.

He returned the ladder to the pantry and flipped on the switch. The repaired globe shone brightly. He strode to the counter with a cadence—heel toe, heel toe—and sat on a high stool. Father brought out another plate of corned beef, and Kip consumed it as intently as the first. I kept him in view, wiping the counter so many times that Aunt Irene, hovering to prevent Father from refilling Kip's plate again, said, "Margaret Ann Toft, you're wearing out that rag."

Father told Kip to store his belongings in the pantry, gave him one of the white aprons that Mother had embroidered with a little bluebird, and set him to work washing dishes in the kitchen. "You'll help us greatly if you can keep on top of that and whatever else you see that might need a spiff and shine."

In the early afternoon, Kip was at the counter polishing glasses and placing them, with precision, in a straight row on the shelf when Mickey ran in. "Hey, Skinbones. Let's go." I was embarrassed by Mickey's nickname for me and looked for Kip's reaction, but he kept on polishing.

Mickey's Brownie camera was strapped on his hand. He had joined the Kodak club and took pictures of common things—a curved trolley track in the cobblestones or a sign in a storefront. He mailed the film to the club, and they returned new film along with small photographs in shades of gray.

Aunt Irene and Father were out of earshot, so I lied. "They need me here."

Men sat biding their time, and I doubted that any would

order a meal. A fortunate few had devoured breakfasts or lunches bought for them by the salaried customers, but the rest had been sipping their cups since early morning, being cooled by the ceiling fan, wearing overcoats that they sported even on days when it was hot enough outside to clarify butter. I could easily have gone to *Tarzan* and returned in time to help with the afternoon patrons, but I wanted to stay.

Usually, the men who worked odd jobs with us disappeared at the end of their tasks, and I was glad to see them go. Kip was different. He was unlike anyone who ever came to us looking for work, anyone who ever walked into our restaurant. The bounce in his step made it seem that our linoleum floor was on springs, as in a story Father told from his boyhood, but Kip's bounce was his own.

"Who's that?" Mickey pointed.

"Just someone helping out. He fixed the sign."

Mickey scrutinized the window. "A little crooked."

"Picky Mickey." I stuck out my tongue. My brother had a keen talent for precise drawing of automobiles and wanted to be an illustrator for magazines. He had tried working as the Bluebird's afternoon dishwasher, but he had let enough dishes slip from his hands that Father suggested he could sell magazines to earn money, polish the Ford, and tidy the back alley at the Bluebird.

I noticed wavy edges on the *R* and *D* and said, "I think it's fine. And curves are hard.

"Not for me, Skinbones. Too bad you'll miss seeing *Tarzan*."

He ran out, stopped in front of the window, and raised the camera, motioning for me to move into the picture frame. Kip stepped out from behind the counter. I waved and, as Mickey snapped the photo, Kip looked my way. All afternoon, I kept him in sight. He washed dishes, swept, and polished the floor to such a shine that as Aunt Irene was taking off her apron to leave she gave him roundabout praise. "Bees knees. It's almost too bright in here. Don't forget to lock up, Elliot."

At closing time, Father signaled to the lingering customers, who shuffled out as he fumbled in his pocket for the key. Kip and I followed. The stragglers headed to the river bottoms and rail yards. Kip watched them go. Father found the key in a pocket and locked the front door.

"You could board with us and help out at the restaurant," Father said. "If you don't mind sharing the basement room with another gentleman."

Kip regarded the street ahead and the BLUEBIRD BUFFET sign, as if they held the answer. "Thank you, sir. I can stay a few days."

"This way then." Father started uphill and Kip fell in, matching his stride, their two hats at equal height. I kept pace behind them.

Ever since times became difficult after the Great Crash, we had boarders living with us. Except for our current one, who had worn our patience after only two weeks, they were usually agreeable men. Near starving when they arrived, they ate our food and paid us a bit when they found work. Mother said that they were good men caught in bad times and we were to count our blessings, which I tried to do when one was lingering in the bathroom across the hall from my room and I needed him to get out. Father enjoyed being a host.

A southward breeze swept the stink of cattle from the stockyards toward downtown. The newspapers reported fifteen hundred men a day coming through Kansas City, hopping off trains in the bottoms, looking for work in the slaughterhouses or rail yards, and escaping their worries at the speakeasies. Crime had increased in the vicinity of the Bluebird, but it couldn't be blamed only on the transients. There was the homegrown corruption of Boss Tom, who was Chairman of the Democratic

Party and had a grip on KC politics. People said he bribed the police to clamp down on some crimes and allow others to run rampant, giving criminals a place to hide out in our town, which was known to be wide open. I had overheard customers' conversations, which Father avoided. He said, "If you can't say anything nice, don't say anything at all."

He had lost bids to Boss Tom, who owned a cement company and had ways of winning contracts to enrich himself and his cronies. Rumors flew that his projects used excessive quantities of cement. "He has friends in high places, but he's a common bully," Aunt Irene often said. "He gets his grunts to tighten the screws and cover up his schemes."

One grunt owned the buildings that housed the Bluebird and also the Hayride Jazz Club where people danced and drank bootleg liquor. A man and a woman wearing a hat with a feather now passed us on their way there. We shared our back alley with the club, and I had peeked into the dark and smoky room, which had a hay-wagon stage, hay-bale seats, and a floor littered with hay and cigar stubs. It seemed a miracle that the place hadn't burned down.

Most transients hopping off trains near the riverfront stopped at restaurants on First Street, but plenty found us on Fourth. Aunt Irene said we should post a sign reading *This way for a handout*. Other places refused to let the hobos linger or the Negro railroad workers hold their meetings, but Father welcomed them all.

He turned away from the sinking sun toward our neighborhood, built on a bluff rising as high as a ten-story building above the rail yards. He often took the direct route to the Bluebird, but, on the way home, he preferred to veer past Millionaires' Row to Cliff Drive, which snaked through Terrace Park, and stop at the Lookout for a view of our city's progress.

Leafy treetops cascaded to the rocky cliffside, which

dropped down to Kansas City Southern and Missouri Pacific trains lined up on their tracks. Across the river, a silvery plane landed at the airfield, where the Transcontinental & Western Air fleet sat with tail tips to the ground, wings wide, and noses to the sky. Near river's bend, where the Kansas flowed into the Missouri, our grid of streets began parading southward.

"That's the Bluebird, Kip. Do you see it?" I pointed. "Four streets from the tracks."

He nodded, and Father said, "From which way did you come?"

Kip pointed east. Figuring Father wouldn't pry further, I said, "New York?"

"Saint Louis. Today."

"Once—I went there with Mother." I almost said that Mickey had once ridden the rails that far, but my parents didn't know about his escapade, and he may have fibbed to me. Traveling to St. Louis was my only train ride, and the farthest I'd been from home.

Kip pointed midtown. "What's the one with all the—oh, the colors changed." The green became pink and then green again.

"That's the Power and Light—the tallest building in Missouri. Thirty-four stories. In New York City, only six buildings are taller. Father and I have located them all on our map. I'll show you at home. And there's the Fidelity Bank Tower. Father helped to design and build it."

"Snazzy," Kip said. "I've never met anyone who built something so—impressive."

We walked along Cliff Drive onto Gladstone, where our church sat among a row of brick mansions that Aunt Irene said were "ostentatious." We passed the grand house that Eugene's grandfather had built long ago when he became a railroad tycoon. Eugene had lived there with his grandmother. His parents lived there, too, when they weren't in New York City mingling with other writers, artists, and publishers. I read a story of theirs in a *Vanity Fair* magazine at the library. Aunt Irene called them "silver-spoon Bohemians."

After Eugene's grandmother had died in early January, his parents had taken him to live with his great-uncle in New York. Eugene wrote to me that they were giving him more presents, not more attention. He had always shared with me whatever he had, never making me feel the poorer. His grandmother had been generous to me, but not to the hobos who climbed the cliff and tramped through the bushes, knocking at doors for odd jobs and food. Eugene had said that his grandmother was afraid of these men because they came from elsewhere. His parents wrote all night and napped during the day and didn't like being bothered by strangers.

Father turned onto Elmwood, where our foursquare house sat in a row of Kansas City Shirtwaist style homes with stone front porches and wood-sided upper stories, painted in blue gray or dusty rose. Ours was yellow. Perhaps the cheery color and the backyard garden were enough to signal a handout, or perhaps a hobo had scratched a symbol indicating Mother's generosity.

When we arrived home, she was chatting with Aunt Irene over a platter of sandwiches. Knowing how Father liked to meander, Mother often didn't wait to serve the family supper on evenings when he closed the restaurant. My brothers had run out to play, and my sister was with her new beau. We were used to the eager boys who courted Betty, a senior-class beauty queen, but this new suitor was shy and older.

Father introduced Mother to Kip, who greeted her with hand to heart and a bow. Our boarder, Mr. Crowley, emerged from the basement. "This is Kip Kelly," Father said. "He'll be sharing the room down there with you for the week."

Mr. Crowley extended his big hairy hand, but Kip again

put hand to heart and bowed. I wondered where he learned this sort of politeness. Mr. Crowley wiped his palm against his trouser leg and scowled. He took two sandwiches and stomped downstairs.

A hurt expression crossed Kip's face. "I didn't mean to offend him."

"He's always crabby," I said.

Mother scolded. "Mattie, don't be unkind. Will you sit with us and have a sandwich, Kip?"

"May I take one with me? I'd like to hit the hay."

"Of course. You must be worn out. Mattie, please run upstairs for clean bedding."

When I returned, Kip took the sheets in his arms with a "thank you."

"Let me show you the way, young man," Father said. Kip followed him to the basement.

I listened to a mumbling from below as I ate. When Father returned, I wrapped half of my sandwich in a napkin, put it on a plate to save for my bedtime snack, and joined him in the living room.

The Philco played "Gee, but I'd Like to Make You Happy" as Mother sang along and painted more leaves on the tin box. Aunt Irene waved an envelope. "This boy is wearing out the postman."

I took the letter. Since first grade, Eugene and I had sat alphabetically side by side in school—Turner, Toft. He always had Life Savers in his pocket and would hand me a candy when the teacher wasn't looking. Used to passing notes under our desks, we naturally began writing letters after he moved to New York. Now he lived in a penthouse with a terrace view of rooftops, trees in pots, and skyscrapers beyond. He got dizzy looking over the edge of the railing to the street below but said he couldn't fall off, unless he climbed over and jumped on purpose. I opened the envelope, *Dear Mattie, I will never find a friend like you here. Come visit.*

I longed to see the New York high life, as Mother had once done with Eugene's parents, who had treated her to a trip as a "thank you" for the special attention she gave Eugene when they were often away. His grandmother had been home to take care of him, but he liked to stay to dinner at our house. A lot more happened around the table in our small dining room than in her big one, where the two of them ate with the butler watching. Eugene didn't like being an only child. If he happened to be visiting me when Mother gave the boys a haircut, she would sit him down and give his curly hair a trim. If Father took us on an excursion in the car when the restaurant was closed on a holiday, Eugene would crowd into the back seat with us. He always fit right in with the family.

Some time before the trip that Mother took with his parents, she and I went to a vaudeville revue in downtown Kansas City at the Midland Theater, where we particularly noticed a young girl from Georgia. Then Mother saw her in a role on Broadway. I liked knowing that a girl could start out singing a bit part and make it big.

Mother had looked out from a high floor in the world's tallest building, the Bank of Manhattan Trust, rising seventy-two floors above Wall Street—over nine hundred feet. She sent a postcard so that Father and I could mark the location on our map, but the building didn't hold the record for long. A month later, the Chrysler Building measured more than one thousand feet with antenna, and now the Empire State Building nearly fifteen hundred feet.

Mother had enjoyed the trip, but said during dinner the night of her return that, even if she had all the wealth that the Turners had, she'd never be comfortable spending money so lavishly or going out on the town every evening. She had smiled at us around the table. "Everything I need is right here with you."

While in New York, Mother had a chance to make peace with the fact that her parents had been injured in the Wall Street bombing of 1920. "They happened to be in the terribly wrong place at the wrong time," she said.

They had never fully recovered and passed away within a few days of one another when I was a baby. Soon after, Father's parents died of heart problems. When Father had a scare with his heart and was told he might not have long to live, our family changed to the church we attended now, where people believed in the power of mind to heal.

On the rug beside Mother's feet, our old dogs grumbled in their dreams. When her missionary cousins moved to Japan, they gave us Sakura, a fluffy white Spitz. Our black-and-brown mutt showed up on our doorstep the year I was born. Father named him Raldo after Ralph Waldo Emerson, whose books were on our shelves, along with those of other philosophers, poets, and writers of adventures whom Father described as being spiritual and worldly. "Journeys into and beyond oneself."

Heart of Darkness promised a journey down a river, but I hadn't read past the first page where "gloom" was mentioned twice. *The Wonderful Wizard of Oz* was tattered from reading. I had outgrown its magical silver shoes, winged monkeys, and a wizard who pretended to have all the answers. *As I Lay Dying,* a book that Father had recently finished, rested askew.

I flipped the pages. "An old woman watching her own coffin being built?"

Father, who was studying his Emerson, glanced at me. "Yes, and a plunge into the minds and souls of people similar to and yet much unlike ourselves."

"I'll read that book when I'm older."

Father believed that when people came to greater self-knowledge and understanding of others, we would embrace our shared humanity and improve the common good. He trusted that I would choose what I was ready to absorb and would always do what was right. I had never wanted anything more than to please him, but I was eager for the June *American Girl* magazine to arrive at the library and didn't want to think about dying. "I'd like a true story with a happy ending."

Aunt Irene muttered. "Happy endings are for fairy tales."

"Not at all," Father said. "Many real-life tales resolve hopefully."

"Baloney. All lives end the same—in a box." She dropped a stitch and turned the dial.

"I Got Rhythm" played and Father said, "It's your tune, Mattie."

I had been memorizing the lyrics for soloing on Sunday, replacing "my man" with "my faith" at Father's suggestion. I wished I had as much faith in my singing as he did.

When the song ended, Father moved to the card table. "Shall we see what stuck?"

I sat beside him with the open atlas and located places he had identified on previous evenings—cities in Europe where our ancestors were born and where he passed through during the war, towns he traveled to in Missouri and Kansas and as far as Oklahoma on trips seeking contracts to build churches, schools, and banks. His eyes lit up when I named a building he had designed in Wichita.

"One hundred thousand bricks in that one," he said. It was built the same year they opened the Bluebird.

"You like being an architect so much, Father. Why did you start a restaurant? It's a lot of work and trouble."

"Don't be cheeky, Margaret Ann." Aunt Irene often criticized me for being brash. Her husband and daughter died in 1918 from influenza, and she moved in with Father, Mother, Betty, and newborn Mickey. I followed in two years and Wiley in seven. Aunt Irene helped Mother take care of us all. "And ungrateful."

"I didn't mean to say that it's trouble for me, Auntie." I was sorry that her sadness had drained her. I wished I'd known her before she became a cup-half-empty person.

"You know that painting of the little bluebird?" Father voice was deep and resonant with a chuckle at the ready. I knew the painting, of course, and the story he was about to tell.

"Shush." Aunt Irene turned up the radio.

A man's voice burst through static. "Foolish optimists . . . dark realities . . . temporary relief . . . top . . . permanent . . . bottom up . . ."

"Did you hear that, Elliot?"

"He's talking about President Hoover, Irene."

"An emergency equal to war . . . take disciplined action . . ."

"I agree with Governor Roosevelt. He's the one most likely to do what's needed, but the ladies are favoring Smith again." Aunt Irene belonged to the Civic Club. When she was young, she saw Emmeline Pankhurst give a speech. Ever since, she had held strong opinions on politics. I liked this about her. She had marched for the right to vote. Every election day, she pinned on her best hat and strode to the polling place, arm in arm with Mother.

Father smiled. "If I were a gambler, I would put my money on Roosevelt. I may be an optimist, but am I foolish?" He liked to goad his sister into arguments and entice her to side with him. "There's a stirring in people's hearts, don't you agree."

"The haves and the have-nots are setting up camps. The veterans marching to Washington to demand their bonuses are a sign of the times. They want action, Elliot—"

"They deserve it after having fought for our country."

"You fought too."

"But we are not destitute."

"Not yet."

"I left my home for the war. I hope never again."

"Hope won't pay Power & Light, much less Edgar Steeken. I wouldn't put it past him to raise the lease or burn the place down for the insurance money." The name of the Bluebird's landlord hung in the air. He was as unpleasant as Mr. Crowley.

"Put your letter in here, Mattie. Be careful to let the leaves dry completely." Mother handed me the tin box. "Go on up to bed so you'll be bright-eyed tomorrow."

I thanked her with a kiss and gave her the envelope for her to scissor apart later and use for her daily writing, along with other paper scraps we saved for her. I went to the kitchen to eat my leftover sandwich. Mr. Crowley stood beside the empty platter licking his fingers.

"That was mine," I said.

He looked down at me. "Was it?" He shrugged his shoulders. "No way of tellin'."

I stuck out my tongue and ran upstairs, where I nudged the tin box under my bed and opened my diary. I licked a pencil lead and put the tip to paper.

Dear diary,

Today Amelia landed safely and Kip Kelly came home with us.

I paused to consider all that had happened. "On the Sunny Side of the Street" drifted from the living room. My parents were singing along. Even when things were bleak, they found happiness every day, unlike Mr. Crowley, who spoiled it for everyone. I drew a doodle, which became his scowling face, and scribbled him into a furious gnarl of gray. Beneath, I wrote in big letters: *GO AWAY.*

CHAPTER FOUR

Two Travelers

Sunday morning, Kip came up from the basement rubbing his eyes. Mother served him oatmeal and said, "Mattie is singing today at early service. Would you care to join us?"

"I'd like to stay here, if you don't mind," he said. "I didn't sleep at all." He wished me luck and ate quickly. Mr. Crowley had already departed for his shift at the train yards. I stood to clear the dishes.

Mother plunked me down to brush my hair and said in a hushed tone, "I thought I heard shouting last night. Did you?"

"Mr. Crowley gets in moods. He's a sour old man who smells like a mildewed towel."

"He has met with great misfortune in the war and ever since. Don't squirm, please." She handed me the wide red ribbon that matched my church dress.

I tied a bow. "And he's jealous of Kip, who is so easy to like."

"Your father has certainly taken to him. We all have."

"Mr. Crowley could try to be cheerier. You tell us that even if things aren't our fault, it's up to us to make them better and get along with others."

"I believe that he is a casualty of these times. Perhaps we can help him find his way. Oh, that's lovely." She took the bow and fastened it tight to my head with a clasp.

"Ouch."

"I'm sorry, dear." She loosened it. "I'll go pin on my hat. Please be sure Wiley's face is clean and round up everyone. We'll be off with minutes to spare."

Mother usually braided my hair, which was thick like hers but dull as weak tea. On Sundays when I performed, she glamorized me. Father wrote skits for the occasional pageants, and our church music director Mrs. Abernathy, a Ziegfeld girl who had married a KC banker, altered her follies costumes to suit the drama and cast me in starring roles. She gave me peppermints for extra rehearsals and a piggy bank, where I saved coins. At Easter, she had dressed another girl and me as flowers. We sang the verses of "Happy Days Are Here Again," and the congregation belted out the chorus. That song had become an anthem of sorts. Everyone wanted to believe it was true, or maybe that singing about happier days would bring them to us all.

Today, walking to church, I lagged behind the others, repeating "my faith, my faith" so I wouldn't slip and sing "my man." Throughout the sermon, my stomach fluttered. During the offering, when I tiptoed out of the sanctuary to put Mrs. Abernathy's sequined dress over my own red one, I was shaking. She cinched a scarf around my waist and pushed me back into the aisle. "Remember to breathe."

I strode to the altar and faced the waiting congregation. Some I knew by first name; others I pinned by surname to a family group—the Andersons, Greens, Tates, Whites. My family smiled from the front pew and Aunt Irene frowned, no doubt in disapproval of the sequins. My heart galloped as the pianist began playing.

I opened my mouth and a sound rose from my belly, filled my chest, and spilled from my throat something glorious, unlike what had happened at our rehearsals. I belted out the lines about not needing money to be happy, but needing birds, flowers, and music, and not asking for more. People smiled. When I spread my arms wide and sang, "I've got my faith," they sprang up clapping.

Afterward, Mrs. Abernathy said, "You could be a professional, up in lights with the Aherns." She had once taken me to a hotel downtown where presidents stayed to see Lassie Lou, an actress in *Our Gang* pictures, performing with her older sister, Peggy. The Aherns asked girls from the audience to join them on stage to sing "The Star-Spangled Banner." Until now, that had been my greatest moment in show business, and I basked in Mrs. Abernathy's praise. By the next Sunday, I would be asking for something more.

We walked to the Bluebird, where Kip was waiting out front. "Was your song a success?"

"Yes," I said, wishing he'd been there to see it.

"Mattie was right on the money." Father felt in his pocket for the key. "I'm about to make a scramble. Are you hungry this morning?"

"I am, sir." Kip grinned.

Father swung the door wide for us to enter. As we all helped him in the kitchen, Aunt Irene took trash to the alley and came back angry. "You forgot to lock the back door last night, Elliot."

"Did I? I'm sorry. I thought I had."

"If you aren't more careful, we'll have vagrants spending the night and eating from cupboards."

"I see nothing out of place today, Irene. Let's enjoy these omelettes before they're cold."

We carried our plates out to the tables, and Father said, "Kip might like to hear your song, Mattie. Could you make it our blessing?"

As I sang, Kip watched me closely. I felt more nervous than I had with the entire church audience. When I finished, he said, "I like that tune. You sang it fine."

After lunch, Mother and my siblings took a streetcar home. Kip proved himself capable at his tasks and charmed Aunt Irene, who paid him attention instead of criticizing me, asking him to do this and that. "Kip, could you fill the salt and peppers? The sugar bowls, too."

"Where is the—?"

"In the pantry. Mattie can help."

I jumped to it, and we began collecting from the tables. By now, his second day, I was used to the sounds his tap shoes made as he walked around the restaurant. We brought the shakers and sugars into the pantry and placed them on the worktable in the center of the little room. A single light bulb hung above us. I unscrewed the lid from a glass shaker and began pouring from the bag into the small opening, spilling a quantity of salt.

Kip said, "Hold on. This won't cut the mustard." He found a piece of newspaper, furled it into a funnel, and stuck the pointed end into the opening. "Now pour."

In no time, we filled the salt and peppers. I opened a bag of sugar, and Kip made a bigger funnel. As the sugar poured into the last bowl, I was aware of his closeness. I didn't want the sensation to end. I wanted him to know something special about me, and I wanted to learn something of him for my own. "Do you have a big dream for your life, Kip? A plan?"

He placed the funnel on the table and it unfurled. "I don't trust in dreams and plans."

"But if you don't have a dream and don't step toward it, how will it come true?"

"You're lucky if you can believe that."

"Father says if I put the power of mind on something, it will manifest. I'm going to be in the pictures someday. I intend to be the star, but I'll start in the chorus."

"Well, then. You'll need an edge." He sized up the pantry and pushed the table against the wall, opening up a narrow space in the center of the room. "Watch me and listen. Steal my steps. It's how you learn to tap. First do a shush. Heel raised."

He slid his right foot forward on the floor and leaned slightly into it. "Then add a chug." He dropped his heel with a clack. He did the left foot, and then the right again, one after another. Shush, chug, shush, chug. He traveled the length of the pantry and turned around toward me.

"It's called the railroad."

I swayed my arms forward and back, as he did. I felt like a rag doll.

"That's a good mimic, but listen for the sound." He shushed and chugged, picked up two sugar bowls, and shushed and chugged out to the tables.

I tagged behind with a pair of salt and peppers in each hand, listening to his steps and my own. The customers glanced up from their cups. Kip and I railroaded until we had delivered all the shakers and sugars to the tables.

Back in the pantry, I said, "My shoes don't make tap sounds like yours." My Buster Browns were boxy, not sleek.

"Tacks in your soles will do the trick, but getting the rhythm is what matters. Now here's the train." He crossed his right foot in the air in front of his left and leaned forward while twisting his whole body in that direction. "Plant your weight on the ball of your front foot, lift the back foot, and stomp as you lean back onto it. Then bring the right foot back beside it, shifting your weight again with a right step, left step. Then cross your right foot in front again. Cross, back, stamp, stamp. Cross, back, stamp, stamp." He repeated the sequence a few times, and I heard the train.

"You can stay in place or move down the tracks." He danced out into the hallway, repeating the sequence with grander stamps and wider swings of the leg. His hair bounced and his eyes shone. It was as if a motor inside of him had needed warming up and now shifted him into gear. He chugged into the kitchen, came out, and headed my way. Grinning, he stopped in front of me. "Your turn."

I stamped and leaned, lifted and stepped, until I found the rhythm. *Chu, chu, chu, chu.*

"All aboard," Kip said with a smile. "Here's a variation. Add a brush back. It's called a spank." This time when he stepped back on his left, he brushed his right foot back and stepped down on it to the right. Then he stepped down on his left foot to the left and repeated.

I tapped it. Cross, back, spank, stamp. I added a slow shush with my left and finished with a hard chug on my right. *Chu, chu, chu, chu,* shush—chug.

Kip repeated my steps. He railroaded out the back door into the alley and waved goodbye. In a few seconds, he was back.

"Where did you learn to tap?" I asked.

"Back home."

"Where's that?"

"Kip?" Aunt Irene called him to the kitchen.

My questions would have to wait, but I didn't mind. All through the afternoon, I moved with a zing that I would have said came from the morning's solo in church, the last week of school, and all the summer days ahead. Later, I recognized something more, something I couldn't name at the time.

For dinner, Mother had prepared cream puffs, as she did whenever a new boarder joined us. I was eager to get to dessert. In the dining room, Mother and Aunt Irene squeezed together at their end of the table and Father sat at the opposite end. Betty was to my right. During the two weeks Mr. Crowley had been with us, he had been to my left at Father's right corner. Tonight I pulled out that chair for Kip. Mr. Crowley had to sit at Father's left corner, beside Mickey, who was all elbows. Wiley was next to him.

Raldo and Sakura, optimistic old dogs as they were, maneuvered under the table. They had lost their bark and bite, no longer able to chew much at all. We were forbidden to feed them at dinner, but a tidbit might fall from my brothers' hands or mine.

As a blessing, Father often recited a few lines of his own. We bowed our heads as he spoke. "A weary traveler stopped on the dusty road and rested a heavy load. He saw an old man and said, 'All day, I've trudged on sharp rocks that bruised, while overhead the sun burned. How's the road ahead?' The old man said, 'As you came, you'll find yonder is the same.' Then a cheerful youth said, 'All day I've traveled 'neath the sun's light. The birds sang, the flowers smiled, and breezes cooled. How's the road ahead?' The old man said, 'As you came, you'll find yonder is the same.'"

Father unfolded his napkin. "Bless us all. Amen."

We chorused, "Amen." The dogs' tails thumped, Kip's foot jiggled, and Mr. Crowley scowled. Mother must have spoken to Father. The parable was his way of talking to Mr. Crowley. Kip was the youth, and Crowley was the bleak traveler. Father's mistake was in believing that a man's small, wounded heart could be healed by a well-intended story. We had learned about the human body in school. Bones decayed and muscles atrophied. I assumed the heart muscle did too. It needed exercise, or it wouldn't expand to hold all the love it was meant to hold. Mr. Crowley's heart had shrunk.

Mother served egg gravy with chipped beef, a meal we ate often. Tonight the beef flecks were more sparse than usual. Mr. Crowley heaped his plate.

"Looks delicious, Clara." Father dished a small portion over his toast and passed the bowl to Kip. "Young man, you are an asset to the Bluebird. Isn't he, Irene?"

"Cat's pajamas. We've never had anyone quite like him."

Father reached to pat Kip on the back. "You made quick work of the dishes and all else today. You're good to have around."

Kip said, "Thank you, sir."

Mr. Crowley glowered. Mickey stared at his plate. Wiley stuck out his tongue, but Kip was busy spooning gravy and didn't see it. In midlift, he glanced at those of us who had not been served, put the spoonful back, and passed the bowl to me.

Father registered the mood shift. My parents usually encouraged brotherly loyalty, but Wiley's behavior was unacceptable at the table. Rather than chastise Wiley, Father praised. "Good job on the automobile, sons. I saw my reflection in the shine." The boys beamed with pride.

Mr. Crowley ate with his head down, shoveling the gravy toast into his mouth. During the first days after he arrived at the Bluebird, cap in hand, he helped us out there, but he was so unpleasant to customers that Father suggested he might be happier elsewhere and offered to ask a friend about the rail yards. Crowley now rose at dawn to stack crates.

"And how was your day, Mr. Crowley?" Father waited for him to finish chewing. "Nice weather for working outside, I'd say."

"How would you know? Sittin' there in your clean white shirt."

Father cocked his head, unsure how to take the comment, but gave him the benefit of the doubt. "Well, sir, I can only imagine that it might have been. Work is a blessing."

"Some ain't as blessed as you see it. None of your prissy aprons in the yards."

"Children—" Mother's voice had a lilt and her toast a smear of gravy. The serving bowl was empty. "I'm sure you will hear this tomorrow. Yancy Clark ran away from home."

"When?" Mickey was Yancy's classmate.

"Mrs. Nelson said that Mr. Nelson saw him in the train yards Friday after school and tried to catch him, but Yancy hopped into a moving boxcar." Our neighbor loved to gossip, which Mother, in her sweetness, rarely challenged. A customer had said that Boss Tom owned Mr. Nelson, a policeman, but I didn't believe that it was possible for a person to own city employees. The Clarks lived up the street.

Wiley gasped. "Holy moley."

"Nancy told me their father hit him," Betty said. She knew Yancy's sister.

"Perhaps a spank?"

"No, Mother. A slug."

"I doubt that Herbert Clark would intentionally hurt any child, even though he is under a great deal of pressure at the bank."

"That's no reason," Betty said.

"It's no excuse, certainly. But what's to be gained from running away from home? The world can be a cruel place, and Yancy may find out how cruel." Mother smiled at each of us children around the table, as if memorizing the comforting picture of it.

"Some boys need their adventures and do fine. It takes gumption," Father said, watching Kip cut gravy toast into squares on his plate and arrange them in a checkerboard pattern.

"I pray he returns soon." Mother's gaze lingered on me because I was the only one returning hers. "Mrs. Clark is broken up. I know how wretched I would be if one of you left me."

"I think it's cruel to name your kids rhyming names." Mickey gulped his milk.

Kip regarded Mickey over a forkful of gravy toast and said, "Elaine and Blaine."

Mickey laughed and snorted milk out of his nose.

Wiley shouted, "Sam and Pam."

The boys yelled over one another, "Frank, Hank. Lloyd, Floyd. Mary, Harry, Larry."

I chimed in. "Errol, Meryl, Carol."

Betty followed with a rhyme that fell flat. "Albert. Robert." Her talents were in sewing.

Giggling, Mother pushed back her chair. "You children know how to ease a mother's fears and lighten a worrisome conversation. Time for dessert."

She carried the platter of cream puffs to the table, making a ceremony of serving the biggest to Kip last. He lifted it from the plate with a "thank you," and we all bit into ours. The cream oozed, and we licked our lips. We watched Kip as a look of confusion crossed his face. He stuck out his tongue, removed a wad of cotton, and dropped it into his napkin. Embarrassment flushed his checks.

We shouted, "April Fools."

"We're delighted you are here with us, Kip." Mother handed him the puff she'd kept in reserve. "Here's a real one for you."

He held it with admiration, as if a gift he might keep. He took a bite and cream decorated the corners of his mouth. We told him how Mother baked the puffs as a joke for us one April Fools' Day. After that, we served them to our new boarders year round as a way of putting them at ease right away.

"No need to feel awkward at the table now." Father smiled. "We do appreciate good manners, but we all relish some fun at the end of a day."

Mr. Crowley scowled. His cream puff orientation had been in early May. He wasn't amused by our prank then, nor when he sat through the initiation of a boarder now departed. The only sign that Mr. Crowley had enjoyed the dessert tonight was the white smudge on his chin. He never showed gratitude for anything, not even a "thank you" for a meal.

After dinner, Kip offered to wash dishes. Father retired to the living room with his newspapers and Irene with her knitting. Betty went out with Albert, who had already become her new steady. Mickey and Wiley played dominoes at the card table, arguing about rules of blocking and scoring. Someone turned up the radio to "Life Is Just a Bowl of Cherries."

Thinking about how we'd be picking tart cherries from our backyard tree in a couple of weeks, I gathered ingredients to bake banana bread for the morning customers.

"Has anyone seen the butter? There's none in the icebox or cupboard."

"We'll use lard," Mother said.

"Ugh." I pretended to gag. A few classmates brought lard sandwiches for lunch.

"That's unbecoming, Mattie. See what you can make of these bananas."

A family friend who owned a grocery store sold us bruised fruit cheaply. With a sharp knife, I cut away stringy bits that were unfit even for baking. I placed the knife on the table, near the edge, and began mashing the pulp in a bowl. The kitchen was warm and steamy with fragrances of Oxydol and ripe bananas. I moved my feet in small shushes and chugs as I mashed.

The door to the basement opened, and Mr. Crowley loomed on the top step behind Mother, who was heaping flour into a measuring cup. He stared into the room with a peculiar expression on his face, as if he didn't quite know where he was or why he was there.

Kip was at the sink, the water running, dishes clattering. Mr. Crowley moved toward the table and, in an instant, had grabbed the knife. He waved it at Kip's back. "You," he growled. "Keep your paws off my stuff."

Kip didn't hear. What happened next felt like when a reel

at the moving pictures faltered—slowing to stopping to speeding up to burning away. In the slow part, Mr. Crowley lunged as Kip leaned right with a rinsed plate. His left hand was near the faucet. The point of the knife in Crowley's hand traveled straight toward Kip's hand, sliced into it and past it, and stabbed into the windowsill. Crowley's face hit the faucet. He stood up, blood pouring from his nose.

I screamed, and began kicking and pummeling Crowley as hard as I had once when Yancy had locked Wiley in a tool shed during hide-and-seek and left him there past dark. Kip snatched the knife from the sill and raised it like a torch toward the ceiling.

"Kip! Mattie!" Father stood in the passageway from the living room to the kitchen. Mickey and Wiley were beside him and Aunt Irene behind them.

I stopped in midpummel, fists clenched. For an instant time stilled. We were posed as if actors in a pageant. Mother held the spilled flour cup, a cloud of white dust drifting to the floor. Mr. Crowley was hunched over. Kip gripped the knife, and blood dripped from his hand.

"What's going on? Put the knife down, Kip." Father spoke harshly.

"He didn't do it." I yelled. "He did." I kicked Crowley again. Father grabbed my arm.

"He attacked Kip, Elliot," Mother said. "He tried to hurt him." Her hands shook as she set the measuring cup on the table.

Father stepped in front of Mr. Crowley. "Please pack your belongings." His voice was calmer, but his face was pained. He had never asked a boarder to leave our home.

Crowley's face was smeared with blood. "You're throwing me out now? At night?"

"The safety of my family is of greater concern now than

where you will lay your head tonight," Father said. "If you would like to find lodging downtown, I will drive you."

"I don't need your charity just so you can feel good about yourself. And what kind of family is this punk kid?" Mr. Crowley glowered at Kip. "I fought the Huns in the war. What'd he ever do? Couldn't count on the likes of him to keep them new Nazis down if we had to."

Mr. Crowley stomped downstairs into the basement, and Mickey said, "He lost his marbles."

"Do not be unkind. Prideful men also need our compassion. We don't know his hardships." Mother's eyes brimmed with tears. She wiped them with floury hands, trailing white smudges on her cheeks and eyelids and white flecks on her lashes. Coming from her, "prideful" was an insult. She didn't approve of name-calling, but I wished she had said it like it was. Mr. Crowley was a bully.

"Are you badly injured, Kip?" Father asked.

Kip placed the knife on the counter and held his bloodied hand over the sink. "Not much, sir."

"Let's have a look." Father turned on the faucet. The water flowed red then pink over Kip's hand, revealing a slice on the fleshy mound below his thumb.

"At least now you don't have to share the room with him," I said, handing him the dishtowel. As he took it, blood splattered onto my dress and socks and his shoes.

"Sorry, Mattie." He pressed the towel against the cut.

"It's okay." The spots disappeared into the flower pattern, but my white anklets now had red dots.

Mr. Crowley stomped up the stairs with a bedroll strapped to his back. He gripped a lumpy, blanket-wrapped bundle tied with rope. "You won't be getting nothin' more off me." He left the house with the slam to the front door.

I looked to Kip and then Mother. "I'll fetch Mrs. Nelson." Our neighbor had been a Red Cross nurse in the war.

"Honey," Kip said.

"Me?" My hand was on the doorknob. I turned to him.

"Do you have honey?"

"Oh." I let go of the knob.

"We do." Mother gave him a jar from the cupboard and a clean towel.

He spooned the amber honey onto the cut and wrapped the towel around his hand. "It will help to heal." He started down into the basement and then turned to us. "I only moved that bundle from one place on the floor to another. I'll sleep better tonight, now that he's gone." He closed the door behind him.

"Holy moley." Mickey said. "Did you see all that blood?"

Wiley nodded, eyes wide. "Holy moley."

"No more excitement tonight," Mother said. "All of you, run up and get ready for bed. Then I'll play a bit. And Mattie, be sure to put your clothes into a cold tub to soak."

My brothers and I donned our pajamas and sprawled on the landing, listening to "Moonlight Sonata" coming from Mother's piano. When she finished, we knew it was time to tuck in, and my brothers went to their room, but I wanted a glass of milk.

My parents and Aunt Irene were talking with an air of importance and hushed as I passed by. I opened the icebox, poured a full glass, and walked back toward the stairs, halting and sipping to keep the milk from spilling, hoping they would start talking again. Mother mended. Father and Irene watched me start up, and Mother called, "Good night, Mattie."

"Good night." I set the glass by my bedroom door and crept back to the landing.

". . . hard getting my fee from Fidelity now, Irene."

"They've owed you the balance on that contract for two years, Elliot. We can't get along without it any longer. Those flimflam men don't deserve another cent on the mortgage until they pay up. Herbert Clark should get off his high horse and see to it. You did the work."

"They are different departments, Irene. Herbert says he's sorry, but if we miss the June first payment, the bank will foreclose on the fourth. Fidelity holds his mortgage too, and they've cut his salary."

"Sorry? He's sorry?" Irene scoffed. "That bank deserves to fail. If I had any nest egg left after our foolish investment in the Bluebird and our stock losses, I'd take it out.

"People losing faith cause the failures. Fidelity is a sound institution."

"It's a grand building, Elliot. You never design anything less. But it's filled with small-minded men, and Herbert is one of them."

"I'd like to think he's done what he can. The Clarks have been good neighbors." Mother must have been patting the dogs, because their tails thumped.

"You paid the Bluebird lease already?" Mother said. "We have until the twenty-fifth. That's Wednesday."

"We discussed it last week." Father rarely spoke unkindly to Mother, but his tone was chastising. "The payment has cleared, Irene?"

"Yes, and utilities are due. We can't run a restaurant without gas and electricity."

"We've never missed a house payment," Mother said. "Surely—"

Irene interrupted. "We can risk losing the house more than the Bluebird, Clara. A little income is better than none. Power and Light will shut us off, and Steeken is getting greedier by the day. He may be bluffing about giving our lease to another speakeasy, but he's raking it in with the Hayride Club. No doubt he has a man inside Fidelity to appraise him of our deposits, little as they are. And Boss Tom to grease some palms."

Steeken's political crony was famous for his lavish gifts, but our landlord himself was known for stinginess. His daughter was nice, but my classmates called her "Stinky." She'd be stuck with it until the day she became Mrs. Somebody Else.

"The church bulletin board has offers of spare rooms. If it comes to that, we'll manage until the time when we can all be—" Mother's voice broke.

"I may yet get the Topeka and Atchison contracts, Clara. And the Sedalia job should finally be starting up tomorrow. If all goes well with the bank loan—"

The conversation lulled. Afraid they would hear me sneaking back to my room, I didn't budge. Mother said, "We'll let the phone and gas go here. I'll use my pin money toward the Bluebird utilities." She regularly painted items from the thrift store, sold them at the church benefits to help the less fortunate, and tucked a bit away for her own.

"Every spare moment goes into that, my love. It grieves me for you—"

"There's nothing I want beyond our family's togetherness."

I heard a kiss and then Father said, "You two go on up. I'll wait for Betty."

Raldo and Sakura padded toward the stairs with Mother and Aunt Irene. I scooted to bed and lay embraced by our house, believing Father would find a way to keep us here. I wanted to feel as I usually did—lucky and rich in the essential ways Mother spoke of, not poor. A breeze lifted the curtain. I breathed river and cattle and locomotive. I heard a whistle, the buckling and unbuckling of rail cars, and a cow's faint bellow. A moan came from beneath the window. I tiptoed to it. Betty and Albert were pressed against each other. The only time I had slammed like that into a boy was when Eugene had tagged me out at second base. I wondered how being in love was different from being in friendship.

I slid the tin box from under my bed and took out the heart locket Eugene had sent for my twelfth birthday. It contained a four-leaf clover from Central Park. I held the locket, imagining living with servants, being chauffeured to school, taking taxis to Broadway, and eating Bordelaise sauce over steak served by waiters wearing bow ties. I wanted to explore his island city and wander along streets where buildings soared higher than any-where else in the world. I opened a letter to the moonlight.

> *We'll see the bald-headed monkey at the menagerie and go by train to the Adirondack Boys and Girls Camps. A Hollywood agent wants my parents to write for moving pictures. Mother likes it here, but Father is melancholy. They go to a communist club where people believe that art is a weapon. Mother says the pen is her sword.*

I saw how a pen could be a sword, but I didn't want the bloody image in my mind while I was trying to sleep. I won-dered if Kip was awake and in pain from the stabbing. I thought a pen was more a spade for digging to free buried memories or a pickax to crack open ideas. Pencils worked too.

Betty tiptoed in, wafting perfume and grease. She unbut-toned her blouse and the moon hit her brassiere cones—high and pointy. When she released the back snap, her breasts emerged, plump and rounded. She cupped them in her hands, admiring herself in the mirror. I giggled.

"Don't spy." Betty snatched her nighty from the dresser.

I pictured her pointy brassiere contrasting with the curves of her body and doubted I had what it took to be in love. All that jutted out from me were elbows and knees. My chest was flat, no curves at all.

"Grow up, Mattie."

"I am." I whispered it so low she couldn't have heard.

Soon my sister was snoring softly, a slant of light on her face. Anyone could see why she had been chosen as high school queen. How could I ever measure up? I lay in bed, railroading my feet under the covers.

CHAPTER FIVE

Leaping Bells

On Monday, I sprang out of bed for the last week of school with my parents' concerns as foggy as a dream. During recess, I stayed in to help my teacher remove student work from the corkboard. When she went to call the class, I slipped thumbtacks into my pocket. As she droned on with the geography lesson, I touched the sharp points of the tacks through the cotton fabric of my dress.

The dismissal bell rang. I rushed to catch the streetcar, dashed along the alley to the Bluebird's back door, and bumped into Leroy coming in from carrying out the trash. He was our weekday cook.

"Whoa, Mattie. Why the hurry?"

"Just hungry, I guess." I had a gnawing, but not for the snack he always prepared. The hunger was in my feet.

"Your milk is poured and bread sliced. Get your jam and a bag of onions from the pantry. We'll talk while I chop. The new fella is making quick work of the dishes, one-handed no less." Leroy gave Kip a pat as he moved past to the chopping table. "He's a good egg."

I had known Leroy Calhoun all my life. He was the oldest son of Cyrus, who was superintendent of the apartment building a few doors down from our house. Cyrus was born in Georgia to slaves who came north after emancipation. He had worked in the rail yards but had been injured and lost his job. Now he spent part of his time growing the garden in our back yard.

Leroy turned on his radio. He lugged it to the Bluebird every weekday morning and home in the evening. An advertising jingle played.

"Hi, Kip," I said.

He didn't greet me or glance my way. Maybe he didn't hear me above the clatter and song. The announcer said, "And now to spice up your morning, here's a tasty little tune—'Need a Little Sugar in My Bowl.'"

Leroy quickly turned the dial. "Lord 'mighty. That's not for your ears, Mattie."

I'd heard the men in the Bluebird guffaw and knew that the song was about sugar, hot dogs, and rolls, but not really. I would have been curious to hear it, but all I was thinking about was being near Kip. I pulled a stool beside the table with him in view, close enough to hear Leroy, but far enough to keep the onion sting from my eyes. I spooned blackberry jam onto the bread.

Whenever Leroy said, "Talk to me," he meant "Listen." Being with him, I didn't need to think about what to say because he rambled on and answered his own questions. I licked the spoon clean of jam.

"Ever wonder how they grow? From a little bulb no bigger than this," he held up his pinkie, "—to this." He secured an onion on the cutting board and sliced. "Did you know it was a symbol of eternal life for ancient Egyptians because of the concentric rings? It'll cure almost anything that ails you." He slipped his finger through a ring, twirled it around, and bit into it. He licked his lips. "Nothing like raw Allium cepa."

I always shoved onions to the side of my plate, but Leroy

believed I would grow to like them. "Their flavor depends on sulfur in the soil. No sulfur, no kick. It's essential for life." For the Bluebird, he used pungent ones. Father loved them, especially in chili.

"I'm finished, Leroy. Is there another task?" Kip hung his towel on the rack.

"Peanut soup is on the menu tomorrow. You could shell the bag that's in the pantry. Mattie can help."

"Hi, Mattie." Kip waved with his injured hand.

"Does it hurt?" I put concern and sadness into my voice so he'd know I cared.

"Not much." He wiggled his fingers. "Leroy wrapped it tight." Some blood had seeped through the white rag bandage and stained it rusty red.

In the pantry, I showed Kip the tacks. He took them one by one from my hand and laid them on the table in a pattern for each shoe. While he shelled peanuts, I hammered the tacks into the soles at heel and toe. Then I railroaded across the floor, tapping as loud as I could.

"Easy, there. A precise sound is better than dull and loud. Make your feet tell the story."

I railroaded again, landing more lightly.

"That's coming along. Now, here's a challenge. The bell kick. Follow me."

In the hallway, he turned his right foot out and stepped forward on it, planting his weight with bent knee. He raised his left leg high to the side, then leapt up and tapped his heels together—*a* bell ringing to the left. He landed on his right foot. "Try it."

I did, but my feet tangled, and I stumbled. Flailing my arms, I fell against him, hitting his face. "Oops. Sorry."

He backed away, rubbing his eye. "You're a real live wire."

I jumped up and knocked my heels together. "Like that?"

"A clacker moves side to side. Like a pendulum. It swings." He leapt, rang his bell to the right, and landed on the left foot.

I tried it and stumbled. "Show me again."

"Your jump is too straight and still. Think of keeping your center down, even when you're lifting up." He tapped a few steps, sunk in the knees, and leapt. His heels met with a *bing*, and he landed. "You're going to come down, no matter what. Gravity is your best friend. Let it cradle you."

We leapt bells until Aunt Irene entered the hallway with a tray of dirty dishes, and Kip nearly toppled into her. "You two are gumming up the works," she said sharply. "Get on with your business."

We returned to the pantry and worked in silence. Kip took the bowl of shelled peanuts to the kitchen. I swept and went to wipe tables. At closing time, I made bell shapes to the left and right all over the restaurant, but no ringing sounds like Kip's.

That evening after dinner, Kip asked about his hat. He thought he had worn it home from the Bluebird on Sunday, but it wasn't in the basement or at the restaurant. I helped him search the house with no luck. Forlorn, he finally said "goodnight." I wanted to find the hat and take it to him, so I kept looking, though in places where I was certain his hat was unlikely to be.

Later, in my room, I practiced bells, landing with a thump after thump. Betty was reading in bed. "What are you doing?"

"Learning to tap." I leapt and landed, hitting the wall.

Betty threw a pillow and yelled. "Mother, make her stop."

Mother didn't come in, Betty rolled over, and I kept going. I must have known at that moment that I'd be dancing for as long as I lived.

CHAPTER SIX

Snakehips

During the math practice quiz on Tuesday, my teacher frowned when I missed an answer in the nine times table and flubbed a division question. I knew very well that trying to reduce some fractions to the lowest common denominator was like trying to divvy up a pie for four when it had been cut into seven pieces and everyone wanted seconds but only three pieces remained.

At the Bluebird, I met Kip coming out of the kitchen. "Watch this." I leapt high and came down with a thud.

"That's it, but land lighter." He did a quick bell. "Keep the lift in your hips while you drop the foot. The sound you're going for is short, then longer. Like this." His bell resounded in the hallway with a *bing bong*.

I stepped and leapt with a loftier bell and landed lighter. I was starting to get it. He did another bell and another, higher and higher, propelled up by an invisible force.

We practiced until Irene called us to refill cups and clear tables. I dashed to make a fresh brew, Kip carried away dirty dishes, and we met back in the hall for more bells.

Leroy exited the kitchen, heading to the alley with trash,

and on his return he stopped to watch. "Do that one again," he said.

I rang to the left and the right. "You have talent, Mattie." He started toward the kitchen and stopped. "You also have a fine teacher in Kip."

"Yes, I do."

Kip shrugged. "Here's one more for today."

He rolled his hips around and gyrated with an energy shooting through him from one foot to the other, lifting him off the ground with two clicks and setting him back down with two more. "Snakehips with a spring."

I swirled, leapt from left to right, brushed past him, and fell against the wall.

He laughed. "You have lift all right, but the snake is more like this." With a hand on each hipbone, he whirled around like a top. His hips seemed unattached to the rest of him.

I tried again, swirling slowly like a marble being rolled around with a fingertip.

"You've got it. Now break down the spring. It's the basic step ball change. Step onto the ball of one foot, drop the heel, then step onto the ball of the other foot."

I stepped and dropped like I was marching in place. *Cluck. Cluck.*

"Okay, now swing your leg out a bit and put a lift in the hips before you step. Transfer the weight from one foot to the ball of the other, and then drop the heel." He demonstrated slowly. Then with a wider swing of the leg and higher hip, he launched off the ground. "Exaggerate the lift to fool the eye."

I did it again and again, my body speaking this new language as if the moves had always been in me. Aunt Irene passed by with a tray of dirty dishes. "We could use your help in here. Both of you." I slithered with Kip into the kitchen, keeping the snake in my hips and a spring in my step.

I stood beside him drying the dishes, swiveling in time with the towel as I rubbed around and around. Kip laughed and swiveled as he handed me a rinsed plate, saying, "We're in sync at the sink."

That evening, Mother and I baked rhubarb pies. I rolled the crust and pinched it, taking time to perfect the fluted edges, while gyrating below my apron strings. "You are about to fly out of here and take the crust with you," she said. "That's unbecoming."

"It's only tap dancing, Mother."

"That may be, but you're growing up, Mattie, and that's not proper behavior for a girl who's almost a woman."

"Mrs. Abernathy did it. Lots of women do. Like this." I tapped out a step ball change. "Then you add the snake." I swirled my hips more modestly and finished with a shush, chug, shush, chug. I smoothed my dress.

"That's better. More ladylike." She smiled. "That's very good, Mattie. You have talent." She removed a pie from the oven. "Call down to Kip. He might like a slice of this while it's warm."

CHAPTER SEVEN

Tanglefoot

On Wednesday, I tapped beneath the desk during the final math quiz, and my teacher reprimanded me. "Mattie, sit still or go to the principal's office." I calculated while trying to glue my feet to the floor, but saw the steps and heard the rhythms in my head. Upon dismissal, I sprinted to catch the streetcar and tapped behind the driver all the way to my stop.

I raced to the Bluebird, filled customers' cups, wiped tables, and retreated to the kitchen stool, tapping my feet in the air to the lazy rhythm of "I Don't Know Why (I Just Do)," while Kip washed dishes. Leroy's chopping added a layer of percussion. He held up a mushroom as dark as charcoal. "Did you know these are called trumpets of the dead?"

"Because they're shaped like—?"

"Trumpets. The ancients saw them as being played by dead people from beneath the soil. They're also called black chanterelles. Hard to spot because they look like black holes in the ground under dead leaves. These were in the park by the waterfall."

I had gone hunting with Leroy in the North Terrace woods after a rain. We had found regular chanterelles and served mushroom soup all that week at the Bluebird. I picked up a dark fruity-smelling trumpet and held it to my nose. "Like apricots." I started to nibble.

Leroy snatched it away. "Not raw, Mattie. You need to be wary of false chanterelles. You won't die, but you'll have a bad tummy ache. The false ones are deep orange in color and don't smell like apricots, but always cook your trumpets if you don't want to die before your time."

The dish clatter ceased. Kip hung up the damp towel and stood beside Leroy.

I jumped off the stool. "What's next?"

"Heel dig." Kip slammed his right heel into the floor and leaned back into it with left foot raised, then dug the left heel and lifted the right." He sounded like a shovel hitting stone.

We shoveled around the kitchen, pots boiling, a cleaver hanging from the chopping table, our heels sharp on the floor, until we were laughing and Leroy was too. "You're both goofy," he said.

"Now try tanglefoot." Kip balanced his right foot on its heel with toe raised nearly straight up and twisted his foot back and forth. "Also known as corkscrew."

I tried. "That's easy."

"Combine it with this." He did the tanglefoot and then stepped his left foot over his right, moving sideways, his arms wide-angled to the ceiling and the floor like a windmill. He nearly toppled, windmilled again, lost his balance, and landed upright with a flat step right, then left. "Falling off a log."

"You fell on purpose?"

"Almost. You try it."

I twisted and tumbled, bumping into Leroy, who chuckled. "Take it out of here. Both of you."

In the hall, Kip said, "Here's rubber legs. Follow along." He started shaking his legs like they were detached from his body.

Mimicking his moves, I flopped my legs around from my

knees, as if they were wet noodles dangling from a serving spoon. It was not at all ladylike. We both started laughing so hard that Leroy poked his head out of the kitchen. "You two whacky peas in a pod could work up a comedy routine."

Kip showed me the barrel roll. With arms out like airplane wings, he turned and turned. I tried, but my wings were bent and going every which way.

He took my arms in his hands and straightened them to ninety-degree angles from my sides. "Stretch yourself, Mattie. Make your fingers point out flat—like arrows." He pressed my fingers together. His hands were warm and strong.

He demonstrated again, spinning in full circles. I tried it and got dizzy. Kip grabbed my elbow as I teetered.

"Focus on one spot every time you turn. Try looking at that switch on the wall. And keep a strong core to spin from." He hit his belly with his fist.

I tried with more success, and Kip joined in. We were rolling, arms winged wide, when Edgar Steeken came storming through the open alley door carrying an envelope. Kip didn't see him and clocked him in the face with his flat hand.

Kip lowered his arms to his sides. "Oh, sir. I apologize."

Steeken glared. "Watch yourself, kid. Where's your aunt, Margaret Ann?"

"In there." I pointed to where Irene had been at the counter keeping an eye on Kip and me, but she wasn't there. Steeken stormed into the dining room.

I peeked around the corner to see her holding a wiping rag and facing him. At the tables, customers stared into their cups. He handed Irene an envelope, but she crossed her arms and refused to take it.

"You can't raise the lease now, Edgar. We've already paid."

"I can and will do as I please through the renewal date, which is today."

"We've been good tenants. A raise is unfair in these times."

"Times are hard all around, Irene. My costs don't quit. Insurance, maintenance."

"We've asked you to maintain very little."

"There are standards for keeping the property value up. You've got the Negro men meeting here—"

"We have every right—"

"Don't test me on this, Irene." He slapped the envelope on a nearby table. "I'll give you until June first to pay the increase. If not, you'll be out by the fifteenth."

He brushed past Kip and me in the hallway. At the door, he growled. "You've got no license for a dance hall." He stomped out, nearly tripping, but caught himself before falling headlong into the alley.

Without skipping a beat and in perfect imitation, Kip stomped down the hallway, pretended to trip, and righted himself with a grin. I laughed and, behind me, Irene let loose a chuckle.

CHAPTER EIGHT

Trading Fours

Thursday was the last day of school. When the bell rang, I rushed out. I had always cared about my report card, but I never found out how I scored on the math quiz.

At the Bluebird, I gulped the milk Leroy poured and grabbed a towel to dry dishes as Kip washed. His injury was no longer bandaged, but he was careful using that hand. I ran through the moves in my mind—shush, chug, railroad, train, spank, bells, snakehips, heel dig, tanglefoot, falling off the log, rubber legs. My feet, tapping beside Kip at the sink, had taken on a life of their own, as if someone other than me were in control.

"Hold on." He stepped away from the sink. "You've got everyone talking at once. Yap. Yap. Yap. Make it more like a conversation. Set a tempo with a time step." He spoke the moves as he showed each one. "Stomp. Hop. Fa-lap. Ball change." He repeated them—clean and precise. "Stomp. Hop. Fa-lap. Ball change. Now you."

I did the moves I saw him do and tried to copy the rhythms I heard him make. He washed a stack of plates and turned on the tap to refill the rinse basin.

He flicked water from his hands and turned to me. "You've got a style going. Now let's take turns. Four measures, four counts each. Here's a simple phrase with your home town. Make the counts even. Kan-sas-Cit-y." He tapped on right toe, left toe, right heel, left heel.

I counted in my head and tried it. I was too long on the "Kan" and short on the "Cit."

"Almost." He did it again. "Even counts. One, two, three, four. Then repeat. Four times." He demonstrated. "Keep the rhythm tight."

I concentrated and stepped it out in steady fours. Kan-sas-Cit-y. Kan-sas-Cit-y. Kan-sas-Cit-y. Kan-sas-Cit-y

"Now change it up. Still four full counts for each phrase, but on the third phrase you add a brush hop to the fourth count. Phil-a-del-phi-a. Like this. One, two, three, four-and." He showed me the new rhythm, then stepped through the phrases. Kan-sas-Cit-y. Kan-sas-Cit-y. Phil-a-del-phi-a. Kan-sas-Cit-y.

I tapped, and it sounded right to my ears.

"Now add a different count. One, two-and, three hold, four-and. Pause on count three. In, di-an, a—, po-lis." He did a hop, shuffle, step hold, shuffle. "You try it."

I tapped, heard the distinct rhythm, and felt the difference in my body. Kan-sas-Cit-y. Phil-a-del-phi-a. In, di-an, a—, po-lis. Kan-sas-Cit-y.

"You got it, Mattie. Now you invent one."

I knew my states and capitals but could only think of city names with two or three regular beats: Lincoln, Topeka. I wanted something special. The Missouri Pacific calendar on the wall displayed a painting of a mesa that resembled a layer cake of red and buff-colored stone—a hot, dusty place under a lonely turquoise sky with no cloud in sight. I put together a phrase with a hop, hop, and leap. I landed on the right foot and fell back to the left. Kip tapped it back with a timing equal to mine. "Got a name for it?" he asked.

"A-ma-ril-l-l-l-o." I let the *l*s bounce and roll to the *o*.

"Aces, Mattie. You're a whiz. Let's trade fours. I'll change up yours first." Kip did my move again, adding his own touch. He tapped even counts on the first two syllables, then leapt wide on the trill, and dropped down for a percussive finish on his heel, soft on the toe.

"Now you riff on mine."

"Heads up!" Leroy shouted.

The sink had overflowed. Kip switched off the faucet and grabbed the mop before Aunt Irene could walk in and holler at us.

Leroy was amused, then thoughtful. "Kip, you ought to get in on the Tickle Your Ribs talent show down at the Hayride Club barbecue on June second. That's Thursday night next week. There's prize money. I can get you signed up. A pal of mine works in the kitchen."

"Do it." I clapped. "You could win."

Kip stared down as if asking permission of his feet. "Could I?"

"You're better than most. Isn't that right, Leroy?"

"That's all I'm saying. It's worth a try. Now, how about you two get out of my way?" Leroy grinned and swatted us with a towel. "I'll finish the mopping." He turned up the radio to a woman singing "All of Me."

I liked the song, though I couldn't make sense of the singer giving her body parts away. I was sure that when I grew up and fell in love with someone, we'd be as happy together as my parents were.

In the hall, Kip and I tapped out my Amarillo. "That's a duet," Kip said. "Now make it more your own. Try shaking out your ankle like you are flicking drops of water."

"Or like I'm stepping on hot stones?"

"That'll do. But be careful not to clutch or force it. Releasing the muscles in your foot and ankle gets you the cleanest sound."

I lifted my heel and toe more quickly off the imaginary hot stones. I let my body go sultry from the heat.

"Snazzy." He smiled in approval and tapped out his like popcorn pinging in a pan.

I soaked up Kip's praise as we did it again and again—me the butter in the kettle, him the popcorn. I flowed into the movement. It was alchemy. I had once read about it in the library and learned a new word. Transmutation. The solids were my bones become hot liquid, then slowly poured into a mold and shaped into something shining new and golden.

"Piece of cake, Mattie." Kip reached for my hand and held it lightly in his.

We danced, switching hands, left to right, right to left, me melting, him pinging, as if an electrical current ran between us. We switched and popped, melted and pinged. The sensations were different from anything I'd ever felt before. It was not only the alchemy that was moving in me. It was the magic of dancing with him as my partner.

Outside in the world, mean people like Edgar Steeken roamed dusty, lonely places like Amarillo. Here, inside the Bluebird, light streamed through the front window, ceiling fans cooled the air, and Leroy sang in the kitchen. I was the luckiest girl who'd ever lived.

The lucky feeling carried me to evening and through dinner, where I was keenly aware of Kip, sitting on my left, joking and laughing with my brothers. He seemed born to be family. Father winked at Mother over his bowl of chili and she smiled back. Crowley's chair was in another room and his annoying presence a faded memory. I knew we would be getting another boarder soon, for we always did after one departed. The new one would throw us off balance again, but for now we counted eight, an even number, four pairs. Mother and Father. Aunt Irene and Betty. Mickey and Wiley. Kip and me. Everything was right with the world, and I wanted to linger on that perfection.

Mother served a rhubarb oatmeal cobbler. I ate it slowly,

enjoying every bite, savoring each moment with Kip sitting beside me. My brothers squirmed and complained, eager to run out to play. I picked crumbs from my plate.

Wiley whined. "Hurry up, Mattie."

As I licked my fingers, the iceman's wagon rolled down the street. Mother said, "Okay, children. You're excused."

My brothers and Kip dashed outside, and I followed close behind. While the horses snorted and hooved the pavement, neighbors emerged from their houses, and the iceman chiseled pieces for us. Then he lifted the frozen block with tongs and hauled it to the side of the house to deliver it through the little door to the icebox in the kitchen.

We stood in the warm evening sucking on chips. Someone yelled, "Let's play capture the flag."

We organized into teams. My brothers, Kip, and I were all together. "Who's got a kerchief?" Mickey asked.

Kip pulled one from his pocket. "How about this?"

I recognized the gingham from a dress Betty had sewn for me that I had outgrown. My brothers didn't care much about clothes and said, "Let's go." I placed it on the fire hydrant on our team's side of the street, and we began playing.

Busy defending it from the other team, I shut off my mind from thinking about it. Later, while lying in bed before I drifted off, I tried to make sense of the fact that Kip's kerchief was exactly like the fabric scraps we had used to wrap the silver salt and peppershakers and sugar bowls.

CHAPTER NINE

Trust

Friday morning I awoke to summer sun flavoring our room. It tasted different than a school day. Betty was asleep, and I lolled in bed with the warm months stretching before me. I heard someone in the bathroom, the door opening, and footsteps down the stairs. By the time I was dressed and in the kitchen, Kip had already left for the Bluebird. I helped Mother finish baking pies, and we carried them in baskets on the streetcar to the restaurant.

I opened the glass case to refill it and lifted a single wedge of lemon meringue. I loved pie anytime of day, even if it was starting to seep juice.

"Leave that be, Mattie." Aunt Irene grabbed it. "Somebody will pay half price, and that's enough to buy lemons for another." She slid the wedge back with the new pies and closed the case.

Mickey raced in, out of breath. "Uncle Vincent's in the taxi. He's taking us to the airfield."

"What a fine surprise," Mother said. "Would you like to come along, Kip? Can you spare him, Irene?"

Kip looked to my aunt and back to us. "I promised to make a sign." She nodded, clearly pleased by his devotion.

"Tough luck," Mickey said.

I grabbed Mother's hand and pulled her outside to the taxi and Uncle Vincent. He was her brother and a pilot working for Transcontinental & Western Air. When he had visited us at Christmas, wearing his leather jacket and looking a lot like Lindbergh, he promised to show us a plane. When he knocked on the front door this morning, Mickey and Wiley were in their pajamas. I had never before ridden in a taxi.

We crossed the bridge over the tracks and river, a drive we sometimes took with Father to watch the mail planes land. We entered the airfield through a gate, not through the passenger terminal, and Vincent guided us to his Ford Trimotor.

Mother patted him on the back. "Daddy would be proud."

"A ticket to New York or Los Angeles costs more than most men make in a year." Uncle Vincent stood taller than I remembered him being at Christmas and said, "Would you like to step inside my Tin Goose? It's a tight fit. I'll take you one by one. Mickey first."

Other than my uncle, the only people I knew who had flown were Eugene's parents. I remembered his mother saying, "Flying is our last chance to pioneer. How dull by comparison to sit on a train being served in comfort with one's every wish indulged." The stewardess had polished his father's shoes, which didn't sound to me much like pioneering. His mother complained about the stench from passengers being sick and the insects that flew into the cabin through the opened windows. In killing a wasp, the stewardess accidentally slapped Mrs. Turner's cheek with the swatter.

"You're next, Mattie," Vincent said.

Entering his Tin Goose felt like being enclosed in a storm drain. Eugene, Mickey, and I had once ventured into one of those cement tunnels we shouldn't have. We'd waded in dank water that rose above our knees. Vincent's plane—built of pieces of metal formed to a tubular shape—had less headroom than the drain. Seats lined up on either side with a narrow aisle between them.

"Sit here." He buckled a strap. "Without this, you'd get bumped around. Flying is more thrilling than all the carnival rides put together."

He extracted a bowl from under a seat. "For airsickness. Our hostesses are registered nurses. They earn half again as much salary as a nurse on the ground and as much as an electrical worker or pharmaceutical salesman."

In the cockpit, he showed me how he steered, the location of the altimeter, and the importance of the knobs and dials. As we exited the plane, he said, "You could be a hostess when you grow up, Mattie, if you don't get much taller. That would be a good job for a smart girl like you before you get hitched."

"I wouldn't want to be worrying about spilling the airsick bowl. I'd rather be a pilot, like Amelia."

He patted my head. "Don't let your dreams get so big that your noggin explodes."

On the drive home, packed into the warm cab, I took in the sights. The airfield disappeared behind us, and the Missouri River lazed below the bridge. I wondered what it would be like to fly through the clouds and look down upon the streets, our house, and the Bluebird. I imagined seeing myself there in all the familiar places.

As we crossed over the train tracks, my brothers boasted how they would pilot planes when they grew up. They raspberried their lips and made engine noises. "Brrrmm. Brrrmm."

Mother tried. "Brrr. Brrr." Laughing, she sputtered again. "Brrr."

Wiley hugged her. "Do you wish you were a little boy like me?"

She kissed him. "But then I wouldn't be your mother."

"Do it like this." Wiley took her lips in his fingers and

pinched them into a pucker. He raspberried close to her face, spraying spit. "Brrrmm. Brrrmm."

"That's a bit too close." She pushed him away gently, found a handkerchief in her pocketbook, and wiped her smooth skin. Other mothers had necks that sagged and creases across the forehead. Mother only had faint wrinkles at the edges of her eyes that crinkled tighter when she laughed.

"I'll sell my drawings to buy us leather jackets like Vincent's," Mickey said.

"Best to put that money toward your school clothes, dear."

Wiley raspberried with his lips against the window. She lifted a strand of hair from across my eyes and whispered, "Why so quiet? Are you feeling well?" Her fingertips were cool on my forehead. "It's a big world, Mattie. Perhaps you'll see it all someday."

When we arrived home, I told her I wanted to take a streetcar to the Bluebird, but she needed help baking mock apple pies. I tried to preheat the oven, but it didn't light, and she said, "Mrs. Nelson offered to let us use her oven for the time being."

I mashed stale soda crackers, rolled crust, and carried the pies to our neighbor's house. When I returned, two hobos were at our back porch. While Mother made pickle sandwiches, Father arrived home earlier than expected. He was subdued but came out and sat with the men. One had been an English professor, his wife a dentist. Before he began his trip west in search of work, he was let go from the college, and his wife's patients were unable to pay their bills. The other man had practiced law and then worked as a janitor before losing that job too. They were both veterans of the war.

Mother presented the sandwiches on one of her painted trays, and the men thanked her. "You've got to feed the spirit, too," Father said. "Mattie, how about 'Of Two Minds' for these gentlemen?"

I knew this poem of Father's upside down and backwards and stood to recite. The men sat in their overcoats in the shade of our porch, chewing as they listened. "'If you have gold and I have gold, and we make a trade, we two. Still you'll have gold and I'll have gold, when the trade is through. But if you have a thought and I have a thought, and we exchange them fair. Why, you'll have two and I'll have two, and be richer for the pair.'"

The men nodded and smiled. I told them about going inside the airplane, and they swapped stories about the war. Father related his recent automobile trips—fourteen flat tires on one of them—and a tornado near Topeka. The visitors talked about riding the rails. They found it as lonely and uncomfortable as the war, but not as dangerous, although they'd both seen men maimed and killed when hopping trains.

While they talked, Mother picked sugar snap peas in the garden, searching for pods among the leaves and vines like she was on a treasure hunt. I went to help her, and she asked me to pick dandelion greens for our salad. I moved about the yard, where ripening purple plums and small hard peaches and apples polka-dotted the trees that Cyrus had planted when I was in first grade. One plum tree was my own to water, but he gave it a drink when I forgot. Every year, he tended a vegetable garden in our yard. He taught me to coax a watermelon from a seed and tap the fruit for ripeness. On every Fourth of July, he and I would split open a melon and spit seeds into the dirt as juice dripped from our chins. Aunt Irene paid him below market price for restaurant produce, and we shared the rest between our families.

Mother claimed she had no green thumb, and Father enjoyed the garden's beauty, but he preferred writing poetry to weeding. Every summer, we looked forward to Cyrus' riot of yellow, orange, and red—the corn, squash, and tomatoes. He could make anything grow, even cotton in Kansas City. He said the prickliness reminded him of what his parents and grandparents left behind in Georgia to raise him up and give him a better chance.

The men thanked us, and Father said, "We appreciate visitors of good will and good cheer." They departed with extra sandwiches and a complement of pea pods. Father leaned back and soon fell asleep. Before dinnertime, we woke him.

Kip had arrived home, and we all sat at the table without Aunt Irene, who had not yet returned from the Bluebird. Father repeated "Of Two Minds" for the blessing. As we were saying "Amen," Irene stormed in carrying a flour sack, which she dropped beside her chair with a thud.

"I hate to say I told you so, Elliot."

"But—?"

"Taken right out of the pantry." She sat and flared her napkin across her lap. "The whole sack of our silver bird salt and peppers. I went to find them to sell, but they're gone."

Mother frowned and paused in midlift of delivering a roll from the breadbasket to Wiley's plate. "That's terrible. Who could have taken them?"

"Who? Any one of these wayward men Elliot has invited into our lives. This is what comes from being too trusting, when it's so easy to be fooled." Irene stared at Kip, who startled, as if he had been slapped. He lowered his head and his leg jiggled.

She continued, "They did not get the silver sugar bowls. I brought them home and will sell them tomorrow. From now on, I'll lock the pantry and keep the key on a string around my neck. Whoever needs something can ask me. Although little of value remains in there now. How many times have I reminded Elliot to lock the alley door?" She glared at Father.

I worried that Mickey and Wiley would say something about the flag that Kip had pulled out of his pocket during our game, but they were busy sneaking bits of roll to the dogs, whose tails thumped under the table. I loved those little silver bird shakers, but I hadn't missed polishing them since the day we wrapped and stored them on the shelf.

"It certainly is a loss, Irene. Those silver birds had meaningful sentiment, besides their monetary value," Father said. "While you're right that we should be careful going forward and not give people a chance to do something they may regret due to their deprivation, I prefer to err on the side of trust."

"As you always do, Elliot. But do you understand that the sale of those would have paid gas and electric for the year? And more."

Father nodded. "And I believe that trusting a person is the greater worth. I was about to ask Kip here if he could see his way to staying another week with us."

"We'll manage, Irene. We always have," Mother said. "Let's not ruin our dinner time. Elliot has already had disappointing news today."

"That's true, I have," he said. "So what about it, Kip? Your saying 'yes' could cheer a fellow up. But I can see that you might want to mull it over."

Kip nodded. "Thank you, sir. I will. Mull it over."

Mother stood. "Mickey, tell Kip and Betty and Aunt Irene all about our adventure with Vincent while I ladle the soup. It's potato. And Mattie picked the salad for us."

Mickey began with the taxi ride and described the plane's cockpit in detail. Betty asked questions punctuated by comments from Irene. Her husband had been a pilot in the war, and she considered herself an expert in matters of aviation. Kip ate and listened with politeness, but turned in his chair, as if readying his legs to make a quick getaway.

Father cleared his throat. "Kip, have you noticed at the restaurant the painting with the bluebird chirping on a branch?"

Kip nodded. "Yes, sir."

"Well, when I was a boy, that little bird came to me in a dream and said, 'Jump for joy, Elliot. Add good cheer to the world.'

"The next day, my friend Harry and I hammered together boards for a floor, topped it with a piece of linoleum, and raised it above the ground using coil springs from a sofa that we found in a scrap heap. We made a sign—*The Jump for Joy Candy Store*—and sold fudge and caramel popcorn prepared by my mother. The spring-loaded floor provided free amusement.

"When I married Clara, her baking started me thinking about opening a restaurant. I liked the idea of making customers happy through good food, which is more immediately rewarding than bricks and mortar. I imagined a place where all people could bring their appetites, be welcomed, and be satisfied. But we were detoured by the war and then becoming established as an architect and raising a family."

He smiled toward Mother and winked at her. "I'm only sorry we waited so long for folks to have the chance to taste those pies. Best of the west. When we opened the Bluebird in the spring of 1929, my architecture business was bustling, and Clara won a Gold Medal Flour recipe contest. We put a sign in the window—*Featuring Clara's Homemade Pies—Best of the West*. With the prize money, we bought stocks and gave a certificate to each of the kids—even Wiley. By November of that year, all that and more became worthless."

Father's stories always had an obvious point, and I wasn't sure he'd made one this time. We all waited to hear him elaborate, but he said simply, "I hope you'll stay on with us, Kip. You're good to have around."

I realized that telling the story was Father's way of including Kip in the family lore, of saying he trusted him. Father never talked about money to strangers and rarely mentioned it to us children. I believe he was letting Kip know that money didn't matter to him as much as good will, which, if Father's could have been banked, would have made him a wealthy man.

After dinner, Kip went down to his room and didn't join us outside. No one had a flag, so we played hide-and-seek.

Mother called us in and my brothers went to bed, but I lingered in the bathtub and then lay awake listening to the thump of Betty's sewing machine treadle as she stitched her graduation dress. I sensed something shift beneath me and crept to the stair landing. The conversation was broken, and I strained to glean bits.

". . . Atchison . . . *thump* . . . Topeka . . . no opportunity now . . ."

". . . Too late . . ."

". . . Sedalia may not . . . *thump* . . ."

". . . Boss Tom's scheme . . ."

". . . Loan losses . . . *thump* . . . Herbert enmeshed with the fraud . . ."

". . . Bank foreclosure . . ."

". . . Steeken knows we can't come up with it . . . *thump* . . ."

". . . Let's not get ahead of ourselves . . ."

No one spoke for several minutes. I scooted closer to the edge of the landing, hoping to hear more about not getting ahead of ourselves, and Father detected me.

"Would you like to join us, Mattie?"

"Me?" I moved onto the stairs where I had a clear view.

"Only for a few minutes, then it's bedtime," he said. "Read to us a bit, will you, Clara?"

"As soon as I finish this passage."

Most evenings, Mother wrote a paragraph or two about our family, the weather, and the price of meat. She said they were keepsakes of her little slice of life and that, one day, we would delight in remembering the events of our growing up.

Betty stopped sewing. Mother cleared her throat and read

from the paper in her hand. "This is quite a siege the world is going through. Men who have commanded wages as high as four hundred dollars a month are working as janitors or doing anything they can to earn a living. Today, one of the men who came by asking for something to eat had been an English professor at a university. We're lucky Elliot still has the promise of the Sedalia job. We hope they award him the contract next week. Irene discovered that the silver salt and peppers are missing."

"Stolen." Irene huffed.

"Perhaps," Mother said. "We all have misplaced something at one time or another. They may yet turn up."

"That reminds me, Clara," Irene said. "I set a letter aside to give to Margaret Ann—"

"On the table?"

"It's not there." She glanced to the stairs, as if accusing me for taking something that was mine, but I hadn't seen the letter. She usually left mail on the card table or sewing machine, but sometimes she took it to her room in the attic or misplaced it anywhere in the house. I would search in the morning.

Mother flipped the paper and continued reading. "Betty is upset that the telephone has been disconnected, but Albert comes by after work every evening no matter how late. Vincent showed us his airplane today. The boys said they would work harder to sell their magazine subscriptions in order to buy leather jackets. Mattie said, 'Clothes do not make the man,' a phrase she's heard often enough, although I do believe that Elliot's starched cuffs, even if a bit frayed, lend dignity."

Mother smiled at Father before finishing. "I told the children they would have to put their money toward school clothes, but there is talk of school being cancelled this fall. In these so-called days of depression, it takes all we can scrape together to keep us fed. But some things are cheap. Yesterday Irene bought one hundred pounds of potatoes for forty cents, and Elliot paid only one dollar for shoes with leather soles. With his old ones worn through, he worried he'd make a poor presentation at the Sedalia meeting next week. We are fortunate to have this home where we can be together."

"You make it sound like I complained," Betty said. "Do you blame me for being upset?"

"No. And I don't equate being upset with complaining, but I will make a note."

I didn't care about the phone being disconnected. Mother said that living without a phone encouraged friends to visit. I didn't have anyone to call, except Eugene, but long distance cost too much, and I didn't like the snoopy operators listening in anyway. Letters were private.

In the taxi, Mother hadn't mentioned anything about school being cancelled. Thinking of the months stretching ahead, I realized that Father hadn't been on a trip to *build* a new project, not merely to bid on one, for a long time.

As if knowing I was thinking of him at that moment, Father said, "Good night, Mattie."

I scurried back to my room and tried to ignore the worries, but they piled on. I had nearly forgotten about the flag. Father had chosen to trust Kip, and I wanted to, but I pictured him pulling that gingham scrap from his pocket. I had used every one of those May Day flags to wrap the shakers and sugar bowls. He must have snooped around in the pantry and opened a sack. Could he have stolen the shakers? We really didn't know much about him.

Earlier in the day, when crossing the river on the way home from the airfield, everything had seemed possible. Now, I felt closed in. I tried to lift my mind above it all, but I couldn't see any other explanation. Kip was a thief and a liar.

PART TWO

CHAPTER TEN

Flight

In a small jet plane over western Kansas, Mattie finishes her diary entry and marks the date—March 9, 2020. She gazes down upon a terrain she's seen many times on visits to the Midwest, but never as close as they are now in this Cessna 510. Snow gathers at the edges of the plowed fields, creating patterns of concentric circles, waves, and stripes in brown and white, dirt and snow—a patchwork cut through by gray roads and dotted by a rooftop here and there.

"Mattie? Need more?" Amoy, her daughter-in-law, offers a thermos. She has the high cheekbones and thick, black hair that Genet inherited, but her curls are silver streaked.

Mattie holds her cup to be filled. "I've been thinking about my call with Genet yesterday and what a good long talk we had. She's become so curious about my past."

"She never asks about mine—"

"Amoy, it's—"

"I know, I know. She needs her space. And I'm thankful she's close to you. I'm not worrying. See?" Amoy forces a smile. "Trying not to. I mean, she's taking on a lot with this marriage. Excluding me from the wedding planning is healthy for her—for both of us—I guess. But I used to dream of her big day being in our garden. It would have been beautiful in the early summer."

"Yes, it would have been. Your roses would be at the height of their glory."

"Tell me, Mattie, in all honesty, wouldn't you prefer living in our cottage close to us and your team's new offices rather than in a retirement community so far away?" Amoy is a Professor of Dance and Performance Studies. She has a PhD in cultural anthropology and is the author of a book on world dance history. She and Charles, Mattie's son, have a house on Potrero Hill in San Francisco.

"You could move from your three-story house and all those stairs, but stay involved with your team. How many years have I been asking you to talk to my students about your dance career? If you leave the Bay Area, that will never happen."

"I never like to say 'never,' but I see your point. And I do appreciate the offer of the cottage." Mattie smiles and glances again to the farms and houses below. "I was mulling over how I've taken my roofs for granted and how lucky I've been in this life. We're flying above land that was once a desert. Indigenous tribes lived on it for centuries before it was portioned to settlers in forty- or one-hundred-and-sixty-acre plots."

Amoy takes in the view. "The grid remains distinct."

"To claim their acreage, my Swedish ancestors had to settle for five years, build a home of sod, dig a well, plant trees, and survive dust storms, drought, grasshoppers, floods, and frostbite."

Amoy caps the thermos. "I have never had to work that hard for a roof over my head."

"Nor have I."

"And underneath it all, the Ogallala aquifer. I heard on a podcast that it could run dry in fifty years."

Mattie sighs. "Seems like no time at all to me now."

"Or to me. And it will take six thousand years to recharge. Anyway, when will you decide about your next rooftop?"

"This trip will tell."

"If you stay with us, you could still dance with your salsa group or stroll up the hill to the rec center. They now have hip-hop, line dancing, and ballroom. Or Charles could clone you. Then one Mattie could go to Kansas City and the other could live among our roses. We want you with us."

"I wish I could be in two places at once, but life seldom gives a second chance such as this one to be with Wiley. I can't retrieve those years I lost with him when I left home, but I can reclaim time now. Even if Genet's wedding weren't this Sunday, I'd want to visit soon to check out the apartment and all else that Sonata Court offers. The timing is good this week. Everyone's busy packing up to move to the new offices, so I won't miss any important work."

"When is the last time you had a vacation?"

"A what?"

Amoy laughs. "Right. Your idea of a good time is starting one of your studies."

"I attribute those to keeping this going." Mattie taps a finger to her forehead. "I've never had a concept of retirement. What would I do with it?"

As the fields glide beneath, she thinks about her team's work on movement and memory. They have been documenting people dancing, their faces and postures appearing more youthful than their years, noticeably more youthful than in the moments before they began dancing. They've tracked how lungs expand, LDL lowers, HDL rises, and hearts pump with the blood pressure of people decades younger. She believes that someday there will be a way to measure HDJ—High-Density Joy.

Snowflakes float against the window. Mattie closes her eyes, contemplating how humans are hardwired to connect with others. Someday her colleagues will chart how the intricacies of those connections improve brain plasticity. They will graph how being fully present in the moment nourishes and heals the soul. The awareness of one's awareness will be tracked like blood sugar in routine checkups. Along with a Hemoglobin A1C, an annual wellness checkup will report on one's capacity for learning and delight.

Someday people will dance as routinely as they floss their teeth, every night and mornings too. They will dance as long as their hearts pump, even if only a wiggle of finger, a tap of a toe. She would like to live long enough to see it.

"It will be good for Genet—honestly, for me—to have you there in Kansas City with her this week," Amoy says. "Oh, I'm sorry. Were you asleep?"

Mattie opens her eyes. "Only ruminating."

"I'm overcaffeinated." Amoy places her cup in the holder. "I can't help thinking about the wedding. I wish Genet wanted my help. I admit that I'm jealous of the mother-in-law being in charge, although I don't blame her for my fragile relationship with Genet. No doubt we'd be knocking heads right now if I were involved. But I can't shake the feeling that she's rushing things. I mean, becoming a stepmother to a young child? Genet is barely out of adolescence, or so it has seemed until recently."

"She has made remarkable strides, Amoy."

"Still, it's a lot. Why not try living together?"

"I can't criticize marrying young. Eugene and I were twenty-one."

"But your times were so different with the war and all."

"True enough."

"With Charles and me, we simply fell head over heels. And I owe it all to you. If it hadn't been for you inviting me to participate in your research—"

"As I told Genet yesterday, some things are meant to be. You two certainly are."

Mattie remembers well that December evening in 1980 when Amoy Abebe, a twenty-year-old dancer, came to the house for a meeting about a movement study. At the end, Amoy had offered to clear the cups and collided with Charles in the kitchen, where he was warming up a late dinner. She stayed past midnight talking with him about John Lennon, who had died that night.

From her room, Mattie had heard Charles and Amoy harmonizing to "Imagine." She had thought it must be that opposites attract—Amoy so outgoing, Charles uncomfortable in groups. At thirty-three, he had been as shy and awkward as he'd been as a teenager. He might have missed out on marriage and family altogether had it not been for Amoy, who was born in Jamaica to a woman who met a man on a beach. Amoy never knew her father.

A week after meeting Charlie, Amoy said to Mattie, "He was family from the first moment and filled something in me that had always been missing. My soul's mate. I knew that we were destined to be together."

On her lap, Amoy opens flat the book she's been perusing on the plane, a slim volume that Mattie brought in her carryon. On the inside of the book's cover is a label: The library of *Elliot Toft*. His signature in blue ink extends the crossbar on the cap *T* of Toft over the whole name, like a rooftop. Amoy flips to a page and reads. "'The common heart of which all sincere conversation is the worship.' To me, 'soul's mate' conveys the seeking and finding of something extraordinary in another human being and holds that idea much better than 'soulmate,' which has become—"

"Trivialized?"

"Yes." Amoy turns to another page. "'We live in succession, in division, in parts, in particles.' I've never studied Emerson, but he's spot on. When was this written?" She searches for the date. "1841? His words are more relevant now than ever. I've seen my students' attention spans go from imagining their fifteen minutes of fame to craving fifteen seconds of influence."

Mattie nods. "So much has changed and some things not at all. My father would be tickled to see me in this private jet and all else that I've witnessed in the decades since he passed away—humans landing on the moon, robotics on Mars, driverless cars. You can't imagine the number of tires he had to repair merely traveling from town to town when I was a girl."

"I wish I had known Elliot. And Eugene, of course," Amoy says.

"I do too." Mattie glances across the aisle at her son.

Charles inherited his father's physical features and investment instincts, but he is as much an introvert as his father was an extravert. Eugene enjoyed a law career enhanced by socializing and sports and died at fifty. Charles has devoted his life to science and, at seventy-three, has no intention of retiring.

He spends his days in his lab, weekends too, searching for genetic markers to reverse aging and extend a healthy lifespan. He maps the genome the way Mattie used to chart the steps for teaching dance choruses—coming together, splitting apart, pairing off for this and that. He thrives on new challenges, as she always did. Does. More lie ahead, but her conversation with Genet has shifted her thoughts to the regrets of her past. She wonders if she'll carry them until the end.

Usually tidy and pale, Charles is rumpled and flushed, having returned to California two days ago on the red-eye from three weeks of meetings in New York and Connecticut. His biotech company has provided the plane and pilot for him to attend a genetics conference in Chicago. They will land in Kansas City, where Mattie will deplane, and then he and Amoy will fly on to the conference and return to KC in time for Genet's wedding festivities, which begin Saturday night.

As Charles scrolls his phone, he coughs and draws a short breath. He sips from a water bottle and coughs again.

Amoy reaches over and places her hand on his forehead. "You're warm."

"It's nothing a good night's sleep can't cure," he says.

Experts are saying that this new virus could be much worse than the flu, but Mattie isn't worried. Only one case has been reported in Kansas and one in Missouri, and none in the metro area of Kansas City. A few cases have been reported in Chicago, but Charles will be at a conference with scientists and medical professionals, not in large public gatherings or on transit. Mattie takes a vial of sanitizer from her purse, squeezes the gel onto her palm, and rubs her hands together. The alcohol stings a scratch on her skin. "Would you like some?"

"Sure," Amoy says. "Charles? Sanitizer?"

He offers his hand for a dollop of gel. "The Dow is down 2,000."

"What are the predictions?" Amoy squeezes the drops.

Mattie admires how Amoy is with Charles. She has made a world for Charles that allows him to be himself, while giving herself what she needs. In loving him as his mother, Mattie has struggled not to give advice, but she worries that he works too hard and misses out on many things. He has often replied, "The same could be said for you, Mom."

The plane banks on approach. Mattie rests her forehead against the glass. Below them, the surface of the wide Missouri has the dull sheen of pewter. The river curves east toward the train yards and the long bluff, upon which perches her old neighborhood with its familiar pattern of streets. The last time she drove through, she noticed the peeled paint at their old

Elmwood Avenue house and the construction beginning on the weedy lot next door where the Nelsons' house had been. The field where long ago she had stepped into an airplane for the first time and where they are landing today now serves private planes, corporate jets, and helicopters. Years ago, a new international airport for commercial flights was built miles to the north.

The window encrusts with sleet as the plane lands and taxis. Mattie hugs Amoy and Charles goodbye and wishes them a good time in Chicago. "See you Saturday at the dinner. Feel better, Charles."

Inside the terminal, she pings Genet. *I'm here.*

Within seconds, Genet replies. *Class ran long. Take Uber. Meet you at house. Hugs.*

Mattie taps her phone to book a ride and rolls her carryon outside to wait. White crystals cling to the nubby wool of her blue coat, and she wraps her neck scarf tighter. The ride app shows a dot moving closer and closer. Within minutes, the driver has stashed her bag in the trunk, and she is on her way.

They cross over the river and the railroad tracks. Her memory lights upon that day in 1932 when her family was returning from the airfield and Wiley asked their mother if she would like to be a little boy. Clara was only thirty-eight then. Mattie is nearly sixty-two years beyond that age and eighty-eight years beyond that day, and yet Clara is alive in her memory—her gentle voice saying, "That's not polite," while Wiley raspberries close to her face.

Now, Wiley is a ninety-two-year-old man who has lost his recent history and most of his long-term memory too. Can Mattie entice what's left by bringing him reminiscences of events from their past, along with shared emotions? She feels determined.

The driver pulls alongside the curb, and Mattie draws a sharp breath. This happens whenever she visits. The house is so similar to the one in which they grew up, it is as if Wiley transplanted his life from their childhood to this address. After their father died in 1960, Wiley moved with their mother and Aunt Irene to this oak-lined street near the Country Club Plaza and the university. It is the same style of foursquare house made of stone and wood and painted the same butter yellow as the Elmwood house, lost to the bank so long ago.

The question surfaces whenever she visits. Had she known when she left in 1932 that she would never return to live with her family, would she have left? The void in that childhood time with her family has haunted her. Now only Wiley and she remain. He never ventured beyond Kansas City nor left his mother's side. After Clara's death forty years ago, Wiley continued as a biology professor at the university until last October, when his dementia prevented him from performing even his limited responsibilities as an endowed chair, which involved no class load but being at his desk to advise students who knocked on his office door. With affectionate joking, people had been calling him the absent-minded professor until they realized that he had fooled them. In his groomed appearance, he was much the same as he had always been, but he had, in fact, lost much of his cognitive ability.

Genet, in yoga pants and tank top without a coat, waves from the front porch. She runs to the curb as the car stops and opens the door. A hot pink headband holds her curls back from her face, glowing and moist with melting snowflakes. "Gram, I'm so happy you're here."

Mattie unfolds from the car into her embrace. Genet takes the luggage and says, "I found more family keepsakes in the attic. Lucky for us your brother is a pack rat."

Mattie recognizes in Genet a familiar path of personality, an eagerness that she herself once had. "Wiley thought of himself as the keeper of the family history. He never wanted to let go of anything. After Mother died, Betty and I offered to come help him sort through boxes, but he refused."

Genet leads Mattie into the house, opens the hallway closet, and pushes aside garments. "Most of this should go to Goodwill."

As Mattie hangs her coat, she breathes the sharp scent of mothballs. Something else forgotten and familiar emanates from the cedar walls and the shoe kit on the floor.

Genet leads Mattie to the dining room. "Everything is here." On the table, boxes and ribbon-tied bundles circle around an aloe vera plant. "I only took a peek so we could go through it together. I'll fix our sandwiches. You make yourself at home."

Genet steps into the kitchen, remembering how her great-uncle spoke those words to her a year ago. She had been aimless, in and out of rehab since high school, and was hitchhiking across the country when she landed in Kansas City during a snowstorm. In distress, she called Mattie, who directed her to Wiley's house. He opened the door and said, "Welcome, Genet. Make yourself at home." He asked nothing of her and didn't judge, and with that, she wanted to help. In caring for her great-uncle, she began caring better for herself and grew in her resolve to turn things around.

She realizes now that so much in life is about being at the right place at the right time. Being here was her right place, right time. She passed her GED, took a yoga class at the Y, joined a recovery support group, and met a woman there who helped her get a job teaching yoga at Sonata Court. The residents liked her and asked for more classes. She stays one jump ahead of them by watching YouTube videos on her phone and teaching the poses she learns—Cat-Cow, Cobra, Happy Baby. Their favorite is Child's Pose.

Layering turkey slices onto bread, she flashes upon the past Thanksgiving. She was preparing dinner, in the middle of basting the first whole turkey she had ever cooked, when one of Wiley's former research assistants, who had become an entomologist, stopped by to visit. Her mother is worried that Ravi is a divorced father and that Genet won't be able to handle the responsibility of being a stepmother, but Genet thinks she can.

On a recent call she said to Amoy, "You of all people should understand how it is to meet someone and know you want to spend the rest of your life with him. Besides, I like playing with kids. I always wanted a little sister. Anyway, she will only be with us half-time. Week on, week off. And she's quite grownup for a five-year-old."

Genet returns to the living room and places their lunch tray on an antique teacart beside Mattie on the couch. She collapses into an easy chair and stretches her spandex-covered legs over the cushioned arm, her feet sneakered in white with pink stripes and laces. "What a morning. My new qigong class, plus chair aerobics and memoir."

Mattie hands Genet a steaming cup of tea, pours her own, and replaces the cozy over the pot. "Tell me about your qigong."

"Well, Qi is vital energy. Gong, the skills you gain through practice. I'm all about helping people renew their life force. For some, it's about healing. For others, it's balance—physical or emotional. A lot of them are stressed out about getting old and all the things they can't do any more. I keep them moving as much as possible, even if they can't stand up."

"Sounds like just the ticket."

"I use it in the memoir and movement class too. I tell everyone to lie silently for ten minutes in the corpse pose and let a memory emerge. I ask them to share their stories, then do some qigong and think about their stories from different angles. They write them as if someone else were telling the story. It's fun. They make things up that never happened."

"That approach could certainly put a spin on it. What might have been. If only—"

"Your life is awesome, Gram. You should write about it. Really, you should."

"How about you write it for me?"

"Maybe I could transcribe our conversations? I have a clear recording of yesterday's. Your memory is amazing. I wish mine was half as good."

Genet is enrolled in a communiversity writing class and has begun a memoir about her turbulent days. She's worried that if she writes the true story, people will be upset if they see them-selves in it, and she doesn't want to hurt anyone more than she already has. Her instructor suggested changing names, trying different points of view, and fictionalizing the events of her ado-lescence. Much of that time in her teens and beyond is a blur of being high on whiskey and pills or curled up in a corner with anxiety.

"Some things are etched forever," Mattie says. "But memory can deceive. What we remember are our perceptions of what happened at the time, and those memories may change over time. Even if we remember what occurred, it may not be the way it occurred."

"Let's keep talking for now. I want to hear it all." Genet reaches for her phone and opens up the recording app. "Are you ever sorry you left home so young? If you had to do it all again, what would you do differently?"

"I try not to dwell on that." Mattie sets her cup on the tray. She wants to avoid triggers that would cause Genet to obsess over past choices that haunt her. As a child, Genet was a vora-cious learner. In middle school, she was in the gifted program. She won poetry and story contests and talked about being a writer when she grew up. Then, in her freshman year in high school, her curiosity vanished, replaced by a dire self-absorption and angst that lasted years past adolescence. Her genes are coded for brilliance and willfulness, eagerness and melancholy.

Mattie proceeds carefully. "We have what was, what is yet to be, and this moment—right here, you and me—and now that has slipped away. My tendency has always been to look ahead, perhaps too much so." Her thoughts are leaping. To stay or leave? Her well-loved Victorian near Golden Gate Park or the garden cottage on Potrero Hill? A studio apartment that's available soon on Sonata Court's second floor or a larger unit with a patio entrance and a six-month wait? Living in the complex with Wiley and near Genet or near Charles and Amoy? New people to meet in Kansas City or her friends and colleagues in San Francisco?

"After all the things that these people have gone through in their lives, they are forgetting so much, Gram. Your parents lived through all those hard times, two world wars, and a pandemic. I don't think we'd know how to do it if things ever got that tough again. Some people are saying this new virus could be as deadly as the 1918 flu, but I can't imagine. And our political situation sucks."

"It does," Mattie says. "But for every step back, another forward. There was tremendous misery in the thirties, but we didn't analyze it as much as people do now. The daily papers and radio were easier to ignore or tune out than all the media we have today. Growing up, if we complained about a small deprivation, we were reminded that others were less fortunate."

"You didn't expect so much back then. Not like when I grew up. But I don't think it helps to know that other people have it worse. Not when you're feeling bad."

"Perhaps not in the midst of it." Mattie stretches to relieve the stiffness in her hip. "I have lived through the best times too. My mother's mother had only an eighth-grade education, never voted, and died in her early forties. My mother graduated high school and voted in every presidential election from 1920 on. She never had a driver's license or flew on a plane, but she lived to be eighty-six. I enrolled in college at fifty, received my doctorate at sixty, and today flew here on a small jet that travels four hundred miles an hour. My doctor, who, granted, is quite the optimist, says it is likely I will be going strong at one hundred and five." She looks for wood and knocks on the coffee table.

"I want you to live forever, Gram."

Mattie laughs. "That might be a little *too* long. I told you yesterday how my father used to say that humans are reaching for the stars, and I suppose I still am, but in a different way than before. I used to believe anything was possible if I put my mind to it, and that kept me going. Now that I have a shorter stretch in front of me, I still think about possibilities—"

"Like a woman being elected president of the United States?"

"I used to believe I'd see that in my lifetime."

"We nearly did four years ago. Just think. The first time I ever voted for president, I got to choose a woman. I sure wish we had a grandmother in the White House to help us through now."

"I'm sorry to see it won't be this election, but I hope for your future—."

"Me, too." Genet's cup teeters on the armchair edge, and she catches it. "Let's look at the attic stuff."

She takes her phone to the dining table and brings out a photo from a box. "This is what I showed to Uncle Wiley yesterday. It's the one that Mickey took, right?"

Mickey's picture, now resting on Mattie's palm, captures the window lettering. Inside the Bluebird, she stands in a flowered dress with a rag in her hand. Kip, wearing an apron, is stepping out from behind the counter and looking her way. She brings the photo closer. "Yes, that's the one."

"I thought you learned tap dancing at that school in

Hollywood where Shirley Temple took lessons. Amoy said you did. She's always so impressed by the fame thing."

"I did study there later." Mattie touches Kip's face on the photo. It's the only picture of him she has ever seen.

Genet has been calling Amoy and Charles by their first names since high school, rather than "Mom" and "Dad." It unsettled Mattie then, but she understands that it serves Genet in finding her identity.

Genet opens a box and removes a bundle wrapped in tissue and tied with a ribbon. She fans assorted papers across the table. Mattie picks up a flattened envelope covered in her Mother's neat script, runs her finger along the deckle edge of the two-cent stamp, and reads.

"'My painted trays brought in a little money at the church bazaar. Without what the Bluebird brings in, we would not be making ends meet. Somehow we get along on twenty-five dollars a month.'"

"Wow. Twenty-five dollars is nothing," Genet says.

"The money went further of course. A loaf of bread cost less than a dime back then." Mattie continues reading. "'The children eat what I fix with little grumbling. My waistline is narrowing and Elliot says I shouldn't deny myself, but the children are growing. They need the nourishment more than I.'"

"Did you talk much about the Great Depression, Gram? You know, on a global scale."

"We didn't know to call it that at the time. I think it wasn't until someone wrote a book with that title in 1934 or thereabout that people began describing it as such. I was young, but I remember thinking that 'horrible' would have been a better word than 'great.'"

"How about little *d* depression. Did anyone take meds?"

"We experienced sadness, certainly, but we didn't talk about being depressed. I wasn't aware of anyone taking pills for it. My father-in-law was melancholic, but he didn't take drugs until the 1950s, near the end of his life. It was a medication for tuberculosis that was used to treat depression."

"Really? That's weird. They seem like two entirely different illnesses."

Genet takes a scrap and reads. "Oh, Gram. Listen to this one. 'We have learned to live and enjoy the blessings of each day and not worry about what will happen tomorrow. A new boarder came to live with us tonight. He seems a sweet boy. A quiet type. Mattie seems to be somewhat smitten.'"

"I never knew she noticed," Mattie says.

"Amoy always noticed when I had a crush. She hovered. Anyway, let's not talk about her. I was awake last night wondering if Kip did break your trust or not. Did he steal the shakers?"

As Mattie regards Genet's finger pressing the record button, emotions arise that she can't readily name. "I suppose that I truly did doubt him. I'm ashamed to say that the lack was in me, as I found out the next morning."

CHAPTER ELEVEN

Apology

Mother woke me early that Saturday to help her bake pies using Mrs. Nelson's oven. It seemed there would be too many for the case. When we arrived at the Bluebird, a customer or two sat at every table and most were eating pie for breakfast. The pies that I had put in the case on Friday were gone.

At the counter, Kip was finishing his new sign, his hand trembling, Aunt Irene hovering. He placed the sign in the window next to the old one about Mother's pies. Some of the letters were crooked, but the overall effect was pleasing. Blue musical notes bordered the cherry-red lettering: *Have Another Cup of Coffee. Have another Piece of Homemade Pie. Best in the West. 2-for-1 special.*

Mrs. Abernathy had recently taught our class the tune about coffee from the new Broadway musical. I didn't like the bitter taste, but I liked the song. I would be performing it on Sunday and had been singing it around the house.

"The power of advertising," Irene said, admiring the sign. "That ought to draw more customers."

"But they're paying less?" I did the math in my head—the sale price less cost of ingredients. "How does that add up to more profits?"

"It's called upselling," she whispered. "We give people the sense of getting a lot more for a little add-on to their meal or tempt them to return for a pick-me-up. Did you notice that we're cutting the slices thinner? By next week, they'll be half of what they were." She raised her voice, "Now, Kip. Clean up that brush, and I'll unlock the pantry when you return so that you can put the other things away. Be quick about it."

Kip carried the paintbrush out to the alley, and I followed. He knelt beside the can of kerosene and, frowning in concentration, wiped the brush with a rag.

"She can be bossy," I said.

"I didn't steal anything. She thinks I did." Tears glistened in his eyes, and he ducked his head.

"Then where did you get the flag?"

"Right there. I saw it when I took out the trash on Sunday. I needed a handkerchief." He pointed behind the garbage can, beside the spot where Aunt Irene stored the kerosene, and rubbed his eyes.

A wadded newspaper lay next to the can. I smoothed it to read the date—*Friday, May 5*. I tried to remember when we had taken down the May Day flags. It would not have been on a school day, but on Saturday of that week. It was morning. I remembered a man coming in asking for work.

"Mr. Crowley."

"Huh?" Kip looked at me.

"He would have seen me wrapping the shakers and Aunt Irene putting the sack in the pantry." I held out the newspaper. "We used this too, along with the fabric pieces."

Kip was thoughtful. "The alley door was left unlocked Saturday night. He could have—"

"Or Sunday morning early before work. He must have had them in his bundles when he left our house that night."

"But why cause trouble with me? It's like he dared to be caught."

"Right under our noses."

"*If* he did it. But you thought it was me, didn't you?"

"I was—"

"Suspicious. You didn't trust me."

"You had the flag in your pocket."

"You jumped quick to blame. I wouldn't steal from your family. Your father believed me."

"He didn't see the flag."

"No, but he *believed* in me. You don't." Kip stood and walked into the Bluebird.

All afternoon, I kept him in my sights, tapping out new rhythms to entice him, but he said, "I don't feel like dancing."

I should have said then that I was really sorry for not believing him. I wish I had, but my apology stayed stuck inside me.

Aunt Irene opened the pantry for him to grind beans and roots for the coffee. He helped plate pie wedges and serve customers. He made sandwiches, carefully arranging the slices of bread and cheese. He carried dirty dishes from the table to the kitchen, walking with faint click-clacks and no spring in his step.

CHAPTER TWELVE

Fireflies

In the fellowship hall after church service on Sunday, while people mingled and Mother and Aunt Irene poured, I sang "Let's Have Another Cup of Coffee." Mrs. Abernathy praised me and gave me a box. "Open it."

Inside were tap shoes. They were made of blue satin with a high arch and delicate strap that buckled across the instep. The heel was sturdy, but graceful with an inward curve, similar to the shoes my mother kept in a box in her closet. Eugene's mother had bought them for her during their trip to New York, and Mother had worn them out to dinner and to see Broadway shows. She had modeled them for us upon her return home and stored them in her closet. Mrs. Abernathy's shoes were like those, but even more lovely. They were the most beautiful shoes I had ever seen.

She lifted them from the box and placed them in my hands. "The soles and taps are scuffed, of course, and the satin could use cleaning, but they have life yet. I wore them on stage the night I met Mr. Abernathy, and they certainly brought me luck in that department." She smiled. "Your mother told me you are learning to tap, and they might fit you."

We both looked at my feet, which were big for my age. They

were long and narrow, like Aunt Irene's and Father's. He had said that once I grew taller, my feet would be in better proportion to my size.

As pretty as they were, the tap shoes didn't thrill me as they would have before Kip started ignoring me. While I was pleased to accept the gift, I was keenly aware of the words that I had sung about things that mattered most in life.

All I truly wanted at that moment was Kip's attention and praise. I wanted things to be the way they were when he taught me steps and I did them well. I wanted Father to go on trips and come home telling stories about the school or bank he was building. I wanted to bake pies in our own hot oven and not ever think about living somewhere other than our house.

On the sidewalk in front of the Bluebird, I strapped on the shoes before stepping inside. Hoping to surprise Kip, I found him in the kitchen, his arms in suds up to his elbows.

He glanced to me and down at my feet. "That's a fine pair. How's the sound?"

I did a shuffle hop, heel, toe. "Dandy," he said, and turned his attention to the sink.

All afternoon, I clicked-clacked around in my blue shoes and red dress, trying to entice him to railroad or barrel roll or leap bells with me. I made up new phrases of four counts to trade with him, but he kept to his tasks and to himself.

During supper he said nothing and afterward sat on the porch with Father, who read aloud, while Mother mended by lantern light, and Aunt Irene nodded off. I kicked the can with the neighbor kids.

I had questions and wished my parents would ask them of Kip, although it wasn't in their nature to pry. I wanted to know those things he didn't seem to want to tell me, like where he was from, and where his family was, and where he might go next. I sallied up to the porch, hoping for conversation, and Mother beckoned me to sit beside her.

"Ah, Mattie," Father said. "My eyes are strained." He handed me the Emerson. "Start here."

I read, skipping words to speed things up. "'We live in succession, in division . . . within man is the soul of the whole . . . the universal beauty, to which every part and particle is equally related . . .'"

The porch light cast a warm glow on the faces. My aunt's eyes were closed. Kip and Mother were paying attention.

"More?"

Father nodded, and I read on. "'The spirit sports with time . . . can crowd eternity into an hour, or stretch an hour to eternity . . . some thoughts always find us young, and keep us so.'"

I felt like the passage was stretching to eternity and read quickly. "'The things we now esteem fixed shall, one by one, detach and fall. The wind shall blow them none knows whither.'"

Father had a twinkle in his eye. I'd heard that word in a sermon at church—"Whither thou goes, I will go"—and, on the way home, he explained it was about destination, not to "whither" from lack of rain.

I gave him the book and mulled over questions of time and soul. To me the soul was like water and time was a container. If I took a full glass of water and poured it onto a big cookie sheet, it would be the same amount of liquid as in the glass but filling a different space. I wondered if Emerson baked or knew his way around a kitchen at all.

Father's soothing voice blended with the warm night air. "'The soul's advances are not made by gradation, such as can be represented by motion in a straight line; but rather by ascension of state, such as can be represented by metamorphosis—from the egg to the worm, from the worm to the fly.'"

As many times as I'd heard those words, I now listened as if for the first time. He was talking about magic. He was describing how I felt transformed when dancing with Kip.

Wiley and Mickey stepped onto the porch, and Betty too. Across the lawn, between the street and the porch, lightning bugs flickered. They were there every summer, and I didn't think much about them, except when we studied insects at school.

"We had fireflies at home." Kip moved from the porch to sit on the grass.

Wiley plopped beside him. "They aren't flies, you know. They're beetles. And their eggs glow." He loved insects of all kinds, especially lightning bugs. I had told him everything I learned in class.

"They are like stars," Kip said. "Constellations revolving. There's a pattern. See how they flash at different times? Fast like that." He snapped his fingers in quick rhythm. "And each one gets brighter. Or that one—longer flash, pause, flash." He snapped with his other hand.

"Why?" Wiley asked.

"Maybe they're talking to each other." Kip snapped left and right.

"Hello, hello." Wiley's little fingers made a shushing sound. He'd been practicing all spring, but hadn't mastered the trick of the snap. Suddenly he did.

"You've got it, little fella."

Wiley grinned and kept at it. "Goodbye, goodbye."

"Sometimes a whole group will flash at once," Kip said.

I sat down beside him on the lawn. "I've never seen that. My teacher said the flashes are signals for finding mates, but she didn't say anything about them flashing at once. It's sad that they become so beautiful for such a short time."

In the lesson, I had been fascinated by how they began as eggs laid under damp leaves in the late summer. As larvae, they lived in the ground or tree bark, shed their exoskeletons and grew larger ones through that winter and spring, and maybe the next. As pupas, they rested in cocoons of mud for a couple of weeks, hanging upside down from tree bark and growing wings. The adults emerged to flash, mate, and die within a couple of weeks. Some didn't take time to eat.

Kip cupped his hands in the air and caught a firefly. Light glowed pinkish between his fingers. He opened to the flashing bug, and it flew away. "At home they did flash together. Sometimes."

I wanted to ask where home was, but at that moment a firefly landed on his knee and rested there. Flash, pause, flash. Another landed on my leg and more landed on the grass. Soon hundreds of flashing fireflies enveloped us.

We sat in silence, watching the bugs. Probably only minutes slipped by, but an hour may well have passed when Mother said, "Cinnamon toast before bedtime, anyone?"

Wiley and I went inside. Kip stayed in the yard alone with the fireflies and all that I wanted to learn about him.

CHAPTER THIRTEEN

Omission

Monday was Memorial Day, and the Bluebird was closed. Before breakfast, I helped Mother hang wash on the line and cut bouquets of dahlias for her, Father, and Aunt Irene to place at the graves of their parents at the Forest Hill Cemetery, which was not in a forest but near farmland at the south of the city. Mother asked me to mind Wiley. "I'd like for you to stay here with him. I don't trust Mickey to supervise, and Betty has plans with Albert."

Given a choice, I liked to visit the cemetery because we took the route south along Ward Parkway. A grassy strip decorated by European statues divided the boulevard. On either side, wide lawns sloped up to mansions in various styles with arched windows, turrets, and gables. A favorite had stately white columns. We liked to estimate the number of bricks and picture the inhabitants living in all their many rooms.

Many of the owners had made Kansas City what it was—like the pioneer Seth Ward and the architect Mary Rockwell Hook. She was the daughter of a Union Army captain in the Civil War, one of only a few women architects in KC, and the only one with any fame beyond it. We liked to pass by the houses she designed for her parents, a sister, and a friend who owned a tin can company. One mansion had a private swimming pool.

More than once, Father had slowed to savor the view and said, "You could design houses, Mattie. Whatever you set your mind to in your life is yours to do." He was always half serious, half teasing—serious about my doing anything I set my mind to, teasing about the architecture, because he knew my ambitions were to fly or perform, not to dig foundations and lay bricks. We often played a game together, imagining the walls peeled away so that we could see the inhabitants going about their lives. He'd say, "Four walls make a house, Mattie, but every home is a world unto itself."

Usually before returning home, we would park at the Country Club Plaza to window-shop and admire the Spanish-inspired mosaic tiles and fountains. We also went there at Christmas to see the lights twinkling along all the building rooftops and archways

This Memorial Day morning, after my parents and Irene drove off with the dahlias to the cemetery and Betty with Albert to who knows where, I joined my brothers and Kip in the kitchen. They were finishing their oatmeal and hadn't combed their hair.

"Let's go to the waterfall," Mickey said.

"An adult needs to know where you are." I said, hearing Mother's voice echoing. *Take care of your little brother.*

"Ah, Skinbones, don't be a spoilsport. We'll be back before they get home. They can sit for a long time talking to dead people."

"Those people are your grandparents."

"I know that. But they're not there in holes in the ground. They're all around us. I can talk to them anywhere, if I want to. Can't you?"

"I guess so."

Mickey surprised me sometimes with ideas he had going on under the surface. He had been just old enough when our grandparents died to remember them.

"Right, Kip?" Mickey said. "Do you talk to people from the other realm?"

Kip nodded. "Sometimes."

"Who—?"

Wiley tugged at Mickey. "Come on. Let's go."

I wanted to know about Kip's conversations with dead people, so I followed him and my brothers out the door and closed it behind us. I traipsed after them to the waterfall that originated from a spring bubbling up from beneath a big flat rock in the woods along Cliff Drive. The water flowed to a brook, which splashed over the rocky cliffside and pooled in a hollow on a ledge far below. Overflow seeped between stones to an underground creek that flowed deep beneath the railroad yards into the river.

Mickey and I often went to the waterfall with the neighbor kids, but Wiley wasn't allowed to go with us. We liked to perch on the flat rock, launch leaf boats from the top of the fall, and watch them cascade down. Whichever boat survived and was the first to float in the pool won. Then we would climb down the rocks, retrieve our boats, and climb back to the top to race again. How we folded and tied the leaves made a big difference in a boat's success, and we were always trying new designs. We showed Kip various folds, rolls, and tucks. He plucked fresh leaves and vines and quickly made a slim canoe.

Mickey scrutinized Kip's creation. "Your boat is skinny." Our boats tended to be flatter and broader like Huck Finn's raft.

"What's your point?" Kip crouched by the start.

"You'll lose," Mickey said.

"Don't bet on it." Kip placed his canoe in the water.

On the count of three, we let the boats go. Wiley's and mine tipped gently into the falling water and bumped down over the rocks. Mickey's raft sped past ours, plunged from one drop in the falls to another, and landed upside down in the pool. Kip's canoe took a nose dive into the first drop, then another and another, pointing downward through the chutes toward the pool, where it landed upright and floated to the edge, surprising the water bugs, who quickly jumped away, stone to stone.

"That's the best boat ever," Wiley said.

Mickey grunted. "Yeah. He got lucky."

We clambered down the side of the cliff to retrieve the boats, and Mickey said, "Let's go to the rail yards."

"No. Wiley is too little." I was feeling more and more guilty that I'd broken my promise to Mother to take care of him.

"Ah, Mattie. He's a big kid now. He won't tell, will you, Wiley?" Mickey patted him on the head.

Wiley said "no," but he reached out and touched my arm. I should have taken him home then, but I didn't.

I doubted Mickey knew much about the yards, even though he had bragged about hopping the train to St. Louis. I wanted to see what Kip knew. He took off his shoes, to protect the taps, I figured. My Ziegfeld shoes were safe in my closet. Kip tied his laces, slung the pair over his shoulders, and walked in bare feet. They were long and narrow with high insteps similar to mine.

We lowered ourselves from rock to rock, taking short paths that angled down in places. Partway, we stopped to rest.

"It's too far," Wiley said.

Scrapes reddened his knees below his short pants. Bruises purpled on my shin and thigh. My dress had snagged on a thorn, and I wished I'd worn my camp rompers. The rail yards loomed below.

Mickey pointed to a clump of boulders. "There's a path beyond those. It's real quick from there." He led the way.

Kip followed, not staying on the trail but leaping from rock to rock as lightly as a water bug and heedless as a billy goat, his arms winged for balance. He teetered and almost fell, but righted himself and leapt, looking ahead. Wiley and I lagged behind. When we reached the bottom, we were in the Missouri Pacific yards. We crossed two empty railroad tracks and arrived at a train extending far to the east and west.

Mickey and Kip climbed a ladder into an open car and sat on the edge dangling their legs. "Climb up. It's easy. That's how you board a train." Mickey puffed himself as an expert.

"Not always," Kip said. "Often they're moving, and you can't squirrel on."

"I know." Mickey protested.

Kip continued. "You have to jackrabbit. You run alongside and scissor your legs to hop on."

"You think I don't know that?" Mickey sounded less confident.

I was pretty sure now that he had never hopped a train, but I couldn't embarrass him in front of Kip. The first rung was too high for Wiley, so I gave him a boost up. The boys grabbed his arm and pulled him into the car. I was the best in my class at chin-ups on the jungle gym and fairly easily hoisted myself onto the ladder and swung into the car. I perched on the edge with Wiley pressing close to my side.

"Ever been on a train roof? Bet I can get up there before you." Mickey reached for the ladder, swung himself on, and started up.

Kip grabbed a latch high on the open door, found a foothold on the lower latch, then on a crossbar and another, gripped the roof edge, and pulled himself up and onto it. He stood as Mickey reached the top of the ladder.

"Huh? How'd you do that?"

"Practice," Kip said.

"Show me."

Kip demonstrated. When Mickey's elbows were scraped

raw, and he finally succeeded in reaching the roof using the door hardware, they descended and sat with Wiley and me. The rocky cliff rose before us. Our long train stretched in each direction nearly as far as we could see. The boys smelled of damp dirt, as they always did, and the boxcar stank of metal, grease, and something putrid. A splinter from the floorboard lodged in my finger, and I sucked the skin until it bled. I was about to say, "Let's go home," when we heard voices coming near our car.

We scrambled back to a shadowed corner and waited, but Wiley's cap was resting where we had been sitting. I crept to snatch it only seconds before two men stopped beside the open door. I flattened myself against the wall of the boxcar and tried not to breathe. I couldn't see them both, but one was our neighbor Mr. Nelson, wearing his police uniform.

"Steeken says Thursday night. Wee hours Friday . . . the whole strip . . . paid if it's done right."

"Oh, it'll be done all right. Right as rain." The second man spoke in a gruff voice. It could have been my imagination, but he sounded a lot like Mr. Crowley.

As Aunt Irene would have said, they were common bullies up to no good. I wanted nothing to do with them. I wished with all my might that they'd go away, and they did. They walked on. When their voices diminished in the distance, I peeked out and motioned to the boys. "Coast is clear."

Climbing up the cliff side, Mickey again led. Kip stayed with Wiley and me, letting us pass and bringing up the rear. As we neared the top of the waterfall, Mickey's foot loosened a rock. It bounced down, smacking Wiley on his head. He pitched backward.

"Wiley!" I shouted. He tumbled past me.

I turned to see Kip teetering on a ledge, gripping Wiley by the wrists, keeping him from falling further down the cliff. As I descended toward them, Kip tugged Wiley back onto the ledge. Blood streamed from my brother's head, and he wailed.

By the time I reached them, Kip had taken the gingham flag from his pocket and pressed it on the cut. He placed Wiley's hand over it. "Hold it tight, little fella."

I gave Wiley a hug. "It's going to be all right." But I was scared it wouldn't be.

Kip carried him up to Cliff Drive. I walked close alongside, keeping rhythm with his step and holding Wiley's hand. I patted his arm, and, in doing so, patted Kip's as well. His face was red and glistening with sweat from the midday heat and strain of carrying Wiley. Mickey was paces ahead and kept glancing back at us. When we reached Gladstone, Wiley was still crying, and I kept saying, "We're almost home. We're almost home."

We passed between the bushes into the backyard. Sunlight filtered through sheets hanging stiff on the line. On the other side, Cyrus hoed. His backlit shape moved up and down on the sheets like a shadow puppet. When we came around, he dropped the hoe. "Lord, 'mighty." With a white dishtowel from the clothesline, he wiped blood from Wiley's face and pressed the towel against his forehead. When he lifted it, I saw the gash above Wiley's eye.

Cyrus threw the bloody flag into the burn barrel and scrutinized us. "What have you kids been up to?"

"Just playing," Mickey said. "Wiley fell down."

"In some places you ought not to be." Cyrus frowned at Kip. "This the new fellow I've been hearing about?"

"It's not his fault," I said.

Cyrus tolerated no nonsense. He was a loving parent to Leroy, but a lot tougher and stricter than Father. I was not about to tell Cyrus that we had been to the rail yards, but the scrapes on our arms and legs and the dirt and grease on our clothes told the truth. Wiley was taking it all in. We were setting a bad example, but it was more of an omission really, not the same as a lie. We weren't telling an untruth, merely not the whole truth. Not any one of us was to blame for endangering Wiley. We all were equally at fault.

Later that night, I crept to the landing. Aunt Irene had gone to bed early, and my parents were talking.

"I don't want them to believe they can lie to us without consequences," Mother said.

"Nothing more thrilling than forbidden territory, Clara. I told my parents a few fibs about those yards. Perhaps the guilt is consequence enough."

"Thank goodness Wiley wasn't badly hurt."

"Mattie clearly feels responsible."

"And she should, Elliot. I'd asked her to take care of him. But what about Kip? Do you think that he is a bad influence?"

"On Mattie?"

"On all the children."

"He's a hard-working boy who is well on his way to becoming a conscientious man. He seems to have some troubles he doesn't want to talk about, but I don't see that he's a troublemaker. He's a good sport."

Being a good sport was Father's highest praise. I tried always to be one in order to please him.

"I'd be more worried about Mickey leading Wiley astray than Kip doing so. Mickey is keener on playing than work. We'll resolve today's event, Clara, I'm sure."

"I'll wait up for Betty."

"Then I'll be off to bed. No need to bother with breakfast for me. I'll leave before dawn for Sedalia."

"Will you be gone all week?

"If things go well."

I heard newspaper rustling, a kiss, and Father's footsteps

toward the stairs. He stopped and said, "It's not like Betty to stay out so late. Would you like me to wait up with you?"

"You go on," Mother said. "Betty is surely smitten. If Albert is the one, I will be pleased for her, but she's quite starry-eyed. This morning the word 'marriage' crossed her lips. I want to talk with her about that. She's much too young."

"Your parents said we were too young, but we found our way." Father continued toward the stairs.

I hurried to bed. I had never thought of my parents as being in love the way Betty was with Albert, and I'd never pictured them finding their way. They'd always been there, having settled in their life together long before I arrived.

CHAPTER FOURTEEN

Letter

When I entered the Bluebird's kitchen Tuesday morning, Leroy was grinning. "He's got a spot in the talent show. Thursday at six." At the sink, Kip concentrated on the suds.

"You could win," I shouted.

"Maybe," he mumbled.

For the rest of the day, Kip was preoccupied with his routine for the show. He did his tasks, but stared past us all—me, Leroy, the customers—as if he were watching a moving picture flickering somewhere behind our heads. He tapped his fingers in rhythms and patterns against his thighs.

That afternoon, when I arrived home from the Bluebird, Father was sitting in his chair in the living room. My mind was on the talent show, otherwise I would have realized that he'd come home from Sedalia the same day he left and known, right then, that trouble followed.

At dinner, my brothers were rowdy. Father said a brief blessing, but not much else. Kip ate the pea soup, tapping his feet under the table all the while, and retreated to the basement immediately after the raspberry Jell-O.

I helped Mother with the dishes, went to my room, and tried to read. When the house stilled, I crept to the landing. My parents and Irene were speaking in hushed tones, and I strained to hear the bits and pieces of their conversation.

". . . Forced the lender to call the loan . . ."

". . . Certainly the city will . . ."

". . . Boss Tom finagled . . . his cronies . . ."

". . . Nothing more to do . . . bank will take the house . . ."

". . . I told you so . . ."

". . . Can't all stay together . . ."

". . . Perhaps Mattie . . . the Nelsons . . . Betty . . . the Clarks . . ."

". . . Not a good time for them . . ."

". . . Another notice at church . . . so many having difficulties . . ."

". . . Wiley . . . with us . . ."

". . . And Mickey?"

". . . I . . . failed you . . ."

". . . My love . . ."

Several minutes passed. As I began inching toward my bedroom door, Mother said, "Will you tell Kip, Elliot?"

". . . tomorrow . . . I hate for him to leave us."

". . . wait up for Betty?"

". . . yes, I'll talk with her . . . you've had a long day . . . go on up."

I returned to my room, where I lay shivering, although the night was warm. I hugged myself under the blanket. No "Moonlight Sonata" comforted me. A train hooted and moaned in the distance, sounding like a wounded animal as miserable and afraid as I was. What would happen to us? Where would we go? This house was the only one I'd ever known. I didn't want to live split apart. I lay awake, waiting for my sister to come home.

When the door opened, Betty was crying. "Mattie? Are you awake?" She sat on my bed and sniffled. "I might as well run away with Albert and get married."

"Did he ask you?"

"You won't tell? Promise? Cross your heart?"

"Hope to die. Stick a needle in my eye."

"He wants us to be settled before his college starts so we can live in married student housing. I want to wait until Thanksgiving so I can sew a beautiful wedding dress. Now, I might as well elope rather than live with neighbors or a family from church."

In the middle of the night, I awoke to Betty's soft snoring. My thoughts were on Eugene and how nice it would have been if he were still in Kansas City and his grandmother were still alive. We could have stayed all together in her mansion. I remembered the letter that Aunt Irene had misplaced.

In the darkened living room, I groped under the card table for the atlas and flipped it open. An envelope fell out. I tiptoed to the kitchen to read Eugene's letter by candlelight over a glass of milk.

Dear Mattie, We are moving to Los Angeles tomorrow. My parents have a job writing scripts for the pictures. Mother said it will take only twenty-five hours of flying. We will stop in six cities and be in Los Angeles in less than two days. We will stay at a house in Hollywood that belongs to a famous actor who the agent knows. He won't be there. Please write to me at this new address.

Back in my room, I lay awake imagining Eugene in Hollywood. I was sorry for myself that some people have more luck than others and mad that Hollywood would be wasted on Eugene. He couldn't dance or sing to save his life.

CHAPTER FIFTEEN

Westward

On Wednesday morning, Leroy turned the calendar page to the month of June. Arizona. A spectacular painting of the Grand Canyon didn't cheer me as it would have on any other day. Kip moved close to read the description. "Coconino County." He clapped out the rhythm and did a shuffle hop step fa-lap to match. "The Grand Canyon would be something to see."

"I'd like to see it too. It's a mile deep."

He nodded. "Maybe I'll head westward."

No doubt Father had spoken to Kip already. He would be leaving soon and I would never see him again. I didn't want to think about that.

All day I stayed close. He was working his mind on the steps for the talent show. Now and then he stopped in the middle of his tasks and tapped out sequences. Some I recognized, others not at all. I tried to copy him and cram in all the learning I could.

At night, as I lay awake listening to the trains, a plan grew powerful in my thoughts. When Kip left, I would follow him on the train, but I would not let him see me until we were far enough from home so that he couldn't make me go back. He could stay with the Turners too. They would have extra bedrooms and plenty of food and comforts to give us. I'd write to my parents once I arrived, and they would have one less worry. When the situation improved, I would come home.

In the morning, I would pack my camp knapsack and hide it. The problem was my hair. I could tie up my braids and wear Mickey's hat, but if it fell off, the men would see I was a girl. Before I left, I'd borrow Betty's scissors.

PART THREE

CHAPTER SIXTEEN

Plenty

"Bummer." Genet taps her phone to stop the alarm and the recording. "I have to go to work, but I'd rather stay in the past with you, Gram. Did the idea of leaving home scare you?"

"I had no real sense of what harm could befall us. Coupled with my innocence, I was probably operating on what we'd now call an adrenaline rush."

Genet lifts the tea cozy. "More? It's warmish. I really do think your life story would make a good book."

Mattie holds her hand over her cup. "I have no intention of making my life more than it is, nor any desire to become an author. I was serious when I said to take it. Write it as you tell your memoir class to do. Embellish."

"My instructor last semester said that a life examined can be story enough. He had us reading books like *To the Lighthouse*, where nothing much occurs. This new teacher says to give our characters trouble. She says to make them go through hell and back. I've been checking out novels looking for ideas. I can relate to the characters who have problems, you know, like ones I had. But should I ramp up the misery? I have no perspective. I'm my own worst enemy."

"I've wondered about that, Genet. I believe you have been hard on yourself."

"Did you struggle with anxiety when you were my age?"

"I don't remember anyone using that word when I was young—"

"And now we have phone apps for it." Genet leans in. "Sorry, Gram. Continue."

"We had everyday worries, of course, and the long uncertainty of the Depression and then the war. Our enemies, as such, were out there more than in here." Mattie places her hand against her breastbone. "Some days I didn't know if Eugene and Mickey and others I loved would make it through. I agonized about their well-being, but not so much about mine."

"Well, this instructor says to keep raising the stakes, to make our characters suffer, have them lose everything, and then figure out how to put their lives back together."

"No doubt your professor knows her business, but I wouldn't relish the job of inventing greater misery. In a life as long as mine, there's been plenty. I've lost my parents and siblings, all but Wiley, and more friends than I can count. When Eugene died, I had known him for fifty years and been married to him for thirty. And now Diego, my longtime salsa partner and companion, is gone. I miss him very much."

"Diego was like a grandpa to me."

"He felt that and loved you."

"I wish you two could have danced at my wedding."

"If only it could have been."

"You're right, Gram. You've had enough grief already."

"So make it uplifting. Surprise me. You always have had quite a lively imagination."

"You think so?"

"I look forward to reading whatever you write," Mattie smiles. "Even if, or maybe especially if, I'm in your story."

Genet laughs. "I want to hear more tonight after my sessions. Yoga Flow at three. Dance mixer at four. Would you like to come to that today?"

"I thought I'd bake a pie for Wiley, unless you need help with something for the wedding."

"With Ravi's mother's contacts at the art museum, everything is going smoothly. Catering and all. She has a knack for entertaining. You should see their house—well, you will soon, of course. It's one of those out on Ward Parkway that you were talking about. Anyway, she's reserved the museum's Italian courtyard for the wedding. We'll have a reception as people come in, and then dinner and dancing after the ceremony. I was thinking maybe you could lead everyone in a salsa dance lesson. Ravi and I want to learn it."

"How many guests?"

"About three hundred."

"That's quite a production."

"Ravi's parents know tons of people, and his extended family is huge. Some are coming from India and England. Our little Turner group will be outnumbered—you, me, Amoy, Charles, and Uncle Wiley. He won't even know where he is, but I want him there."

"We wouldn't be complete without him." Glancing to the window, Mattie notices that the sun has broken through the sluggish sky, and the snow on the street is melting. "While you're gone, I'll walk to the store for the apples."

"Take the Toyota. I'll bike to work."

"Shall I pick up something for dinner?"

"I made soup, but you could get a loaf of whole grain and bananas. And I don't have much baking stuff. Let's make a list."

At the market, Mattie wheels a cart past colorful produce mounded high in bins. From the display of shiny apples, she selects ten firm Honeycrisp. Her senses are heightened, as if seeing the grocery store for the first time, though the market where she shops at home is the same chain. The array and abundance of food never fails to astonish. She finds the items she came for and checks out.

"Have a nice day," the cashier says. "You saved two dollars."

Mattie slips her debit card into her purse, wondering if the woman has any idea how much those two dollars once bought. A young man with a badge on his shirt pocket announcing "In Training" stands at the end of the checkout counter. He studies the groceries that have slid from the conveyor belt and accumulated in front of him. He opens a paper sack and bites his lower lip in concentration. He bags the packages of flour and brown sugar, box of butter, and jars of cinnamon and nutmeg. He puzzles over the apples and ripe bananas, deciding on apples first, and smiles.

His resemblance to Kip Kelly is striking: the careful attention to task, his height and lean build, the eyebrows bridged above his nose, and one crooked tooth of a teenager lacking orthodontia, a sight more common when Mattie was a girl than it is today. He layers bananas, then bread. In a moment of recognition, not of her, but of the task—he knows how to do it better—he reaches in, lifts the bananas, rearranges the crusty loaf, and nests the fruit.

"Need help out, ma'am?"

"Yes, thank you, if you'd like the exercise." She could carry the bag herself, but she wants him to accompany her. He follows her through the open automatic door.

"I'm over there. The hatchback." She points to the far edge of the lot beyond rows of empty spaces. "I like to park far from the door."

He nods and shifts the bag. Watching for icy patches on the asphalt, she adds a spring to her step over a puddle. A penny shines in the slush. She stoops to claim it, rubs it between her fingers, and slips it into a pocket, thinking to herself, "All day long you'll have good luck."

At the car, she lifts the hatch, and the young man leans in with the groceries. His forearm brushes her hand. His skin is firm, resilient. It electrifies hers. A sensation travels up her arm, spills warmly across her breastbone, to her ribs, waist, and pelvis. He backs out and stands tall against the sun.

She wants to lean into him and rest her cheek against the curve of his collarbone. She wants to press her ear against his shirt and hear his heartbeat, touch his cheek, and push back the wayward dark hair shadowing his eyes. Talking with Genet has brought Kip Kelly alive in her memory, and now here he is, or nearly so, in front of her. Is the choice of checkout line and seeing this young man a coincidence? She is certain that Genet will think it is not.

The hatch slams shut. "That's chill you can drive," he says. "They took my grandma's license away. She ran into a light pole."

"Yes, well, I try to avoid that." She smiles and catches his earnest look. "I pray she wasn't injured. Actually, this is my granddaughter's car. I gave away mine last year because I rarely used it in San Francisco, what with Lyft and Uber so handy when I need them."

"Sweet." He smiles. "Have a nice day, ma'am."

He hops a stray grocery cart and rides it with a beautiful carelessness—one foot on the bottom bar, the other pushing against the asphalt to pick up speed, then both feet on the bar, bending his upper torso for thrust—to the front door of the market where he dismounts and, with precise force, slams the cart into a queue of them. He raises his fist to the sky. He is a boy, after all, with his whole life in front of him.

She breathes in the brisk air and his image—slamming the cart, raising his fist. Another stray cart, abandoned by a departing customer, rolls across the parking lot toward her. She grabs the handle, orients it to the curb, and shoves. It hits, bounces, and lodges with a wheel over the curb. She lifts both arms to the sky.

In the car, Mattie turns the radio dial to an oldies station. She pumps the volume high and sways in her seat. Her own voice has lost dimension, but she joins in "Ever Changing Times" along with Aretha, who sings with passion.

At the house, Mattie hangs her coat in the hall closet and carries the groceries to the kitchen. It's arranged identical to the one in her girlhood home: the sink by the window, a wooden table at the center of the room. She peels the apples, slices them into a bowl, and stirs in spices, sugar, and lemon juice. She measures flour and salt into another bowl, dices the butter into the flour using two knives, and sprinkles cold water over it all. She crumbles the dough with her fingertips, thinking about how the young man bending into the car with the groceries brought Kip Kelly alive beside her for an instant. She hears the train whistle and Kip's voice within her.

She rolls the bottom crust and presses it into the pie pan, tumbles the apples from the bowl, rolls out another round of dough, places it over the apples, and pinches the two crusts together. As she flutes the edges, Genet enters, perspiring from her bike ride home.

"What a day. We had an incident in Yoga Flow. Mrs. Armstrong keeled right off the chair while doing leg lifts and passed out. We called an ambulance."

"Is she going to be alright? Tea? Lemon verbena?"

Genet nods. "A bruise on her elbow is all. Turns out she was dehydrated. And guess what? In memoir class this morning, Mr. Nguyen told me that he has a new heartthrob. The staff thinks it's Mrs. Gupta, but I'm pretty sure it's Ruth. She's only forty-five. He wrote in class about his habit of sending a dozen red roses to his wife. They'd been married seventy-three years when she died. And Ruth received a dozen roses this afternoon with a card signed by an anonymous admirer. The handwriting looked like Mr. Nguyen's."

Mattie raises her cup. "To love and anonymous admirers." The tea burns her tongue. She has seen the residents' names in the acceptance packet from Sonata and heard personal details from Genet. Ruth is the front desk receptionist who has befriended her. Mr. Nguyen is ninety-five.

"Love *you*." Genet smiles and sips. "Yikes. Hot." She sets the cup on the table. "I'm not trying to twist your arm, or anything. I get why you wouldn't want to leave California, but I'd love for you to live here in KC. I think you'll like the people at Sonata Court. A lot of them have led fascinating lives.

"Mrs. Hall was a Red Cross nurse in London in World War II. And rumor has it that the newest resident was in the CIA. He has trouble walking, uses a motorized chair, and has impaired memory, but he was a really lively dancer today at the mixer. According to his bio, he used to perform on Broadway. It's like he gets switched on when the music starts. I signed you up for the Thursday mixer so you can meet some people and get the lay of the land. Okay?"

"I'll try it."

Mattie often tells people what studies have shown—that forming new relationships helps to prevent cognitive decline—but she is not eager to meet a host of people all at once. At Sonata, she could putter alone in her small kitchen and bake the occasional pie, but she would take her evening meal with one hundred and twenty other people of her generation. They will share reminiscences of their pasts, and she will share hers, but to what and with whom will she look forward? If she finds Sonata Court tolerable—yes, that is her criteria—and if she can see that being there with her brother will ease his final years, the decision to move will be made.

"Who knows, Gram, you might meet a new love."

"Or improve my Downward Facing Dog. At any rate, I would enjoy being able to take your classes and see you often."

Genet places her phone, along with a notebook and pen, on the table. "To jot down a few ideas. Do you have the energy to talk more now?"

Mattie regards her granddaughter's eager expression. "I do. But let's remember the pie."

"I'll set the timer. We can break for dinner then." Genet pulls the soup kettle from the refrigerator and turns a burner to low. She settles back at the table and presses record. "Ready?"

Mattie nods and closes her eyes. "Where were—? Ah, yes. The knapsack."

CHAPTER SEVENTEEN

Silver Dollars

On Thursday morning, I had no intention of missing the evening's talent show, but I pretended to have a headache and stayed in bed. Sitting beside me, Mother said, "It is so unlike you to be ill, and I have faith you will work through it beautifully. You rest while the boys and I go to the market." She gave me a kiss and left the bedroom door ajar. I heard my brothers roughhousing and then Mother herding them out the front door. Father and Irene had already gone to the Bluebird and Betty to a fabric store downtown to apply for a job.

I got up and packed my knapsack with my tap shoes, the tin box of letters, underwear, socks, and my church dress. I figured I wouldn't need a coat in Los Angeles, but it might be chilly on the ride, so I tucked in my best sweater that Aunt Irene had knitted, along with Mickey's cap and my ceramic piggy bank.

When I lifted the knapsack, the coins clattered inside the pig. I emptied the money into a sock, tied it with a ribbon, and stuffed the sock in with the underwear. In the living room, I tore out the map of the United States from the atlas. I would only need the western half, but I folded both the left and right pages into the knapsack. Upstairs, I hid it under my bed.

From the hand-me-down bin that Mother kept in Mickey

and Wiley's room, I took a pair of Mickey's suspender trousers and a shirt. Wiley wouldn't be growing into them any time soon. I hopped in bed and stuffed the clothes down by my feet under the covers.

When Mother returned, I told her I was much better and wanted to go to the Bluebird. She placed her hand on my forehead and cheek. "You're good as new, Mattie. Run along, then."

The restaurant was busy because of a railroad meeting. The Negro men filled half of the room. Only one other restaurant in the neighborhood would serve them, and no other would let them meet without buying meals.

Kip was jittery, and I didn't blame him. I was jittery, too, for his sake that the talent show loomed in a few hours and for my sake that I was about to have a real-life adventure beyond anything I'd ever imagined. I said I didn't feel like dancing today because I forgot my tap shoes. He didn't guess the real reason—I could barely put a shuffle hop step together.

In the afternoon, Aunt Irene said, "Finally, Margaret Ann, you have the sense not to be prancing around on a hot day. You ought to go on home if you're still feeling poorly."

"I want to see the talent show."

"You are not allowed to step foot in that place. Is she, Elliot?"

Behind the counter, Father polished the walnut top in slow swirls, moving one arm clockwise, the other counter clockwise. He could cover twice as much surface in the same amount of time as doing it one-handed.

"No daughter of mine is going into the Hayride Club," he said without looking up.

"Please, Father?" I had imagined going inside, but I offered a compromise. "I'll watch from the alley."

He kept on polishing.

"Please? Leroy will be with us."

"It's no place for young girls."

"I'm almost thirteen."

"Or for young ladies."

"But I won't go inside. Cross my heart."

 He stopped in midswirl. "You'll listen to Leroy?"

"Don't you trust me?"

"And you'll stick close to him?"

"Like cheese on toast. I promise."

"Then you may watch the show from the alley."

"Thank you, Father." I waltzed behind the counter and hugged him.

"I do trust you, Mattie." He released the hug, held me at arm's length, and looked me steadily in the eyes. "If you heard doubt, it's only because growing up is a bumpy road that tests one's moral compass, no matter how strong and true. We each are enticed to lose our way at times, and you're at the age where you will soon be tested."

My stomach churned. He was giving me all of his trust, and I was planning to leave home without his permission in the morning. But I would travel with my moral compass and, once I reached Eugene's, Father would be relieved and proud that I made it all the way there.

The hands on the clock above the radio in the Bluebird's kitchen barely moved all afternoon. I checked it frequently. It seemed that closing time would never come.

Finally, it was five-thirty, going on six o'clock. Kip and I stood in the alley outside the back door of the Hayride, waiting for Leroy, who had ducked in to talk to the cook. Smoke from cigarettes and cigars wafted from the club into the alley, along with the smell of hay, barbecue, and whiskey. Leroy returned to us with a plate of ribs. I gnawed two of them to the bone, but Kip didn't eat a bite.

I patted him on the arm. "Don't be nervous. You'll be really good."

"Easy for you to say. You're not doing it." He shrugged me away. A minute later he said, "Do you think so?"

I was still dishing out the encouragement when his turn came. He entered the Hayride Club with his head down and fists in his pockets, as if he didn't have a friend in the world. I guess he wasn't counting Leroy and me waiting in the wings, where we had a clear view.

Kip stepped up onto the hay-wagon stage, where a jazz quartet sat. He stared at the audience without a grin or a grimace, his mouth set in determination, his eyes narrowed toward the task. He put hand to heart, nodded to the musicians, and tapped out a beat. Then he started dancing, and they played. He traded fours with them, making it a jazz quintet.

As Kip tapped phrases, the musicians riffed. It was like stealing steps. Kip did rubber legs, and the trumpet player wobbled his notes. He railroaded, and the double bass player plucked out a low rumbling. He rang bells left and right, and the pianist jingled the high notes.

The audience clapped and whooped, and so did Leroy and I from the alley door. "Lord 'mighty. He's got the chops."

Kip shuffled, hopped, and put a snake in his hips. He did the Kansas City and Amarillo and fell off a log. He dipped and stretched, collapsed and expanded, twirled and spun, jumped and landed. I had never seen him put it all together in a long, continuous dance. It was magical.

Leroy snapped his fingers. "They got a groove going."

When the music ended, Kip took an outro on his own, tapping and winging his arms across the stage and back to center, where he landed on toes, then heels, with triumph. The audience stood and cheered.

Other acts followed—an opera singer, a banjo player, a ventriloquist, and more. The master of ceremonies conferred with a group of judges down in the front row, stepped back up on stage with a grin, and said, "Well, folks, you might have guessed it. The winner is our talented young hoofer, Mr. Kip Kelly."

Kip had won twelve silver dollars. Leroy exclaimed. "Lord 'mighty. That's more than I earn workin' a week in the kitchen."

We walked home together, said goodbye to Leroy at his building on the corner, and continued up our street, where Mickey and Wiley played.

I shouted. "Kip won!" The boys ran toward us and followed us up to the porch, where my parents and Aunt Irene were sitting.

"Congratulations," Father said. "We're proud of you."

Kip bowed, hand to heart. He reached into his pocket and brought forth the silver dollars. "I would like to give these to you—Mr. Toft, Mrs. Toft—to help with the situation."

Father shook his head. "That's generous, young man, but it won't change what's about to come."

"Holy moley," Wiley said. "I never had a whole dollar of my own."

Without hesitation, Kip gave Wiley the shiniest coin. "Now you do."

"Holy moley." Wiley held it lightly on his open palm, as if it were a firefly about to flit away.

"That's very thoughtful of you," Mother said. To Wiley, she whispered, "What do you say?"

"Thank you, Kip." Struck by his good fortune, Wiley went into the house muttering. "Holy moley."

"You hang onto the rest of those, Kip," Father said. "You'll be needing them."

"I could give you a hand tomorrow with the move—"

"We've closed the Bluebird for the day, so we'll have Irene to help with the sorting and packing. And Leroy has offered to help. We'll make quick work of it."

"I'll be heading out early then—"

"We wish it could continue," Father said.

"But it's time for me to be moving on, sir."

Father nodded, and I did a shuffle and a new pattern that I had put together myself. "Steal that, Kip."

He tapped out my rhythm. "Stolen."

After we'd given our "goodbyes" to Kip and he'd gone to the basement, Father said, "Through the kindness of neighbors and church friends, we will weather this stretch together, though living apart."

I hadn't thought about my parents having to clean up after me or pack my things. Betty was out with Albert, so I threw socks from the floor into the hamper and arranged the books on the nightstand between the beds. I opened the bureau drawers that contained my clothes and folded everything neatly in piles. I tucked my empty piggy bank between the piles, put on my pajamas, and lay in bed thinking about the morning. It wasn't too late to change my mind.

CHAPTER EIGHTEEN

Smoke

Before dawn, I heard Kip coming up the stairs. The bathroom door opened and closed and the plumbing grumbled. He retreated down, rummaged in the kitchen, and left the house. I knew it was now or never. I rolled out of bed on the opposite side of how I usually got up, so as not to pass near Betty. I tiptoed out of the room with the knapsack, clothes, and my diary. In the bathroom, I put on the shirt, trousers, and my Buster Browns, washed my teeth, drank a big glass of water, and rolled the toothbrush and diary with my pajamas into the knapsack. When I opened the door to the hall, Wiley was there, half asleep. "Mattie? Is it morning?"

"Not yet."

"Where are you going?"

I hugged him close. "I'll come back, little brother. I promise."

He stared at the trousers. "Why are you wearing Mickey's?"

"Because I need them. Now goodnight, sleep tight."

"Don't let the bed bugs bite." Wiley smiled sleepily and turned back to his room.

I crept downstairs to the living room, where I took Betty's scissors from her sewing basket. In the kitchen, I put a note in the icebox, so that Mother would find it, but not before I was well on my way.

Dear Family,

I am going to stay with Eugene in California. Don't worry. I will travel with Kip.

Love, M.A.T.

My foot slipped on a dog's blanket edging out from under the table. I bundled the frayed thing around slices of bread and a banana, stuffed it into the knapsack, and unlatched the back door.

In the garden behind the plum tree, I cut off my braids and placed the scissors on a stump beside the watermelon patch, where Cyrus would see them. I picked four plums that were ripe to touch—two for me, two for Kip. I nestled them, along with the braids, into the bundle. I put on Mickey's cap, strapped the pack onto my shoulders, and made my way to the waterfall. As long as the moon and stars shone, I wasn't afraid of the night, but the rocky trail down along the waterfall was more difficult to maneuver than it had been in the day. I stumbled and slid, getting dirt on my hands and trousers, then had the idea to rub some on my face so that I'd look more like a boy.

In the train yard, I hunched beside a pile of crates and tugged Mickey's cap low enough to shadow my face, but so I could still see from under the brim. I'd watch for Kip and steal his steps to hop the train.

Something skittered across my shoe and ran behind a crate. I shrieked. Mickey once had a rat for a pet, and I wasn't afraid, but I was losing my nerve. Dawn crept in, turning the dark to dull gray without the reassuring moon and stars. I was already homesick and hungry for a hot breakfast. A large presence loomed behind me. I yelped, and a thick hand clamped against my mouth and nose. "Shut up, kid."

A dirty face hovered close to mine. The man spoke in a low,

gruff whisper. "There's bulls in the yard." His breath was foul. I pictured horned cattle loose from their pen but realized, of course, that he was talking about the railroad police. I planned to act as young as I could. They probably wouldn't be too hard on a poor orphaned boy, but if they were, I would reveal that I was a girl. I figured they would then treat me more kindly.

The man didn't let go, so I bit his finger hard. "Criminey," he growled. "Yuh feckin' pipsqueak." He swung at me, knocking off my cap.

I grabbed it and crawled away, the bitter taste of his skin on my tongue. I burrowed deeper into the space between the crates, and yanked the cap snugly on my head again. Gripping my knapsack, I gave the man the stand-down glare I had perfected playing capture the flag with the boys, but he was looking out into the yard, paying me no attention.

"Hey." I threw my voice to him while keeping it low. "Are you planning on hopping a train?"

He turned, angered. "Whad'yuh think? I'm out here for my health?"

"I'm going too."

"Where're yer folks?" He spoke harshly. "Young uns oughtn't be ridin' alone."

I mustered sadness. "I'm an orphan."

"Ain't yuh got some relatives what could keep yuh?"

I shook my head. "Going to see my friend Eugene in California. His family will take me in, most likely."

"Well, yer lucky to have somebody." His voice softened to near tenderness.

I moved closer to him. "I never hopped a train before. What's the knack?" My confidence that I could do it based on what I had learned on the excursion to the yards had begun to vanish.

"Ain't no knack, so to speak. Ain't gonna have much luck

boardin' a sittin' train of any kind. The bulls and dicks will roust yuh out. Ain't much space to ride on a passenger train anyway, 'cept in the blinds between the cars. Slip under there and get yerself mangled or killed. Best to hop a freighter on the fly." He seemed satisfied with his explanation and stood to peer over the crates.

I tugged at his trouser leg. "What's the fly?"

He looked down. "Yer a pipsqueak, ain't yuh?" He sounded annoyed but sat beside me. "Gotta catch it when it's movin' slow at the edge of the yard, where it's convergin' to the main track. Someone yer size has gotta grab onto the deck of an open car. Then scissor a leg up and thrust yerself in. With some luck, yuh don't get yer limbs chopped off." He axed his hand against his forearm.

"Yuh never know once yuh start runnin' where it's gonna end up. Just hope if the scissorin' don't work, yuh get good hold of a ladder next to an open door and heave yerself up and in. Someone could give a small kid a haul in, if they cared to. But first timers don't have much of a chance when they catch out. They get hurt."

"Could you help me?" I said it sweet and humble, as if I were asking Aunt Irene for the last piece of pie in the case. I heard a rustling and saw the rat's tail, but I didn't budge.

"It's every man for hisself in this business. If I was to see yuh runnin', I'd give heave-ho if I could but wouldn't linger in the open to do it. Sure can't take yuh on as my charge. Once yer in the car, best to hunker back in the shadows until the train's long gone from the yards." He scrutinized me. "What's yer name, kid?"

"Matti—" I stopped short. "I'm Matt. What's yours?"

"Called Whistler." He hoisted his knapsack and strapped it on. "Yuh might be able to make it by jumpin' high and grabbin' the ladder. Then hang on tight and swing yerself into the car.

But yuh got to be further down the tracks or a bull's gonna catch yuh."

He stepped past me between the boxes and sniffed the air. "Smell that?" His body alerted, his gruffness returned. "Somethin's burning."

I inhaled and looked to the sky. Smoke filled the air. An orange light glowed in the west. If it were in the east, it could have been the sunrise. Whistler slipped behind another stack, out into the open, and then behind another stack and another. I tried to keep up.

By now the dawn and the fire had given the whole dusty train yard a rosy wash. Shadows moved along the edges of the yard and down the tracks, which stretched out into the gray pinkish light in both directions. I caught up with Whistler as he entered out into the open. I paced myself several feet behind him, watching for Kip's movements among the dark shapes.

The train on the closest track loomed black and oily, much bigger than it was in daylight. From a distance, I tried to gauge if I should jackrabbit onto the open edge of the boxcar or chin-up on the ladder and then swing into the car. Chin-up, I decided. In that moment of what Mother would call being too full of myself, I lost sight of Whistler. All the shadowy figures had disappeared too.

Only one shape was moving, and he was striding toward me—a bull. His brass buttons and belt buckle shone dully against his dark uniform, and he wasn't smiling. It was Mr. Nelson, slapping his billy club into his palm. He never paid me much attention even when I was in their kitchen using the oven. I doubted he would recognize me with the cap and short hair, but I hid beside a crate. He stopped a body length away from me, close enough so that I could see the swirls engraved on his buttons.

Another man came out of the shadows. "It's done," he said. It was Mr. Crowley. "You got the money for me?"

"Is Steeken happy?" Mr. Nelson said.

"Sure is. Went off without a hitch. Fire crew was slow to respond, just as the chief guaranteed. Likely now to burn to ashes."

Mr. Nelson handed Crowley a packet. "Here you go. The amount Steeken promised."

Crowley took it. "Oughta be more. He's insured to the limit and with a fella to blame. I'd sure like to see that roustabout get his comeuppance and put in the clinker. Wish I could be here to watch, but I'll be long gone from this town."

"Never saw you here." Mr. Nelson walked away, slapping his billy.

Crowley crossed the yard and into the shadows between stacks of crates. I stayed hidden between mine. Whatever these men were up to, I was glad it didn't concern me. I was hoping Crowley would be heading east, but if he caught the same train as I did, I'd steer clear of him. I doubted he'd recognize me because he never paid me attention other than to scowl my way.

The train on the nearest track hissed, and a clump of shadows moved toward it. I looked for the sway of Kip's shoulders, the length of his stride. I hooked the straps of my knapsack over my shoulders and moved into the open. The train started rolling, letting go a stench of oil and metal that scorched into my nose and throat. The clump of figures moved faster, breaking up into smaller clumps and single shapes spreading along the train cars, running fast and then faster as the train picked up speed.

I was certain I'd seen Kip jackrabbit into the open side of a car, so I grabbed for the rungs of a ladder on the car behind it, missed, kept running, and aimed for the next open door. I tried to jump, grab the edge of the car's floor, hoist myself up, swing a knee over, and then haul the rest of me onto the floorboards, but the floor edge was higher than I'd judged. I missed that car and kept running until the next edge was above my head. I leapt for it and grabbed onto the boards. Something jagged hurt my hand. I was losing hold when my trousers were hitched up from my backside. I flew in and landed hard, my chin slamming into a dusty boot. I rolled over to see a man towering above me.

"Hi, Whistler."

He glared. "Could've got yerself killed."

"Thanks for saving me." My hand smarted.

"Feckin' kid." He turned away into the car. I crawled to the wall near the door and sat sucking my palm, tasting blood.

Dawn was breaking and warming, but inside the car was dim and cool. Men slumped against the boxes. I tended my hand, convincing myself that Kip was a few cars ahead and, in the next second, worried that he wasn't even on the train.

I glanced up to see men staring past me to something happening outside. The train had pulled beyond the yard and cliff to where the tracks paralleled First Street. A few blocks in, a fire burned. Smoke covered the area but I could see clearly, there on the corner of Fourth Street, flames leaping through the roof of the Hayride Club.

As the train thundered out of Kansas City, some men bent their heads and fell asleep. Others stared out toward the open door or rummaged in their bundles, one uncapping a bottle, another pulling forth socks to cover his bare toes, which poked out from the ragged ones he wore. Another man unwrapped something in brown paper, put a lump into his mouth, and chewed.

I slid the pack off my shoulders and reached inside for a plum. I felt the plumpness, the smooth skin, and an oozing spot. I curled my fingers around it, brought it to my mouth, and bit into the bruise. Juice ran down my palm and stung the cut, but I didn't mind. A plum had never tasted so good. I licked juice from my wrist. A man stared, open-mouthed. I'd seen that look on the men at the Bluebird eyeing the pie. I moved my hand closer to my mouth and bent my head down to hide the nibbling, going slowly to make the fruit last. All the while, the man stared and the plum lost its deliciousness. I mouthed it, finished slurping the pulp, and sucked the juice until the pit was rough on my tongue.

By that time, the sun poured bright through the open door. All that whizzed past were dry fields and a few trees here and there. My chest rattled with the ride and the dust, which drifted into the car with the warm air. I was thirsty. I sucked the rough pit against my cheek. The man who had uncapped the bottle did so again, glaring me down.

Some of the men now moved around, a few came over to the door, faced out, and relieved themselves. They weren't all as old as they looked in the shadows. Some of them were as young as Kip and Mickey. I was glad I hadn't drunk any more water than I had that morning. When the train stopped, I would find a bush or an outhouse. Until then, I wouldn't give the tingle of urgency another thought. I would use power of mind to overcome.

A drop splashed from the doorway onto my cheek. I wiped it away with my shirtsleeve, lowered my hat and head, and began practicing what I would say to Kip when he saw me. I thought about telling him that I had asked Father and been given permission to go, but I was certain Kip would know I was lying. It was better to make an ally of him. If he said he wanted me to turn around and go home, I'd say I was too scared to travel alone with the hobos. I'd say I nearly died hopping the train and was afraid of being beaten up.

In truth, I was sure I could slip the punch of any of these tired old men and most of the younger ones too. If Kip said he'd take me home, I would plead that my parents couldn't find places to put us all. I would tell him that, once I got to Eugene's, they would have one less worry. Kip would run out of arguments at that point and agree that we could go together to California.

By my calculations, almost seventeen hundred miles lay between Kansas City and Los Angeles. Even a slow train could go eighty-five miles an hour, so I calculated twenty hours or so of traveling time. With stops, I figured we could be there in two days at most. I reached in my pack for the sock of coins, reassured that there would be no way to spend them all, even if we ate in restaurants along the route. I planned to find stores or stands selling bread and fruit. I craved an orange, but if I splurged on one I'd be out fifteen cents, and that was worth two loaves of bread.

The car heated up and became stifling. I scooted closer to the doorway to get some air. The train sped past a small town, but the dust obscured the sign. I coughed, nearly swallowed the plum pit, and spit it out. Nearby, a man plucked a banjo, working out a lonely tune, making it up as he went along. "I'm a . . . I'm a hard times traveler . . . don't you . . . don't you worry 'bout me . . ."

A man eased beside me. "Hey, what's an Angelina like you doing out here?"

He had a broad face and kind brown eyes, but his hands were knobbed with knuckles and scars. I didn't know at the time what he was calling me, but it sounded like an insult that Mickey would have made if I threw underhanded. Later, I found out the man was only saying I was an inexperienced child.

"I have a boy about your size back home." He offered a stick of gum. "Got a name?"

I chewed, stalling for time. Until I found Kip, I didn't want to let on that I was a girl or scared of anything. I needed a moniker that inspired respect and said I meant business. I considered Mickey's "Skinbones." Eugene often called me "scrappy," and he meant it as a compliment. Betty said to "grow up" and "act your age," which suited her purposes by confusing me so that I had no retort. Mother said I was nearly a woman, and Irene said I was a tomboy.

To Father, I was right on the money. When I first learned

to pour a cup without spilling a drop, he said, "Right on the money, Mattie." When I made lemon meringue that turned out too lopsided to serve but still tasted good, he took a bite of the pie, melted it in his mouth, and said, "Right on the money." The phrase came from putting a shiny nickel or dime onto a post so a surveyor could see the top of it through his transit and get things level. I did like things being even as much as possible in the world—"fair and square," as Father said. I thought for a moment of calling myself "Even Steven," but decided against it. I had been taught that the best way to inspire respect was to give it and that respect was in the person, not the name.

"I'm called Matt, sir."

"Matt it is. I'm Knuckles." He fisted his left hand and punched it into his flat right palm. Then he offered that hand, and I grabbed on. Mine stung. "Where're you from, kid?"

I chewed and smacked the gum, licked my fingers, took the glob out, and rolled it between them. If I named a town that I hadn't been to but he had, he could trip me up on some detail. I wanted him to believe my story. I popped the gum back in my mouth.

"Ever heard of Independence?"

"Up by KC?"

"Yes." I knew this could go either way.

"Never been there. Only through it."

"You didn't miss much, sir. I was born there. Put in an orphanage when my folks passed."

"I grew up in an orphanage myself. Run by nuns. How about yours?"

All I knew of orphanages was what I'd read in books. "I didn't take to it, so I left." He seemed to believe me, and I didn't want more questions. Mother said that empathy and interest fed good conversation, so I said, "That's all behind us now. Where's your kid?"

Knuckles settled back against the wall. "He's back home in St. Louis with his grandmother. It's no life out west for a motherless boy."

"No, sir, it isn't." I forced a solemn expression, but I was smiling inside. It was no life for a young boy, but one for a girl pretending to be, if she used her wits.

Knuckles closed his eyes and drifted off, perhaps dreaming of his son or a cooler place. The car was getting hotter and dustier by the minute, and I was full to bursting. I clenched against that morning glass of water, using my mind control to concentrate on something else, trying to picture the Atlas pages in my knapsack and where we were heading on the map. I stared at the dirt fields flying past. If we had been going east, I might have recognized a few things along the route to St. Louis, but we were heading southwest, a direction I had never been.

CHAPTER NINETEEN

Caught

I awoke to a scrambling of legs stepping over me, feet stepping on mine. My fellow travelers jumped out the open door onto a graveled strip and browned grass that sloped away. I had only worried about hopping onto a moving train, not leaping off. I stood at the opening, terrified. Although the train was slowing, the ground below seemed to whiz by. Soon everyone had jumped, and I'd missed my chance.

Ahead in the distance, a flag waved on a pole above a depot. Hobos were rolling down the slope and running away, others climbing back up, their dark shapes silhouetted by the sun. One shape darted out, moving like a leaf on a stream. He stopped and looked at the train. It was Kip. My car rumbled toward him, and I prepared to leap from the open door, but I froze. As we passed him, I yelled his name.

He couldn't have been more confused and surprised if I'd had two heads. As the others scattered away from the depot— Whistler and Knuckles among them—Kip ran toward it, toward me. The train chugged and came to a stop alongside the platform. Climbing down, I spotted Kip and lit out in his direction. I needed to find that bush or outhouse really soon.

I ran smack into a bull. He grabbed me and held tight;

I yelled and kicked. As he dragged me away, I lost my mind control and wet myself. It ran down my legs into my socks. We walked some blocks, passing a billboard with a picture of a cow piloting a plane. *Welcome to Wichita. The Cowtown that Knows How.*

The officer pulled me into a building, pushed me past the front desk, where another officer sat, and into a narrow hallway. He yanked off my knapsack and shoved me into a cell occupied by several men hunched on benches. One of them moved to make room. "Tough luck, kid."

When I sat down, his arm behind me brushed against my back. If any of these men touched me, I'd bite them. I leaned forward and hugged my arms around my chest, thinking of my knapsack, the plums, and the coins. The bench was hard. My underwear and trousers were clammy against my skin, my socks damp in my shoes. Above our heads, a small window let in a square of sunlight, which reflected on the opposite wall. I hugged myself tighter and watched as the light patch moved by fractions of an inch toward the ceiling. It must have been past noon.

It seemed an eternity, but the patch had moved only a few inches when the hallway door opened and an officer entered. He was the one who had been at the desk. He unlocked the cell and said, "Come with me, boy." I followed him into the office where Kip stood, unsmiling.

"This here's the kid?" the officer asked.

"Yes, sir." Kip nodded. His palm cupped silver dollars.

The man took them and sat at his desk, which was littered with papers and odds and ends. He lined the dollars at the edge above the opened drawer and counted as he slid them in. "That's eight, ten, and eleven."

He reached for my pack, which was on the floor beside his

desk. "Let's have a gander in here." From the radio on the shelf behind him, Bing Crosby crooned "Just One More Chance."

The meaning wasn't lost on me as the officer dumped the contents of my pack onto the desk and handled each thing—blanket, bread, plums, map, box of letters, sweater, underwear, dress, diary, braids, tap shoes, sock tied with a ribbon—and arranged them on top of his papers. Plum juice stained a page, and the officer handed me the squashed fruit.

"Well, well," he said, holding up the underwear and dress. "These don't look to me like no boy's." He stuffed them into the pack, followed by the sweater, socks, and bread. He touched the braids, pinched one between his thumb and forefinger, and held it above the desk. "This neither." He examined the tap shoes and set them aside. He picked up the sock of coins, shook it for the jingling sound, enjoying the tease, and slowly untied the ribbon.

"Well, well." He stacked my pennies, nickels, and dimes, scraped his hand across the desk, and sent the coins clattering into the drawer. He shoved it closed.

He stuffed the sock and my other things into the knapsack, except for the tap shoes. He held them up by the straps. "Now, where'd you steal these fancy things?" He put them in the pack and snickered. "Best be on your way—*boys*. No place for you fellas in Wichita."

I walked out behind Kip. He paced ahead until we arrived at a corner, then he turned to me with an expression that I'd never seen on anyone's face—a mix of anger and scare, sorrow and caring.

"Why are you here, Mattie?"

"I'm going to Eugene's."

"In New York? But—"

"He moved to Los Angeles."

"Does he know?'

"Not yet, but he'll be happy."

"Did your folks—?"

"I'll write to them from Eugene's. You can stay there too. It's a mansion."

Kip crossed the street, and I followed close behind him for several blocks, until we came to a park with picnic tables, benches, and a drinking fountain. The plums, which I had put in my trouser pockets, were warm and oozing juice. I placed the mushed fruit on a table. "Want some bread and *jam*? All that's missing is the sugar." I thought my emphasis on "jam" might sweeten Kip up and make him laugh, but he didn't. I had imagined offering him the plums whole and beautiful.

At the fountain, we washed our hands, splashed water over our heads and necks, and drank. I spread plum pulp on the bread, handed Kip a slice, and we chewed without talking. When he finished his, he sat rolling the pits around and around on the table with his finger.

"What if your folks believe I talked you into this?"

"You didn't."

"No matter. They trusted me. I'm taking you back on the next train. We're going to the depot. Now."

Walking away from the park, we passed a boarded up Cessna aircraft factory. "Kip, did you know that they make more airplanes in this city than any other? I bet we could find the airfield." I felt badly that he had missed the trip to ours and was hoping to stall our departure with a diversion.

"They're not making any planes in that place now, Mattie."

"They will again. When things get better. Wichita is the aircraft capital of the world." I winged my arms and smiled.

"Do you ever get tired of being so optimistic?"

"No."

"You have no idea how things really are."

We walked on toward the afternoon sun. I was working my mind, wondering if I could stall by trying to locate the brick building that Father had designed and have more time to talk Kip out of taking me home. Did I have the nerve to go on to California alone? I doubted it. And I liked being with Kip, even if we didn't talk.

At the depot, we waited. Nothing came or went. So much had happened since we left Kansas City that I had forgotten to ask him about the fire. "Did you see the Hayride Club on our way out of town?"

"What about it?"

"It burned up."

He shook his head. "I was way back in the boxcar."

"It was a firetrap. All that hay." At that moment, I saw Knuckles and yelled his name. He ambled over, full of news.

"A tornado ripped up tracks to the north. Until they fix 'em, nothing's coming or going that direction. Could be days."

"This is Kip. My brother. He's an orphan too." I patted Kip on the arm, and he scowled at me. "Knuckles helped me on the train."

"Pleased to meet you," Knuckles said.

Kip put hand to heart. "Any idea how we can we get back to Kansas City?"

Knuckles pointed to a set of tracks. "Up these, come mornin', you can catch a Missouri Pacific freight to Amarillo. Bulls won't bother you when you're leavin' Wichita. They want you gone. From Amarillo, take a Southern Pacific across to Oklahoma City, then head northeast to Springfield. From there, you can catch a milk run to KC or a fast train Springfield to St. Louis and backtrack to KC. All depends. For sure, you want to get the heck out of this cow town. I'm keepin' on west." He started to walk away, but turned around.

"You two watch yourselves in Texas. They'd soon as put you

on a chain gang or have you pickin' cotton for thirty days as keep you housed and fed in the clinker." He tipped his hat and ambled across the tracks.

Kip seemed angry as we walked back to the park and sat in the shade of a tall tree's spreading branches. "Why did you say I'm an orphan?"

"I had told him I was."

"Well, I'm not. Don't say I am. It's bad luck."

I pictured Kip meeting Knuckles, hand to heart, not an orphan but a mystery to me, and I remembered a question I'd been meaning to ask. "Where did you learn to greet people the way you do?"

"My grandpa."

"Tell me about him."

Kip plucked a blade of grass and twirled it around his finger. "He was a good man." He kept twirling that grass until it shredded and said nothing more.

The evening darkened, and we ate the bruised banana for dinner. Kip lay on a bench, and I lay on another. Other men wandered into the park. Although the night was warm, I pulled the dogs' frayed wool blanket over me and breathed in the comforting scent of Raldo and Sakura. Above, stars flickered. Nearby, the bushes rustled. A dog slunk out, sniffed at the blanket, and moved on. My stomach growled. The moon shone on the trees and on ghostly shapes beneath. I wondered if anyone would try to harm us.

As if reading my mind, Kip said, "We ought to be as okay here as any place."

My first day hoboing had been the worst day of my life so far, but I hadn't lost an arm or leg. I truly believed things would be better in the morning. Father said if a person got out of bed on the right side, he'd have a good day. I had rolled out of bed wrong in the morning, but this bench had only one side.

In the dawn light, the hobos under the trees began to stir and mumble to each other. Soon they'd picked up their bundles and left the park. Kip and I scrubbed our teeth and faces at the fountain, ate the remaining bread, and walked toward the depot.

He was solemn while we waited for the Amarillo train. It moved slowly along the track, and we ran beside. He scissored on and reached down to give me a lift up. He hadn't made more than necessary conversation, and I wondered when he would start being friendly again.

Other travelers filled the car—men with their bundles, a family with small children, and a quartet of three boys and a girl about Kip's age. They were laughing and sharing food from a basket and sips off a bottle, as if they were out for a picnic. The girl had long, curly red hair. The kids at school would have called her "Carrot Top." She squinted at Kip and flashed a pretty smile from beneath the brim of her summer hat. She wore a lilac frock and white stockings. My sister would have been envious of that dress. It had a draped white collar with a pearl button.

"Want a sip?" Carrot Top passed Kip the bottle. He drank and passed it back, not offering any to me.

"Nice." She gestured to Kip's tap shoes. "You a hoofer?"

He nodded and smiled, leaned against the wall of the car and closed his eyes. The girl kept glancing over. A couple of times he opened his eyes and smiled at her. She flirted with her pals and flapped her eyelashes at Kip with the same sort of open-mouth expression I'd seen an actress in a moving picture poster give to the actor. Soon, she started singing "Need a Little Sugar in My Bowl"—the song Leroy hadn't wanted me to hear. I knew enough about metaphor to understand that the song wasn't about sugar bowls or hot dogs, but about something that this girl was offering to these boys. Whatever it was, I knew that

I couldn't compete, but I wanted her to know I was a girl and that Kip was with me. I took off my hat.

Kip turned away from me but kept the redhead in his sight. We rode in the hot, dusty car, sleeping and waking and sleeping again, lulled by the constant clickety-clack and jostled by the occasional swerve or stop at a town. We had no view out the door and no bulls rousted us.

Kip woke, his eyes searching for the girl, who had moved to the opposite side of the car with her pals and was fast asleep. He became a bit friendlier to me and began explaining his technique for leaving a moving train.

"It's all in the timing, Mattie. Sort of like doing bells—you have to leap and catch it just right. You spot a smooth stretch ahead so that, at the moment you jump, it will be passing right in front of you for a good landing."

As the train lumbered into Amarillo, we stood at the open door of the car, and he glanced back toward the girl. It seemed she would be sleeping her way into the depot and the arms of a bull. He shook his head and turned his attention back to the moving landscape.

"Now!" Kip yelled and leapt. He landed in a crouch, somersaulted, and sprang to his feet. I followed.

I landed on my right side on the gravel and rolled down the weedy slope. I lay there with the thistles pricking my face.

PART FOUR

CHAPTER TWENTY

Comfort

"The pie." At the buzzing of the timer, Genet jumps up and opens the oven door. "What do you think? Done?"

As Mattie stands for a closer look, she teeters. Regaining her balance, she understands from deep in her bones that the arthritis in her hip may have begun with that hard landing long ago. She peers into the oven. The piecrust is golden, the edges slightly browned. "Yes, take it out."

The kitchen is warm and fragrant from the steaming pie and soup. Genet fills two bowls and sits back down across from Mattie at the table. "I was arrested in Wichita once and jailed, like you."

"When was this?"

"Not long before I came here to Uncle Wiley's house. I was with a guy I'd met hitchhiking one morning. We had stopped for gas and gone into the mart for smokes and stuff. He slipped some packs of batteries into his coat pocket. I didn't see it but the cashier did. We walked out and a cop, who was on the property, took us to the station and put us in separate cells. I was there for a few hours before a woman came to search me. When she found nothing, they let me go."

Mattie tastes the soup, thinking how often she had worried,

along with Charles and Amoy, about Genet's safety. She had imagined whom her granddaughter might be with and where. She isn't sure now that she wants to know those details but will let Genet reveal as much as she needs to. "I hadn't heard—"

"I've never told anyone. Only you, Gram."

Mattie nods. "It sounds like a difficult time."

"It sucked. Anyway, luckily, I'd left my backpack in the car. Something in there would have gotten me into trouble. When they let me go, I returned to the car. In the glove compartment, I found an envelope with a one-hundred-dollar bill and took it. I've felt bad ever since, but maybe what goes around comes around. You lost money in Wichita, I found it."

"I don't think it works that way," Mattie says.

"I'd pay the guy back now, if I could, but I don't know his last name. I've done a lot of things I'm not proud of, but that's the only time I've stolen."

"Most everyone has done something they can't admit to."

Genet stirs her spoon in her bowl and looks up at Mattie. "It feels good to have told you. Now, let's continue. Were you injured in the jump?"

"I don't remember feeling anything other than Kip's praise at the time. Seconds after I landed, Kip came running to me saying, 'That was swell.' He offered a hand up, and I was pleased to take it. We dashed toward the station, but we'd missed the last eastbound."

CHAPTER TWENTY-ONE

Players

The train to Oklahoma City didn't depart until the next afternoon, so we explored the bustling town. Automobiles lined up bumper to bumper along the curbs, and people milled on the sidewalks, going in and out of the shops and restaurants. We asked at doorways for food in exchange for work but were turned away without so much as a "sorry, kid." We passed a handbill nailed to a post. *Kiwanis Club Theater. Musical revue.*

My growling stomach gave me an idea. "This is tonight, Kip."

"We've got jack for that. Nada."

"But we could dance in front of the theater. People might give us a few coins." I smiled sweetly at him.

He smiled back. "They might."

We found the theater next to an alley where a man in blue striped trousers and a top hat was smoking a cigarette beside a stage door entrance. We must have looked as hungry as we felt, because he gestured to us, went inside, and came back out with rolls and two cups of something steaming. He said, "My younger brother is on the rails somewhere. I'd hope someone might help him out." I thanked him, ate the roll, and sipped the hot brew. I tasted bitterness, but with a sweetness of molasses that lingered on my tongue.

A few people had queued next to the front doors of the old brick theater. A sign noted the time they would open. I strapped on my tap shoes, placed the knapsack on the sidewalk, and coiled my sweater into a nest to hold the money. Kip did a shuffle-step right, shuffle-step left, and shuffle ball change right and left. His arms hung loose. It was new to me. "Shim sham," he said. "You try it. Repeat and reverse."

I shim shammed it my way, missed a few shuffles, but kept going. A couple stopped to watch. They were dressed in fine clothes, linked arm in arm, seeming all the world as smitten with each other as Betty and Albert. They laughed and dropped coins into the nest.

I did rubber legs with a new combination of my own. Kip joined in with high kicks. We were not actually performing, but stealing steps. Soon the people waiting in line clustered around us, smiling and clapping. We added snakehips and people cheered. We barrel rolled, turned, and winged our arms to windmills, tipping this way and that. Kip did bells, tapping his heels together high in the air. We stepped a grapevine up and down the sidewalk. I fell off a log.

In my head, I was humming "All of Me," the song we had danced to at the Bluebird.

I wasn't a great hoofer yet, but Kip made me so much better. I could have danced forever with him. Many more people gathered, leaving us little room to move. We traded fours, first Kip tapping out his best four measures, almost dancing in place, slipping in the subtleties that maybe only I noticed. He looked at me to "top this." I tapped out my best four, miming a subtlety of his to make more a game of it, and looked at him to "top that." As the crowd grew larger, the space closed in and our steps tightened. The audience clapped and hooted, louder and louder.

When the doors opened, people hurried past us, dropping coins into the sweater nest on their way into the theater. In the alley, we counted our haul. We were rich enough for a restaurant meal and maybe a hotel room. I put the money into the sock in the knapsack.

"But we have to eat tomorrow too," Kip said. "Let's find dinner, and then we'll see about the night."

A few doors down from the theater, lights shone in the windows of a diner. *Open 24 Hours.* We parked ourselves in a booth near the back. The restaurant had a checkerboard floor like the Bluebird's, but in black and white. The booths were brown leather, not blue, and one big booth was circular, which the Bluebird didn't have. Overall, the place wasn't as neatly kept as ours. If Kip and I hadn't just struck it rich, I'd have offered to sweep in exchange for our meal. The waitress, Shirley, treated us as kindly as Father treated the Bluebird customers, bringing us brimming plates of stew and the biggest pieces of pie. Kip gave me half of his second piece. "That was some idea, Mattie."

"We could do it again." I mumbled with my mouth full. It was decent pie. "Work our way to Los Angeles."

"I'm taking you home."

"But—"

"Button your lips."

"But—"

"Taking. You. Home."

His words stung me. The tears welled up, and I choked down the pie. Mother would have said I was overtired, brought me hot milk, and tucked me in. Kip looked away. I blew my nose on the napkin. "You don't have to be mean."

"You follow me. I bail you out with my money and change

my plans. Who's the mean one? I ought to take off and leave you to fend—"

"You doing alright, honey?" Shirley reached for our empty plates and stood with the dishes, waiting for my answer, scowling at Kip.

"I'll have a cup of warm milk, please, Shirley." I said it sweetly.

"You got it, honey."

When Shirley returned with the milk, she said, "You two can stay here as long as you want. I'll be here all night. My manager won't be in until morning. Use the washroom, too. Spiff yourselves up. You both could do with a scrubbing."

I thanked her, sipped the milk, and settled against the booth. My eyelids drooped, and I saw through the slits that Kip was nodding off. When we awoke, it was to the laughter of a group entering the diner, including the man we'd met in the alley. He waved.

"That's them," I whispered. "The Players." They sat in the circular booth.

Kip glanced over his shoulder. Attending them with her coffee pot and menus, Shirley called them by name. "How'd it go tonight?"

Most of them were a bit older than Betty, but one woman had gray hair. They were all talking at once, and I made out snatches: "Sold old out house . . . missed your cue . . . won them over . . . rig it right tomorrow." Men had their arms around women, and two women embraced. They seemed to be a big, happy family. The gray-haired one motioned to me, and I went to their table.

"We saw you two out front. Did you make a good haul?"

I wondered if they had rules against us dancing there or wanted a cut of the profits, so I said, "Not too much."

"Well then, take this." She gave me a handful of coins. "You warmed up the audience for us." The others smiled and nodded. The woman said, "I'm Phyllis. If you're here tomorrow, come to the show. I'll leave two tickets at the door for you and—is he your brother? What's your name, honey?"

"I'm Mattie. That's Kip. He's not my brother." Kip had been watching us, but he turned back around.

I thanked her and went to show Kip the coins. He acted unimpressed and watched as I put them in the money sock. I wrapped my arms around the knapsack and sat back on the cushioned bench. I was sleepy, but I was working my mind. Eugene's big house and the soft beds were waiting for us in California, but first I had to get us there and not turn around for home.

The Players left, waving goodbye and throwing kisses to Shirley and to us. She cleared our cups and wiped the table. "That Phyllis is a talented woman. She used to be an opera singer in New York and Europe, but now she's stuck here. Big fish, small pond. She directs the theater company. Married to a big muckety-muck railroad commissioner."

"Does he own the railroad?"

"Better than that. He's the man to know if you got an oil well in your backyard, and lots of people do. He regulates transportation and all the oil and natural gas in Texas."

As Kip took his turn in the washroom, I pondered ambition. It seemed better to have it in some amount and stick with it in spite of things turning out differently than planned, like Phyllis had done, than not to have it at all or give it up at the first big disappointment. I reviewed my own plan. I had made it to Wichita and Amarillo. If I could sweet-talk Kip into not taking me home, Albuquerque would be next. The name inspired a new step, and I began working it out in my mind.

We'd seen kindness in the world and a streak of meanness in some people, but if we could find the good ones and steer clear of the bad, we would make it to Eugene's. Kip would be glad that he had stuck with me, my parents would be relieved, and I could keep on believing that I could be a moving-picture star or a pilot—anything I put my mind to do. If we turned around for home, I could lose my confidence forever.

I hugged the knapsack tighter. It held all the money we had in the world. Kip would be going nowhere without it, and he'd have to wrestle me for it, even though, in all fairness, half the money was his. I would be sleeping in this cushioned booth, sure to get up on the right side—the only side possible.

After Kip had returned and closed his eyes, I visited the washroom. The girl who stared back at me from the mirror above the sink was not familiar. On the right side of my head, the hair fell uneven at my jawline; on the left side, the cut was above my earlobe. My face was streaked with dirt. Aunt Irene would have said I looked like a ragamuffin, not like a girl with ambition for the stage and screen. I yanked at the short side, hoping it would grow longer by the time we got to Los Angeles. I washed with soap and water and dried with the damp, soiled towel.

Back in our booth, I unbuckled my tap shoes, put them in the pack, and set my Buster Browns on the floor, ready to go in the morning. I caught up my diary with our adventures and wrote what I wanted to manifest: *Tomorrow will be a good day. We have the knack for traveling. I will put my mind to keep us heading west together.* If I had known then what would happen, I would have counted out Kip's coins and wished him well on his way.

In the morning, Shirley shook me gently awake. "You two ought to get going now. My boss will be here soon."

On our way out, she gave us a warm packet of something wrapped in greasy newspaper. "Toast and sausage. If you need a meal later, head over to the Salvation Army. To the west. Near the station." She held the door open and pointed to the left.

We ate as we walked. Between bites, I made my case for delaying the trip back to Kansas City. "A few more nights in front of the theater, we can go home with a lot of money." Several hours remained until the eastbound train.

"A few more nights for your folks to worry. We're going back today."

I was thinking about ways to stall for time when I saw in the clear blue sky ahead a big yellow-and-red striped balloon with a basket hanging from it trailing a banner, *Amarillo Balloon Festival*. "Look, Kip." I waved and people in the basket waved back.

"Let's go. We have time." I started running before Kip could disagree.

At the fairground, people milled about the rows of booths. Some lined up to buy tickets under a banner, *Helium Capital of the World*. Colorful balloons were tethered with their baskets on a field of dry grass. As we watched, waiting for one to lift off, a man and a woman with a head scarf approached. "Hello, Mattie. Hello, Kip." It was Phyllis from the diner.

"I see you found the festival. This is my husband, Harvey. Honey, these are the two tap dancers I was telling you about."

He grinned at us. "I bet you two would like a ride."

Kip and I looked at each other with glee.

"Then come along. We have room for you both."

They led us across the field to a balloon. We left our packs on the ground with the attendant, as instructed, climbed up a small ladder into the basket, which Phyllis called a gondola, and waited as a few other people came aboard. When the balloon lifted off, my stomach fluttered more than when I sang in church. I gripped the edge of the gondola, looking down at my feet, instead of over the edge, and gasped for air.

Phyllis said, "It's quite safe. You'll get your bearings."

Maybe she was right, but in that moment, I let go of my

ambition to be a pilot. Kip peered over the side and into the distance. He seemed to soar out on his own lightness and was miles away from me.

I held on tight and looked out as we sailed above the festival grounds. I saw that a long cord still tethered us to the earth and relaxed my grip. Mesas of red and buff-colored stone stretched in all directions below a turquoise sky like the picture I'd seen on the Bluebird's calendar. The air around us was clear and cool.

We floated so quietly that I could hear my own breathing becoming slower and deeper as I calmed. We rose higher and higher. The river below ran north and south. Train tracks ran east and west. I squinted, wondering if I could see as far as the Pacific Ocean, but mesas filled the western horizon. Far beyond them was California. I pictured myself there with the palm trees, a vision so clear that it had to come true. If only I could convince Kip.

After a time, which might have been an hour or merely minutes stretched to feel as long, we descended and landed. Kip and I thanked Phyllis and her husband and grabbed our packs. As we walked across the field, we both seemed to float.

"That was swell!" Kip shouted.

"I was scared at first."

"What?"

"Never mind."

"I wish I could do that every day of my life." He leapt into the air.

"You do?" I had never heard him wish for anything.

"Don't you?" He ran ahead.

"Not really." I tried to catch up.

Seeking a way out of the festival, we took a path between rows of booths, tables, and blankets on the ground attended by people selling honey and jam, knitted shawls, and sculptures of animals carved from wood. Children spun tops. A woman wove at a loom.

A banner across one booth read *Conversations with Shakespeare*. A man held a parrot, who squawked, "Penny for your thoughts . . . what's the question." People lined up to drop a coin in a bucket and talk to the bird. He climbed onto a woman's outstretched hand and squawked compliments to her. "Pretty girl . . . quite the looker . . . hot damn . . . gimme a schmooch."

"We gotta go, Mattie." Kip turned away into another row of booths. I followed. At the end of the row, a man knelt on a blanket, unwrapping a bundle.

He stood up and blocked our way. "Well, well." It was Mr. Crowley. He growled at us. "Got the hell out of town, did you?"

"What's it to you?" Kip said.

"Yeah, what's it to you?" I tried to sound tough, but I was trembling. Crowley had sprung out of nowhere. With his nasty snarl and menacing eyes, he looked exactly like the sketch I had drawn in my diary.

"No matter, I suppose." His laugh was mean-hearted. "Just wonderin' if they found your hat.

"My hat?" Kip said.

"Hard to mistake them polky dots."

"Where—?"

"In the alley."

"What alley?"

"Where you set the fire."

"I didn't set any fire."

"Not what I heard."

"What are you talking about?"

"Burned down the Hayride Club. The whole block."

"I didn't—"

"Some might say you did."

As they argued, the pieces snapped together in my mind. *Fire crew . . . insured to the limit . . . roustabout . . . jail time.* I shouted at Crowley, "You did it. You tried to blame Kip."

"That can of kerosene made quick work of yours too. Poof." He flipped his fingers at my face.

"What are you talking about?"

He grinned wide. "I'm talkin' about your precious little Bluebird, what your high and mighty father thinks is too good for some of us."

"What did you do? If you hurt him, I'll—"

"Burned the place down. Oughta have shut him up come that morning. All his opinions."

I kicked at Crowley, hitting the bundle. It opened and silver bird shakers tumbled out.

"You little runt." He bent down to gather them.

I kicked him again. "You stole those!"

"They're mine now."

I picked up two near my foot. "You're a thief. And my parents took you in."

"I've had enough of you people and your kind deeds. There's a price to be paid for making a man feel small, not good enough even to wipe your tables or pour your damn coffee." He caught my wrist and tried to pry open my fingers. "Gimme those."

"No." I gripped the shakers and kicked hard. He pried harder. I punched at him, landing a solid hit near his eye. The head of the bird shaker in my fist slipped between my fingers. The sharp point of its beak sliced Crowley's cheekbone.

He staggered back and lost his grip. Kip grabbed my arm and pulled. "Let's go, Mattie. Now."

"Give 'em." Crowley yelled and chased after us.

Kip and I dashed past booths as people stared. We dodged

around those who didn't back out of our way. When we passed the parrot, he squawked at us. "Atta girl."

We reached the open field, and I looked back. Crowley had tripped and fallen near the parrot's booth. The bird's squawks became fainter and fainter as we left the fairgrounds. "You slay me . . . killer diller . . . killer . . ."

We ran up the road and across several streets, until we saw a shady spot beside a shed near the depot. The magnitude of what Crowley had done hit me, and I fell onto the weedy dirt, crying.

Kip leaned back and caught his breath. "What the—?"

I still had the shakers in my hands. I slid them into my pockets and held them while I told him about overhearing Mr. Nelson and a man that day in the rail yards and about seeing Mr. Nelson with Crowley the morning we left Kansas City. I mentioned the insurance and payment for the deed.

"Why didn't you tell me?"

"I didn't know what they were talking about. If I'd known they were planning to burn down the Bluebird, I would have told Father. We have to go back now."

"You should never have left. You don't know how good you had it with your folks. How lucky you were to have that family."

"I still have them. I didn't leave forever."

"No way to be sure about that." He stared out to the tracks. "I can't go."

"Where?"

"Back to Kansas City. Not now."

"You didn't do anything."

"The police won't believe me. Not if they find out about—"

"Father will."

"He's not the police, Mattie. There's something you don't know—"

"What?"

"Something that happened back home. Maybe someday I'll tell you—"

"Well, I don't understand why Crowley is so angry at you, at us."

"That's because you've never been so hungry—"

"I have too."

"Not so that you had to eat your dreams."

Slumped beside the shed, he looked defeated. All the lightness from the balloon ride was gone. I wanted to find a way to lift his spirits. "Maybe—"

"You always think things are going to work out."

"If you put your mind to it—"

"But it doesn't happen that way for some people."

"For you?"

"You've never been without a place to go where they'll take you in."

He was right. I was not without a home, only in between having one. I didn't doubt that Eugene's parents would welcome me. I wiped my eyes and nose on my shirtsleeve. "Do you have a family somewhere? Back home?"

He stared past the tracks toward the distant mesas. "My mama is in a place where she can't have me. My pa passed away."

This was worse than the worst I had imagined. I had thought he might be like Yancy Clark, running away on a whim, but more likely that he had left his family in order to work and send money home, the way the stories of roving youth that I read about in the papers told it.

Questions paraded from my mind, tripping over each other trying to get to my mouth. How did your pa die? When? Where is your mama? Why can't she have you? But I kept my lips buttoned. If Kip had been Eugene or another of my schoolmates or Leroy, I'd have lobbed the questions at him, but Kip had taught me that tap dancing was all about the timing. I sensed that getting answers from him was too. "Do you want to talk about it?"

"Not so much."

"Okay," I said, though it wasn't really. I wanted to know what deep sorrows lived in him.

Something seemed to shift. His jaw clenched and his expression hardened. "I'm going to keep heading west. You can come along or not."

"To Los Angeles? To Eugene's?"

"Sure. Might as well."

"And you'll stay with—?"

"I'll get you there. That's all I'm promising."

Of the choices to return to Kansas City alone or travel with Kip all the way to Eugene's, I was certain. Things at home were now worse than they had been. Father wouldn't need me to work in a restaurant that didn't exist. He would approve of me keeping my moral compass pointing west with a companion rather than traveling by myself.

"Then I will. I'll come with you."

At our next stop, I would send a postcard and let my family know that Crowley set the fire. I would tell them that I loved them. The only way I could continue on was to believe they were okay, so I decided they must be. No one would have been at the restaurant that morning, not even Leroy. They would have all been packing to move.

Waiting for a westbound, I couldn't sit still. I stood up and jammed my hands into my pockets, touching the shakers again. I pulled them out to examine them—a salt and a pepper. They had dulled, not having me around to polish them for the past weeks. I put them back in my pockets and rubbed them with my fingers while I walked away from the shed and around stacks of crates.

Other people milled about. A man with a sweat-stained red bandana tied around his head stood near the track, watching me.

"I wonder when the train will be here." I looked to the distance and back to him.

He leaned down and rested his hand on the track. "Feel that? You get that tremble comin' before you hear it or see it," he said. "It'll be here soon."

I stepped near the rail and touched it. It vibrated ever so slightly. Within minutes, a whistle sounded from afar. A small dark spot grew larger and larger until, slowing and groaning, the engine reared up black and smoky above us. As railroad workers unbuckled cars, I waited with Kip beside the shed, keeping watch for bulls. The freight train moved onto side rails and backed onto another string of boxcars. The workers buckled them and soon the train began rolling. Kip and I ran toward an open boxcar with the other transients. More riders emerged from seemingly out of nowhere. By the time we reached the car, it was full. People sat in the open door, their legs dangling over the floor edge, making it impossible to grab hold. Others scrambled into the next car and the next.

The man with the red bandana clung to a side ladder and yelled. "Up top!" He climbed to the roof. Kip and I grabbed onto the next ladder and found a place on that roof along with others. We perched on the wooden plank that ran along the center of the roof, ashes drifting down on us. On the rooftops to the west and east of us sat hundreds of transients. I started counting them, but was scared to lean forward enough to see down the line. The press of our bodies side by side helped us to stay upright.

The train picked up speed, and Amarillo disappeared behind us. We passed a field with rows of cotton, and I thought of Cyrus, and his caring for the prickly plants in our yard. Here the blooms were not yet full bolls, but like a dusting of snow. Children playing in the field chased after the train, waving. I waved back until they diminished in the distance. I imagined their mothers calling them to supper and all of them running home.

The flat land rushed by. Homesickness swept over me a thousand times stronger than what I had felt at camp my first year, which was the first time I had been away without either of my parents with me. Kip and I had now been gone only two nights and not yet three days, but it seemed like forever. I held on tight to the plank, knowing that, if I nodded off, I might pitch forward or backward. As far as I could see, the tracks ran straight ahead with no curves.

We passed miles and miles of dull brown fields dotted with little oil wells everywhere. My great aunt back in Kansas had an oil well in her backyard—a big black praying-mantis contraption. We passed swarms of them rocking back and forth, pecking at the ground as we flew by.

The late afternoon sun beat down. I did math to stay awake, calculating the miles Kip and I had traveled. Adding six hundred or so KC to Amarillo and a hundred since we had left there, I figured a thousand remained until we arrived in Los Angeles. We'd be in Albuquerque before dark.

CHAPTER TWENTY-TWO

Snake Dance

Near Tucumcari the train slowed. Rooftop riders descended onto the ladders and jumped from the rungs.

"Have you ever done that, Kip?"

"Yeah. But let it slow more. See how they leap so far they don't get sucked under? Use your timing. Wait for the right moment, and fly. Don't hesitate."

Our turn came for the ladder, and Kip jumped, but I held on until the train was almost in the station. Bulls were rounding up people and herding them into a fenced area. I dashed toward Kip, who motioned to me to follow as he dove behind bushes. We hunkered there without speaking and waited for the next westbound. When one started rolling, we dashed out and climbed on top. This time, we lay flat.

The scenery changed from mesas to desolate landscape with blue-black mountains in the distance. We passed a pueblo far from the tracks, but close enough to recognize it as similar to the one I had seen pictured in the calendar at the Bluebird when I peeked ahead to July, New Mexico's month. The structures were like apartment buildings, several stories high with ladders leading to the upper doorways.

I yelled to Kip over the din of the train and wind. "Those

were built hundreds of years before Christopher Columbus discovered America. Built by the Puebloan people."

"What?"

"Those are the oldest houses in America."

He nodded. If Father had been with us, he would have
wanted to get off the train and walk around, hands clasped
behind his back, inspecting the thickness of the walls and the
wooden beams that protruded from the top of each floor.

As we neared Albuquerque, the sun was setting. We were
not yet in the town, but a settlement came into view. It looked
something like my Scout camp, but these tents were white,
not brown, and bigger. They sat among scruffy pine trees and
bushes instead of oaks and maples.

Kip jumped from the ladder. I took a flying leap onto an
embankment of soggy grass and somersaulted across mud. A
rainbow curved in the sky. The landing didn't hurt.

Kip was further down, coming to me. We met and walked
toward the tents. I wanted to find one that housed the kitchen,
as there had been at my camp. Later that night, Kip told
me he had worked last July in a steamy kitchen tent, but as we
approached, all I knew was that we were hungry. I hoped some
adults would be kind to us.

An elderly gentleman wearing a hat, tie, and wrinkled white
shirt sat in a chair in front of a tent. He coughed and waved us
to stay back.

"Is this a summer camp, sir?" I asked.

He shook his head. "It's for lungers."

"What's a lunger?"

He broke into a deep hacking fit and held a white handkerchief to his mouth. Red bloomed across the fabric.

Kip whispered, "Tuberculosis."

I knew about TB from the newspapers and a girl at church.
Millions of people all over the world had died of it, more than

any other disease, but seeing the rows of tents was a different kind of knowing. They were like rows of tombstones, not marking deaths but, instead, a long slow suffering.

A nurse in a white coat and cap approached the tent and darted us a disapproving frown. "Let's have a listen, Mr. Montgomery." She put a stethoscope to his chest.

"I can't breathe—" He choked on his words.

"Let's get you into bed." She helped him stand up and motioned to us. "You two wait there."

They went into the tent, and she came out a few minutes later. "Did you touch anything?"

"No, ma'am."

"That's good. Why are you here?"

"We were hoping to work for a meal," Kip said.

She scrutinized us. "Yes, I can see you might be hungry. Ask at the kitchen tent." She pointed to the far end of the row. "They'll give you something to eat."

Kip put his hand to heart. "Thank you, ma'am."

"We can't have you working here." She looked directly at me. "The camp is highly infectious, especially for children. You best be on your way."

The cook ordered us to wash our hands and heads with soap at the pump. He gave us hard-boiled eggs and hardtack and sent us away into the dusk.

We walked far from the camp, our hair drying in the warm air, and found a flat, smooth ledge among a ridge of rocks. We climbed onto it and made our supper. We peeled the eggs and nibbled. I had never known hardboiled eggs to be so delicious. We broke off bits of hardtack, which was bumpy on my tongue, dry as sawdust, and flavorless. The fact that it was hard to chew made the meal last.

We lay on our backs, side by side, bundles under our heads and the dog blanket over us in the cool night. Above us, more stars than I'd ever seen splashed the inky sky. Perhaps the timing was right, or perhaps Kip had held things in so long that he needed to spill them out. Without my asking, he began talking.

"My mama had to go live in a lunger sanatorium in North Carolina. But she used to be a clogger, a good one. She performed solo at the Folk Festival and with the Smokey Mountain Dancers. That was before the stock market crash and things in Asheville collapsed. And before my pa died."

I had many questions and didn't want to risk silencing him by asking the big ones first, so I said, "What's a clogger?"

"The steps come from our kin in Ireland and Scotland, and from England, and Africa. Depending on where you are in America or what holler you're from in Appalachia, you might be doing flatfooting, low to the ground, or buck dancing with higher steps, but it's all clogging. Mama taught me to clog as soon as I could walk. I danced at house parties and her quilting bees and went on stage with her team at the festival."

"Is it like tap dancing?"

"Sort of, but different. The shoes have wooden soles, and you keep the rhythm with your heels. You piece steps together the same way, but they're different steps, like 'wringing the chicken's neck' and 'shoveling coal.' Mama said the steps contain the history of our kin and place, but they change over time, you know, depending on who's doing them and how they remember them and pass them along." He lay staring at the stars. "I learned tap in school."

"Regular school?"

"Physical education class. Tap dance and basketball. Not at the same time." He turned his face toward me, smiling at his own joke, his teeth white in the moonlight. "Mama said that dancing is like quilters putting their pieces together in their own way. She was a fine stitcher too, better than anyone. She made the band on the hat that I lost."

"That Crowley stole."

"Yes, stole."

"He's a creep."

"Worse than that. But, anyway, it's gone."

I wanted to give him something. I reached into my trousers for a shaker and held it up against the stars. It gleamed in the dark. "Keep this in your pocket for good luck, and I'll keep one in mine." A sprinkling of pepper fell onto my face, and I sneezed.

"Bless you." He curled his fingers around mine, and I let go of the bird into his hand.

"Will your mother get better? So you can go home?" I wondered why he was going west instead of east. Sounds came from a distance; I moved closer against him.

Yip yip yip . . .

The howling grew louder.

Eee . . . eee . . . eeerrr . . .

I'd seen coyotes at the zoo, but not in the wild. I was glad to be with Kip, even though the rock was hard on my spine and shoulders. I wiggled until I found a comfortable position and was nearly asleep, lulled by the eerie lonesome song, when Kip spoke softly.

"After Pa died, Mama shriveled up from sadness and then got sicker from the TB. Her doctor told me she might never be able to come home, and we didn't have a place of our own anymore, anyway. We'd been living in miner housing until Pa's accident. Then they kicked us out."

"Coal miner?"

"Mica."

"What's mica?"

"A mineral used in many things, like radios and electrical stuff and automobiles. It's flaky and shiny. People used to decorate graves with it. Some say it's lightning preserved in rock. Might as well be. The mining of it killed my Pa as surely as if he were struck."

"When did he die?"

"Last year."

"What about your grandpa? When did he—?"

"No more questions." He rolled to his side, and the cold air seeped between us.

In the morning, we roused ourselves from the rock and, shivering, found a trickle of cold water in a rocky streambed where we washed. By the time we arrived in town, we were hot and sweaty. We looked for a place where we could dance for coins. Kip and I didn't mind spending some of our sock money, but we agreed to be frugal in case of emergency.

Few people walked the dusty streets, and many of the buildings were boarded up. At the post office, a line had formed at the door, so we set up nearby on the boardwalk. I strapped on my tap shoes for the performance, and we began. People showed interest, but no one tossed money into my sweater nest.

A boy who was about Kip's age stopped and watched. He had shoulder-length dark, straight hair and coppery skin. He was dressed in a shirt and pants made of an animal's hide, like the rug that Eugene's grandmother had in her library. He wore a belt, hung with beads and a bag of feathers. Barefooted, he began subtly mimicking our movements, a slight touch of the toe and heel to the road, a shift left and right, a brush hop lifting dust. When we stopped, having given up on earning anything in that location and ready to use some of our savings for breakfast, the boy came forward.

"I am Tawa," he said. "I have never seen your kind of dancing. Will you show me more?"

"Sure," Kip said.

While he demonstrated steps, I took my turn inside the post office. I spent a penny on a postcard and addressed it to my family in care of our church. I wrote in tiny script to fit in all the news.

Dear Toft Family, I am in Albuquerque, New Mexico, halfway to Eugene's. Don't worry. I am with Kip. I am so sad about the Bluebird. I pray you are all safe. I believe you are. We ran into Mr. Crowley. He set the fire and tried to blame Kip. Mr. Nelson is in on it, so don't let anyone in our family live with them, even though Mrs. Nelson is nice. He is a bad man. Love, M.A.T.

I drew a little heart by my name and then thought of more to say and put it around the edges of what I'd already written.

PS. Father, you would like the Pueblos. They mixed straw with clay for bricks. Big logs stick out from rooftops. I wonder how people lift them so high.
PSS. I'm lucky you are my family. I miss you. Hugs + Kisses.

By the time I returned to Kip, Tawa had learned a few steps. He picked them up more quickly than I had when Kip had first showed me. The people in line yelled out suggestions. "Kick higher . . . to the right." A few tossed pennies onto the boardwalk and into the dirt.

I picked them up. "Let's get breakfast."

"Come," Tawa said. He led us to the end of the main street behind a pharmacy, where a man patted cornmeal dough into rounds and baked them in a brick oven. We bought three. Mine burned my mouth and tasted delicious.

"You're a good dancer, Tawa," I said.

"I practice." He smiled. "In my village, we do the Kachina Snake Dance to bring the rain in August. Last year, I was Snake Youth and my sister was Antelope Maid in honor of our ancestors. They have lived on this land for thousands of years. Next year I will dance in the ceremony."

"A snake dance? We can do snakehips with a spring." I swirled my hips and leapt.

Tawa tried to repeat it and laughed. "You are missing the snake."

"A real snake?" Kip said.

"Yes." Tawa gestured to the sun. "It is too soon for the rain. I am not allowed to show you the ceremony, but I will show you something."

He walked away from the oven into the sagebrush, stepping carefully, stopping to listen. He dipped his arm into the brush and held up a long snake, gripping it tightly below its head. The snake coiled and thrashed against him, its mouth open, tongue darting, and tail rattling.

Tawa extracted a feather from his belt bag and stroked it against the snake. The animal relaxed into its full length, its tail touching the ground.

Tawa placed the snake in his mouth, holding it between his teeth at the narrow part below the head. Stomping his feet and rocking back and forth, he feathered the snake. He danced across the dirt and around in a wide circle. A harsh sound rose from deep in his throat. He swirled and stomped, swooped and shook.

He took the snake from his mouth and held it and the feather toward Kip. "You try." The snake jerked and rattled.

"Uh—I don't—" Kip glanced my way. I didn't like snakes.

"Do not be afraid," Tawa said. "You will see." He again put the snake in his mouth and began feathering it, showing Kip, and then held out the snake and feather to him.

Kip stepped forward and grabbed the snake, but held it away from his body. The tail jerked and Kip swirled his hips, barely missing the tail as it whipped around each time. He brushed the feather against the snake and it relaxed. Keeping it at arm's length, Kip stomped his feet and shook his body.

Tawa pointed into his mouth and gnashed his teeth. "Bite."

Concentrating, Kip held the snake closer, feathering it all the while, and drew it toward his mouth, but it whipped its head around, startling Kip. He let go, and the snake slithered away.

"You are brave," Tawa said. "You will have a long life." He said goodbye and walked away from town.

"A boy in my class died of a rattlesnake bite," I said.

Kip sniffed his hands. "Smells like watermelon."

That reminded me of our summer garden, and homesickness flooded over me. I wanted to ride with my postcard back to Kansas City and my family. I started to cry.

"I'm okay, Mattie," Kip said. He put his arm around my shoulders.

I let him believe that I was crying for him, and in a way I was. He was my family now, much like a brother, but something more. When we got to the end of the journey, he would be going his own way, unless I could convince him to stay with me in Los Angeles.

We returned to the station and caught the train west to Flagstaff, the Coconino County seat. Sitting in the boxcar, Kip clapped out the rhythm and practiced a step with his feet. *Co-co-ni-no. Co-co-ni-no.* "We're going to see the Grand Canyon."

CHAPTER TWENTY-THREE

Nomads

The air chilled in the high altitude, and we shivered as the train climbed toward Flagstaff, home of the Lowell Observatory. When I was ten, Pluto had been discovered through their telescope. I thought of Father again and how he would have wanted to take us to see it. Near the depot, we waited in line for dinner and cots at the Salvation Army, but they filled up before our turn came.

We walked down the street past families sleeping in parked cars. The only hotel with a vacancy would have required every penny of our savings and more, so we wandered to the hobo jungle on the edge of town. I knew about these encampments from the newspaper, and we probably had them around Kansas City, but I had never seen one. Discards formed rickety shacks. Tin cans and bottles littered the ground.

For a place to settle, we chose a rusty Model-T missing doors and a hood, but with two beds made of linoleum scraps on top of springs in the seat frames. It reminded me of Father's Jump for Joy candy store, and I longed for home. Nearby, four men sat on logs around a fire and a woman tended a steaming pot nested in the ashes.

One of the men plucked a banjo and sang. The song sounded

oddly familiar. "Seen woods in Carolina, hills in Tennessee, rivers in Ohio, flowing to the sea . . . . . . don't know where I'll settle or when it will be . . . I'm a hard times traveler, don't you worry 'bout me . . . Don't you worry 'bout me." I'd heard some of it in the boxcar.

When the song finished, the woman said to us, "He got that from a fella who came through here last night." She ladled out spoonsful from the pot into tin cans. "You kids hungry?"

"Yes, ma'am," Kip said. We sat close to the fire.

"You got something for the mulligan?"

We shook our heads. She passed the bowls to the men, not to us.

"Where you kids from?"

"Kansas City," I said.

"Where you headed?"

"California." Kip and I spoke at once.

"Better get there soon. Heard they gonna be turning people away at the border. They don't want no Okies or auto nomads—none of us Midwest migrants coming to take their jobs."

"We have a friend there. He's bound to let us in."

"Say so? You got some nice dancin' shoes, boy, don't he, Stanley?" The banjo player nodded.

"I'm a dancer too," I said, patting my knapsack. "I have real tap shoes."

The woman cocked her head. "Reckon you could dance for your supper? Wouldn't we like a show, Stanley? Me and him used to hoof it a bit ourselves. It's been a while."

Kip and I dragged the linoleum scraps out of the car to the dirt. I buckled my Ziegfeld shoes, and we started to tap. Other people came into the firelight from the shadows, peered out from under tent blankets, or watched from the seats of junked automobiles. We shuffled, spun, windmilled, and leapt bells. Stanley picked up the tempo, and we traded fours. He finger picked; we tapped and tilted. *Co-co-ni-no. Co-co-ni-no.* We finished with rubber legs to loud hoots and clapping from the audience. The woman served us stew in tin cans, and we ate in gulps.

"How far is it to the Grand Canyon?" Kip asked.

"One hundred miles and worth the time, that view from the rim. But like I said. Don't dally getting to Cali. In case they close the border."

We thanked her for the food and her kindness. She nodded and smiled. "You kids set those dancin' shoes out tonight, and I'll spiff them up for you in the morning. I have a blue ink pen that oughta hide that worn spot on yours, girl—" She kicked the kettle with the toe of her worn boot and looked at Kip. "And I can do yours with the potblack. Shine 'em up good. Happy to."

We replaced the linoleum in the Model-T and set our tap shoes on the running board. Kip lay down in the front seat; I couldn't see him from the back. Stars lit the sky even brighter than our night on the mesa. A rat scurried by, its tail flicking my face. I was afraid Kip would want to go north tomorrow to the Grand Canyon, and I was sure we shouldn't waste time getting to California.

"Mattie? Are you awake?"

"Yes."

"I do want to go to the Grand Canyon someday. But tomorrow, we'll keep going to Los Angeles. I promise I'll stay with you all the way."

"Thank you, Kip. You're a good person."

"You don't know some things about me."

I waited, but silence filled the front seat. "You can tell me," I said. "Maybe I can help."

Kip finally spoke, his voice breaking. "You can't fix it, Mattie. No one can. Don't even try. I'm not your problem to solve."

"Maybe it will help to look on the bright side. Things aren't as bad as they seem, not if you see the goodness in people. We found a place to sleep, nice folks giving us a hot meal."

"The bright side," Kip said, as if he were considering it. "Like these stars."

In the morning, our tap shoes were gone. We searched the camp and asked around but found nothing. The campfire ashes were cold; the woman and her banjo player were nowhere to be seen. I realized my beautiful shoes were lost forever and began to cry.

"Where's the bright side now?" Kip said.

"They are stinking rotten thieves." I was bawling so hard I choked.

"Easy, Mattie." His voice was steady and calm. "It's not as if somebody died. They're shoes."

We walked to town—Kip barefooted, me in my ugly old Busters. A farm stand near the depot sold onions. We bought two and ate them at the edge of the yard while we waited for the westbound. I peeled a layer, sucked the juice, and chewed the crunchy pulp. Leroy was certain that onions were some kind of miracle food, curing what ails you, but this one didn't relieve my anger at the thieves or my homesickness for Leroy, the Bluebird, and my family at all.

CHAPTER TWENTY-FOUR

Partners

We hopped a train and traveled for a short time before slowing onto a side rail outside of Williams. Kip and I walked to the depot, where a crowd was gathered around the caboose of a new passenger train. A man stood at the railing giving a speech. It was Governor Roosevelt. The crowd shoved against us. A few people sat on the low roof of the depot's porch. We climbed up for a better view and to hear.

As the Governor spoke, someone yelled, "Hooray for Hoover." Others joined in.

He waited for the chanting to end and began again. "On this trip . . . observing . . . listening . . . we want prosperity restored . . . all industry . . . classes."

I was wearing the sweater Aunt Irene had knitted and hugged it to me. I now had big news to send. The speech ended and, while waiting for the tracks to clear, Kip and I went to the post office, where a line had formed.

Carrot Top came out the door, looking even prettier in the bright sunlight than she had in the boxcar. She noticed Kip's dirty feet and laughed. "Hey, dancer boy. Lose somethin'?"

Kip did a quick shuffle hop step in the dust. "Guess not what counts." He grinned.

Her hair glistened shades of red, orange, and gold. She ran her fingers through it. "I'm in a jam. Where are you two headed?"

"Los Angeles," Kip said.

"Mind if I come along? Is this your sister? She's cute as a bug's ear."

Kip nodded. "Yes—"

"No," I said.

"Well, which is it?

"We're partners." I wanted to claim Kip for my own and for something more than a brother. "Dancing partners."

"Are you his filly?" She winked at me.

I hesitated, wondering if Kip would set her straight on all counts. I wasn't his filly, and we didn't want her with us all the way to Eugene's.

"You can come along," he said.

"Aces." She grinned. "Ring-a-ding-ding."

"Where are your friends from the train?" Kip asked.

"My pallys ain't worth squat. They split with all the moolah, the twits. But they didn't get my hootch." She held up a bottle. "When do we leave?"

"Wait for me," I said.

"Shake a leg, sis." She fluffed her curls.

Inside the post office, I wrote my family a hurried message. *We saw FDR speaking from a caboose. Only 400 miles to go. Love, M.A.T.* I didn't mention the stolen shoes. It would have worried Mother that we met with bad company.

With the red-haired girl in tow, Kip and I returned to the train yards. "I'm Gladys. Call me Gladdie," she said. To me, she remained Carrot Top. She dreamed of being an actress in the moving pictures and spoke in the voices of characters she wanted to play. She said she knew a lot of gangsters, but I doubted she had ever met a real one.

When the train pulled out of Williams, my stomach was queasy. It could have been the morning onion, or it could have been that Gladdie, who had attached herself to Kip, was making me sick. He seemed to have lost his better judgment, because nothing about this girl was worth a fraction of him. She shared her hootch with him, but not with me. "Sorry, road sister," she said. "You're too young for this rotgut."

I leaned against the wall in the boxcar. Deep green pines raced past, replaced by scrawny bushes. The land flattened and lost color. We were in the Mojave Desert. I knew about this from geography but didn't envision the harsh nothingness as far as I could see. A person could easily get lost here without a street sign, building, or tree to guide them. I thought about all the people who had crossed this vast, dry land. I imagined the folks who had left their homes to make new ones—the westward pioneers, Spaniards, and Anasazi tribes long before trains and automobiles were invented. Those people had braved heat and drought, snakes, and storms. I could certainly put up with Gladdie for the remaining hours of our journey.

She didn't shut up for more than a few minutes at a time. Kip and I listened as she talked. Yap. Yap. Yap. "The summer Olympics are coming up. There's jobs to be had in Los Angeles for Joes like us, 'til our ships come in, but this ain't no trip for biscuits. I'm gonna make somethin' of myself out there. My folks say I'm nuts to be thinkin' I can make it in the pictures, but they can't deny I'm a sweet patootie. Say so?" She put her hand to chin and gave a coy smile.

"My mama's a looker too. But she settled for marrying rich instead of making her own way. My daddy's an oil baron. His moolah keeps her togged to the bricks, and she's some dresser, believe you me. This here is one of her hand-downs." Gladdie stroked her dirty dress, which upon close inspection was silk, finely stitched and cut on the bias. "But I'm no gold digger, you know what I mean?"

I was unsure if she was talking to Kip or me, but she didn't give either of us time to answer. I'd never met anyone like her and never wanted to again. He caught my eye and shrugged, but moved his attention back to her.

"It was making whoopee with my daddy, before he became my daddy, that got her into trouble young and got me born. That put the kibosh on her ambition. She had to kiss her dreams goodbye. No one's gonna take mine." She gulped from the bottle.

"What's your story, morning glories? Why are you two pips on the road? Want some more of this giggle juice? Not much left." She gulped again and swung the bottle toward us. Kip swigged and handed it back.

I sat up straight and as tall as I could. "We're going to my friend Eugene's in Hollywood. He's living in a famous actor's mansion, and his parents write scripts for the pictures. We're going to find work as dancers—as hoofers." I wanted her to know we had an edge on her, and she wasn't included.

"Well, if you got the gams, that's kippy." She winked at us and leaned back against the wall of the car. "Gonna close my peepers for a sec."

As she slept, drool escaped her open mouth. She wasn't pretty now. I wanted Kip to notice how ugly she was, but he didn't seem to realize or care. His feet tapped on the dirty floor. The steady clacking of the wheels on the rails and the heat inside the car lulled me. I was grateful she'd stopped talking, and he seemed to be, too. I rested my head against his shoulder, wishing we could travel again with only the two of us. Soon his head rested on mine.

"Kip?" He didn't answer, and I didn't move away, even though my neck was in a crink. I was hoping that Gladdie would wake up and see us close together.

CHAPTER TWENTY-FIVE

Uncoupling

A sudden descent jerked the car, and everyone stirred. A long bridge over a wide river came into view. A man gathering his belongings saw my questioning look and said, "Topock. Entering Cali."

We rattled across the bridge with water far below. Riders gathered at the open door preparing to jump. As soon as the car left the bridge, they leapt onto the embankment. When the train slowed into the yards, Kip and I climbed out with Gladdie. Bulls chased some of the riders, but we escaped. We hid under the bridge, biding our time to catch a westbound in the cover of darkness. Only a hundred and fifty miles remained until Barstow and then an easy hundred to Los Angeles. With luck, we'd get to Eugene's in the morning.

The sun had set when two men wandered nearby and stopped. They eyed Gladdie and nudged one another. She sipped from her bottle and offered Kip a swig, but he said, "No thanks." He was watching the men.

They ambled over, and one said, "Hey, there, dollface. What're you doing with these punks? A gal like you needs protection."

"Get lost, you greaseballs," Gladdie said.

They bristled, and Kip stood up. "You heard her. Get lost."

As the men closed in on Kip, the train hissed. The west-bound was rolling. We all dashed up the embankment to the tracks. Kip and I made it into a boxcar, but we lost Gladdie. Kip thought that she had caught the one behind us or the next one or one after that. He was worried that the greaseballs had hopped on with her. We leaned against the boxcar wall as the train picked up speed. Kip was thoughtful, and then he spoke. "Can we bring her along to Eugene's with us?"

"Why?"

"She's all on her own."

"It's not your problem to solve. Isn't that what you said to me?"

The boxcar was warm; the wheels clacked steady and strong beneath us. I was hoping Kip would forget all about Gladdie and the greaseballs. More minutes passed.

"I should go find her. Those men were no good."

"Then stay away from them."

He slumped against the wall of the car, his expression an unreadable mix of emotions. He seemed to slip further away from where we were.

I tried to bring him back. "She'll be okay. We'll be in Barstow soon."

"There's no one to protect her."

"But why do you—"

"It's important to me—"

"Because you like her?"

"She's okay, I guess. But there's something I—"

"You'd have to cross over the rooftops."

"I can make that leap." He stood.

I grabbed him by the wrist. "Don't go." In the car were other travelers, mostly men, but also a few couples and a family with two children, who were watching us.

"I need to do it, Mattie. Let go of me," Kip said.

"It's dangerous."

He looked down at me with concern and nodded toward the family. "Will you ask them for help if you need it?"

"I'm not a baby." I kicked at him, still holding on, and missed.

"Whoa." He arched back, trying to shake free. "Listen, Mattie. I won't be gone long. I need to do this. I'll explain later."

A fury overtook me. "Go on then. Go find Gladdie. Go away." I released my hold and yelled. "Go away. Now. Just go away!" I kicked with full force. My heel hit hard against his shin.

"What the heck, Mattie. That hurt." He backed toward the open door, turned, and reached out. Moonlight caught him and, for an instant, he was aglow. He yelled into the car. "Wait for me here. I'll be right back. Wait for me." The last I saw of him were his bare feet as he ascended.

I wondered whether I should follow. Gladdie had lured him the way nectar attracts a bee. What if he didn't return? What if he stayed with her? I began to cry. I had never been so lonesome in my life. The train's whistling pierced into me, reminding me how far away from home I was. It felt like years since I had listened to that sound in the safety of my cozy room with Betty nearby. The mother of the family sitting near me asked, "You okay, honey?"

I nodded. "Fine. I'm fine." I wiped my eyes. I was determined not to be Kip's problem. If he came back soon, I didn't want him to see me crying.

The train sped along for what seemed like an eternity. When we stopped in Barstow, I would find Kip and tell him it was okay to bring Gladdie along. It would be better than not having him with me at all. Eugene wouldn't mind. He would find her entertaining.

Suddenly, the car lurched. A deafening sound of metal

grinding on metal filled the boxcar. A piercing squeal cut through me. I pressed my hands over my ears.

The mother yelled, "What's happening?" Her husband wrapped his arm around her and the children. They were frightened.

The car reared, and the family tumbled. I fell into a space between crates. Wedged there, cushioned by my pack, I was unable to move. Screeching metal swallowed the screams of other passengers.

The boxcar heaved and swayed. A loud groaning and splintering knifed into my ears. The crates fell, and I with them. Everything stopped. The crushing noises subsided. The wailing in the car grew loud.

I became aware of my own whimpering. My arms were pressed against my side. The pointy beak of the saltshaker in my pocket pierced into my thigh.

The next thing I knew, someone was above me with a lantern. "Are you hurt? Grab hold." A man reached into the crevasse, his hand almost touching me. "Grab my hand."

"I can't," I cried.

He placed himself more securely above me, straddling the crevasse, and reached down with both arms. With effort, he jimmied me up until my arms were free. I grabbed onto him. "What happened?"

"We've been derailed. Let's get you out of here."

The boxcar now rested at an angle. What had been the wall was now a slanted ceiling with a door. We climbed on top of crates out to the slant far above the ground. My rescuer lit the way for me to slide down to a man below, and then he lowered himself back down into the opening. As the man led me away by torchlight, I turned to see empty tracks behind the car I had exited. At the bottom of the embankment, a boxcar lay smashed.

People from the train walked along the tracks toward a road crossing. Some were helping others away from the wreckage; some were lying bloody on the ground, not moving.

Two automobiles had crashed on the road. A truck teetered on the edge of the embankment beside the crossing. People pointed and screamed, "Watch out."

I jumped back as the truck flipped and somersaulted down. It landed on top of the boxcar with an explosion. Flames leapt high into the air.

More transients emerged from the train, and we watched as the boxcar burned below. Someone herded me away from the wreckage to a safe spot beside the road with others who had escaped the train. A truck slowed and stopped. The driver rolled down the window and yelled, "Need help?"

The woman from my car spoke with him and assisted her children and husband, who was bleeding, into the truck. Then she saw me and walked over to where I was sitting. "That nice farmer is on his way home from delivering a truckload of apricots to Barstow, but he'll turn around and take as many of us as can fit in the truck bed."

The others stood and started walking, but I remained sitting, watching the fire below. The woman said to me, "Come on, honey."

"I need to find Kip." As soon as I spoke his name, I began crying. "He might be in there."

"If by some miracle he survived, he'll be taken to the nearest hospital in Barstow." She pulled me to standing and gave me a firm push toward the truck. "You'll be safe there. Now go on."

"No." I shook her off, sobbing, and planted my feet. "Kip said to wait for him. He said to wait."

She put her arm around me. "Come on, honey. Come with me."

As she began dragging me toward the truck, I looked back at the flames and smoke. "No. He said to wait."

"Honey, if your friend hasn't climbed out of that boxcar by now, he won't be coming out. She tugged harder. "You can't stay here. You're a young thing."

PART FIVE

CHAPTER TWENTY-SIX

Adoration

Tuesday morning, Genet is washing the soup bowls when Mattie enters the kitchen. "Ravi is back in town and will bring dinner at sixish. If you could teach us a few salsa steps afterward, then we'd be ahead of everyone at the wedding. Sound good? Coffee? Tea?"

Mattie yawns and sits at the table. "Yes, please. Anything hot. And the dinner with Ravi. And dancing." They had talked until late, and Mattie had been too tired to do more than change into her nightgown before bed. She hadn't done a shimmy, much less a twirl around the room, and had awakened at three a.m. from a nightmare.

Genet fills a cup and sets it before Mattie. "When we have time maybe later today, I want to hear how you got to LA and all that happened then. For years I've felt so guilty about running away from home as a teenager, but I feel less so now because you did it too."

Mattie sips and swallows. "I didn't see it as such. Only that I was making it easier on my parents by leaving."

"Still, you don't seem to have regrets."

"Don't I?" The words that she spoke to Kip reverberate in her mind and body. *Go away.* She feels the kick she gave him.

Had she not held him back, or held him a bit longer, might he have survived the wreck? Had she not gone with him, but stayed at home with her family as she should have, he would not have been on that train at that precise moment. "But I do." Mattie's voice is lost to a clatter.

"Oops." Genet bends to retrieve a dropped spoon. "Sorry. What did you say?"

"I do have regrets. I do." Mattie speaks with force. "Overwhelming. More and more so."

Genet pauses with spoon in the air and glances at the stove clock. "I really want to hear about this, Gram. But right now we should go see Uncle Wiley, because he's more alert in the morning. Let's have a long talk when I get home from afternoon classes."

At Sonata Court, the sun shines on the white columns and dove-gray exterior. The building could be the grand hotel it once was, except for the wheelchair ramps attached along the front porch. Inside, a bouquet of white lilies rests on a grand piano beneath a chandelier.

"Hi, Ruth." Genet waves to the red-haired woman behind the reception counter and points to Mattie. "This is her. My gram. We're going up to see Wiley and then check on that apartment she might move into."

Mattie, carrying the pie, nods a greeting to Ruth and takes the elevator with Genet to long-term care on the third floor where, in a brightly lit room, a television blares. White-haired residents sit in wheelchairs before it and elsewhere around the room. Most are sleeping. On the far side, Wiley is strapped to an upholstered, straight-backed chair.

"I'll get the plates and forks." Genet takes the pie from Mattie, places it on a table, and goes to the kitchen.

Mattie crosses the room and kisses her brother on the forehead. His thinning white hair has not been combed. She smoothes it with her hand, brushing against the faint scar from the long-ago accident at the waterfall. She kisses him again on the brow and on his rosy cheek. It's overly warm in the room. "Hello, Wiley." He sees her but doesn't greet her.

"Do you know who I am?"

He stares. "Mother?"

"It's Mattie."

He nods. "Dancing boy."

She takes Wiley's hand. "You remember Kip, don't you?"

Wiley nods. "Silver dollars."

On cable news, a sign flashes across the screen. *CORONAVIRUS OUTBREAK*. The president is speaking. "Be calm. It's really working out. A lot of good things are going to happen."

"Do you mind if I turn it down?" Mattie addresses the people sitting in front of the TV, who don't respond. She doesn't see a remote handy, and the monitor has no volume control.

An aide approaches. "Are you Mr. Toft's sister? Genet said you'd be coming today. This will only take a minute."

The aide takes Wiley's blood pressure, oxygen level, and temperature. "Good marks as always, Mr. Toft." She pats Wiley and smiles.

"Why is he strapped in?" Mattie asks.

"So he doesn't wander off to the elevator—he loves to push the buttons. Don't worry. He doesn't mind being restrained. Some of our residents get quite cantankerous as they get more forgetful, but so far your brother is a sweetheart."

"Yes, he always has been. I'm wondering if you could turn down the volume?"

The aide shakes her head. "Most of them are hard of hearing." She moves on to another resident.

Mattie sits beside Wiley and takes his hand. On the monitor, an image of a heavyset woman appears next to an image of a thin woman talking about a weight-loss drug. It's the same person. Wiley is transfixed.

As drowsiness overtakes Mattie, a memory of Wiley as a boy rushes in. She walks beside him that long-ago day on the way home from the railroad yards, holding his hand. He is bleeding from the forehead. His body is limp against Kip, who is carrying him, but the grocery store bagger has replaced Kip. He puts Wiley in the shopping cart and rolls away up the road, and she tries to catch up.

"Gram?" Genet gently shakes Mattie's shoulder. "Were you asleep?"

Mattie blinks awake, and time tumbles forward. She is beside her brother, and it has all come to this. Whether in her own apartment or here in the long-term care unit, Sonata Court would be the last place she lives before she dies. Her future, which has always stretched before her, feels confined within these walls. An inner voice says, *Moving here would be a mistake.* She shakes it off.

"A catnap." Mattie stretches. "Let's have pie and see if we can interest Wiley in a game of gin rummy before we see the apartment."

They devour half the pie, Wiley wins two hands, and the aide returns him to his room. Mattie and Genet descend to the second floor and peek into the studio apartment. It's a small room with a view to bare tree branches. A woman in overalls is painting the walls gray. A man atop a ladder is painting the ceiling pearl. The admissions booklet had listed three choices of color for the walls: dove, butter, and pearl.

She reminds herself to stay positive and says, "The lighter above the darker makes the room feel expansive." Her voice echoes. The painters wave their brushes and continue working.

Later that afternoon at the house, Mattie awakens from resting as Genet returns from leading classes at Sonata. They sit at the table with the ribboned bundles and loose papers spread before them.

"Did your mother write about your leaving?" Genet extracts a paper and scans the handwriting on both sides of the page "Mattie, look, she wrote on the back of your note."

"Let me see—yes, that's it."

Genet reads. "'Mattie was not in her room this morning when we were awakened by news of the fire. I was called to the hospital to be with Elliot. His wounds are serious, but the doctors say he will have full use of his hands. I couldn't stay but went home to help with the packing. Betty looked for Mattie everywhere in the neighborhood, and Mickey searched the rail yards. In emptying the icebox, I found this note Mattie had left saying not to worry, but we are worried sick. I cried all day as we worked and have no appetite. Irene brought me a piece of cinnamon toast, but I couldn't swallow it. Wiley refused to leave the hall closet. He sat on the floor among the boots and shoes, waiting for Mattie to return. I had to lift him out and carry him to bed, sobbing. He kept saying, 'She's coming back, Mother. She said she is coming back.' He doesn't yet understand that if she does come back, it won't be to this house. Tomorrow I will have to tell him.'" Genet pauses.

"Poor Uncle Wiley. Maybe that's why he never left home. Too traumatized by your leaving. I must have inherited my wanderlust from you. Dad never mentioned a thing about you hopping the rails. But then, he doesn't say much at all to me ever since—you know."

"I never told Charles about riding the rails, only that I went to California to stay with Eugene. And you may be right about Wiley. I never thought about how protective of my parents he must have felt. They were certainly hurt by my leaving, but they never expressed anger, only relief that I was safe. I wish for your sake and Charles's that he could forgive you as easily as they forgave me. Or seemed to."

When Genet ran away from home the spring of her freshman year in high school, Mattie talked to Charles many times every day. He cried and said, "Why is she doing this? We gave her everything a girl could want." When Genet returned home after being gone for thirty days and eleven hours, he met her with a stiff embrace and veneer of self-protection that he has yet to shed fully, even though it has been a decade. He told Mattie that Genet's leaving hurt him so profoundly that he could never love her quite as much as he had before she left that first time. Amoy and he became used to Genet taking off with no warning and no communication for days, weeks, or months. They kept her mobile phone on their family plan so that she could call from wherever she was, and they paid for treatment programs when she was willing to go.

"He does love you deeply. The first time you left home, he lay on the couch trying to breathe. He felt as if he had a heavy stone on his chest."

Genet groaned. "They always take it so personally and make it all about them—why I left. I just needed to leave."

Mattie reaches to squeeze Genet's hand. "Do you want to talk about it?"

"It's complicated, Gram. I can't really. Not yet."

"Whenever you're ready."

"Let's get back to you. Did you find out what happened to Kip?"

"I was told that no one made it out alive from the wreck."

"How horrible."

"I've lived my whole life with the thought that if I'd said or done something differently that night, Kip wouldn't have been in the wrong place at the wrong time."

"How could you have prevented the accident? My therapist says I can't control everything, and that when I try to, it causes problems."

"I've never been in therapy, but I would agree with that." Mattie pauses. Genet is silent, waiting.

Mattie's feelings bubble up from a well of sorrow and spill over. "When you asked about regrets yesterday, I wasn't truthful. I'm haunted by what might have been. I had a nightmare about telling Kip to go away. He was only trying to help someone who was in danger, and I selfishly took it as if he were abandoning me."

"You were twelve, Gram."

"And now I am nearly one hundred. I've lived every day since that day with a young girl inside me wanting to take back those words. If I could—"

"Dinner's arrived." The slam of the front door reverberates in the hall, and Ravi appears carrying a white sack inscribed with golden lettering: *Saffron.*

He's not wearing a coat, and raindrops have darkened his blue shirt. The cuffs are rolled up over his forearms. Thick black hair rises in waves above his forehead. His smile conveys a cheerfulness that seems not specifically of the occasion, but of his being. He glides across the room and kisses Genet on the lips. She says, "This is my grandmother, Mattie. You finally get to meet her."

He takes Mattie's hand. "Very happy to."

The way he moves with an elegant economy of motion, not so much sitting on the chair next to Genet as alighting there and perching, reminds Mattie of Kip. She shakes her head to dislodge a tickle in her ear. Why does she see Kip in these young men? Years ago, she stopped having dreams about him, but then last night in her sleep, he vanished from a train. She reached for him and woke up in terror. In trying to calm her mind, she tried imagining that she saved him somehow. She always tries to save him.

"So, did you two figure it all out yet?" Ravi smiles. "The world's problems?"

"You're one to talk." Genet turns to Mattie. "He is about to solve the climate crisis."

"How's that?" Mattie asks.

Ravi leans toward Genet. "I love your boundless enthusiasm but, honestly, I'm working on a small slice of the problem. Bioluminescence—"

"Fireflies." Genet kisses him. "Their energy is one hundred percent efficient. The average light bulb produces only ten percent as light, the rest as heat."

He smiles at Genet and then Mattie. "She read my dissertation."

"Charles—my son—mentioned to me recently that they use luciferase in bioengineering as reporter genes. Perhaps you know about this?"

"Firefly enzyme." Ravi nods and looks at Genet. "You've never told me about his work."

"He doesn't say much about it to me, or anything else for that matter." She shrugs. "Maybe I don't ask the right questions. Gram and he have the same kind of scientific brain. I'm more artsy, like Amoy."

"I'm excited to meet them both." Ravi walks around the table with its piles of papers and scattered photos. "How's the walk down memory lane going?"

"Gram ran away from home with a boy named Kip when she was twelve and went to Hollywood. That's him." She points to the photo. "There in the window."

"Not exactly ran—" Mattie stops herself. She sees that already Genet is taking from the story what has meaning to her.

Ravi studies the photo. "The Bluebird Buffet? Is that still around?"

"It burned up. Gram had to leave home because of the Great

Depression and all. It's really different from my own experience, but I can relate. And that's what my writing teacher said I needed to do. Put myself in someone else's shoes and see how it feels."

"Speaking of someone else's shoes, let's eat dinner so we have time to learn the dance steps." Ravi carries the food to the kitchen and dishes out fragrant chicken curry and rice from the cartons.

As they eat, he listens to Genet with visible adoration. He points to his chin, indicating a wayward kernel on hers, and she wipes it away with a napkin. They talk excitedly of their honeymoon. Ravi has purchased plane tickets and reserved a suite at a resort in Hawaii. Mattie watches them with pleasure, imagining how they will find their way in marriage, even with the challenges of parenting Ravi's young daughter.

"Dessert?" From the refrigerator, he takes out three small cartons and dishes the contents into soup bowls.

He sets Mattie's before her. Swimming in a creamy broth is a round of something that could be cheesecake without crust. She dips her spoon and takes a bite. "This is delicious. What is it? I taste almond." She takes another bite. "And cardamom?"

"And saffron." Ravi says. "It's called ras malai. Genet's favorite."

"It's my new comfort food, Gram. Do you love it?"

Mattie nods. The sound of spoons against bowls makes a pleasing rhythm.

Genet pushes back her chair. "Time for our lesson. I'll do dishes in the morning. Let me run upstairs and put on a skirt. I want to feel sexier than this." She frowns at the yoga clothes she's wearing.

Ravi smiles. "You look great to me."

"I'll be right back."

She returns wearing a red dress with a hemline well above

her knees. Her calves are shapely above her ankles, which are wrapped by thin red straps attached to her high heels.

"Even better," Ravi says.

"I bought it for Saturday night. I was going to surprise you, but I couldn't wait. Do you like it?" Genet twirls. The skirt flares, revealing her thighs. Ravi takes her hand and leads her into the living room.

Mattie says, "We'll start with a basic sequence that will serve you well for all else. Salsa, as in so many things in life, is about tuning into your partner. For now, we'll start with you side-by-side. Feet together. That's home. The neutral position."

Mattie guides Genet next to Ravi and stands in front of them. "Follow me. Eight counts. Here we go. One, step forward on the left foot with your whole body. You're looking ahead to where you're going, arms bent at the elbow and relaxed, like you are starting out walking. Your right heel naturally lifts off the floor and your weight rolls to the ball of your foot, but you don't actually travel.

"On two, drop your right heel back in place. On three, bring your left foot back beside the right again. A return to home. Four is a pause, no step. Let's try that again. Left step forward, right roll in place, left back home, pause.

"Good. Now on five, step right foot backward with your whole body. Your left toes naturally lift off the floor, but don't travel. Six, roll your left foot back in place. Seven, step your right foot home, feet together. Eight, pause. Let's repeat that. Begin to feel the rhythm in your body.

"Now, let's put those together. Forward, two, three, pause, and backward."

She moves beside Genet and Ravi and steps through the counts again. "You've got the basics. Let's work on lead and fol-low. Genet, be my partner. I'll lead. You follow. Lift your right hand and hook it over my left, lightly, like your fingers are on the throttle of a motorcycle, ready to rev, but resting. This is the close position. We can communicate with the slightest pressure."

Mattie lays her right hand lightly on Genet's back beneath the shoulder blade. "Now place your left arm above my right, held by attraction, as if by a magnet. Your elbow rests in the crook of mine, your hand at my shoulder. Arms neither fully extended nor bent. We frame a lovely empty space between us that moves with us, not too close, not too distant.

"The steps I take are the forward half of the basic sequence, and the steps you take are the backward. You'll step back on your right when I step forward on my left. Let's try it. I go forward, you go back. Then we each step in place. Yes, that's it. Now bring it home. And pause. Beautiful."

Genet grins and counts through the steps again, exaggerating her hip movement and swishing her skirt. "It's easy."

"Let your sway be easy too, as in walking." Mattie presses her hand against Genet's back. "I pull you gently forward, as I step back. You learn to read your partner's intention through the slightest pressure. Now we step in place and each come back to home. And pause. Let's try it again."

They run through the steps a few more times, and Ravi says. "You've got it, Genet."

"Your turn, Ravi." Mattie stands before him. "Let's practice your lead. I'll follow. My right hand hooks lightly over your left. Your right hand is on my back. Higher up. There. Lightly on the shoulder blade. A bit more firmly. Let me know you're there. Indicate with a slight pressure if something is changing, if we're moving in another direction."

For all the years that Mattie has enjoyed social dancing, her partner's hand on her back has always thrilled. Ravi is tall with a graceful presence and his hand presses more confidently against her.

"Lovely," Mattie says. "Now you step forward on your left

foot, and I step backward on my right. Give me your intention with the slightest push. Two, in place. Three, bring it home. Now you step back, I step forward. Gently, but assuredly, pull me toward you. Yes. In place. Home. Pause."

"Let's try it again," Ravi says.

He leads, and she follows. "One, two, three, pause. Five, six, seven, pause. Again."

Genet claps. "Let's practice with music. I put some Latin beats on the playlist." She taps her phone and "La Vida es un Carnaval" fills the room.

Mattie takes a turn again leading Genet and following Ravi. Then Genet and Ravi dance together. "Wonderful." She smiles. "Now, let's add a right turn. It's simply a half-clockwise pivot on count five and finish the full clock on six. Less complicated than it looks." Mattie steps them through the turn.

"I don't get it," Genet says.

"Here, I'll lead you." Mattie takes Genet's right hand with her left. "We lift our paired hands and draw a J in the air down and back up as you step forward and pivot. Here we go. Yes. Now a full turn back to me. That's it. Again."

"This is fun, Gram. Try it with Ravi."

Leading and following, Mattie shows him the turn. He's a natural. She hands him to Genet. The two dance together, and Mattie says, "You have the steps, but you're narrowing the space between you. Hold it open. And Ravi, on the turn, look to where you want to finish."

Mattie moves about the room with an imaginary partner. When the music stops, Genet goes to her phone. "Oops. Needs a charge." She looks around for the battery cable.

"That's all for tonight." Mattie sinks onto the couch. Genet plops down beside her.

"Hold it right there, Genet. And Gram—May I call you that?" Ravi pulls his phone from his pocket.

"Of course."

"Lean in. Heads closer. Smile. That's nice. I'll get a few."

After Ravi has departed and Mattie has gone into the guest room, Genet knocks. "Gram? Are you still awake? I just want to tell that you're my hero."

Mattie opens the door. "I've hardly done anything heroic."

"You've evolved. You still are evolving. Lots of people don't. They stay the same."

"I wonder about that. Especially when I'm back here. I feel much as I did when I was a girl. Only older. And with wrinkled skin."

"You're beautiful to me." Genet kisses her on the check. "Sleep tight. Don't let the bedbugs bite."

Before the mirror, Mattie regards her cropped white hair, knobby shoulders, and slack breasts. She slides her hands across the round of belly and over the pucker of scar from the C-section that brought her Charlie. She presses over the protruding hipbones and reaches around and down the buttocks to her hamstrings. Her long legs still have something of their shape, her spine is straight and strong, and she isn't too tired from the day to dance. She slips the silk nightgown over her head, finds her phone, and plays "Can't Stop the Feeling."

She moves around the bedroom, singing along, "Dance, dance, dance." In her bare feet on the wooden floor, memories arise. Some moments are easily recalled. She can live again in the instants she heard the news that Pearl Harbor was bombed, President Kennedy was shot, and two airplanes flew into the Twin Towers.

With her whole being, as readily as if it were yesterday, she experiences the sensation of holding Charlie for the first time in her arms. If there had been a measure for her happiness then, it would have been off the charts. Because she was fully immersed in that moment, it was encoded and consolidated in her brain regions for retrieval through her neural pathways. Her understanding of the science doesn't make it less magical.

Many memories have been eclipsed or take prompting, but she easily recalls her partners. There have been three.

Eugene Turner.

He has been gone from her life for as long as he was in it. The letters he wrote to her in childhood, along with those from the army when they were newlyweds and from a long business trip when Charles was a baby, are in the tin box with the painted lid. Reading Eugene's neat cursive, she can sense his reliable presence.

She remembers asking Amoy if she felt Charles completed her. "No, it's not that." Amoy paused for a moment. "It's that when we talk, when we're together, a quiet space between us fills up and overflows into each of us."

Mattie realized then that Eugene and she had been like two wheels on a bicycle, spinning together in their life in Los Angeles. They had moved efficiently in the same direction—building careers, starting a family. He avoided dancing at weddings and parties, but she didn't mind because she danced at work every day. What had been missing between them? Amoy had put a name to it—the silence, filling up, overflowing.

After Eugene died in 1970, she moved to San Francisco intending to make a home for Charles while he attended medical school. In 1980, she completed her PhD in neuroscience at the University of California San Francisco. The evening following graduation, she went to a salsa class and met the teacher.

Diego de la Fuente.

He was forty-five years old to her sixty. At first, they shared a flirtatious romance only on the dance floor, where he showed her how to express her desires to her partner through the slightest touch. One night, they also shared her bed. The next morning, they talked and laughed over the newspaper and cups of coffee, and she told him that the lovemaking was better with him than with Eugene.

On that day, she didn't foresee how much pleasure Diego's caresses—his strong hands, smooth fingertips—would give her, even though she knew that the statistics about women deriving more satisfaction from sex as they age were in her favor.

With a blend of affection and teasing, he often asked her to marry him. "You are the woman of my dreams. If you have a problem, I will be around to take care of you in your old age. My name is *fountain*—of youth."

One night she remarked, "There's a term I learned from a colleague of mine. Limbic resonance. We have it."

He grinned. "Is that a professor's way of saying we're meant to be? We are tuned together. We are happy. And unless you will marry me, that will have to be enough for me. Is that enough for you?"

"Yes. Not on the marrying, but let's grow old together dancing."

She liked telling Diego about her team's studies. On that last morning, five months ago, she had said. "There's no doubt that dancing improves brain plasticity and cognition, cardiovascular health, and sexual enjoyment."

"No doubt about that, my professor. Dance is the language of love, and love is what humans can do well until the last breath." Then he loved her tenderly.

"We'll do more research on that tonight." He kissed her before riding away on his scooter to teach a salsa class. He would still be loving her, and she him, had he not crossed paths with a man in an SUV who turned onto a one-way street going the wrong direction.

Diego would have been the best dance partner of her life, except for the fact that someone else had secured that place in her heart and soul long ago.

Kip Kelly.

As she moves around the room to the music, she catches a glimmer of something and then a bright burst of memory. She can hear the traffic on the streets of New York City when she arrived for the Dance Teachers Convention on that glorious day decades ago. She will have no problem remembering it to tell Genet in the morning. The nineteenth of October, 1960, is sparkling clear.

CHAPTER TWENTY-SEVEN

Parallel Lives

"So this is Fifth Avenue." Mattie said. "It's more than I ever imagined."

"Never been?" The driver of the town car glanced at her in the rearview mirror.

"No. My brother lives here, but this is my first visit. We usually get together with the family back in Kansas City."

"Born and raised?"

"I moved to California when I was twelve." With that simple answer, Mattie usually could avoid questions that might require more from her than she could give, and she didn't want anything to diminish her delight in this moment. The driver glanced again in the rearview. She smiled to convey that she appreciated his interest and preferred to enjoy the rest of the ride to her midtown hotel without talking.

In store windows, gold watches and jeweled handbags sparkled. Chrome bumpers glistened on black Cadillacs idling beside the curbs. Men in tailored suits and women in fitted dresses emerged from the limousines to enter the shops. From those doorways, shoppers carrying bags stepped out to the sidewalks and entered the restaurants. Mattie imagined the purchases being taken from coat checks home to closets and jewelry chests brimming with more belongings than any person needed. At the start of this new decade, how had all of these people become so fortunate? How had she?

At the hotel, she thanked the driver, whom Mickey had pre-paid on her behalf. In the glittering lobby, she asked at the desk for Virginia Lee's room number and took the elevator up.

When Virginia opened the door and saw Mattie's suitcase, she said, "Good decision."

As Mattie's business partner in SPARK, their performing arts school in Los Angeles, Virginia had booked a room with two beds, so that that Mattie could overnight at the hotel during the convention rather than sleep at Mickey's place. His penthouse was spectacular, and Eugene and Charlie were staying there, but Virginia thought that, after the sessions, Mattie would prefer to mingle with teachers and presenters, who had come together from across the United States to investigate the rapid growth of dance education.

"What about the ticker-tape parade?" Virginia said. "If we leave now, we can get downtown and back before your panel presentation this afternoon."

"First let me hang this out." From her suitcase, Mattie unfolded the red cocktail dress with its full skirt, cinched waist, and plunging V-neck. "What do you think? Too much?"

"You'll knock 'em dead."

"Eugene says that red is my color." Mattie draped the dress over a chair beside the window and fluffed the hem. "Now, let's go."

With the doorman's assistance, they caught a cab in front of the hotel. When they reached Lower Broadway, the street was blocked for the parade. Mattie asked the driver, "Could you take us as near as possible to forty Wall Street?"

The map in the guidebooks she and Virginia had picked up in the hotel lobby showed the downtown streets, bridges, tunnels, and waterways—the conduits for arriving by car, bus, and ferry. The driver negotiated what felt to Mattie like a maze. "Here you are. Forty is that way." He motioned west. "Broadway is just beyond."

Virginia paid the fare, and she and Mattie stepped from the cab. They stood on the corner reading their guidebooks, looking up at the buildings and to the ends of the street that Mattie had heard about in childhood—the bombing that injured her grandparents, the visit her mother made with Eugene's parents. The pamphlet described how the street had been named for a succession of walls built by the Dutch to defend their occupied lower tip of the island against Native Americans, pirates, and the British.

Over time, Wall Street had become the epicenter of American investment, where trades were tracked and measured as markets rose and fell and rose again. Mattie was grateful that Eugene was an astute investor, or a lucky one.

"Do you understand the Dow, Virginia? I guess I don't, not really." Mattie looked up from reading. "Here it says it's an index of only two-and-a-half-dozen large companies—chemicals, tobacco, mining, manufacturing—"

"And oil." Virginia said. "Greasing America's gears."

Mattie turned a page. "I always thought of the Dow as a doctor who takes the nation's financial temperature daily, monitoring a patient who is always succumbing to or recovering from illness."

"Dr. Dow Jones." Virginia laughed. "But do you remember the crash? You were what, Mattie? Nine? I was five. It's been thirty-one years. I'd always thought it happened overnight, you know—*wham*—everyone is busted. It says here the market nosedived and then lost ninety percent of its value in three years."

"My Aunt Irene was sure we'd never recover."

"Well, the patient is in full recovery now at the start of this new decade. The Dow hit a high a few months ago. Nearly six hundred and eighty, wasn't it?"

"Eugene thinks we should invest more money, right now. He says things are only going to improve after the election."

Mattie had awakened this morning next to her husband in Mickey's guest room with a nervous energy, a sense that something momentous was about to happen, but it wasn't about financial wealth. Her anticipation seemed greater than any in recent memory. She had been eager to see Wall Street, but now, walking with Virginia by her side, the fluttering in her stomach didn't diminish and her heartbeat didn't slow. She was aware of the press and height of the buildings, but they were merely bricks and mortar, after all. Something else was exciting her.

Virginia pointed. "We're here, Mattie. Look up." On the street sign, *Canyon of Heroes* was spelled out under *Broadway*.

"And look down," Mattie said. With the toe of her shoe, she touched a black granite plaque embedded in concrete. The feet of the people next to her obscured the name and date, so she stepped back against a building and read from the guidebook. "The Canyon of Heroes honors ticker-tape parades of years past—George Washington's inauguration in 1889, Amelia Earhart's first transatlantic flight in 1932. How I would have loved to be here for that one."

Virginia and she found a spot among parade-watchers spilling from the walkways onto the street. Someone shouted, "Are they coming?"

Virginia stood on her tiptoes. "I can't see anything, Mattie. Can you?"

"Not really. Not yet."

People chanted, "JFK. JFK."

A flurry of ticker tape fell onto coats and stuck in people's hair. Shivering from the cold, Mattie brushed at a curl of paper and strained for a view of the motorcade, but a young woman in red lipstick and a low-cut dress pushed in front and shoved a leaflet into Mattie's hand. The man pictured on it was Richard Nixon. Mattie tried to give the leaflet back, but it slipped from her grasp and was trampled.

"I can't take this any longer!" The woman threw her stack of leaflets to the street and tried to squeeze between Mattie and Virginia. "Let me through."

Mattie reeled. "What's wrong?"

"Those liars. They said we'd be helping Mr. Nixon, but no one told us it wasn't his parade. He wanted the leaflets to be dropped from a plane but couldn't get a permit, so they hired a bunch of us to distribute them. I'm all for him, but I'm getting out of here." Mattie made way.

Virginia exclaimed, "I was about to say how *lucky* for us that the dance convention coincided with JFK's parade."

Mattie's "yes" was swallowed by the noisy crowd. She wished Eugene and Charlie were here to witness this—a new era in the making. If she could have reached them, she would have told them to come, but they were at the planetarium by now. Charlie's school report on satellites was due when they returned home. She pictured their house in California—the curving driveway, palm trees, and glass doors that opened onto a patio and pool. It was their dream home where they had lived for five years, but it seemed at this moment to belong to someone she once knew, not to her, the woman standing on a crowded sidewalk in the city which had ignited her girlhood imagination. The buildings whose heights her father and she had noted and the Broadway show whose starlet her mother and she had admired were not merely fantasy to her. They had been as real to her back then in Kansas City as they were now that she was here in New York.

A chill ran through her. What would have happened if Eugene's family had stayed here instead of moving to Los

Angeles, and she and Kip had come east in 1932 instead of going west? Who might that girl have become by this October day? What might have become of him? There would have been no train wreck, and he would possibly be somewhere in this city right now, dancing. They would no doubt be friends. What might he look like now as a forty-three-year-old man?

The phantom Mattie would surely be a grown woman like herself, but different. It was almost as if that other Mattie were here somewhere among the millions, living a parallel life, never having performed as a girl and young woman in films but on Broadway stages, never having been the mother of Charlie but of a boy exactly like him. There would have had to be a Charlie, the same sweet boy. She wouldn't change that for anything in the world.

A child sitting on a man's shoulders shouted, "There they are, Papa."

"Mattie, through here."

Virginia nudged Mattie toward a gap between two men, one smoking a cigar. The women sidled between them, tasting the smoke, and squeezed into a space on the curb.

A curl of tape caught on Mattie's eyelash. Fragments of printed numbers patterned the white. She flicked at the scrap, and the motorcade rolled into view. The man in the convertible was facing away, waving, but he was unmistakable from the magnificent crest of honeyed hair, now covered with paper snow.

"JFK. JFK." The chanting grew louder as the car drew closer. The Kennedys waved, their smiles radiating confidence and warmth.

"They're beautiful. Both of them," Virginia exclaimed.

Mattie held the moment, enraptured. Time divided—before seeing the couple and now, after. She tried to find words to describe her emotions to Eugene and Charlie and wished again that they were here.

"Imagine having people of our own generation in the White House." Virginia hugged herself. "He is only a few years older than we are, and she's younger. Do you have goose bumps? I do."

"Yes." Mattie pulled her coat tight and shivered, but not from seeing the Kennedys or from the temperature. A sensation rocked her, another dividing moment—she was riding on the roof of a boxcar, with Kip beside her, as they passed by children playing in a cotton field. The children ran after the train, waving, and became small in the distance.

"Watch out." Virginia yanked Mattie's arm.

A horse loomed before them. A mounted policeman forced people on the street back to the curb as the motorcade approached.

Virginia spoke loudly in Mattie's ear. "She looks so—"

"Regal." The women often finished each other's thoughts.

"So slender and elegant in her pillbox hat—"

"And long white gloves—"

"And taller than I had imagined."

Mattie was bursting with hope for the country—for everyone and everything. What a glorious future to behold. As the motorcade passed close by, one of Jackie's buttons began to slip its buttonhole. Mattie watched until the Kennedys—her hat, his head—were blocked from view.

"We should start back to the hotel," Virginia said. "The session begins at four."

Unable to move from the curbside in either direction, Mattie checked the time. Her watch—platinum with diamonds—had been a gift from Eugene in honor of the ten-year anniversary of SPARK. Because of the school's growing reputation, Mattie had been asked to join the afternoon panel and contribute on three themes—her background as a child performer, why she became a teacher, and the state of dance in America. She felt confident talking about herself, but she doubted her authority to speak to the broader matter of the art form. So much in modern dance was happening beyond her familiar world in Los Angeles.

"Are you ready for the panel?" Virginia asked. They were still hemmed in by the crowd.

"I'm not sure—"

"Tell them about your life—your big break in the thirties and all that happened after that, and how you started the school. People will find it inspiring."

A siren wailed. Someone pushed Mattie from behind. Thrown off balance, she widened her stance and relaxed her knees to steady herself.

Should she start with her arrival in Los Angeles, alone and grief-stricken over Kip? Or start when she left Kansas City and tell about traveling with him on the trains but not how the journey ended? She didn't believe any of this was relevant to the topic today, even if she could find the words to talk about it.

She turned to Virginia. "But where to begin?"

"How about that afternoon when you were discovered by the producer? Isn't that everyone's dream come true? Most dance teachers have probably had that one."

"Could be."

In June of 1932, a week after she arrived at Eugene's bedraggled and hungry, she was out on the patio by the pool with him. Wearing a swimsuit his mother had bought for her, she showed him barefoot bells on the clipped lawn. The grass prickled the soles of her feet. A producer, sitting by the window in the living room discussing a script with Eugene's parents, saw her as she leapt and exclaimed, "I've been looking for a young girl to do that exact move. I need a slight awkwardness for the role, not the polish of a professional dancer."

After he'd worked with her for a few days, he told the Turners that Mattie had natural talent, which could be developed through dance lessons. Eugene's mother bought her tap shoes and signed her up for classes.

"It was serendipity." Virginia yelled. The siren's wail came closer.

"Yes—" The horse's tail swished against Mattie's face. She turned her head and pressed back into the crowd, stepping through her speech.

She would tell the audience about her luck by the pool. She would mention how the contract with the movie studio enabled her to send money home—the often-told story of "kid makes it big in the Great Depression." But she wouldn't tell how the demanding schedule kept her from returning to Kansas City for many years, even after things improved for her parents and they were able to bring the rest of the family back together under one roof, along with Betty's husband and their baby. Her parents were grateful for that but couldn't pay for everyone to travel to California to visit Mattie. Eugene's parents bought tickets for Clara and Elliot to travel out by train together once; Clara came another time with Mickey and Wiley. Elliot's pride in caring for his family kept him from accepting more help from the Turners.

She wouldn't say to the audience that a few years had passed after her arrival in Los Angeles before she learned that her father had been injured in the fire. A church friend, who lived in a house near the Lookout, had been up at dawn and saw the flames along Fourth Street. He ran to the Toft house and woke Elliot, who rushed to the restaurant, hoping to save the painting of the bluebird. He was taking it from the wall when a ceiling beam fell. With effort that belied what he knew of his own strength, he pried himself out from under and escaped before the roof collapsed. No one told Mattie about his injuries because they didn't want her to worry. She didn't know until she saw the scars when he came to visit her in California.

"If I'd only known what nasty old Crowley and Mr. Nelson were up to, I could have warned you, Father."

"You're not to blame, Mattie. I cared for that little painting, but it was foolish of me to risk my life for it. My love for all of you is far greater." He took her hand in his scarred one. "You're growing up well here. Your mother and I are proud of your accomplishments."

Mattie wouldn't say how she often cried herself to sleep at night missing her family and Kip. She wouldn't mention how the night and day after the accident, she sat at the depot, her hopes of Kip being alive fleeing by the minute. While at the Western Union window sending a message home, she had spotted Gladdie. Her dress was filthy and torn, her shoes and stockings gone.

"No, I didn't see your fella. I was way back with the grease-balls. They weren't too bad after all. I'm here to get Daddy to send moolah enough to stay in Cali 'til my ship rolls in. Hey, how about your Hollywood friend? Does he have room for me?"

Mattie wouldn't mention the railroad official at the depot telling her that the workers dug through the rubble and found no survivors. They could only estimate the number of transients killed in the wreck. Many of the bodies in the burned boxcar could not be identified.

She wouldn't tell the audience that she used the savings from the sock in her knapsack to purchase a passenger car ticket to Los Angeles. She sat on a polished leather seat in her dirty shirt and trousers, famished and thirsty, while the other riders in their tailored travel clothes stared at her. An apricot rolled down the aisle to under her seat, and she retrieved it. A child at the other end of the car watched as she ate it. A basket of fruit rested on the seat beside the boy and his mother.

She would say only that she took a long train ride to California. When she arrived at the borrowed Hollywood mansion, Eugene's mother said, "You're going right into a bath, young lady." She wouldn't mention that she ate and slept, woke to eat, and slept again for three days.

She wouldn't tell the teachers that there has been an empty space in her life—a skip in time. She has had a recurring dream about trying to return to a place but not finding it, about hoping to find Kip and save him, but finally having to accept that he died in the train accident.

The siren screeched as an ambulance made its way on the street. The Kennedys' motorcade had moved a half block, and the horse followed. The crowd began to break up.

"Come through here, Mattie." Virginia started across the street.

As the two women slogged through the paper river, ticker tape wrapped their ankles. When they reached the sidewalk, they stood on their left legs to shake the ribbons from their right feet, then stood on their right legs to shake their left, naturally synchronizing their movements, as if rehearsed. They looked at each other and smiled. They were both tall and possessed a sense of balance earned through decades of daily dancing.

"I'll hail a cab," Virginia said, trying to flag one of the many yellow cars making their way in the slow traffic.

As that cab and another passed them, Mattie wondered if people wanted to hear about loss these days, or only about promise and opportunity. She would tell the audience how she took classes and performed in films during the thirties. She would tell them how, after the war broke out, she sang and danced at the USO clubs stateside at the Hollywood Canteen. She would mention the stars she had met—Jack Benny, the Andrews Sisters.

She would tell them that she stepped back from stage and film after the war. In 1947, the year Charlie was born, Eugene graduated from law school. He joined a firm that represented talent being boycotted by the studios, including his parents, due to being accused of un-American activities. As his father's melancholy deepened and his mother's drinking increased, they needed more than legal help. Mattie had her hands full with baby Charlie, but she cared for Eugene's parents, as they once had for her.

In 1950, Mattie opened SPARK and took Virginia on as a partner. The regular hours of teaching were compatible with being a mother and homemaker. In the evenings, she'd dance and sing in the kitchen to the radio—"If I Knew You Were Comin' I'd've Baked a Cake"—making treats for Charlie and his playmates or dinners for Eugene's clients.

Several SPARK students had scampered away to become Mouseketeers. Others went on to perform in MGM musicals, on television, and in the award shows. Many became actors skilled at moving through their scenes as bit players or stars. Mattie encouraged their ambitions and was eager to expand classes to meet the demand. Everyone wanted to dance. They gyrated on TV, did the Twist and all the others. Virginia had hired a young teacher for rock-and-roll, and Mattie planned to join in when she could.

If time allowed, she would tell the audience about her most meaningful achievement—Charlie, her shy, curious eighth-grader, who surely would not follow in her or Eugene's footsteps, but would find his own brilliant way in the world. Lately, he had become moody, and she worried he had inherited Eugene's father's melancholy.

Eugene's emotions, on the other hand, were steady. He was always practical. At their wedding in 1941, they lined up at City Hall with all the other couples in a ceremony presided over by a justice of the peace. Mattie cried, upset that she would not be married in a church surrounded by her family and that she and Eugene would soon be separated. He gave her his handkerchief for her tears and said that at least he could now go off to war knowing she would be waiting for him.

Should she talk about how new fears pressed upon them along with the war? The teachers of her generation didn't need reminding, but could those who were younger possibly imagine all the sacrifices people had made?

Should she leave out her age entirely? If she told them she was twelve years old in 1932, they would know she was forty now. She would say she was a schoolgirl and leave it at that. Even though she was a woman of middle age, she felt young and eager for whatever was next.

"Taxi." Virginia waved. The cab slowed. A man in a suit stepped in front of them, opened the door, and slid in. "How rude. Let's try the next block."

The women walked west and stood at the corner. "Look at this." Virginia pointed to a mimeographed flyer among other weathered posters on a utility pole. "I'm guessing that word is 'thrilling' but is it 'pling dancers'? Something-pling?"

Mattie scrutinized the poster. T_RILLING NEW __ PLING DANCERS. L_CK OF THE DRA_. Tacks had torn the paper. Silhouetted dancers were drawn lifting one another in poses that were not balletic, not graceful, but intriguing. "I have no idea."

"I haven't heard of them, have you?"

"Looks like we missed it, anyway. What's the presentation tonight? The one after my panel?"

"As I recall from the schedule, it's 'Three Choreographers on the Rise.' But at this rate, we'll be late for yours. Every cab has passed us by."

"There's still time." Mattie checked her watch. She was anxious about the panel presentation and something else. She again sensed something so near and strong that she might have split into two of herself. One Mattie would return to California where her familiar life spread out among the palm trees and miles of new freeways. The other Mattie would stay here in

New York, where she might have been all along, where her deepest feelings were waiting to be released. She might have had a life with Kip among these tall buildings. The nearest one at the moment rose as high above her as the cliff in her old neighborhood. So many things today have recalled her childhood. Wayward ticker tape floated above her. She thought she saw a hand extend from a window, but it could have been the shadow of a bird.

"Finally." Virginia rushed to grab the taxi door handle.

"Where to, ladies?"

"Times Square." The women chimed in unison. They entered the taxi, and another ambulance screeched past.

In the hotel lobby, a dance teacher they knew from California waved to them as she ducked into the bar. Virginia waved back. "Shall we stop for a cocktail, Mattie?"

"You go on in. I want to take a bath."

In the room, Mattie's red dress caught the light streaming through the window, which was framed by gold-flecked curtains that matched the bedspreads. Virginia's clothes were hung in the closet, her valise and makeup case stacked neatly beside shoes, and bottles of perfume and lipstick tubes arranged beneath the mirror on the bathroom vanity.

Mattie bathed, dried her hair with a towel, and ran her fingers through her new bob. The last of the old perm had been chopped for a cut that angled toward the cheekbones. Her hair, with only a few gray strands, was still the color of diluted tea. She donned the hotel's white terrycloth robe, drew the double curtains to dim the light and traffic noise, and sprawled on the bed.

Hearing Eugene's voice would have been a comfort, but he was probably with Charlie at the zoo by now, their last stop as planned for the day. She would see them soon enough at the panel session, though they might be late.

She stretched out, raised her arms above her head, and let them fall. She raised a leg, bent the knee, raised the other leg, and bent it. With both feet and palms flat against the bed, she lifted her buttocks and stretched her spine. The robe fell open. She lowered herself, lifted again, and lowered. She had a dancer's body—long and lean. She would admit to vanity about her muscled buttocks, firm thighs, and still shapely calves, and about her feet. They were slender and her arches hadn't fallen. They served her well.

She raised one foot and then the other. Her breasts had always been small, and she considered them now. They sagged more to the sides, and she wondered if Eugene had noticed. He hadn't commented. He used to say he liked their shape and size, but he was a leg man, and recently had told her that she still had other women her age beat in that department.

Mattie didn't like that he qualified it with age. She didn't want to think about growing old, not today, when this city had aroused her desire. She longed for something that she couldn't name, something absent in her life. Was she missing Eugene? They had spent yesterday traveling with Charlie to New York. It was rare for her to spend a whole day with Eugene, as busy as he usually was. She would tell him of this expansive feeling, if she could find the words.

She stroked her skin, dragging the tips of her fingers lightly over her breasts and belly. She slid her hand down along her thigh and up between her legs, where it was still warm and damp from the bath. She heard a key in the lock and rolled to her side. She was drawing the robe closed as the door opened.

"Oh, I'm sorry. I didn't think you'd be sleeping." Virginia switched on the desk lamp and rummaged in her briefcase.

"Only resting."

"They're showing off their kids." Virginia held up a photo. "I forgot about mine." She giggled. "Can you believe it? One

Bloody Mary, and I'm plastered. They make them stronger here. Seems like everything is a bigger deal in New York—life is lived larger. Couldn't you bust wide open, Mattie? Couldn't you burst? I want to bundle up all the energy, take it home, and give our students a taste of New York."

She crossed the room to the door. "Shall I meet you in the ballroom?"

"Yes. I'll be down soon."

"This will be fun tonight. You'll be great. I'll save us seats." Virginia stepped out into the hallway. "I can't wait to see the modern dance demo after your panel. Someone in the bar was raving about one of the choreographers. He won a Rockefeller grant. She said he's far out. It's another world here, Mattie. Day and night from Los Angeles. See you downstairs."

Mattie opened the curtains to the cityscape and drew a deep breath. She pulled on a new pair of Panti-Legs, snapped on a lace bra, slipped on the red dress and high heels, and chose a matching lipstick from Virginia's cosmetics display. Regarding her image in the mirror, she drew a breath, exhaled, and spoke to the flutters in her stomach. "After all these years, why can't I make you go away?"

They continued as she stepped into the elevator, entered the ballroom, and sat beside Virginia in the first row. The flutters intensified as she took her place on stage with the other panelists, listened to the histories, and thought about how her story compared.

The fluttering nearly overtook her when she heard her name. "Please welcome Margaret Turner, Director of SPARK, the School for Performing Arts and Repertory Kids in Hollywood, California."

Mattie stood before the crowd of five hundred fellow dance educators and, on cue, the flutters dissipated. She projected her voice beyond the gilded chandeliers and brought her focus back to Virginia. It helped to speak to a familiar face.

"I was lucky one summer day in nineteen thirty-two, and that's why I'm here before you today." She told about leaping bells beside the swimming pool, meeting the producer, performing in movies and at the USO, and starting the school to teach children and now adults too. She talked about the health benefits of dance for all ages. Audience members smiled and nodded.

As she was about to mention her greatest achievement—Charlie—he walked through the door at the far end of the ballroom with Eugene. Mickey was right behind them. At the sight of her brother taking a seat in a folding chair, a little laugh escaped her. Her world was much different from his of penthouses and chauffeured limos, but their personalities were so similar, their optimistic natures in tune. Their Aunt Irene had once said that Mickey's hopes were too lofty for his own good, but he'd only set them higher. Mattie admired him for it.

"Thank you, Mrs. Turner. We'd like to hear more, but let's move on to the discussion." Mattie sat down with the other panelists as the moderator continued. "Each of you had an interesting journey on the way to becoming a dance educator. To start off discussion, if you could go back and do anything differently, what would it be?"

A voice within Mattie spoke loudly. "Find Kip. Save him." The clarity and resolve surprised her. Could she have? Saved him? She was twelve. In all the years since, she had not allowed herself to dwell on it, so why had he arrived so fully in her mind today?

She heard, as from a tunnel, the other panelists. "I would have stopped dancing before I injured myself . . . would have brought my partner into the business sooner . . . would have moved to New York."

"And you, Mrs. Turner? Different choices?"

"I—" Mattie cleared her throat. What would she have done? Should she have done? There in the back row was the top of Charlie's head.

"My father used to say, 'Life is what you make of it.' I've been lucky in so many ways, and I wouldn't change what that luck has brought me." She strained to see Charlie next to Eugene and smiled at them both. Mickey was checking his watch.

The panel ended and Virginia met Mattie beside the stage. "I have to dash to the room before the next session. Meet you back here or up there?"

Before Mattie could respond, audience members gathered around. She saw Virginia leave the ballroom.

A woman with curly red hair said, "I was a child performer too. If you ever want to talk about old times, give me a call. I'm in San Bernardino. Let's get together."

"That's kind of you," Mattie said. "I'd be more interested in talking about what you're doing now or next rather than reliving the old times. If that entices, you can reach me at the school."

A slender man reached to shake her hand. Wisps of gray threaded his dark hair. "I'm designing a study on dancing and aging. You'd be perfect to participate."

"The dancing or the fact that I'm getting old?" she said.

"I meant to say that we're making remarkable findings about the health benefits of dance for longevity." He handed her a business card. "Jim Bloomfield."

She took the card. "Oh, Doctor Bloomfield, I was teasing. Tell me more—"

Eugene interrupted. "Well done, Mattie. You look sharp." Charlie and Mickey were beside him.

"Enjoyed your presentation, Mrs. Turner," Jim said. "Please call and I'll give you the details."

Eugene embraced her and she pressed against him—the

damp wool of his suit jacket, a whiff of cigarette smoke. She had reminded him to bring his raincoat on the trip, and he had left it in the coat divider on the airplane. "Sorry we were late."

His voice soothed her. It was one of the things she loved most about him. "You're here. And Mickey. I'm so happy you came too. Is it raining?"

"Drizzling."

"You were good up there, Mom." Charlie offered his cheek for her kiss. His skin was bumpy and prickly. Only a few months ago, it had been smooth.

"Yeah, good job." Mickey fanned four tickets in his hand. "We have tickets to *West Side Story*."

"How—?" She had wanted to see the musical's revival at the Winter Garden and had tried to buy tickets when the travel agent booked their plane reservations, but it had been sold out. The sensation that something momentous was about to happen hadn't gone away after the Kennedy parade or the panel. Seeing the show must be what she had been anticipating.

"He knows the producer." Charlie beamed. "Uncle Mickey knows everybody."

"Called in a favor, Skinbones. We did some pro bono work." The nickname that she'd hated in childhood had long since become a term of endearment.

Mickey, who had drawn in the margins of his schoolbooks and done poorly as a student, had found his way in the world as an illustrator in New York after the war and then as the head of his own ad agency. He had made more income last year alone than their father earned in his lifetime before Elliot retired this year—not as fulfilled in his own career as he might have been in this new era of prosperity, but full of pride for his son.

"Let me get my coat and tell Virginia."

She walked with Eugene, Charlie, and Mickey toward the ballroom exit, where they encountered a hotel maintenance man carrying a ladder. "Excuse me," he said. "I thought all you folks would have already left this session."

"On our way." Eugene nodded and put his arm around Charlie. "Is there time to eat? We're hungry. Right, buddy?"

Charlie shifted away slightly from his father's embrace, but smiled. "Yes. Hungry."

"I know the perfect place," Mickey said.

"I knew you would." Mattie followed them out the ballroom exit. "I'll meet you back here in the lobby—with an umbrella." Going up to tell Virginia that she was sorry to be missing the evening session with the choreographers, she felt a tinge of regret. One of her goals for the trip had been to check out the avant-garde dance scene, but how could she pass up tickets for Broadway?

She returned to the lobby and walked with Eugene, Charlie, and Mickey to a deli near the theater. When they entered, she gasped. "This reminds me very much of the Bluebird." The floor was checkerboard in white and black, not blue, but the cushions were blue vinyl.

"I thought so too, first time I saw it. Figured you'd like it," Mickey said. "Let's sit here by the window."

Mattie munched a dill pickle from the bowl on the table and watched people pass by on the sidewalk. She wiped juice from her chin, smudging the napkin with red lipstick. The napkin fell from her lap to the floor and, as she reached to retrieve it, the waiter bringing their plates said, "Leave it. I'll get you a fresh one."

She slid it out of sight under the table with the toe of her shoe. They dug into their sandwiches with thirty minutes to go before the curtain rose.

Mickey lifted the heaped pastrami on rye to his mouth and read from a newspaper someone had left on the table. "Listen to this review. 'Everything contributes to the total impression of wildness, ecstasy, and anguish—'"

He took a bite and spoke with his mouth full. "'Hostility and suspicion between the gangs . . . the terror of the rumble . . .' Hmm." He glanced at Charlie and said to Eugene and Mattie, "Are you okay with this?"

"I'm not a baby," Charlie said. "We have gangs too. In LA."

Eugene nodded and said to Mickey, "He's heard me talk about a case I had a couple years ago. The litigants were Spook Hunters out of Southgate. They are white racists who couldn't deal with the growing Negro population in LA. Then the black youth gangs formed for protection. And so on. Yeah, we've got them."

Charlie dipped a straw into his chocolate shake. "It's just a musical, anyway. Not real life. And kids at school fight too."

"Did it used to be easier for people to get along? May I?" Mattie took the paper from Mickey. "Or did we Tofts miss out on the conflict gene? Father and Mother hate arguments. Any kind of friction. If you can't say anything nice—"

"Don't say anything at all." Mickey bit into his pastrami and chewed.

"Friction is good if you want to light a match or brake a car." Charlie slurped his shake. "It's not so good when you're reentering the atmosphere. Too hot."

Eugene tousled Charlie's hair. "That's my son. Bound to be a scientist, maybe an outer space traveler one day. Nothing so pedestrian as law."

Charlie shrugged. "It was in the exhibit today."

"Mind like a steel trap." Eugene said. "That's youth for you."

Mattie wished this moment could last forever, here with her family, their crusts on the plates. Euphoria filled her. But they would miss the curtain call if they didn't leave now, so they paid the bill and dashed to the theater.

They took their seats in the dark and the show began. Some minutes into it—the Sharks and the Jets rubbing each other the wrong way, setting off sparks, friction—she had a vivid memory of Kip in the boxcar the night of the accident. *Wait for me.*

She had been sitting forward, tense, and settled back into her seat, then leaned forward again as "Something's Coming" built palpable tension in the theater. Sparring tribes danced in confrontation, taunting, egging each other on. The men moved, sharp and angular. The women swished in voluminous skirts, raw and sexy. Charlie sat mesmerized beside her.

The dancers kicked and spun, leapt and lifted. They joined together, needing to belong to one another. Their longing conveyed danger, hope, conflict, and determination. The women sang America's praises as a land of opportunity and wanted to stay. The men wanted to leave or destroy it and each other.

At the end, she clapped until her palms stung. She gathered her coat and purse, flowed with the crowd through the lobby, and skipped with Charlie into the night air humming the tune "Somewhere," with Eugene and Mickey close behind.

The rain had stopped. The city pulsed with energy. They came to the deli. At the table where they had sat earlier, a man and woman had finished their meal. Mattie hooked her arm onto Eugene's and paused on the sidewalk.

"Shall we go in for a slice à la mode? We could grab our same spot." She pointed toward the couple. The man was bending to retrieve something from under the table. With dismay, she realized that it was the same lipstick-stained napkin she'd dropped. Why hadn't she picked up after herself as she had been raised to do? She looked at Eugene.

"It's late." He checked his watch. "How early is your first session? We should get you back to the hotel."

"Maybe a quick bite? For some odd reason, this place seems to be calling to me. Nostalgia for the Bluebird, I guess."

"It's up to you," Eugene said. "You're the one with a schedule to keep. Charlie and I can sleep late."

Mattie started toward the door and paused. She wasn't really hungry for pie. Nothing in this glorious day had yet satisfied her craving, and she realized that no amount of pie would do so. Eugene was a sport. He'd go in with her if she wanted to, but he was right that she should get a good night's sleep.

"Let's go, Mom," Charlie said.

In front of the hotel, she kissed them all goodnight and waved as the limo drove away. She tiptoed into the room so as not to wake Virginia. The blackout curtain was open. Green and pink neon flashed from the street. She slipped between the sheets with "There's a Place for Us" repeating in her mind.

"Oh, hi, Mattie," Virginia whispered. "How was it?"

Mattie rolled to face the adjacent bed. "Absolutely wonderful."

"I'm glad."

"And you?" She thought of saying how her feelings of expectation had carried her through the day and hadn't been fulfilled. Would something always be missing from her life? Would that mysterious place where she dare not go remain within her forever? She would think about it another time.

"It was good," Virginia said. "Interesting. Not what we're used to seeing. Especially the first presentation. It was far out, as that woman in the bar said it would be. Anything goes here, I guess. Standing still. Following each other around. Falling off a ladder. Everyday movements. It's all dance. Kind of heady, you know. Avant-garde. The choreographer has agreed to give a workshop tomorrow, so I signed us up. It's early, before the main session."

"How early?" Mattie strained to listen.

"I've requested a wake-up call for 6:30 a.m. Okay?"

"Yes, I'd like to go."

"I wish you'd seen this session tonight, Mattie. It's funny, well maybe not funny, but you know, odd for a choreographer. He had a noticeable limp."

A siren wailed. Neon lights flashed.

"Mattie?"

"Definitely. Wake me. I don't want to miss a thing."

As Virginia rose to close the curtain, Mattie drifted on thoughts of a choreographer with a limp and imagined a troupe of dancers hobbling across the stage with canes. What had Virginia said? Mattie wiggled her toes under the cool sheet and trailed her fingers across the starched pillowcase. Any movement could become dance if you noticed it as such.

CHAPTER TWENTY-EIGHT

Luck of the Draw

In a tenth-floor studio a block off Broadway, seven dancers sat on the polished hardwood warming up with feet together, knees splayed and bouncing gently. The white walls pulsed with reflected sunlight, a siren wailed from the street below, and a distant ferryboat bawled over the thrum of traffic. The studio doors swung open and the company director backed in dragging a mattress. It thudded onto the floor.

He shed his black overcoat, aware that the dancers were studying his every movement. They leaned toward him in expectation—Yuka, Solomon, Livia, Hannah, Frank, Juan, Judith—and he absorbed their tableau for future use. His choreography was known for moments of people coming together, splitting apart, holding, releasing, returning.

"Today we're flinging." Dark hair shadowed his eyes, which gleamed copper.

The old mattress had ripped at the last rehearsal, its coils spiraling out from the cotton batting. Four dancers moved to prop this new one vertically—two gripped either side; two braced from behind. The other four queued across the room.

Aidan was first in line. He rubbed his right thigh, pressing into the quadriceps, sliding the heel of his palm hard toward the knee, and again, hip to knee, kneading his fist into the thick cord of scarred flesh. The ache was always present, along with the gap in his memory of the accident twenty-eight years ago. He loped across the wood floor, gathered speed, and threw himself into the mattress. He rebounded, landing in a crouch to absorb the bounce, rose with arms out, and limped aside, motioning to the dancer who had stood behind him in line. "Yuka, go. Your way."

Her raven hair fell past her shoulders; a magenta headband framed her face. She ran, slammed into the mattress, and stumbled backward. Dropping to the floor, she folded her arms against her chest and said softly, "Like a lover." She replaced a dancer at an edge of the mattress and alerted the ones supporting it from behind. They widened their stance and braced for impact.

Solomon stripped off his shirt, baring his dark-skinned chest. The tallest dancer, he flew at the mattress, hooked his arms over the top edge, and hung suspended above the floor, knees bent, then slid down to toes, shins, thighs, belly, chest, palms, chin. "Forgiving," he said, rolling over. "Forgiven." He went from prone to upright in two moves—sit, stand—and stepped to take his turn behind the mattress.

When Yuka's turn came again, she ran and bumped against the fabric. "You hedged," Aidan said. "Do it like you're throwing yourself into the deep end of a swimming pool."

"I'm not a good swimmer."

"Use something else. Your own impulse. You had it that first round."

Aidan was preparing the dancers for a performance in which they would fling themselves into each other's arms. Timidity in anyone endangered everyone. The piece was inexpressible in words, as were all his dances, though reviewers would write paragraphs about trust and tolerance, courage and fear. By the time a reviewer wrote about a piece, it would have died for Aidan. Its life was in the studio, in the invention, rehearsal, and the heightened moments in front of an audience. He wanted the performance to be inevitable each time. He didn't choreograph a piece for any group of dancers to repeat in repertoire; he created for his dancers to become one in unanticipated ways.

One critic had understood and wrote in the *Village Voice*: "On any night, in any concert hall, the up-and-coming choreographer Aidan Kipling and company startle the audience and themselves with the unexpected. They are gritty, energetic, and driven by a mysterious force."

Two years would pass before "improvisation" appeared in reviews, but Aidan had long been improvising from the unforeseen and seeing the possible in each moment.

Yuka pulled her hair into a ponytail. The dancers held the mattress. She ran and lightly bounced.

"Again," Aidan said.

She tried repeatedly until she hit the padding with her full weight and fell to her knees. "I give up," she said in tears.

"You can't quit," everyone chorused.

"Break." Aidan clapped.

At the sound, the dancers dropped the mattress and gathered around Yuka, who cuddled against it. Dark half-moons under her eyes bestowed the haggard look of a defeated prizefighter. A collision with an elbow last week had purpled her jaw. She wiped her face. "Not quit. Give up. Surrender."

Solomon stood. "I've got her." He bent and lifted Yuka, who went limp as a rag doll. He tossed her above him and caught her. The dancers clapped and whooped.

Aidan imagined her flung from dancer to dancer, a human hot potato. On a darkened stage, dancers would fall from ladders in the wings into the light. In the presentation they would be giving this evening, the ladders would be exposed. Let the audience see some dancers climbing, others waiting below. Anticipate. Tonight, he would join them. Later, when he cast himself for the performance season, he would be the only one not catching or being caught.

He had always asked more from his troupe than they believed they could give, but this was why they worked with him despite salaries that barely paid for flats with floors that sagged and roaches that skittered across them at night. As director of this new company, this family of his making, he could have kept more of the Rockefeller Foundation grant for his own, but he sliced it into eight equal parts after the low overhead was paid. The rehearsal space, though not ideal, came with the grant. He waited for the group to settle and said, "Freedom is self-mastery."

The dancers, except for Yuka, murmured and nodded. They would have seen him as their guru, but it would be another decade before the idea of following a guru became popular in the US.

Yuka and Aidan have been talking about her moving into his flat, and he had asked that she not say anything to the others yet. He was with Hannah before this. Yuka understood that he wanted to protect his freedom at this critical time of his career, but regarding "self-mastery," she wondered why he would care what the others thought about him choosing her. It was one of his contradictions, which were what attracted her, along with his grace and perseverance. She had never been with a more beautiful, complicated man.

Bits of white, like winter's first snow flurries, floated outside the floor-to-ceiling windows, but it was only mid-October.

"A ticker-tape parade today . . . Yeah? . . . The Kennedys . . . Can you see it?" The dancers moved to the windows. Yuka and Solomon—shortest and tallest—stood side by side, their legs powerfully muscled and toned. A curl of paper had stuck to the glass. Yuka cranked open the window and reached her hand toward the scrap, but it drifted away.

Aidan watched, thinking about scale and height, about floating free of gravity. He waited for a siren to diminish before he spoke. "We're in the hotel ballroom tonight. Small stage. We'll be in front of it."

"What is this for again?" Livia asked.

"A convention of dance teachers," Yuka said. "A demonstration of how our pieces get made." She knew that Aidan had little patience for this kind of event, though it fulfilled a requirement of their funders, and he had even less patience for dancers who didn't pay attention. "We're one of three companies presenting this evening. So take a break, get nourished, and meet in the green room next to the ballroom to warm up at—Aidan? Six o'clock?"

"Right." He would have kept them in the studio all afternoon, but the Rockefeller grant came with a stipulation requiring overtime pay and extra accounting, so he cut rehearsals short on performance days. If he could have avoided paperwork altogether, he would have. Tracking the details felt like a punishment. Gathering the proof to show he deserved the grant was difficult enough. Now he had to prove his worth in order to keep it and be considered for another year of funding.

In the years since leaving home when he was not yet fifteen, he had never planned that far ahead. When he did spend a few years at a stretch in one place, it was due to circumstances, not ambition. He knew now what he wanted to be doing with his life and it was only this: making dance in this moment and the next for as long as he could move.

"Costumes?" Solomon asked.

"Your choice," Aidan said.

The dancers circled around the thrift-store bin. They held up skirts and vests, pants and shirts. "Give me that . . . suits you . . . put this with it." Livia flung off her sweatshirt and slipped a pink sundress over her green leotard and tights. Solomon buttoned a gray tuxedo vest across his bare chest and pulled red plaid boxers over his sweatpants. As soon as the dancers had selected items for the presentation, they bundled their things and left. Their chatter from the hallway drifted back to the studio.

Yuka stayed with Aidan. "Want to go back to my place to nap?"

He shook his head. "Not tired."

"I wasn't really thinking we'd sleep." She moved close and stood on tiptoes to kiss him on the cheek, which was rough from not having shaved that morning. He had stayed over with her the night before and hadn't brought his razor. "You seem all bottled up about tonight. We can remedy that."

"They want me to talk about my life."

"Mmmm. I'd like to hear it."

She had met him a year ago and, in spite of their physical intimacy, he was a mystery to her. Most of her boyfriends had been like puppy dogs, eager to please, staying close at her heels. This one was like a cat whose trust she had yet to earn completely. He would be generously affectionate, and then the next moment not let her come near. She was pretty sure he'd been hurt deeply in the past and wished he would open himself to her. He was like kintsugi. A beautiful brokenness.

She remembered her mother carefully wrapping their family's kintsugi bowl in clothing and carrying it in a pillowcase to Wyoming from their home in Los Angeles. Of all their treasured possessions, the five-hundred-year-old cracked and mended bowl was the one thing of value they took with them. During the three years of internment during the war, her mother kept the bowl hidden under a dusty floorboard of their bunkhouse and brought it out for special occasions. "So that we remember our dignity," she had said.

Yuka saw it clearly in her mind's eye—a celery-colored tea bowl that she could cup in her hands. Gold-flecked resin held the shards together, the golden veins making the bowl more beautiful than it would have been before it was broken.

"Shall I stay? Go?" She bent to kiss him.

"Go." He caressed her jawbone with his fingertips. "Nap. We'll be together tonight afterward."

In the years years since coming to Manhattan, she had danced in other companies and been with other choreographers, but she had never met anyone like Aidan. He was part of the New York modern dance scene, yet seemed to exist partially in another realm, untethered to the earth. Sometimes watching him dance she saw him skipping through a galaxy all his own, lightly touching down, from star to star.

"I love you," she said.

"Love you too."

He always responded this way, leaving out the "I." It was always "love you too" in response, never saying "love you" first. She would be patient. Like the kintsugi bowl, his movements were not flawless, but flawed perfection. His limp was part of his grace and beauty. There was more brokenness inside him. She would be his golden repair, but it would take time. As she left the studio, closing the door behind her, she decided that being with him was enough for now.

Aidan's skin was clammy with sweat. He put on his coat, sat on the floor, and pulled from his pocket a stubby pencil and an envelope containing a utility bill he hadn't paid. The organizer of tonight's event had said, "Talk about your life's twists and turns and what led you to start your company. A brief autobiography. The teachers will be inspired."

What facts about his life could have meaning for anyone in the audience tonight? He had no degree, did not go to college. He had no theory of teaching, only a theory of learning. Study with the best. Try new things, whatever you could do.

His entire life had prepared him for this moment, for having a troupe of dancers to perform his work. What were the turning points of the years since he left home? If he were a cat, he would have used up most of his nine lives. He had been marked by it all—accident and intention. If he told about only a few of the twists and turns, what would they be? He licked the tip of the pencil and, on the back of the envelope, began jotting notes about how one thing had led to another.

> *the train wreck–kindness of strangers*
> *conservation corps–heart mountain*
> *uso tour–tap again*
> *german capture–escape*
> *ballet–modern with Martha*
> *black mountain summer–merce*
> *west side story–jerry says "use your limp"*
> *changing my name–starting the company*
> *luck of the draw–the grant*
> *ask questions–release your fears*

He didn't want to talk about himself. He wanted to make pieces where each dancer moved distinctively, becoming as one—a strangely beautiful animal, the way a bird with beak and feathers, claws, and wings seemed incongruous and yet was fascinating and absolute.

He read the list and crossed through all but the last three words—*release your fears*. It was the one piece of advice he had found to be true, no matter the circumstance or challenge.

He stood, walked to the window, looked down on the

graveyard beside the Trinity Church, and wondered if the descendants of people buried there so long ago attended the graves. He had visited his folks' graves during the summer that he spent at Black Mountain College dancing with Merce. The cemetery was green and cool in the shade. He bought two small tombstones and had them placed side by side—Rose Kelly McKillip and Magnus McKillip, next to his grandma. For his grandpa McKillip, there was no grave that he could find.

He used to believe he would die young and didn't mind the idea of it, but now he trusted he would live another decade or two. The possibility of that filled him with relief, because he had much yet to do, and lifted him with the ballooning promise that he might be able to do it. At forty-three, he now knew his purpose. No more detours. Dancing was akin to flying. He would soar in this life and leave a trace, like the jet contrail streaked across the sky.

Standing at the window, he was aware that this radiant moment would blur, along with this day, into other days of coming and going, rehearsing and performing. Yet, there would be a quality that he retained of time well spent. He didn't realize he was smiling until he noticed his faint reflection in the window glass smiling back at him. He remained there until the white wisps in the blue sky had evaporated.

The afternoon beckoned with time to work in this room that came with the grant—an empty office suite in a building undergoing renovation. He imagined some day having a rehearsal studio in an old church or factory, a building of human proportions that retained evidence of the souls having passed through—echoes in vaulted ceilings, scuffs on the wooden floor, an entrance off the street or alley where the dancers could go to smoke.

He moved across the room, improvising as he recalled events of his life, starting with the traveling time. Leaving

North Carolina, landing at the Bluebird, his stay with the Toft family. Mattie by his side on the train. The dark hole in his memory. Surviving the accident. It was his material, his essence. He had explored it all before, and yet he had only begun to make meaning from it, much less to make dance that would stand on its own.

Propelled by an inner force, he knotted his fists at his chest and pounded them against his heart, knocking at his own door. Open up. He flung his arms wide and brought them back across his chest—open, closed, open, closed. He imagined Yuka flinging herself full force at him, being held, slipping from his grasp, and spinning away. He would use the dancers' own propulsion in the presentation and forget the ladders; they needed no props tonight. They would show the audience how movement was born when you put dancers with heart in an empty space and welcomed what arrived.

In the rainy twilight, he made his way to the hotel where the Dance Teachers Convention was being held. He found the green room empty. A door led into the ballroom beside the stage. At the far exit, two men, a teenage boy, and a tall woman in a red dress were walking out. Attracted to something in her stride, he made a mental note. *Quartet. Woman walking in the wake of three men.*

A maintenance man unfolded a ladder at the edge of the open space in front of the stage.

"The chairs," Aidan said.

"Sir?"

"We'll need the first several rows removed."

"Yes, sir. I'll get the crew on it right away."

"Five should do."

"Men?"

"Oh, no." Aidan smiled. "Rows."

"Yes, sir. And another ladder's coming."

"Sorry for your trouble, but we don't need the ladders, after all.

"I'll have the crew remove this one."

"Much appreciated."

Aidan returned to the green room. His dancers were shedding their damp coats and scarves and shaking off the stiffness in their muscles. They yawned and stretched. He told them there would be no ladders tonight and helped Yuka with her coat.

Dancers from the other two companies arrived. Some were friends or acquaintances, having performed or studied together; others made introductions.

"Hey, Aidan. Yuka."

"Hey." They greeted Gordon, whom Aidan had met when he performed with him—a Jet, a Shark—in the original run of *West Side Story*. Now Gordon had his own company.

"I heard you got the Rockefeller. Lucky bastard. Dominoes, huh, Kipling? Sounds like things are falling in place." He slapped Aidan on the back.

"What can you do?" Aidan shrugged.

They were all in this quest together and wished each other well, but they competed for the same few modern-dance grants. Aidan had been awarded his for "Boneyard," a piece he developed with his dancers using dominoes to structure improvised movement. The number of dots on either end of a tile determined the number of participants in each sequence. A double-one commanded two solos, a two-three a duo and trio. In the performance that captured the award, the final draw was a one-six. When the sextet spontaneously queued and fell backward, Aidan, at the end of the line, held their weight and stopped them from toppling.

The final show of their three-night run might have been the company's last, unable as Aidan was to pay the performers or studio rent, but the rave reviews caught the attention of the funders. The company had been assured another year of survival.

"You got it made in the shade," Gordon said. "Hey, have you seen Jerry lately?"

"No. You?"

"There's something on tonight—old cast, new cast thing—backstage at the Winter Garden after the performance. I'm stopping by. Come if you can."

"Maybe." Aidan would consider it later. He didn't want to infuse the sensations of tonight's demonstration with those of a Broadway show. He wanted to stay open to what happened in the moment and not be penned in by a script. That was why he had left Broadway behind.

First on the program, the Kipling dancers walked out and stood in front of the stage. The propped-open ladder had not been removed from the edge of the open space. The ballroom was full, other than one vacant seat, like a missing tooth, in the front row. Aidan waited as people drifted in. He had found that the best way to call attention to oneself, when speaking to a room full of people, was to stand still and say nothing. Soon all conversation died in the ballroom, all eyes focused forward. "Hello. We're the Kipling Dancers. I'm Aidan Kipling."

The dancers introduced themselves, one by one, and came around again to him. "Tonight's organizer asked me to give you a brief background and some teaching advice, so here goes. Where I've been and what I've done goes into the work. What we're making now will be created tonight in this demonstration, as in rehearsal. We'll show you how we do it. My only advice, the only sure thing I know is—release your fears. Whatever you do, go in with all you've got."

He began slapping his palms against his chest and flinging his arms open and close, moving across the floor. Yuka responded, mirroring him. Soon all the dancers were slapping and flinging. They clustered in pairs or trios on the slap and then flung themselves wide apart. Cluster, *slap*—fling. The slaps reverberated in the ballroom and layered into a rhythm. They went with it, accelerating to a speed that blurred the distinctions, dancer to dancer. They moved as one.

Yuka circled wide and bumped into the ladder. She responded by climbing to the top rung. She slapped her chest and opened her arms.

Aidan saw this in his peripheral vision and framed it in his mind, like a photograph, which he would come back to time and again in his pieces over the next decade. He would name them "Precipice" and "Plummet," "Transgression" and "Capitulate," and they would garner rave reviews. In interviews, he would say they began in this moment, but he knew they were within him from long ago. He would continue trying to seize memory from the black hole and unwrap the terrible beauty of it.

Yuka threw herself off the ladder like a rag doll, and the audience gasped. The other dancers instantly melded into a line, shoulder-to-shoulder, with arms extended and hands clasped in the exact spot, miraculously, it seemed, where Yuka's trajectory ended. They caught her, and the audience whooped and applauded. The dancers gently released Yuka to standing, and they all bowed.

"We didn't rehearse that," Aidan said. "Only the trust." At this moment, he realized that when he said earlier to go in with all you've got, he should have said to go in with all your love. That was what he meant to say, but it might have sounded too soft, even though he knew that love was the toughest thing in the world to do.

The other two dance companies gave their demonstrations, all three companies came together for questions from the audience, and the conference session ended. As Aidan was leaving the green room with the dancers, the organizer of the event caught up with them. "That was something. Several teachers have asked if you could give a workshop. We have an early morning time slot where we could slip you in tomorrow. Is it possible? There's a stipend."

Aidan glanced at Yuka—his brave Yuka—who had never been more beautiful than at this moment, disheveled as she was from the performance.

"We should do it," she said, and looked to the other dancers. "I think we can all be there. Right?"

They nodded. "Yeah . . . tomorrow . . . how early?"

Aidan said, "I'll agree to it if we can have four ladders. We'll invite the participants to trust and fall with us."

"Terrific," the organizer said. "And Mr. Kipling, can you talk more about your background? Where you're from. How you got to where you are? Your influences. The main highlights and some of the obstacles, too. The painful stuff. They'll eat it up."

"I'll do what I can."

"Much appreciated."

As Aidan and Yuka walked to a deli near the Winter Garden Theater, she slipped her arm through his and said, "I know you don't like to talk about your past."

"Not so much."

They ate sandwiches, and Aidan sipped a second beer while they waited for the performance of West Side Story to let out. He had nearly nodded off when Yuka said, "Looks like people are leaving. Shall we go?"

"Give the cast time to pop the cork," Aidan said. He didn't like entering a dressing room full of half-naked, sweaty dancers when he hadn't been one of them on stage. It made him an outsider, more of one than he was in most situations.

Aidan glanced to the window where four people were paused

on the sidewalk. The tall woman was familiar, something in her gait. He knew her, but from where?

Oh, yes. It was the same quartet he saw at the hotel. *Woman with three men—two men and a boy.* He made a mental note for a piece. *Entrances and exits. Coming and going in ones, twos, threes, fours.*

Under the table, his foot slid on something. He bent and reached to pick it up. The napkin wasn't Yuka's. She didn't wear red lipstick, only pink.

He folded the napkin across the sandwich crusts on his plate. His body knew the language of this place and others like it where he'd worked odd jobs. Picking up napkins. Sweeping the floor. He imagined a dance of these rituals—bodies bending, swaying, and folding themselves across one another. The stage set would be a large checkerboard.

When Aidan and Yuka arrived at the stage door, some dancers were in the alley with their cigarettes, rehashing the performance. "A little late on that cue . . . nearly missed the lift."

Aidan and Yuka wandered into a crowded, noisy dressing room and found Jerry. "Good to see you, Aidan. Were you in the house?"

"Not tonight. Heard the reviews are good, though." At one time, Aidan would have seen anything Jerry choreographed, but he had grown wary. He wanted to be free of his mentor's influences, freer to experiment.

"And I've heard you've come into your own," Jerry said.

Aidan had never understood that expression. How could he come into something that was already his? If it were his own, he must have always been in it, but hadn't identified it. Did others see it first? He drank in Jerry's praise, while wishing he wasn't so thirsty for it, and raised his voice above the noise. "This is Yuka Hashimoto. A member of my company."

"Good to meet you," Jerry said, shaking her hand.

"An honor, Mr. Robbins."

"Call me Jerry. So you've pinned your star to this fellow?" He rested his hand on Aidan's shoulder. "One of my best." His gaze shifted to someone across the room.

Yuka glanced to Aidan, wondering if, indeed, she had pinned her star, but Jerry had turned away, replaced by another cast member whom Aidan seemed to know. She stood in the packed room with the music of praise and heat of bodies all around her. She loved this backstage dancers' world in the steamy aftermath of a show gone well, loved it as much or more than the rehearsals and performance. When she left Minneapolis five years ago to come to New York City and make her way as a dancer, she dreamed of this and now she was here. She reached for Aidan, who was talking to a cast member.

"If you can't laugh at your failures, what's the point of them?"

His comment surprised her. She hadn't heard him laugh much at all. He was usually so serious. She touched his coat sleeve, pinching the wool between her fingertips, ever so lightly. He shifted against her. She slipped her hand over his arm, as if to show other people in the room that she and Aidan were now together and that she would gladly pin herself to him.

They exited the theater onto the neon-lit street and walked in the black night with no stars to his darkened neighborhood. His leg ached and, by the time they arrived at his place, they were arguing. She wanted to tell the Kipling Dancers that she and Aidan were together. He wasn't ready.

Later, he lay awake in bed, remembering the conflict—their first real fight. He relived the making up, the softness of her skin, and her long, unbanded black hair falling across her bare shoulder blades in the moonlight. He relived the kissing and the letting go into her eyes.

He set the alarm and spooned against her as she slept,

breathing deeply of her fragrance. She was trying to break through to his heart and mind, but he didn't see how he could devote himself to her the way she wanted.

In seven hours they were due back at the hotel for the workshop where he had promised to talk about himself. What events of his life would matter to an audience of dance teachers? It had all started with losing his pa suddenly, his mama slowly, and leaving home. Then there was Mattie. Those few weeks in Kansas City and traveling out with her were shrouded in him. She had been a bright light, and then she vanished into a void that began with something percussive and ended with searing heat and pain. He had dragged himself away from the burning boxcar across an orchard to the back door of a farmhouse, where he pulled himself to standing and knocked. A woman opened the door and he fell in.

When he regained consciousness, the woman was washing his right leg. A bone protruded. "This will hurt," she said. As she wrested it in place, he blacked out. When he awoke, his leg was wrapped from hip to toes, and his hands, left foot, and throbbing head were bandaged. She was beside him with a cup. "Drink this for the pain."

The woman, he soon learned, was Mrs. Garcia, the wife of an apricot farmer. She knew the healing ways of her ancestors, who had lived in the Mojave for centuries. Luck of the draw.

Through her kindness and that of her husband, he fought off infections, and his leg healed enough to walk. The headaches eased, but the gap in his memory remained. The next summer, he climbed orchard ladders to pick the apricots, trucked them to market, helped with other farm chores, and attended high school in Barstow.

The physical education teacher befriended him and encouraged him to try dancing again. He learned to leap and land while ignoring the rope of scar tissue in his thigh and the pain.

Would he have worked so hard to become a dancer had he not been injured? His leg always ached, as it did now, lying beside Yuka.

He rose from the bed, careful not to disturb her, and went to the kitchen for a glass of water. Moonlight shone through the window. Should he tell the audience about entering the Civilian Conservation Corps? Mention that he had sent his monthly salary of twenty-five dollars to North Carolina for his mother's care until she was no longer alive to need it? Mention that he thought daily about trying to locate Mattie's family. Her father had trusted him.

From his bunk at the CCC camp, tonguing his teeth for the grit that never washed away, his body spent from digging a canal in the parched Wyoming soil, seeing the looming silhouette of Heart Mountain—a chunk of moonlit rock—he was better able to ask forgiveness.

He wrote to the Toft family in care of Leroy, guessing his address on Elmwood Avenue, and to the church on Gladstone. Had Mattie made it to Los Angeles? But he received no response. The shame and guilt of not seeing her to safety would have overwhelmed him if he had let it, so he didn't. He hadn't.

Should he mention that his crew didn't finish the canal? He didn't know while digging that he would be contributing to building an internment camp. The Japanese Americans finished the job of irrigating the land that they were then made to farm. He had never talked about it, not even to Yuka, although they shared this bond. They had lived at separate times in that place of cruel contrasts with a view to the hard, dark heart of a mountain. It was where, at last, he came to terms with his pa's death and his mama's confinement, and he grew stronger.

Perhaps he should mention only that he went to New York to study ballet shortly before the war broke out. He could tell the audience about performing at a USO club in a castle in France, celebrating with his buddies afterward, and being captured by Germans. One of his unlucky nights. He could tell about how they escaped—one of his lucky days.

He studied and danced with the best—Graham, Cunningham, Robbins. He landed a role on Broadway in *West Side Story*. He took his stage name and never looked back. Yuka knew him only as Aidan Kipling.

A sanitation truck groaned on the street beneath the kitchen window. In only a few hours, he and Yuka had to be back at the hotel for the workshop. He gulped the remaining water in the glass and returned to his bedroom. Yuka was sprawled across the sheet, unaware that he'd been born Aidan McKillip, and once called Kip Kelly.

He has tried to forget the dark history of McKillip, and often relived the moment when Mattie's father asked his surname that first day at the Bluebird, before he knew he would be staying on in Kansas City. His middle name, his mama's maiden name, came to his lips. *Kelly*. As days with the Tofts passed, it became more difficult to correct the lie of omission.

His stage name came easily. His mama had often read Rudyard Kipling's *Jungle Book* to him when he was small. She had nicknamed him Kip, her own little wild child, because he played for hours every day in the Appalachian woods behind their log house a mile from the mica mine. Aidan was his given name. At its Irish roots was the Celtic god of sun and fire— ready to blaze bright. Aidan wanted to do that, but he was skilled, as Yuka had said, at hiding within himself.

In the morning, he would try a new approach. He would give the audience a few highlights from his life and answer their questions, but would not talk about the pain or loss. He'd keep that close to feed the work ahead.

CHAPTER TWENTY-NINE

Anticipation

In the dark hotel room, the phone rang. Mattie groaned and buried her head under the pillow. "Ten more minutes."

"Oops. I forgot to cancel the wakeup call," Virginia said. "I've been up since six. I'm so excited for this workshop with that choreographer. I was going to let you sleep until the last minute."

"I'm awake now." Mattie removed the pillow.

"The choreographer said to wear comfortable clothes. We're going to be improvising with him and the dancers."

"I only brought nice things."

"You can borrow—"

The phone rang on the bed table, and Virginia answered. A look of shock crossed her face. "She's right here." She handed Mattie the receiver. "It's for you."

"Skinbones." Mickey's voice trembled. "Wiley called. Father had a heart attack."

"Is he—?"

"He's gone."

Mattie listened to Mickey sob, her own tears spilling. Moments passed, and Mickey spoke again, all business. "Eugene and Charlie are showering. My travel agent is making reservations for the next flight to Kansas City. My driver will pick you up in thirty minutes. I have to call Betty now."

Wiping her eyes, Mattie tried to fold her red dress into the suitcase. "Let me help you," Virginia said. "I'm so sorry, Mattie. He was a peach, your dad. A real gentleman."

"Yes he was. A truly gentle man. And always my moral compass."

As Mattie walked out the door, she said, "I'll stay past the funeral, spend a few days with Mother, and probably be back in California at the end of next week. Could you give me a report then about all that I will miss at the conference?"

"Will do," Virginia said. "I'll take notes."

Mattie, Eugene, and Charlie flew with Mickey to Kansas City, where Clara, Irene, and Wiley waited, along with Betty and her family. On a Midwestern autumn afternoon, the Tofts prepared for Elliot's funeral. They cried and comforted one another. They asked, "How would he want to be remembered?" In one of his notebooks, they found two lines of a poem to engrave on his headstone.

At the Forest Hill cemetery, the leaves had turned crimson and gold. Mattie stood beside her mother at the graveside. She could almost hear her father speaking the words they had chosen. She choked back tears as she read them.

I wonder what your life will be when mine has run. What may the future moments hold?

Each member of the Toft family said something, recounting a story of Elliot's, a joke, a memory of him. Eugene and Charlie contributed too. The spoken words were a mumble in her ears, and she cried. She could think only of how she must have disappointed her father terribly when she left home as a girl. He had never admonished her, and she had lived her life ever since, in great part, to gain his praise, as if that could make up for her leaving. He had said many times how proud he was of her, but now he was gone.

Afterward at the reception, she spoke to her siblings who were gathered in the kitchen. "I feel like I've lost forever the person who knew me before I knew myself, the person who helped me grow into myself."

"We still have Mother," Wiley said.

"Yes, luckily we do." Mattie understood then that she had always felt accepted by her mother unconditionally, but she'd needed to please her father.

Back in California, more than a week after Mattie had left New York, she sat in the SPARK office talking with Virginia over sandwiches. "The day we spent together in Manhattan seems long ago, doesn't it? So much has happened since then. I can't believe that tomorrow will be November already. How was the rest of the convention?"

"Quite inspiring," Virginia said. "I'll go over all the details of the sessions with you when my luggage is found." Her suitcase had been lost by the airlines, along with notes from the conference, including those about the choreographer whose workshop she attended the morning that Mattie departed.

The phone rang. While Virginia was enrolling a new student, Mattie took another call. The moment for reminiscing passed.

That evening, Mattie cleaned out her handbag and found the business cards from the convention. Her first call was to Dr. Bloomfield, who was delighted to hear from her. He explained his study on dance and aging and added her name to a list of participants.

In the next decade, she would engage in one study and then another, fitting the commitments in with her teaching schedule, becoming intrigued with his findings about movement and memory and curious to discover more. It would be a few years before anything was known about neurogenesis. People would continue to argue about the human brain, whether there was a sharp drop in the formation of neurons as it aged, or whether neurons persisted in developing well into older age.

It would be two decades before studies of the songs of canaries and finches showed that neurogenesis happened on a grand scale in the avian brain. It would be three decades before science accepted adult neurogenesis as a legitimate topic, and universities and granting organizations funded studies, such as the ones Mattie led.

At the moment she hung up on her conversation with Dr. Bloomfield, she didn't have any idea how much her life was about to change. She knew only that she tingled with anticipation.

CHAPTER THIRTY

Ever-Changing Times

After that October night at the backstage party, Yuka began staying often at Aidan's flat. She left a robe in the closet, underwear in the drawer, and Kotex in the bathroom. Soon no one doubted that they were living together, and she moved in the rest of her belongings. They danced at rehearsals during the day and made love at night, fought and made up, and danced. When she had missed two menstrual cycles, she didn't tell him, but telephoned a dancer friend who had an abortion the previous year. Yuka asked for the name of the doctor who had performed it.

On the morning of the appointment, a snowy day in January 1961, a baby bundled in a stroller on the sidewalk smiled at Yuka. She saw it as a sign—not only was abortion illegal and dangerous, she was thirty-one, already old for a dancer. How many more years would she have to bear a child?

That night, she told Aidan that she was going to have their baby. He held her and said, "I want to be a papa." They made love so tenderly that, by the end, they were wiping tears from each other's cheeks. In the years ahead, he would remember that the kissing with her was better than with anyone.

She danced with the company until the flinging and falling

on her rounded belly became dangerous for the baby, who was born in July of 1961 at seven pounds and named for her sweet pink lips, puckered like a rosebud, and for Aidan's mother, Rose.

The first time he held baby Rose, he believed he could give up everything for her, would give his life for her, and he was sincere, but a voice within warned that he had failed before at protecting the people he loved. Aidan and Yuka didn't marry, but they gave their daughter his surname.

On a day in August, when Rose Hashimoto Kipling was barely a month old, Yuka said, "My parents want us to come to Minnesota for a visit. They're sending money for the plane tickets."

Aidan shook his head. "I can't leave the company now—"

"It's only for a week—"

"Not even for a day. Too much is at stake with the autumn performances. You go with Rose. Tell them we'll come over the winter holidays."

At the cabin by the lake, as sailboats skimmed the water, Rose slept in a bassinet covered by mosquito netting. Red bumps blossomed on her cheeks. Yuka tried not to scratch at the welts on her own arms.

In mid-September, she returned to Manhattan for the season and took Rose along to watch the rehearsals and performances. Nestled against her mother in the warm theater, the baby cooed and slept.

In January of the new year, Yuka, eager to rejoin the company, wheeled Rose through the snow and slush to the studio every day. Sometimes, the child napped while the dancers twisted and leapt, fell and caught. Sometimes, Rose squirmed and cried.

On St. Patrick's Day, Aidan's forty-fifth birthday, he was at home in the morning with Yuka and nine-month-old Rose. They had a performance scheduled for that evening. Rose fussed from an ear infection and couldn't be pacified. Yuka stopped cleaning a desk drawer, leaving items in a heap on the floor, and went out to buy eardrops. Aidan tried everything he could think of to soothe his baby girl. He held her in his arms, walked around the flat, and made silly faces. He sat with her on a blanket and danced her fluffy toy—Miss Kitty—across it, making Rose laugh. He reached his arm to keep her penned on the blanket.

She had been slow to crawl but now was capable of scooting quickly around the apartment, putting every little thing she got her hands on into her mouth. The phone rang and Aidan answered, keeping his eye on her. She beelined to the heap in the corner and grabbed something.

"What the heck?" His shout startled the baby to tears. She sobbed and gulped air. He swooped to pick her up. "Little one, little one."

She held the silver bird peppershaker tight in her chubby hand. When he tried to pry it from her fingers, she screamed and wouldn't let go.

When Yuka returned, she put drops in the baby's ears, and Rose calmed. Falling asleep, Rose released the bird. Aidan placed it on the kitchen table, where in the months ahead he delighted her with it during meals or any time of day. He chirped and danced the bird across her plate and flew it over her head. She giggled and said, "Bir. Bir." It was her first word.

In July, Yuka packed the bird in her suitcase when she took Rose again to the cabin by the lake. As Yuka played with her daughter on the lawn sloping from the porch to the lake, she pictured her own childhood. She and her school friends had roamed the green backyards of Los Angeles until a frightening day in 1942, when her family was sent to an assembly center at the fairgrounds, and then to a relocation center on the desolate Wyoming plains below Heart Mountain. Barbed wire rimmed the windy camp, and guards in towers watched over it.

She lived with her family and people she didn't know in a crowded dormitory, enclosed by tarpaper-covered walls. Those first months, she wet her bed in the middle of the night rather than brave the walk to the latrine in the dark. They stayed there for three years in frigid winters and parched summers. Yet, when she played in the snow or dust with other children, she felt the affectionate gaze of her parents, aunt, uncle, and other adults. Her overwhelming memory of that time was that she had been loved.

In September, Yuka broke her ankle during rehearsal. Aidan held her hand in the emergency room as she sobbed. "I can't possibly go now." The company was leaving the next day on a four-month tour of Europe. She had planned to go and had arranged for her cousin to accompany them as a helper with Rose, but now they would only be a burden for the company. Aidan would have to pay the salary and expenses of a substitute to dance her part.

Staying in Manhattan without him and the others felt as desolate as Heart Mountain, but without the comfort of family. She packed her belongings along with Rose's clothes and toys— the rompers, Miss Kitty, and Bird—and flew to Minneapolis for Thanksgiving with her parents.

At their house, she took the kintsugi bowl from the mantle and held its broken beauty, choking back tears from missing her life as a dancer and missing Aidan. She stayed in Minneapolis through the Christmas holiday, into the New Year, waiting for his return. He called from Germany to say that the European tour had been extended through the next summer. Yuka was firm. "It makes no sense for Rose and I to live in New York without you. We'll stay in Minnesota while you're gone. I can teach a bit and keep in shape for next season."

Yuka felt certain that the love and security that her parents offered Rose was greater than she trusted herself to provide alone or with Aidan, even when he returned. Many nights, she stayed up late talking with her mother and father. "Is it me or him that's the problem? Am I trying hard enough?" They listened, wanting her to find happiness with Aidan and secretly hoping that she and Rose would stay in Minnesota.

In the living room one evening, Yuka held the kintsugi bowl and touched a resin-filled crack. "I was certain that I could have been his golden repair. Now I need him to be mine." Her parents exchanged glances.

"Might that be putting too much on him?" her mother said.

"He seems like a good man," her father said. "But can he be what you and Rose need him to be?"

"Maybe if I could dance with the company another year or two." Yuka's friends had said that her ambitions would return once Rose was older. In her heart, Yuka knew that she no longer had much interest in rehearsing and performing. Her only instincts were maternal.

After the Kipling Dancers returned to America, she brought Rose to New York for each performance season, birthdays, and some holidays. Aidan came three Augusts in a row to be with them by the lake. Then he skipped a year, and several more passed before he made the trip to Minnesota again. Her trips to New York with Rose dwindled to once annually and then more time passed between visits, until she and her daughter were not so much estranged from Aidan as disentangled.

Aidan loved Yuka, loved Rose, but his work was an elixir he had to drink daily. He thrived on the sore muscles, the sweat, and the freedom to explore movement with partners, in groups, and alone. He had other lovers, although no one he cared for as much as Yuka. He saw her and Rose more rarely and called less frequently. He didn't write letters.

In 1978, when Rose was eighteen and applied to colleges, she said to Yuka, "'Hoshimoto' would give me a more competitive edge than 'Kipling' in meeting some of the schools' diversity quotas."

"But he has a reputation, and that might also help," Yuka said.

"In dance, Mom, not in sculpture. Besides, I don't know him well at all." Rose dropped "Kipling."

Aidan limped, ached, and carried on. Grants flew in. Opportunities knocked for his company. Young dancers joined. Older ones retired. He traveled with the troupe to Canada and Mexico, Russia and Greece, Japan and Brazil. He choreographed a performance in a castle in Germany and in an ashram in India. They danced atop the Great Wall in China and in Egypt's ancient ruins.

When funding dried up during a tour of Australia, the dancers returned to the states, but Aidan stayed down under, taking a position as choreographer in Sydney and then Melbourne. He was invited to Thailand, Sweden, and South Africa. Time and again, dance sent him around the world.

Wealthy patrons, corporations, nonprofits, and governments paid him to do what he loved. When being interviewed for a grant, he said, "I'd do this for free, if I could." Afterward, he was sure his offhand statement had ruined his chances, but he received the funding.

Two decades passed. When he returned to New York, improvisation was mainstream and contemporary dance everywhere—on and off Broadway, at the Y along with aerobics and yoga, and in pop-music videos. Young dancers in the New York scene had heard his name, and older ones esteemed him. At seventy-five, he was asked to teach dance workshops at Jacob's Pillow in the Berkshires and at several colleges.

The next century arrived. The Internet defied fears of collapse from the Y2K computer bug. Terrorism escalated within America. New wars were declared on foreign soil. The song "I Hope You Dance" played on the radio.

And people danced.

NASA hired him to work with astronaut crews in weightless environments, improvising movements for use when confined in capsules and walking in space. He traveled to festivals around the globe to speak about the history of modern dance. Film studios called him to coach actors portraying astronauts living on space stations. Organizations dedicated to prison reform invited him to improvise with the incarcerated.

And people danced.

In the autumn of 2019, now a centenarian plus two, he was eighty years older than most people in a North Carolina audience comprised of students from graduate arts programs across the United States. He walked out onto the stage and spoke about the evolution of dance from clogging to tap, tap to ballet, ballet to modern, contemporary, and improvisation. Many people were looking at their phones.

"Before I go, I leave you with the one directive that has served me well. Release your fears." He stepped away from the podium and did a shuffle and hop. The audience clapped. He did a bell kick, leaping as high as he could. *Bing. Clack-k-k.* They gasped as he tumbled. He regained his balance, lifted higher, and landed surely. They cheered. He bowed, aware that after all he had done and been, he could still leap inches off the ground without breaking a bone.

Afterward, a professor approached him. "When I was a dancer in San Francisco ten years ago, I participated in a research study on aging. It involved movement and the benefits for cognition. It was a life-changer. I say to my students that dance is not a class they take nor steps they learn. It's a way through life. You've shown them this, Mr. Kipling. Thank you for sharing your journey."

"I'd be interested in seeing the findings of the study," Aidan said. "When people ask me about how I keep going in body and mind, I say that the habit of standing on the right foot and then the left foot each morning to put on my socks and moving all day long on most days means I haven't yet stopped being able to do it."

Lately, he sometimes forgot why he had come into one room of his apartment from the other. He found that when he paid attention in the moment to one task at hand, not to several, and when he was conscious of his movements, he more easily remembered what he came to do.

"The research was led by a Dr. Turner, as I recall," the professor said. "You might google it when you have a chance."

"Thank you. I will." Aidan put hand to heart and made a mental note. *Movement and memory. Turner.* He didn't have a pen.

While in North Carolina, Aidan visited his parents' graves. His hometown had become a tourist stop on the way to national parks and a haven for river-rafting guides. At a curio shop, he palmed a hunk of mica. Glittering crumbs of it could be found in everything from plastics and concrete to the paint on his hotel room walls and the lipstick that the last woman he'd been with had left on his medicine cabinet shelf.

He turned the mica in his hand to catch the light. Decades ago, his pa had died in pursuit of this mineral that the world couldn't do without. At forty, Magnus McKillip, whose given name meant "great" and who named his son to blaze bright, tunneled into a dark hole to follow a streak of glimmer. What was his sacrifice worth, Aidan wondered. What was the value of any man's life beyond his time on earth?

PART SIX

CHAPTER THIRTY-ONE

Kinfolk

On Wednesday when Mattie visits Sonata Court, Wiley is strapped to a chair in front of the television. Bold letters—*GLOBAL PANDEMIC*—fill the TV screen. The words dissolve and a doctor stands beside a sink, talking about preventing the spread of the virus. The camera zooms in on his hands. He washes with soap and water, counting to twenty. He cautions against handshaking, hugging, and touching your own face. The image changes to the president, who is saying, "It's going away. We want it to go away with very, very few deaths."

Numbers scroll beneath the newscaster as he resumes the coverage.

U.S. Cases 1,271. Deaths 38. Global cases 118,319. Deaths 4,000.

Wiley darts his gaze around the room with a look of panic and tries to stand. As Mattie unstraps him, an aide rushes over. "Let me get this first." The man takes Wiley's blood oxygen and temperature.

"The news is distressing," Mattie says. "May I turn off the TV?"

"It gives them something to do," the aide says. "I can't keep an eye on everyone."

Mattie wants to say that Wiley needs to be active, not sit in a chair all day staring at a screen, but no other aide is in the room and this one has his hands full.

She kisses Wiley's forehead. "Good morning."

He looks past her to the doorway, as if expecting someone else. "Dancing boy?"

"You remember Kip. He was kind to you, as you have always been to others."

Mattie leads him to a chair at a table and deals. Wiley holds his cards in his shaking hands. He seems unaware of her, and she wonders if they should stop the game, but Wiley slaps down his cards. "Gin." He counts Mattie's and writes the score on a notepad. He has trouble holding a pen.

"You've always been good with numbers, dear brother."

Behind him, *PANDEMIC* flashes on the screen. The U.S. death toll advances by seven, the cases of infection by hundreds.

Later that afternoon, back at Wiley's house, Mattie waits for Genet to return from errands. She unties a bundle of letters and finds ones she wrote during those first years in California, when every day she thought of returning to Kansas City, and her family members still lived in other people's houses. *I could stay with Mrs. Nelson. I'm mad at Mr. Nelson, but it would be okay.* Eugene's parents had written too, although she didn't know it at the time. *Mattie is welcome here indefinitely. She is having wonderful opportunities.*

She told her parents that she was happy, and it was true. Of all the things she learned as a girl that shaped her life, the most important may have been that two things can be true at once. She was happy taking the dance lessons, performing, and having Eugene as her substitute brother. She was unhappy being far from home and missing her family more than she could say. She wanted to be a good sport and to make them proud. After a day of dancing, she played with Eugene in the pool. Before she fell sleep, she prayed to go home.

Among her mother's scraps, Mattie looks for words that might comfort and finds a poem of her father's. She knows it by heart and speaks the last line softly. "Yet some day may befall just a little touch of sorrow, making kinfolk of us all."

He wrote it when the roving men began coming to their door, asking for food or to work in exchange for a meal. She recited it to the ones who sat on the porch and shared the bounty her mother offered. In winter, the thin broth was seasoned with a bone that had already given up most of its marrow to a previous pot. In summer, the garden grew along with their belief that things couldn't get worse. And then winter came again.

"That's how it goes," Mattie says aloud to her parents' ghosts. "We may be heading into a difficult time, perhaps as bad as the 1918 influenza. This new disease is now on our doorsteps. Will sorrow touch us all?"

She tries calming her mind with thoughts of home and family, past and present, but the questions trespass. Will this new pandemic draw people closer together or further apart? Does it matter who knew about it first? Who spread it? Already, people are blaming countries and individuals, and distrust abounds.

She wonders how everyone at work is faring. They are probably managing fine without her, but she is not doing as well without them. If she moves here, what will happen to her? The work keeps her going. Her identity is indistinguishable from it. She stands to find her phone to call a colleague and the front door opens. Genet enters carrying a garment bag.

"Gram, you've got to see this." She lifts out a wedding dress and holds it against herself. White lace shapes the long sleeves.

The bodice narrows to a low waist, and the skirt spills to the floor. Across the satin, lace roses bloom. At the center of each, fine thread holds a tiny pearl. "Isn't it beautiful?"

"You will be a stunning bride." This, Mattie thinks, is why humans have children. Without them, many meaningful rituals would disappear and celebrations cease. Children make history, become the keepers of it, and pass it to next generations. She and Wiley are the remaining keepers of the family history who have also lived it, and now only she remembers. She wonders what Genet will do with all that she's been told.

"Oh, no." Genet reads a text on her phone. "Ravi's relatives in India have cancelled their reservations. They're afraid if they leave the country, they won't be able to get back in."

"It's wise to be cautious."

"But the wedding will still be great. Won't it? Everyone else will still come?"

"I'm sure it will be wonderful."

"Even if there's no hugging? No touching?"

"Even then."

"Ravi's grandfather is flying in tomorrow. I can't wait to meet him." Genet checks the time. "Yikes. Gotta get ready. The game starts at six, and Ravi likes to arrive early. Will you be okay here alone, Gram? We tried to get an extra ticket but—"

"I'll be fine. You go on with Ravi and have a good time."

At the Sprint Center downtown, thousands of people are waiting outside to be let into the basketball arena for the Big Twelve tournament. "What's the hold up, I wonder?" Ravi says. "It was supposed to open at four-thirty."

When they're finally let in, a row of tables blocks the way. Told to sanitize their hands, Genet and Ravi squirt gel onto their palms and rub it between their fingers.

"This stuff is gross. It makes my skin dry." Genet wipes it on her jeans, takes a tube of hand cream from her purse, and offers some to Ravi before lathering it on herself.

In their seats, waiting for the game to start, they scan the program. An ad for T-Mobile fills a page. Genet is not sure how it all works, but Ravi said that the deal with Sprint is worth billions, and his father owns stock. She scans a paragraph about Sprint's origins. *Abilene 1899 . . . small telephone company . . . built a legacy . . . home for the aged . . . Great Depression . . . bankrupt.*

A footnote about the founder stops her. As a ten-year-old boy, he injured his arm in his father's gristmill, and it had to be amputated. He wore an artificial limb and decided he would succeed in life by using his head instead of his hands.

Genet flashes on some of the crazy things she did as a teen. Hitchhiking one night, she took a lift from a truck driver. They hadn't traveled far when he pulled off to a side road and shoved his hand between her legs as he slowed. Before the truck stopped, she jumped from the cab and ran. A voice within says now, "I could have lost a limb or died. But here I am. What am I to do with my life?" One day, when she's gone from this earth, what will she leave behind? Not a building or a business, but maybe a book? A trace of other lives and times, or of her own.

She closes the pamphlet. "Everyone's getting 5G. Are they going to rename this place for T-Mobile?"

"Once the merger is finalized, so my dad says."

Ravi's father has already departed Sprint with a retirement package, and his patents in voice-recognition technology provide additional income. His new ventures in recognizing speech patterns for communicating across spoken languages have potential in the voice-commerce market to make the family wealthy beyond Ravi's imagining.

Ravi doesn't understand the aspects of artificial intelligence and machine learning that his father is involved with well enough to explain it to Genet. He has only and always been interested in the natural world. Insects are his first love, fireflies his passion. There's nothing artificial about them and so much to learn from them.

A noisy crowd fills the arena. People laugh and bump elbows. Tonight's game is Oklahoma State versus Iowa. Genet and Ravi will cheer for Iowa; tomorrow, they'll cheer for Kansas.

A voice comes over the loudspeaker. Ravi and Genet strain to hear. "Tonight's games will be played . . . precautionary measure . . . no fans . . . allowed to attend . . . remaining games."

"No fans?" Genet says. She had bought the tickets for tonight and tomorrow as a gift for Ravi. "Can we get the money back?"

"I'm trying to wrap my head around the magnitude of this thing. Did you hear that guy behind me talking about a travel ban—?"

"It feels like a scary movie. Did you ever see *Contagion*?"

"Do you want to go home and stream it?"

"I need sleep, Ravi."

When Genet returns, Mattie is waiting up. "I was worried you'd be upset if you'd heard the news."

"Ravi's London cousins can't come. I'm going to bed."

Upstairs in her room, Genet unzips the dress bag that she had earlier draped over the chair. She caresses the lace roses and pearls. Tears well up. She lays the dress across the bed and curls up under the comforter, crying. She hears music coming from the guest room. Mattie is dancing.

Dreaming of her wedding on Sunday, Genet drifts to the thrum of the song. It's the one she used to move to on the days she cut class and came home to an empty house, while her parents were at work. She would spill her troubled thoughts into spiral notebooks and drink whiskey hidden in her bedroom closet. She would scrawl dense lines of free verse and autobiography thinly disguised as stories. She would play her parents' old *One World* LP, stomping and swirling to "I Just Want to Celebrate." Sometimes she drank until she passed out. Amoy and Charles had worried that she was suicidal and sent her to a therapist. They never understood how difficult it was for her.

Without the whiskey, she couldn't see her way to a tomorrow. It wasn't that she wanted to die and leave this earth and everything she loved, it was that each day demanded greater effort than she could summon.

The song stops, and stillness descends on the house. Genet wipes her eyes with the edge of the sheet. She believes that she can now see tomorrow, which will be Thursday, followed by Friday, Saturday, and Sunday—her wedding day. Then her new life with Ravi will begin, and with his daughter too—people to take care of other than herself. She's beginning to make sense of it all. In the recovery group, and in the treatment programs she attended, they talk about making amends. She knows her list by heart. Can she now act upon it?

Moonlight shines through the window. The pearls on the dress glow. She touches them. What had Mattie said? We have what was, what is yet to be, and this moment—right now—and it slips away. On her bedside table, the red numbers on the digital clock read 11:59 p.m. The numbers change. It's midnight—now 12:01 a.m. The one becomes two, three, now four. She counts the hours until Sunday. What else can possibly happen in that time? What if no one from out of town is able to travel? She tells herself that she'll be able to cope if everything else goes according to plan.

CHAPTER THIRTY-TWO

Confidence

Thursday morning, Amoy calls Mattie. "They cancelled the genetics conference late yesterday. We thought we'd leave today, but Charles has a slight fever, so we'll stay put in the hotel for now. He should be well enough to travel by Saturday afternoon. I'll try to book a flight to arrive in time for the dinner. The corporate jet is no longer an option. Keep your eyes on the news. Things are changing by the hour."

Genet opens her laptop on the kitchen table. "Oh, wow. Listen to this. The mayor of Kansas City has declared a state of emergency, canceling all events involving a thousand or more. It's a good thing we're only three hundred and two. Well, two hundred and ninety-four now, without India and England."

Across the country, things are shutting down. In New York City, events with over five hundred people are cancelled and Broadway closes. In California, the caps on gatherings are smaller—two-fifty, one hundred, or fifty, depending on the county. Genet receives a text to call Ruth at Sonata. She puts it on speaker so Mattie can hear. "No classes the rest of this week and no visitors," Ruth says.

"We can't get in to see Wiley?"

"No visitors in or out. Residents can't leave or gather together. That means there's no mixer today."

"Bummer. I wanted Mattie to meet the CIA dancing man. Keep us posted, Ruth."

Genet refills her cup, sips, and peers over the rim. "Oh, well, Gram. There will be plenty of time to get acquainted after you move in." She jumps up and tips her coffee into the sink. "I'm over-amped. Really stressed out. This is too scary. I don't even want to go anywhere. Let's just stay here and talk. Tell me more about your times."

"I thought it might be best to focus on the present over the next few days—focus on you."

"But I need to take my mind off the wedding problems." Genet wanders into the living room.

Mattie's thoughts are seesawing. To move here or stay put in her life? To be near Wiley, or accept that she long ago missed her chance to be close to her younger brother? To believe life is full of possibilities or downsize those, along with her home, activities, and possessions? She is used to asking questions, designing productive studies, and reporting findings, but she has lost confidence in her ability to make a decision. She goes into the living room and sits on the couch.

"I could use a diversion too, Genet. Would you like to hear about when I performed with the USO during the war? I had just married your grandfather before he shipped out."

Genet slumps in the easy chair. "Talk to me."

A mile away in a red-brick, white-columned house on Ward Parkway Boulevard, Ravi's mother is on her mobile phone in the study, where her husband is watching cable news from his recliner chair. Anik says, "The Dow is falling to what could be one of the worst percentage drops in history."

A video clip shows the president saying, "It's going to all bounce back, and it's going to bounce back very big—"

Anik shouts, "I'm for optimism, but whatever this thing is, we need the truth, not a campaign speech." A soft-spoken, measured man on most topics, Anik can become easily riled by the president. "He's blamed the Chinese and the media. He said the number of cases would go down close to zero, and now he's banning travel—"

"Shhh, I'm on hold with the museum." Ravi's mother, who is their curator of Asian Art, has taken this week off to prepare for the wedding. She circulates the room, holding the phone against her ear with one hand, feather duster in the other. Her cleaning team came earlier in the week; she's touching up.

Anik lowers his voice. "He says not to shake hands and then he's shaking hands."

She passes behind her husband, noticing how his hair has thinned to reveal a spot of scalp, marveling how fortunate she has been. The fellowship she won to study in Bombay led her to meet Anik Kumar, the love of her life, who had been born there, emigrated to the United States with his parents when he was ten, and happened to be back in India visiting his grandparents the summer of her fellowship. A year later, she married him. They both are now sixty.

She would be content with Anik wherever they lived, but this house provides pleasure unlike any other she's known. It's a grand home with six bedrooms. All the rooms are spacious, the ceilings high. The heating bill alone is far more than they paid in rent for their first apartment, where they lived while she was in graduate school at Stanford and working part-time as a waitress. Anik flipped pizzas by day.

At night in the spare room, with his computer glowing green and papers strewn across his desk, he played with ideas to replace dynamic time warping in speech recognition. He calculated algorithms and practiced speaking vowel sounds with varying emotions. One of his discoveries was the basis for his first start-up in the cellular industry.

When they bought this house in Kansas City in 2000, the stock market was on the rise. When it bottomed out in 2008, they were heavily in debt. She thought they should sell and get out from under the mortgage. Anik was convinced that the value would return, and he was right. If Anik and she had their wish, Ravi and Genet would move in after the wedding, but Ravi has said, "We need our own space. We'll stay at Wiley's house."

She doesn't understand why people want to live far-flung. Growing up, she lived with her mother and grandparents in a small house in Minneapolis. In the summers they went to their cabin by the lake. She was rarely alone in those summer months when relatives came to stay. At meals, they crowded the dinner table and carried plates to the mosquito-infested lawn. The cousins fought over who would sleep in the top bunks in the bedroom. She wants always to be surrounded by people she loves.

When her own children were young, the thought that they would one day leave home filled her with a mix of sadness in imagining their absence and happiness in seeing their independence. She has read articles about couples renewing their relationship or divorcing once their children were grown. Anik and she lamented their empty nest and had begun to accept it when the nest began filling again. They were alone for only two years before Ravi returned—divorced and with a young daughter.

His twin sisters, Dahlia and Daisy, have also returned home to live. This week they are on vacation but are expected back tomorrow. Dahlia left college without a degree, but with a following as a fashion influencer on her Instagram. She posts designs that she has created with clothes repurposed from thrift shops. Daisy, who had moved back home to complete her nursing degree, is newly licensed as an RN and will start a job at a local hospital in two weeks. The sisters will return from vacation tomorrow in time for the wedding.

The museum event planner comes on the line. "Mrs. Kumar? I spoke to the caterer. We're making adjustments due to the virus. No family-style platters, finger food, or dips. Servings will be set out on individual plates, paper cups, or cones."

"That sounds—sensible. I guess no one really knows the right thing to do. And the beverages?"

"The waiters will wear latex gloves and serve drinks from trays. Guests will not be allowed to stand around the bar.

"People will understand, won't they? It's good to be cautious."

"We're playing it by ear, Mrs. Kumar. We've never confronted a problem like this. I'll email the menu to you."

Ravi's mother slips the phone into her apron pocket and continues dusting. As she passes by Anik, she bends to kiss him. He looks up for a quick peck and returns his attention to the news.

She steps into the living room with her housekeeping carryall of cloths and lemon sprays. She feels embraced by this welcoming space where they've hosted one hundred guests or more in nice weather with the French doors opened onto the patio and swimming pool beyond. She dusts the end tables, checks the water level in the vases of flowers, straightens a short stack of books on the Japanese red lacquered bench that serves as a coffee table, and plumps pillows on the sofa, exciting Miss Paws, their Himalayan Persian, to stretch, fluff her white fur, and curl up again on the cushion.

Everything in the room has been chosen for comfort and beauty. The hardwood floors gleam. A lit wall of glass shelves displays art objects she has collected over the years. Some have significant value, as specified on their homeowner's insurance policy. Some are mementos, priceless only to her.

She touches a silver sugar bowl found at an antique shop downtown and admires the craftsmanship. Silver twigs soldered together form a nest. A silver twig serves as a handle on the lid. She marvels at how well it goes with the little silver bird with the holes in its head, her first toy, the only keepsake she has of her dad. She was three or four years old before she understood that it was a peppershaker. With her fingers, she lifts a translucent cat hair that has landed on the bird's tail.

Again, she is grateful. Had it not been for her son's obsession with fireflies, she might never have seen her dad again. The estrangement had not been intentional on anyone's part at first, but it became so. When Ravi was born, she began questioning how her dad could have chosen his career over being with her and her mother, and why he had chosen to visit them so seldom. She saw him as selfish and told him she wanted no more contact. Nearly three decades passed—Ravi's whole life.

Then, last summer, Ravi showed her the YouTube video of a dance called "Synchronicity" and the interview clip with the choreographer, a centenarian. She located her dad in Connecticut. He wasn't difficult to find. Occasionally, she had googled him to know if he were still alive. She isn't sure she is ready to see him now, but she doesn't want to deprive Ravi the chance to know his grandfather.

On the glass shelves, next to the silver bird, sits her mother's celery-green kintsugi bowl. It is lit by a track light in the ceiling and is glowing. She runs her finger along the golden veins and thinks of how her mother held their life together without her dad. Perhaps, wherever Yuka is in the spirit world, she has forgiven him by now and found peace.

Anik calls it samskara—a psychological imprint. "A deep imprint in your mind from your dad's abandonment has diminished your sense of self and formed hidden expectations. You surround yourself with beautiful objects to elevate your self-worth." He said this to her not as a criticism or judgment, but as an observation with love. "I see the suffering in you as the energy that drives you. To me you are perfect in every way."

Anik is not a psychologist, but an inventor and a deeply spiritual man who lived one summer in an ashram, watches a guru that he finds inspiring on YouTube, and meditates twice a day. He has an innate understanding of how people communicate or don't, of what they intend to say and miss saying.

"Rose? Rose?" Anik calls now from the study. "Can you come? You have to see this to believe it." His laugh, in a register higher than his voice, never fails to delight her. As she goes to him, the pendulum clock chimes, and she wonders if the flight has arrived. When Ravi dashed out earlier, he hadn't much time to spare.

At the airport, Ravi is running late to meet his grandfather's flight. He checks the monitor for arrivals from White Plains and finds the gate. They haven't met, but Ravi has spoken to him on the phone and googled all he can find about him. The photos posted online are from a decade ago or more, but the video clip about "Synchronicity" is recent. Ravi is sure he'll recognize him. His grandfather said on the phone yesterday, "Look for a centenarian with a limp."

Passengers have begun funneling from the jetway through the gate. There's a white-haired man walking stiffly and a gray-haired man with a cane, but their faces don't resemble the photos he's seen. More people deplane—families, singles, couples—and then there he is. He has white hair and is limping, yes, but with grace. When he spots Ravi, he places hand on heart and comes toward him.

"Ravi," he says. "My grandson."

"Good to finally meet you." Unsure about shaking hands with a man who has just deplaned, Ravi extends his elbow for a bump.

As they walk in the direction of the baggage carousel, Ravi leads by a few strides. Aidan notices his grandson's gait, similar to his own, but without the limp. It's in the hips, the length of the thighbone, the long narrow feet, and in the shoulders—those wide flattened scapulae—and erect spine. This young man carries his genes, all that Aidan has ever given him.

Up ahead, a cluster of people stare at an overhead TV monitor. The Dow has fallen again more than 2000 points. Aidan has no investments in the stock market and doesn't track these things, but he understands the significance. It is a trust exercise, like he always rehearses with his dancers when preparing for a performance. A loss of confidence is contagious and can infect the whole group.

CHAPTER THIRTY-THREE

Cadence

On Friday, many businesses and buildings close, including the art museum. Rose phones Genet to tell her.

"Now what? My stomach is in knots." Genet has been watching news all morning.

"We'll find another venue. Perhaps the Saffron. I'll talk with Anik's cousin about hosting the wedding there." The cousin owns the Indian restaurant where they are planning to hold the rehearsal dinner Saturday night. "We'll work this out. Don't worry. How is your dad doing?"

"Amoy called from the hotel. He isn't well enough to fly today and may not be by tomorrow. And my maid of honor from Florida has a fever and cough. She flew out of White Plains two weeks ago, and now an outbreak is reported in that area." Genet sees new statistics scrolling beneath the anchorperson talking on screen. "Six cases in Connecticut."

"She isn't still planning to come, is she?"

"If she feels better by tomorrow morning, she will. It might be a twenty-four-hour thing. Anyway, people my age don't get the coronavirus. Only older people."

"I'm not sure about that—"

"She does triathlons and everything. She's never sick, so—"

"Then may she be better soon. I'll let you know what I find out about having the wedding at the restaurant. Talk with you later."

As Rose ends the call, the small monitor on her kitchen counter shows the president speaking. "I am officially declaring a national emergency—two very big words." The screen image changes to a life insurance commercial.

At the refrigerator door, Rose fills a glass with water and ice and observes Ravi and Aidan at the table, where they lingered over breakfast so long it became lunch. Now it's midafternoon. They are talking about Aidan's firefly dance, which she has watched many times on YouTube. The dancers, wearing black, are at first barely discernable on the dark stage. Little lights blink slowly here and there, and then more lights slowly contour the dancers' bodies. The dancers swoop and swirl, trailing glowing arcs across the stage. The blinking becomes synchronized into a tour de force of movement and light. Then gradually, it dissipates, and the dancers vanish into the dark.

"The little LED lamps they're wearing were programmed to flash at varying speeds and then to sync up and diminish." Aidan pulls out a chair for Rose. "Join us?"

"What inspired you?" she asks.

"Memories of the fireflies in North Carolina when I was a boy. I've had that dance in me my whole life."

"It reminded me of watching the lightning bugs by the lake in Minnesota. Do you remember visiting us there?"

"Yes. I do." Aidan is careful with Rose, letting her lead the way into the past, where the hurt is deep. He had visited Yuka and her in Minnesota only a handful of times. "I have that memory in me too, of course. The fireflies revolving over the lake, their moving reflections mirrored on the water's dark surface. I have good memories of being by the lake with you and your mother, other than the time you had a serious infection from a mosquito bite. You were miserable."

"I remember my mother talking about that summer. I was probably two?"

"That's about right."

"Do you still have a company of dancers?"

"Not for many years, since I began teaching at the Hartt School. I hire them under contract for performances, which have become fewer, but with a bump of activity for 'Synchronicity.'"

"Genet loves the fireflies here in Kansas City," Ravi says. "They aren't common in California where she grew up."

"Tell me about her, Ravi. How did you two meet?"

"Her great-uncle Wiley had been my professor. She was there when I visited him last Thanksgiving, and one thing led to another." Ravi grins.

"I once knew a boy here named Wiley. Wiley Toft." Aidan pauses, picturing the five-year-old he knew back then. "He'd be in his nineties now."

"That's him. How did you—?"

"When I was young, passing through Kansas City, I stayed with his family."

"You did?"

"He had a sister named Mattie."

"That's Genet's grandmother." Ravi says. "She's here for the wedding."

"Mattie's here? Where?" Aidan turns toward the doorway, wondering how this could be possible. Is she in this big house somewhere?

"We're back." Two sunburned women enter the kitchen. One wears a halter pantsuit with flowing bell-bottoms, the other a t-shirt with sequined letters proclaiming "Life Is Good."

"My darling daughters. I was afraid your flight might be cancelled." Rose gives them both a hug as her phone sounds with a text. "Oh, I need to respond to this."

"These are my sisters—Dahlia and Daisy," Ravi says. "This is Aidan. Our grandfather."

"Hello," they chorus.

"Good to meet you both." Aidan smiles, hand to heart. "And Mattie? Is she here?"

"She's with Genet at Wiley's—" Ravi taps his phone photos. "I met her Tuesday night. Have a look." He shows Aidan the photo he took of Genet and Mattie.

"That's her?" Aidan seeks something familiar in the face of the white-haired woman. Ravi scrolls through more photos.

There, Aidan thinks, and says, "Something in the smile of that one. That could be the Mattie I knew."

Dahlia and Daisy peek at the photos and then settle at the table with cups of coffee and sandwiches. "Did you have a good time, girls?" Rose asks.

"Yeah, it was fun, but things are getting weird," Dahlia says. "The plane smelled of hand sanitizer, and people were kind of freaking out. I mean, I don't know, it's weird out there."

"My start date's been moved to Monday," Daisy says. "The hospital has a surge of people coming in who are worried about the virus. So they're staffing up."

"It's reassuring to have you home," Rose says.

"Aidan, how did you know Mattie and Wiley's family?" Ravi asks.

"I boarded with them and worked in their restaurant. The Bluebird Buffet."

Ravi blinks. It sounds familiar—the lettering on the window in the photograph. "You're Kip?"

Aidan nods. "Though no one has called me that for a long time."

"I've got to tell Genet. She'll flip out." Ravi taps his phone.

"Wait," Rose says. "This weekend is turning out to be a letdown for her. What if we surprise her and Mattie with this tomorrow at the rehearsal dinner?"

"It could be too much of a surprise," Aidan says. "I haven't seen Mattie since 1932."

"You lost touch?" Rose asks.

"Yes." He has a vivid sensation of dancing with Mattie, coming together and spinning away. They are trading fours with perfect timing, and he's happy to be with her.

"No contact at all? For eighty-eight years?"

Aidan nods. "My fault."

"Apparently, that can happen." Rose doesn't intend it to sound sarcastic, but she realizes that it does, more than a bit.

Aidan searches her face and sees the injury he has inflicted upon his daughter. "I apologize for hurting you and Yuka."

He has said it to Rose on the phone and in emails, but it helps him to say it again. "I am grateful that you reached out to me."

"I am too. Truly. I wish I had sooner. We lost many years we could have been together."

"Now we are." Aidan drinks in this moment here in the kitchen with his daughter, grandson, and granddaughters. He feels the weight of the shame that he has carried for so long becoming lighter. "And Mattie? Is she well?"

"I haven't met her yet," Rose says.

"She's great," Ravi says. "For someone who is almost one hundred, she's amazing." Ravi pauses and looks at Aidan. "I mean—you are amazing, too."

"For someone who is almost one hundred and three?"

"You're a supercentenarian."

"Not quite. Maybe at a hundred and ten? I'm not sure what it takes these days. But seriously, would a surprise be too much? When I knew her, she liked to plan, anticipate—"

"Genet does too. Let's bring her in on it," Ravi says. "She's really into Mattie's past."

"Could she keep it a secret until tomorrow night?" Rose asks.

"Probably not. I'll call her tomorrow afternoon so there will be less time for her to slip up. I'm not going to see her tonight. We're having dinner with Aidan and the family, right?"

"We're home!" Anik calls from the hallway.

"Nanna. Daddy." Cadence runs into the kitchen and throws her backpack on the floor. When she sees Aidan, she stops. "Who's that?"

"He is *your* great-grandfather, and he's *my* grandfather," Ravi says. "And he's Nanna's dad."

Cadence puzzles her face at Rose. "He's your—*dad*?"

"Yes. But I haven't seen him for a long, long time."

Cadence walks around the table and regards Aidan. "Is that why you're so old?"

He laughs. "It is."

"I'm five." She holds up her fingers. "Do you want to come watch my butterfly dance?"

Aidan smiles. "Yes, I would." He looks past Cadence to Rose.

Rose shakes her head. "It's her lyrical dance class. The recital was supposed to be tonight. That was her teacher texting. I'm sorry, Cadence. They are postponing it."

Cadence twirls. "What does it mean—post pony?"

"They will have it another day soon, in the future, when we don't have to worry about people getting sick."

"Oh." She twirls again and hops next to Aidan. "Do you want to watch *Dancing with the Stars*? Can we, Nanna?"

"If Aidan—if your great-grandfather wants to."

"I do." Surrounded by more activity than he's seen in a kitchen in a long time, Aidan thinks he does want to watch the show with Cadence and participate in whatever else this family has planned. He was going to leave Monday after the wedding, but if they will have him, he'd like to extend his stay.

CHAPTER THIRTY-FOUR

Gifts

Saturday morning Genet is in tears. "They aren't coming?"

"Charles has a high fever." Mattie speaks calmly, but she is frightened. Amoy called to say that she drove Charles to the emergency room at midnight because he couldn't stop coughing. The hospital wouldn't allow visitors, and Amoy was back at the hotel, waiting to hear. "She says not to worry and to have a good time tonight and tomorrow. They are so sorry to miss it."

"They didn't want me to marry Ravi anyway."

"This isn't intentional. I'm sure you realize—"

"It's just that I thought this would make everything better for us—being together and all."

"Genet—"

"I know. Don't say it. I hope he's okay, but nothing is turning out like we planned." Genet wipes her eyes and sniffles. "I wanted it all to be perfect."

Mattie hands her a tissue and reviews the situation as it stands this morning. The guest list for tonight's dinner has shrunk by half. All the people from out of town who haven't already arrived have cancelled. Guests who live locally have called with concerns about the risks of gathering. The band that was booked for the wedding reception is stuck on a cruise ship in quarantine with the passengers.

"We can use my playlist," Genet says. "And I better get some hand sanitizer for the dinner tonight."

"And no matter who comes this evening, it will be wonderful even if only a small group," Mattie says. "Your marriage isn't dependent upon tonight. You will have countless celebrations together."

"Not if the world falls apart."

"It's not going to fall apart—"

"You don't know that."

"But if it does, or until it does, Genet, we'll make the best of things."

Amoy has promised to call with any developments. The news reports twenty-eight hundred cases of the virus in the United States and sixty deaths. Back in California, things are shutting down. People are staying home. She calms herself with the thought that it is more likely Charles would die of heart disease than a virus and immediately feels concerned about his heart, wondering if he has been taking his statins, as forgetful as he can be about things like that. Surely, Amoy is on top of it. She certainly would have informed the hospital.

"I wish Uncle Wiley could be there tonight, Gram."

"I do too. But the dinner will last beyond his bedtime, even if he could come out."

Genet drives to stores looking for sanitizer, but finds the shelves empty. On return, Mattie and she make a batch with rubbing alcohol and gel from the aloe plant on the table.

Mattie changes into a black silk dress with red, blue, and green polka dots and enters the kitchen where Genet, wearing only a bra and panties, is ironing her red dress. Genet's cell phone rings and she picks up. "Hi, Ravi. What? You're not coming here first? What? Yes. A surprise? Okay, okay, wait while I—" Genet takes the phone upstairs to her room.

Mattie wonders what the surprise will be and remembers her gift for Genet. The silver bird saltshaker is still in her travel bag. She had intended to wrap it for the wedding tomorrow. She'll have time to take care of it in the morning.

In a few minutes, Genet returns to the kitchen for her dress. Her skin and hair shine. She struggles with the zipper. "Can you finish the zip, Gram? We've got to go."

Genet drives erratically, turning the wrong way down a one-way street. Mattie grips the door handle. "Are you alright?"

"Just excited, I guess." Genet swerves to miss an oncoming car. "Oops, sorry. It's a good thing there's not much traffic."

Mattie is excited, too, anticipating meeting Ravi's family and something else. In this instant, riding down the dark street next to Genet, Mattie senses something unexpected around the next curve of her life. She doesn't want to leave Wiley, so why can't she see herself at Sonata Court?

"We're almost there." Genet reaches the Plaza and parks at a curb. Every year during the winter holidays, twinkling, colorful strands decorate all the buildings and fountains. Now, weeks past the season, everything is bathed in golden light.

Genet carries the hand sanitizer and walks fast. "We can't be late."

"I'm right behind you." Mattie hurries to keep up.

Inside the restaurant, the chandeliers, gold-rimmed charger plates, and crystal glasses shine at each table setting. Several people have already arrived. Genet introduces Mattie to those friends and relatives of Ravi's whom she knows. Her out-of-town bridesmaids have cancelled. She waves to a woman across the room. "There's Ruth. Let's stand nearer the door, Gram. So we can see everyone as they come in."

Ruth walks toward them, along with a waiter wearing latex gloves and carrying a tray of glasses. Ruth and Genet pluck sparkling waters. Mattie takes a champagne flute and sips.

"I didn't know if this party was still happening tonight," Ruth says. "So many things are being cancelled." Her tight-fitting green dress shows her ample figure. Her reddish hair is gray at the roots. "What a day. I'm sorry, Mattie, that you won't be able to move into Sonata."

"What do you mean not move in?" Mattie takes another sip, thinking that this must be the curve she'd anticipated. The bubbly rushes to her head.

Ruth darts her gaze from Mattie to Genet and back. "I thought someone might have called you."

"No. No one—"

"As of late this afternoon, no move-ins."

"For how long?"

"Indefinitely."

"But you could still live here in Kansas City, Gram," Genet says. "With Ravi and me. And Cadence."

"That's sweet of you, but you'll need your time together with your new husband and young stepdaughter."

Mattie wonders how she will fill the hole in her heart now. Can she restore the memories of home for Wiley and herself another way? The decision about Sonata has been made for her. This must be why she couldn't see herself living there. She will return to California and visit Wiley again once this virus scare has passed. Making the move back to Kansas City isn't meant to be, at least not for now.

A familiar refrain repeats—had she not hopped the train, had she not stayed in California. But she did those things, and they are irrevocable. Life is full of choices to stay or leave, come or go. She has made hers. This is her life. She has found gains in the losses, but a do-over is not possible.

She envisions the yellow cottage behind Charles and Amoy's house where she could fill her days keeping up with her team's research and learning new dance steps at the rec center. The garden is clear in her mind, but she isn't in the picture.

"They're here," Genet says. "Ravi and his family."

Mattie turns as a group enters through the open door. Ravi is holding the hand of a child, who must be Cadence. Two young women and an older couple, who must be his sisters and parents, are next. Behind them is a white-haired man wearing a long black coat. He pauses, and his shape fills the gold-rimmed doorway.

When he steps in, the lilt in his gait startles her. He walks with a limp, but his bearing has grace. Why is yet another man reminding her of Kip? At that moment, his gaze meets hers.

There she is, he thinks. The tall woman with the short white hair. The one holding the glass of champagne. That's her. That's Mattie. When he saw her last, she was a brown-haired girl. Would he have picked her out in a crowd if he hadn't seen the recent photo? Perhaps not. But he has seen, and he's certain. His pulse races.

He moves to her, hand to heart, unable to speak.

He is before her, thinner, older, but is it him?

"Hello, Mattie."

Hearing his voice, she knows. "Kip?"

"Yes," he says, and wonders how it could be that he is here with her."

"I thought you—"

"I didn't know if you—" He hears himself about to absolve himself and stops. Any excuse he could offer would only diminish this moment.

"They said everyone died—"

"Isn't it great, Gram?" Genet is beaming. "Ravi told me on the phone and it was so hard not to tell you. And this is the whole family."

Everyone circles around Mattie. No one shakes hands, but fists bump and elbows knock. Kip stays motionless, waiting, his coat over his arm. When those introductions end and other guests come forward to greet the Kumars, Kip and Mattie slip away to a spot beside a potted palm tree. He hangs his coat over a chair, and she sets her glass on the table.

"I'm overwhelmed to see you," he says. "And grateful."

"I can't believe it's you." She wants to say she blames herself. "All these years. What happened? The train—"

"A head wound, cut feet, and this bum leg." He raps on his right thigh with his knuckles. "Nearly lost it. But you appear to be as good as ever."

"I'm well." She wants to say she regrets everything. "I am so sorry, Kip."

He shrugs and stomps his leg. "It's okay as long as I keep it awake."

"No, I mean—I'm sorry I kicked you and told you to leave. I didn't mean it."

"You kicked me?" He stares at her and into the black hole in his memory of that night. "When was this?"

"Before you went up top."

He shakes his head. "I don't remember."

"Or Gladdie?"

"Who?"

"The red-haired girl? You went to find her."

He shakes his head. "I don't remember." He dredges his memories of the trip. The balloon ride. Snake dance. Lungers' camp. The incessant clackety-clack of the long, dusty rides. His shame at not taking her home, at breaking her father's trust in him.

Mattie watches his face. She hasn't identified until this moment the raw jealousy at the heart of her actions. She could not have said until now how much she loved him then. He is an old man. Skin wrinkled, cheeks hollow, lips thin, and eyebrows wiry. His eyes are paler than they were, but they are still coppery. "The girl had been traveling with us. I called her Carrot Top. I guess I was scared you would leave me and go with her."

"You were?"

"I didn't wait for you, as you asked me to do. I left without knowing for sure what happened to you. I am so sorry."

"I should have tried harder to find you." The shame rises, and he tries to accept it rather than push it back down. "I wanted to."

"You tried?"

"I wrote to what I thought was Leroy's address and to a church on Gladstone, hoping to reach your folks, but I didn't hear back. I should have kept trying. In recent years, with the Internet—"

"I searched online for 'Kip Kelly tap dancer.' I didn't really believe you had survived, but I dreamed that you had."

"Try Aidan Kipling."

"Who?"

"I've been using that name for decades. I will tell you about it, but for now, I want this moment." He opens his arms. "Are you okay with this—? I can't promise I didn't catch something on the plane."

"May I still call you Kip?"

"I hope you will."

She steps into his arms. His ribcage is against her, his collarbone hard under her cheek. They stand by the palm tree, embracing. He is a solid presence against her rapid heartbeat. In the restaurant's golden light with Kip so close, a new memory is forming somewhere along her neural pathways. She feels it take hold.

It could have been an eternity or only moments before they are aware of a commotion across the room. People are hurriedly putting on coats and saying goodbye. Something has happened.

"Gram." Genet runs to them. "The restaurant is closed. The chef has a fever."

"Wait," Ravi says. "I want a picture of you two before we go." He points his phone and snaps this moment in time—Mattie and Aidan beside the potted palm at the Saffron Restaurant on March 14, 2020.

Later, Ravi will text the photo to Genet. One day in the future, she will print it and place it in a silver frame on the mantel beside the one of Mattie and Kip in the Bluebird Buffet.

CHAPTER THIRTY-FIVE

Tango

On Sunday, no gatherings above fifty are allowed in Kansas City. The wedding has been postponed until Memorial Day weekend. "It's only two months until then," Genet says. "This stupid virus will be gone and everyone will be able to come. The weather will be nicer in May anyway."

She drives with Mattie along Ward Parkway Boulevard and pulls into the driveway of the Kumars' house. Mattie recognizes it as one of her favorites from the outings with her father long ago, when they guessed at the number of bricks used in its construction.

Kip is on the front steps, ready to tour the old neighborhood. Genet hands Mattie the car keys and waves goodbye.

As Kip and Mattie drive, the silence between them fills to overflowing. They cross under a downtown freeway and up past Millionaire's Row, where one mansion is now a museum, while others are apartment buildings. They stop before the old Elmwood house, which has been painted gray, and pass by the church on Gladstone. They turn onto Cliff Drive, park, and stand on the sidewalk above the waterfall. It is clogged with cans, bottles, cigarette butts, and potato chip bags. Nearby, in a homeless encampment, a few people are visible, and the presence of more is palpable.

On her last visit to the neighborhood several years ago, a few tents nested among the trees. Now, makeshift houses meander across the hillside. Walls and fences built with shopping carts threaded with rags and trash define rooms. Roofs of corrugated plastic and patio awnings connect them. Broken lawn chairs and tables set with mismatched dishes furnish lean-tos fashioned from cardboard boxes and trash bags.

These human-scale burrows house a tribe brought together not by ethnicity or ancestry, but by consequences of circumstance, misfortune, and choice.

She turns to Kip. "I have tried to imagine what it would it feel like to be homeless. When I moved to San Francisco, my neighborhood was reeling from the Summer of Love. My Victorian had seen better days, but the area had character. Over the years, I've enjoyed rock concerts in the park, musicians playing on the sidewalks, and breakdancers spinning on their heads to the beat of a boom box. As housing values have risen, the number of destitute has multiplied. I fold dollars into cups and guitar cases, but if I gave all I had it would not be enough to solve the problem. I called a friend this morning about donating my house to her nonprofit. It's only a drop in the bucket. That's the truth that makes us want to look away. What can we do?"

"Look and listen. See the hope that's here. All over the world, I've seen people banding together for a safety net, performing high-wire acts to survive war, migration, economic upheaval. History is full of people in a state of impermanence."

"And the problems are getting worse with climate change, climate refugees," Mattie says.

"I agree. Yet, there's never been a better time on earth to be alive. We have more ways to solve human problems than ever before. Some would say the people in this encampment have given up, but they haven't. They exert effort, stringing their laundry on an overcast day and feeding the birds."

"Listen to you. The optimist."

Kip smiles. "I had teachers. You asked me to see the bright side. Dance taught me to leap out of the darkness. It gave back my life."

A woman scatters breadcrumbs to starlings pecking at the ground. In the trees, they chatter and trill their high-pitched whistling.

"We call these people 'homeless,' but they are homemakers, doing the best they can with what they have." Mattie says. "Everyone desires a place to be. We all surround ourselves with belongings for assurance. We hang clothing in a closet—on a tree branch—to say, 'This is my place.'"

"Dance has been mine. In the moment." Kip regards the woman feeding the birds, noticing her lithe movements, the way her hand opens to release the crumbs, reaches into the bag, and again releases.

Mattie nods. "My tendency has always been to look forward. But recently it's been to the past."

She scans the encampment. Digging among the soggy leaves and dirt, a man pulls up something and puts it in a pot he carries. When he sees her looking at him, he holds his treasure in the air. "Trumpet of the dead," he says. "Delicious if you cook them just right. But don't eat them raw."

"So I've been told." She smiles. "Have a good day."

The man nods and continues searching the ground. The woman who was feeding the birds comes to his side and searches with him, as in a duet. They bend and move in tandem across the mulched leaves.

Mattie turns to Kip and whispers, "Did that sound flippant? Telling him to have a good day? With him scavenging for food?"

"He deserves a good day as much as anyone. Why not? Tomorrow isn't guaranteed for any of us."

At the Lookout where they stood long ago with her father, the view of downtown and the bottoms has changed remarkably and yet not at all. New buildings reach greater heights, but the curves of the two rivers are familiar. The Kansas meets the Missouri, which is still the longest in the United States and still flows east and south to the Mississippi.

The city skyline to the south is much changed, and the neighborhood where the Bluebird once was is unrecognizable. To the north are the train tracks and the airport into which Mattie flew on Monday.

Kip is standing close. A train whistles in the distance. Mattie's cell phone buzzes.

"Oh, Amoy. How is he? Good. Take your time. I'm not moving into Sonata. A lot has happened. No, not back to California. No, not now. I'm thinking of staying here." She looks to Kip and reaches a hand to him. "I don't see how I could possibly go away now."

Her touch on his wrist sends a jolt through him. The words tumble into the dark hole of his memory and find their echo from a long-ago night. *Go away.*

Mattie spoke them in the moment he left her to climb onto the rooftop. He remembers going after the red-haired girl. He leapt to the next car back, crossed the roof, and began climbing down. The car lurched. He held on. The train groaned and rose up beneath him. His instinct was to hold tighter. Metal screeched on metal. A voice from within or somewhere beyond screamed, *"Let go."*

The sound swallowed him. He released his grip and flew backward. He fell onto the embankment, rolling and rolling. In this part, a black hole remains. When he came to, he was under a bush and the boxcar was burning.

When Mattie ends the call, Kip says, "I remember that girl now, Mattie. The red-haired one."

"You do?"

"I wanted to help her."

"I didn't understand why you wanted to so badly."

"I had to try. I needed to prove to myself that I could protect her."

"I believed only that you left me for her and because of that you died. Reflecting years later, I realized that you acted out of empathy. That quality was one of the things I liked most about you. Loved most."

They embrace and hold one another for a long time, though neither is aware of time. They drive back south past the Plaza, along the boulevards, to the Forest Hill Cemetery, where the bare-branched trees are budding, and walk to the section where Mattie's family is buried. The graves of Mattie's grandparents and those of Irene and her husband and child are beside those of Mattie's parents.

Kip reads aloud the inscription on Elliot's headstone. "'I wonder what your life will be when mine has run. What may the future moments hold?'"

"We get to the end and wonder how it all went by so fast." Mattie snaps her fingers. "I was forty when Father died. It's been sixty years since then and only an instant. I hope you know how much he took to you."

"And I to him. He was, briefly, the father I lost. I must have disappointed him greatly by not returning you home."

"He never said so. He was so saddened by your death. We all were. If we'd only known—"

"Something happened long ago that I couldn't tell you. I couldn't face it myself. It has influenced the dances I've made, but it's also kept me from deep commitment to the people I've loved."

"Can you tell me now?"

"Let's sit." He motions to a wooden bench inscribed with the names of a man and woman, along with their dates of birth, marriage, and death. He reads it and says, "These two were married seventy-five years and died within days of one another. That could have been us if I'd done things differently."

"We've little time left for regrets." Mattie takes his hand. "But I do want to hear whatever you want to tell me."

"It happened when I was eleven. One night, my pa and grandpa went out for a nip right before my bedtime. I fell asleep, woke up to a thumping sound, and went into the hallway. I could smell whiskey and see my mama in her bedroom. Two men were with her. One was holding her down. The other had his trousers around his ankles. It was the manager of the mine where my pa worked. I heard him say, 'Tell your husband this is what happens when he organizes for the union. You tell Magnus that no McKillip is going to change how things are done around here, not on my watch. You Irish need to know your place.'

"After they left the house, I went to her and covered her up with a blanket. In tears she said, 'Don't say anything to your pa. He will kill those men.' I didn't know the words then for what they'd done, but I knew it was something unforgiveable. It now seems unforgiveable that I said nothing. She was a fiercely private person, and I held the secret as she asked me to do.

"Three years later, Pa died in the mine accident. When the manager was merely fined for negligence, and not held accountable in any other way, I figured he had planned to kill Pa or had not cared enough to keep Pa safe. I couldn't hold the horror of what happened to Mama any longer, so I told my grandpa. He took a kitchen knife and went to the tavern looking for the mine manager. The prosecutor at the trial called it 'cold-blooded murder.'

"The jury never heard evidence of the manager attacking my mother or being negligent in Pa's death. My grandpa said the manager deserved to die. People said that Grandpa lacked remorse.

"A cartoonist drew him as 'Killer McKillip' in the newspaper and people in town stuck the nickname onto Mama and me. People said I came from bad blood, as if I'd inherited a tendency for evil the same way I had come by my dark hair and long feet. Mama got sicker and sicker in body and soul and went into the sanitarium.

"I hopped trains, worked at odd jobs, and ended up in Kansas City. You and your family were so cheerful. I didn't know how to tell you about the sadness. When we ran into Crowley at that balloon festival and he told us about the fire, I was afraid if we returned to Kansas City, the police would discover my real name was McKillip, find out about my grandpa, and believe I could commit a crime. It felt like a curse."

"And you carried that alone, Kip? I'm so sorry I didn't make it easy to talk about it."

"We were kids. And you tried. Anyway, we're talking now."

"Yes."

"I don't believe it was empathy that night on the train. I think fear drove me to find that girl. I hadn't been able to protect my mother long ago."

"You did as she asked."

"But that meant we held onto the terror of it together. As much as Mama was worried that Pa would go after the mine manager, I think she was too ashamed to tell. She didn't want Pa to know what had happened to her. I held that shame too. People didn't talk openly about those things. Today a kid would have the vocabulary and more courage, I hope, than I had to tell the truth. If I'd spoken up, or if she had, things could have turned out differently. Maybe the manager would have been held accountable for the negligence at the mine before Pa died in the accident, and Grandpa wouldn't have killed the manager. Mama and I both blamed ourselves for what happened to Pa and Grandpa."

"It wasn't your fault."

"I believed it was. When I let go of the boxcar ladder that night, I began letting go of the shame and blame, but it was deep within. I layered on more guilt and shame when I didn't get in touch with your family to find out what happened to you, and more in the years later when I didn't take care of Yuka and Rose."

"And now?"

"It's lifting from me each day that I'm here. I can't remember feeling this light since I was a boy running in the woods or that day we flew in the helium balloon."

They sit with the birds chirping in the tree branches above them. He says, "Do you think about being here with your family one day? In the end?"

She looks across the cemetery. "They aren't here, and I don't want to be. They are in my heart and mind and with me in spirit. Maybe when all is said and done, I'll be sprinkled in Amoy's garden with the roses blooming above me. I have made no formal requests or plans. I haven't been able to imagine it, although I've had the opportunity to decorate my own coffin."

"How's that?"

"A colleague runs workshops on weekends for people to decorate their own cardboard coffins for cremation and sculpt their own urns from slabs of porcelain. The coffins go into closets and the urns onto shelves until needed."

"I wouldn't like seeing my empty urn every time I turn around."

"Better than passing by a cemetery knowing one of those plots could be mine. I find that lonely and terrifying." She blinks away the image of her parents in their coffins underground.

"I should be dealing with all of this but I'm not," Kip says. "In the past, I've pictured my near death, but not what certainly awaits in my future."

"Another colleague, who does visioning sessions with our

research team, also works with people facing end-of-life. She draws their imaginings of death and beyond and depicts their wishes for memorial celebrations."

"I assumed I'd have my ashes interred in North Carolina, but this has me thinking I'd like to be with my family here, if they'd have me on their shelf or would scatter me to the winds."

"That had better not be any time soon." She smiles at him.

He laughs and takes her hand. "Not if I can help it. I love life and you in mine—again."

"We've come a long way, you and I."

"We have."

"Did you ever get to the Grand Canyon?"

"No. Did you?"

"Not yet, but I saw an Amtrak ad in the paper. A train leaves every day from Kansas City to Grand Canyon Village."

"How long is the trip?"

"Thirty-seven hours and twenty-eight minutes."

"Time well spent."

CHAPTER THIRTY-SIX

Pair

Monday morning, gatherings of more than ten are not allowed. Schools are closed. People are sheltering in place, venturing out only for essential work and supplies.

Mattie and Genet are gathered with the Kumars around the breakfast table. "You must stay with us," Rose says. She raises her orange juice in a toast. "We'll have a two-day birthday celebration for you and Aidan."

"I wish Wiley could be here with us," Mattie says.

"Let's go get him, Gram."

"But Ruth said they've closed the whole facility. They aren't allowing residents to gather or to come and go, and not even deliveries into the lobby."

"We'll take the back entrance. I'll ask Ruth to help upstairs. You can drive, Gram. Kip can ride shotgun. Ravi and I will go in and get Wiley. He'll fare better with us than if he stays there."

As they pull out of the driveway, the radio plays low. Genet says, "Turn it up."

They drive to the beat of "Reach Out I'll Be There" on streets strangely empty for a Monday morning. They pass a woman wheeling a trashcan to the curb and a man walking a dog. In the parking lot of the market, people roll shopping carts brimming with grocery bags, bottled water, and jumbo packs of toilet paper. A few people wear facemasks. Cars line up bumper to bumper at the drive-by coffee kiosk.

In the alley behind Sonata Court, Mattie and Kip wait in the Toyota with the windows down, engine idling. Genet takes Ravi in through a back entrance that leads to a service elevator up to the third-floor galley kitchen. He waits there, blocking the elevator doors from closing.

Genet walks the empty hall and finds Ruth in Wiley's room, tossing his belongings into a black trash bag.

"Where is everybody?"

"In their rooms. We're supposed to be taking every resident's temperature and helping them place calls to relatives." She pats Wiley. "His forehead is cool and you're here, so my job is done." She looks out into the hallway to see if it's clear. "Let's go."

As they reach the kitchen, a motorized scooter hums behind them. It's the CIA gentleman, the lively dancer. "Oh, hello." He looks puzzled. "Is there coffee?"

The carafe is empty. "All out, I'm sorry," Genet says.

"I would like a cup."

"I'll make a fresh pot," Ruth says.

In the elevator, Wiley pushes the buttons, the doors close, and they descend. At street level, Ravi and Genet lead Wiley to the waiting car.

At home in Rose's welcoming living room, Mattie, Kip, Wiley, Genet, Ravi, and his family sit in armchairs, on the white sofas, the yellow-cushioned window seat, and the red lacquered bench. Miss Paws curls on Rose's lap and watches Cadence gallop around the room in her butterfly costume to her own silent rhythm. Daisy, wearing her nurse uniform, carries in warm cinnamon rolls. Their fragrance fills the room. She is scheduled to report in three hours to the new wing of the same hospital where Mattie was born.

"All together, we're ten. We'll manage fine with six bedrooms and the sleeper sofa in the library." Rose says. She calculates the clean linens and the pairings for the rooms. "The sheltering may last a few weeks, perhaps a month or two. We'll have groceries delivered and stay safe."

Wiley is studying Kip. "Dancing boy." His eyes shine. "He carried me."

"Yes, he did, dear brother. He carried you home."

Mattie's phone chimes. Amoy's face fills the screen. "Happy Birthday, Mattie," she says. "Much love to you from Charles and me. His fever is still high. They won't let me in to see him, but we spoke. We wish we could be there to celebrate with you this week, but now they're saying we may have to quarantine before flying. Is Genet nearby?"

Genet leans in with Mattie. "I'm here."

"We're sorry about the wedding," Amoy says.

"Things happen."

"You must be terribly disappointed. We are."

"I can only control what I can."

"Who is with you?"

Genet scans the room with Mattie's phone and brings it back to her face. "Did you see? We got Uncle Wiley out. And it's Kip's birthday too. Tomorrow he turns one hundred and three."

"Charles wishes he could be there."

"I do too. Both of you."

"Call me later," Amoy says. "Enjoy your time and don't worry about us. I love you."

"You too." Genet pauses. "I love you, Mom. And Dad. Tell Dad I love him. Please tell him."

She cues her playlist. "Let's have some music. We can't go to Hawaii, but we can bring Hawaii here."

A tenor voice sings over the strumming of a ukulele. "Ooh, ooh, ooh, ooh, ooh—"

Mattie and Kip stand and face each other as "Somewhere Over the Rainbow" pours into the room. They touch hand to hand, a perfect fit. To each it feels completely natural, yet also surprising. After all this time, how has it come to this? They dance across the living room, passing in front of the glass shelves, which hold the kintsugi bowl and two little silver birds.

This morning, Mattie took the saltshaker bird from her travel bag and gave it to Genet, who placed it on Rose's shelf beside the pepper. Mattie smiles at the pair of them, reunited. She thinks of the Bluebird Buffet and Elliot. Aunt Irene is nearby while Mattie wraps the shakers in the flags. Clara, Betty, Mickey, and Wiley are in the memory too, around the dinner table. Kip is playing capture the flag on the street. He is in the Bluebird's kitchen, teaching her to dance while Leroy chops onions that Cyrus has grown.

Kip is on the train, showing her how to leap and roll. Eugene is beside the pool in California and at her side a few moments after Charlie was born. Virginia is there with her long legs and high kicks. Diego with his Latin rhythm. And Amoy with red roses from her garden. Genet is here now, embracing new possibilities. The people whom Mattie has loved, and been loved by, throughout her life have taught her to love more fully. Her heart is expanding to contain it all.

"What a Wonderful World" plays, blending blue skies and babies' cries with cinnamon, aftershave, and lemon fragrances. Rose and Anik sway cheek to cheek. Dahlia and Daisy twist slowly. Wiley sashays to the music with Cadence, mimicking her butterfly motions. She flaps her arms. "We got this, Uncle Wiley."

Life is full of choices to stay or leave, come or go, to and fro. Mattie knows where she's been. More memories flow into her awareness. They are encoded in her. Yet she can't hold them all at once, so she lets them go and releases herself into the dance, moving in time with Kip. She senses his steps and where he's leading. They turn away and return their gazes to one another.

He is the tallest person in the room. She is fully present and at one with him. The moves they make are not salsa, not swing, ballroom, ballet, modern, or tap, but a bit of each and something of their own. She is following, and now leading. He is leading, now following. They are partners in a dance of time, creating an ephemeral being that exists for only this instant—now this—and vanishes.

She has held the illusion throughout her life that, with skill and persistence, she could get things right. She lets that go. Cadence whirls around them, her butterfly wings lightly brushing against them, the silky ribbons of her antennae caressing them.

Mattie and Kip shuffle and slide, dip and glide, twirl and rise. They touch hands, mirroring motions, moving close, diminishing the space between them, and then moving apart, opening a wide chasm. They bridge the divide with their arms and sweep it away, coming together now, touching cheek to cheek—his breath, her breath.

They bend and reach with effort and ease. Their hearts beat and pulses race, but they don't stop. The room is alive; the walls thrum. Synapses fire. Everything syncs. Everything is possible. Among the people in this room are dreams still to dream, and yet nothing lacks in this moment.

If she had lived her whole life for this, it would have been worth waiting for.

It has been.

It is.

If she could, she would hold the expanse of possibilities within this one moment, and the next, and keep on dancing to the playlist of her life.

The song finishes, and Mattie and Kip gulp air and laugh.

They remain standing and facing one another while everyone else flops onto cushions. Ravi sees that they don't want the moment to end. He sits beside Genet on the red bench and says, "How about some old love songs?"

"As Time Goes By" comes on and Kip places his hand on Mattie's back. He pulls her close, and she rests her cheek on his collarbone. They press into one another, touching along their ribs, hips, knees, and toes. "Skinbones" echoes in her memory. She again fits that childhood nickname. Kip's body is equally lean. His cotton shirt is damp with perspiration. The heat penetrates the silk of her dress. They sway to the music together.

They move across the room, their steps cushioned by the deep pile of the carpet, their faces glowing from sunlight streaming from the stone patio through the glass doors. She barely knows him, he barely her, and yet they know one another well. Their old story is tucked between them. Another song begins and they match their tempo to "Young at Heart."

Something new emerges. She turns her face to Kip, and they kiss. The first brush of lips is tentative. Their lips are soft and unsure. They come together again, a longer one. When they pull apart, they are aware of the hush and the faces smiling at them.

The music ends. They laugh and kiss—pecks on the cheek this time—and sit on the couch across from Ravi and Genet. Cadence, in limp butterfly wings, comes with Wiley in tow to sit beside Mattie. Miss Paws jumps onto Mattie's lap and settles there, purring.

Genet leans toward Kip. "Did Gram tell you? I'm going to write her life story."

"That's an ambition." He smiles. "It'll be a long book."

"I'll begin it the moment you two meet in the Bluebird," Genet says.

Mattie is petting the cat, and the underside of her wrist

grazes Kip's trouser leg. Beneath the fine weave of fabric, she feels the knotted rope of his scar.

"Or begin the evening before," she says. "I remember it well."

"So you can anticipate?" He takes her hand.

His grip is strong and tender. She gives a soft squeeze in reply. "That was the night you were traveling to us. Synchronicity. It's your story too."

"An even longer book." He kisses her cheek and then turns to Genet. "How will the story end?"

She looks at Mattie and Kip sitting side by side. "This way. Exactly this way."

Coda

Dear Reader,

Some days it seems that only weeks have passed since the sheltering-in-place of March 2020, and yet months and now years have flown. Ravi and I are still together, although I sold my wedding dress, unworn. Last October, we had a small ceremony on the patio, and our baby boy will be born in June. Cadence is now ten and a semifinalist on *America's Got Talent*. I know Gram would be proud. We all miss her so much.

Most of those days that we spent sheltering and many events since then are a blur, but writing about my grandmother brings her clearly to me, straight into my heart. Ending the story sends her away again, so I've continued to revise and tweak the manuscript to keep her close, trying to tell her tale in a way that would please her. In honor of her birthday, I've brought this final draft with her dancing boy to completion.

My teachers and mentors have continued to tell me that a writer must make her fictional characters suffer, but my grandmother was real—a real girl, a living breathing woman. She experienced hardships enough without my piling on more. I can hear her now. *There's difficulty enough in this world. Why add misery?* She would want me to leave you hopeful. I listen to songs from her playlist and watch the online video about roving youth. I fast forward to a moment where she laughs.

When people we love disappear from this earth, we hold them in spirit and recall them in stories. Through remembering and speaking their names, time expands. They live on in this dimension, and all the love remains.

What then, is the measure of a life? If you reach a century, you will count more than thirty-six thousand days or fifty-two million minutes or three trillion seconds. By the clock, time passes at equal pace for everyone. *Click.* Another moment vanishes into another day, another year. By the heart's calculation, some moments linger for lifetimes. I've tried to capture a few of those for safekeeping.

When Mattie handed me her diaries and sat for interviews, she gave me the courage to begin, along with the tenacity to finish and the heart to start again. Is this draft number ten? Twenty? I've lost track. Life doesn't allow a do-over, but we can do some things differently next time. As long as we have time, there can be first times and second chances. It's not too late for a last chance until the end. For now, this version stands. I believe that Mattie and Kip would be happy with this love story. Yes, I know they would.

Genet Margaret Turner-Kumar
March 16, 2025

Mattie's Playlist

"Can't Stop the Feeling"
"Bye Bye Blackbird"
"Dancing in the Dark"
"As Time Goes By"
"Gee, but I'd Like to Make You Happy"
"I Got Rhythm"
"On the Sunny Side of the Street"
"Happy Days Are Here Again"
"The Star-Spangled Banner"
"Life Is Just a Bowl of Cherries"
"Moonlight Sonata"
"Need a Little Sugar in My Bowl"
"I Don't Know Why (I Just Do)"
"All of Me"
"Imagine"
"Let's Have Another Cup of Coffee"
"Ever Changing Times"
"Just One More Chance"
"La Vida es un Carnaval"
"If I Knew You Were Comin' I'd've Baked a Cake"
"Something's Coming"

"Somewhere (There's a Place for Us)"
"I Just Want to Celebrate"
"Reach Out I'll Be There"
"Somewhere Over the Rainbow"
"What a Wonderful World"
"Young at Heart"

ABOUT THE AUTHOR

CHRISTINE WALKER is a visual artist and writer living in Northern California. Born in Kansas City, Missouri, she grew up in suburban neighborhoods on the Kansas side in a close family who encouraged her interests in art, writing, and music. Her paternal grandmother's diary kept during the Great Depression inspired her novel *Tap Dancing at the Bluebird.* Christine is the author of *A Painter's Garden: Cultivating the Creative Life,* a personal narrative about creative process explored through insights from the garden and studio and accompanied by her paintings, and the co-author, illustrator, and lyricist of *Wooleycat's Musical Theater*, an award-winning children's book with song CD. Early in her career she moved to San Francisco, California, where she painted and ran a graphic design business. Her affinity for dance led to collaborations as a stage designer with contemporary choreographers. She now lives in Sonoma County with her husband, composer Dennis Hysom, and continues as a painter, writer, and consultant in strategic visioning. She is also a writing teacher and avid reader involved with literary communities. She has an MFA in Writing and Literature in Fiction from the Bennington Writing Seminars, an MA in Creative Arts Interdisciplinary from San Francisco State University, and a BFA from the University of Kansas.

ACKNOWLEDGMENTS

Tap Dancing at the Bluebird is fiction built on many truths. My parents and relatives taught me the meaning of family and encouraged me toward the arts. For all of them, here and gone, I have tremendous love and gratitude. This novel would not exist without them. My parents, Robin E. and Ramona, always said that they were the conduits for the creative genes, but they did more than pass on genetics; they instilled in me essential habits of self-discipline for pursuing artistic passions. I learned from them a certain tenacity and dedication that has served me well in five decades of balancing a creative life devoted also to family, friends, and community.

My paternal grandmother, Carolyn, painted and kept a diary of family life during the 1920s and 1930s. My paternal grandfather, Robin A., who died when I was two, was an architect, painter, and twice poet laureate of Kansas. My grandmother collected his poems into a book for the grandchildren. My colorful, gregarious Aunt Marilu collected my grandmother's diary writings and printed them as a keepsake. My Aunt Peggy taught art, painted, made museum-quality miniatures, and researched the family's genealogy. My Uncle Mort was a well-known cartoonist whose strips we read in the paper every morning. In our home, we had trays and pitchers painted by my grandmother and great aunt and oil paintings from my father's family and my mother's brother, Lloyd. My maternal grandfather, Walter, told jokes at Sunday dinner after church. My maternal grandmother, Mildred, was a piano teacher and taught my siblings and me to play. I have her piano in my home in California. In our suburban Kansas City home where I grew up, we practiced on a baby grand piano that had belonged to my father's family.

I could not have managed, much less thrived, without my siblings Carol, Robin, and Lloyd. My first brush with dance as a child was as a sister swan with Carol to a set of younger tap-dancing ducky twins. Neither Carol nor I had much dance talent, but those early formative experiences, prancing in our tutus or curtsying in our long dresses that our mother and grandmother had sewn for our piano recitals, cemented a love for the arts that I continue to share with her and my younger siblings. They all have their own remarkable careers and talents, and they are always there for me in my most joyous and also darkest times. I am also fortunate to have cousins with whom to share memories of our relatives.

In 2004, I had completed writing two novels, both yet unpublished. Inspired by my grandmother's diary and an anecdote about my Aunt Marilu tap dancing down the street, I asked my aunt and father to expand upon the family stories and began writing *Tap Dancing at the Bluebird* a few months before I entered the MFA program at Bennington. I had the idea then for a young girl named Mattie to follow a roving youth named Joe riding the rails, but I set the manuscript aside to write my thesis novel, an interweaving of the lives of five mothers.

When I picked up the *Tap Dancing* novel again several years later, I re-read my grandmother's diary, intent upon capturing the essence of this good-hearted family who made the best of difficult times. My MFA teachers had said, "Give your characters trouble." I knew that Mattie must leave home in order to propel the story forward. Aware that her close family would then be fractured, I resisted putting her on the train. Finally, she hopped on, but I didn't know how I would end the book. During this time, my Uncle Lloyd, who was in his eighties and a widower, told me that he had located his WWII girlfriend and gone to meet her. I liked the idea of rekindling youthful love and future promise in older age. I finished a version of the manuscript in which Mattie and Joe danced together in a retirement home and witnessed the election of the first woman President of the United States. After the electoral votes were counted in November 2016, I set the book aside, unsure how to end it.

In January 2020, I was working again on the book when my husband and I experienced a tragedy beyond words. Our son died. Soon after, the world shut down due to Covid. I had time to work on the novel, but I was so bereft of our son in the present that I found it difficult to enter the fictional world set in an era long before he'd been born. I renamed the Joe character Kip and gave him some "Quinnessence," which reignited the story. In honor of Quinn and of my parents, aunts, and uncles, who have all now passed away, I wanted to end the novel hopefully. We keep the spirits of our loved ones alive by telling their stories, whether how things truly happened or how they might have happened. People we love live on in our hearts and imaginations.

Crafting a novel with an historical time frame requires research. In addition to writings by family members, many books, articles, films, and photographs informed this story. I visited the California State Railroad Museum, walked old neighborhoods in Kansas City, took salsa lessons, and watched tap dancing tutorials on YouTube. Particularly informative were the books *A General Theory of Love* by Thomas Lewis, M.D., Fari Amini, M.D., and Richard Lannon, M.D., *Riding the Rails: Teenagers on the Move During the Great Depression* by Errol Lincoln Uys, *Dancing in the Dark: A Cultural History of The Great Depression* by Morris Dickstein, *An American Journey: Images of Railroading During the Depression* by Mark S. Vandercook, and *A Map of Making Dances* by Stuart Hodes, along with the documentary film *Riding the Rails* by Michael Uys and Lexy Lovell.

Music fills my life. My husband, Dennis Hysom, is a

musician, composer, and audio producer. Together we've written several albums of award-winning children's songs and a Top-40 country hit. Growing up, my family sang around the house. I was in a church choir with my mother. I sing to CDs in my painting studio and in rehearsals and performances with the Acorn MusEcology Project, a Sonoma County community ensemble. I thank and acknowledge all songwriters, singers, musicians, and composers whose soundtracks make life richer and whose music carries personal meaning and memories.

Dance has had a profound influence on my visual art and writing. When I took dance classes as an adult after I moved to San Francisco in the 1970s, I discovered (again) that I didn't have a talent for it, but I wanted to be involved. I was fortunate to collaborate as a stage designer on many productions with contemporary choreographers Brenda Way, Kimi Okada, and KT Nelson of ODC/San Francisco and to watch many hours of rehearsals. I thank them, the company, and dancers everywhere for all they do. Last year, I discovered Monroe Hall, a gem of a community resource for dance in Santa Rosa. Line dancing, anyone? I still don't manifest any particular talent, but I love it.

I have long been interested in neuroscience, longevity, memory, music, and movement. I've seen evidence of people being rallied from their wheelchairs by hearing a tune from their past. My father and other relatives succumbed to dementia in their later years, losing their memories and ability to live independently, yet retaining certain key traits. My dad, who close to the end of his life didn't recognize me, could still play a game of gin and keep score. At times, he might have seemed unsure of my mother's name, although she reminded him, but he would burst into singing "You Tell Me Your Dream, I'll Tell You Mine," a song popular during their courtship years. I'm interested in how physical activity and learning new things contributes to vitality. I'm eager to continue forming new neural pathways in my own life journey. The old ones are wonderful, and there are so many places yet to go.

I am lucky to enjoy a wealth of friendships. The Girl Scout motto of my early years has served me well: "Make new friends and keep the old." Many of those friends have read my manuscripts and offered their critiques and encouragement, including fellow writers who listened and responded to early pages and free writes which seeded this novel. All readers' interest and comments have informed the development of this final version. I especially want to thank Barbara Baer, Carol Koffel, Carol Walker Dobbs, Chris Smith, Clare Broussard, Cynthia Jensen, Dennis Hysom, Doug Zesiger, Joanne Hartman, Kathy Parker, Kimi Okada, Linda Woodsmall, Lydia Belot, Lynn Peck, Margaret Thomas, Marlene Cullen, Merrill Vargo, Michelene Stankus, Robin Eschner, Robin Walker-Lee, Sally Dawson, Sandy Jost, Sheri Joseph, Susan Hillery, Teresa Book, and Teresa Cuseo. I'm grateful for my writing buddies Ann Grant and Gillian Parker with whom I've been meeting for more than twenty-five years. Thank you to my discerning and supportive editor Maureen Jennings. A shout out to Vicki DeArmon, who as a critique partner urged me to "Get Mattie on the train!" I'm thrilled that she's now my publisher. My favorite childhood book is also hers: *The Little Engine That Could*.

Finally, I thank two people without whom I would not be who I am. Dennis, my husband, is my true soul's mate, creative partner, and sounding board in all things. Quinn, our deeply empathic, kinetic, and poetic son, gifted me with motherhood and much love. He leapt into my heart and there he will always be.

BOOK CLUB QUESTIONS

1. Family relationships play a key role in the story. How do they contribute to Mattie's confidence? What indicates her self-awareness, sexual awareness, and coming-of-age? How does her upbringing prepare her for the journey? Did you believe that Mattie, who loved her family, would have followed Kip? How did conditions of 1932 influence her? How might things have turned out differently for her and Kip if she had not gone? Would she have followed Kip if she hadn't received Eugene's letter? How might a young person's life be different today than in 1932?

2. The story covers a century of change in America through themes of movement, memory, transportation, politics, communications, and media. What did you notice? What impact did the changes have on the characters' lives? In what ways are the concepts of America as a "melting pot" and land of opportunity woven as subtext? How does dance reflect the changing times? What is your experience of the United States—where you've lived, worked, or visited? How has your hometown changed? What are your thoughts about home as a place or state of being?

3. At ninety-nine, Mattie harbors regrets. What are they? Do you have regrets that have been buried or have haunted you? How might you confront and overcome those regrets? Even with her regrets, Mattie lives a long, fulfilling life with careers in the arts and science. What aspects of longevity interest you or worry you? What opportunities for health, happiness, and fulfillment do you value? Reflecting on your life, what choices are pivotal for you today?

4. How does the story address the questions: "Whose story is it? Whose is it to tell?" What is the first clue that Mattie is giving her story away to Genet? Did you anticipate Genet's authorship as revealed at the end of the book? If so, what indicates that Genet is writing the story all along? Ultimately, do you believe that Mattie and Kip danced together again or that the scene only occurred in Genet's imagination? If your life story were told, would it be more compelling from your first-person point of view as the main character, from another character's selective point of view, or from an omniscient narrator witnessing it all? How does someone else's story become another's to tell?

5. This is a love story without being a romance. How are many forms of love expressed throughout? By whom? To whom or what? Is there someone from your past whom you'd like to see again in order to explore a new relationship or complete an old one? Can you imagine how that might evolve? What would you tell this person?

6. In the novel, there are many prompts to remembering: sight, sound, touch, smell, taste. The touch of wool propels Mattie to a childhood memory of being in the coat closet with her brother. What are powerful prompts for your memory? Where might those prompts take you?

7. Do you enjoy dancing? Which forms of dance mentioned in the story have you tried? Which have you watched live or on film or video? Tap, modern, improv, contemporary, rock & roll, musical theater, salsa, ballroom, hip-hop, line, lyrical. Others? What do you notice about the forms of dance and their relationship to the eras of the story? How does

dance express emotion and meaning through its various forms?

Enjoy other Sibylline Digital First titles by visiting www.sibyllinepress.com or online retailers.